The Wind Shifts

ALSO BY ALAN SHARP

A Green Tree in Gedde

THE WIND SHIFTS

By Alan Sharp

WALKER AND COMPANY
New York

First Printing

First published in the United States of America in 1968 by
Walker and Company, a division of Walker Publishing
Company, Inc.

Library of Congress Catalog Card Number: 68-14002
Printed in the United States of America.

This book is dedicated to Greenock,
to its buildings and chimneys and streets
and the glimpses they have afforded me
of the river and the hills.

*The wind across wildernesses leaves no wish, is
desolate air, till it finds green groves and manifests
itself among the growing trees. Through dry sticks
it makes no song and at the barren branch is silent.*

*God's love, the which God is, so searches to make
His shapes, to utter His word, and without such
utterance God is mute and nohow heard. So must
we nurture our foliage the greater to glory the
wind.*

ROBERT GIBBON, *Preacher*
b. 1866   d. 1925

ONE

The House of the Solitary Maggot

TWO

Roots and Leaves

THREE

The Unalterable Animals

One

The House of the Solitary Maggot

*—'Tis I that do infect myselfe, the
man without a navel yet lives in
me, I feel the original canker
corrode and devour, and therefore
'Lord deliver me from myselfe'—*

SIR THOMAS BROWNE

In the brief pre-dawn the city achieves true sovereignty. The streets lead here and there, unfollowed, the buildings multiply their aphonies and a great cold emptiness exudes. It is a mortuary, a catastrophe of desolation. Silent empty corridors odoured by the acrid brood of mute existence. A silence which is not the mere absence of sound but a thunderous stone hush, a deafening cataract of empty noise falling upon no ear. It is the wilderness made manifest.

Like great brown scarves of sand the birds leave, spiralling out from the centre, radials in the centrifuge of exodus, countless grains of flight. Their going ushers the day and its denizens.

Through the window, unseen but heard, faint, high, the flying sound of countless chittering starlings. Grey seeping light, eroding the dark litho of the room, defining chairs and table, the screen around the gas ring, the wardrobe with its long mirror echoing the wallpaper in a faded panel, small red roses on writhing stems. Books on the mantelshelf, bookended by alarm clock and Chianti bottle, both dead. The bed creaked. He turned down into the pillow, muffing his face in it and feigned sleep only to pierce the deception and roll back, open-eyed, to see the yellowing whites of the ceiling. He pulled the clothes over his head, smelling his warm, night-long odour, while there perhaps a clock struck? He came up to listen. Silence full of suggestions of chime, one of which became a cistern emptying on the floor below. Thus reminded Moseby's bladder clenched and demanded relief. With guilty sloth he buried back into the bedding. Lazy bastard. Still, it's me that has to suffer. Nobody else. Which reminded him. He brought his knees up in an expulsive motion. Unexpelled his deserted wife and distant daughter lay in their dear distant deserted sleep. Wouldn't be awake yet. Perhaps Edna coming up from decorous dreams was lying a moment remembering where and when and why and what before easy tears crumpled her mouth and plastered her hair into an ear. Carol would ask why. Is it Daddy, Mummy, is it Daddy? Gone but not forgotten. His bladder pained. He thrust down-legged at it. See you in hell first and heaped sackcloths upon his dark head and in the ashy dark again sought sleep.

He woke again and it was much later, lighter and with noises, in the house and without. A train and footsteps batting downstairs. He rose and watched from his window into the back garden. A train bowelling below trembled the whole house, a small firm burr. Down at the end of the garden the big elephant ears of rhubarb trumpeted in a wind. Mr. Schonfield emerged and went up and down the lawn spirtling a small green rain ahead of him from the trundling mower. Once he looked up as he turned at the end of the garden and Moseby nodded a nod of approval to Mr. Schonfield who did not see him. This failure somehow affected his bladder and caused him to dress hurriedly and go downstairs.

When he got out the barber's clock advertising Durex said twenty to one. He walked along and left into one of the slow curving streets that lead up to Finchley Road. The trees in the gardens were releasing a few leaves, coming away from the branches at some secret, inescapable moment, their slow spinning drift masking the finality of departure, falling sideways in the late summer light. Someone in an upper room was practising piano scales. Up they went like white stairs and then down, over and over. The leaves coming down from the trees and the bright rises and falls of the notes. The sun coming on him from the right and behind, his neat shadow. He walked, his feelings falling in him and his thoughts going up and down the same staircase.

Edna. Carol. The house in Dempster Street looking over the roofs to the Clyde. His flight, without a word. A letter on the mantel to replace the one he'd found. The train, sawing through the night, the dark country outside the window. Remorse, sick turning remorse, carrying him further and further away. Guilt and loss. Pain, loneliness, fear, self-pity. His face reflected as it watched the hostile night-time landscape. And the absurdities. Would he meet some drawn cool beauty in the corridor. The rally of dialogue. Mutual admiration. Copulation

4

in the toilet. How could he think such things when Edna was still staring in disbelief at his scrawl. "Going. Must. Sort things out. Sorry. Must. Only way. Please try. Understand. Love. You. Carol." Shit.

A letter in the gutter. Only one page. Page three.

> might all try to get down that week if Alec is keeping as well as he is just now. He never complains but it's not a very nice thing to be suffering from and I better than anyone know that. Will Madge be there if we come? I never seem to catch her on my visits and she really is the nicest one of that side of the family, not so stubborn as the

Good brave Alec. What was it he didn't complain of that wasn't nice to suffer from? Piles? Cancer of the crotch? Boils in the nose? Stigmata? Agenbite of inwit? And much missed unstubborn Madge. Would she be there on the day? When the Great Auctioneer divided the sheep from the merdes. Depart from me for I know thee not. Down to the old everlasting torment. Don't make waves.

The piano had stopped, the sun went behind a cloud. The street was sudden grey and several-at-once leaves came tumbling out of a tree and blew around Moseby's feet, making scurrying noises and causing him to move, with involuntary awkwardness, out of their path.

The Montmartre was quiet until after ten. Moseby came on at six and spent the time until the rush making the odd coffee and lemon tea and postponing taking the free meal for as long as possible. The management allowed the staff only spaghetti or ravioli but the cook would often smuggle a fried egg or a piece of liver under the pasta if he could. The cook was Spanish and hated the Montmartre and the proprietors and the manager and the customers and the waitresses. He did not hate Moseby because Moseby earned less and worked harder than he did. Moseby was his inferior and as such he despised Moseby but he did not hate him. Thus Moseby often found fried eggs in his spaghetti, a garnish he did not at all care for,

5

but he always nodded a grateful nod to the cook who would grin sourly and say something in Spanish which Moseby took to mean "anything stolen from these Jewish bastards is a blow for liberty."

The dishwasher took his meal in the back kitchen. The waitresses had theirs at one of the side tables and the cook usually snacked behind the counter as he cooked. But Moseby received his plate and went off behind the curtain into Helen's domain.

Helen did the vegetables, peeled and chipped the potatoes, washed the sprouts and leafed the cabbages. She was always surrounded by peelings and outside leaves and carrot tops and trodden peas and turnip skins. She was a thick woman, with a nose mole and brown hair on her upper lip and wide calves, mottled from sitting too close to direct heat, and her broad face was constantly glimmed with moist. She moved in a crabby surge among her pots, wiping the table clear with a forearm brush and hoisting sacks about, grunting with effort, talking all the while in her nasal Belfast voice, midway between snarl and whine, talking when Moseby entered and talking when Moseby left, and, as he assumed, throughout his absence.

"Them that knows knows and damned if the rest ever will in a thousand years of grace. Never. That cow'll buy the cheapest she can get and think she saves but I could show her different if she'd stop a minute to hear, look," and to Moseby proffered a potato peeling with nicotined and starchy fingers. He nodded and pursed his mouth to convey sagacity. "Need twice as much bloody peeling as good ones do. But then what's it matter here anyroads when we're all Christ's leavings on this earth, dirt under his feet, human dirt do you understand, take my meaning, it's what them that sees sees and the rest never will in a thousand years of grace. Christ's leavings."

Moseby twisted up his slick strands of spaghetti and waited for the yellow spreading stain of his gratuitous egg. Helen's voice went on and her knife skirled around the earth brown potatoes, the light died over Kilburn and the Underground throbbed beneath. The big bins of refuse stank quietly, their twisted intestinal depths echoed in Moseby's spaghetti and it in

6

turn implied the tortuous tracks of the city's transport, and all, all in the labyrinths of his brain.

"You see they think they are something and that's their mistake, pride, consumption of pride, think they're chosen or those others, think they're God's chosen and that's their sin, don't see in their pride they're nothing but filth, nothing but Christ's dregs and spittles, down here you're nothing, but look at them, how can they be, eh, muck, eh, do you understand me, no, what would a lad like you know."

Moseby escaped to his dishwashing and the increasing tempo of the evening's custom. By twelve the place would be packed and the waitresses would be eeling through the tables to collect their orders. Over Moseby's rampart the eaters ate, cut and mashed, pressed and spooned, forked and fingered into their maws the food of their desiring. Grouped around their tables, bent over their plates they made a composite eating noise, knives on plate, cup on saucer and the dull monotone of chew and crush, muffled in the mouth and silent in the throat as the mangles slid down to await metabolism. Then some subsequent where the tensed squat and the short drop and the surreptitious glance before consigning the penitential stools to the underworld. Amid such unending ingestion hunger became as nausea and Moseby gazed in disgust and anger at the endless stomachs that entered, clad in flesh and disguised with clothes, but all one, all pits awaiting their filling. As a child, urged to eat something at which he baulked, they would say "down the wee red brae." He shuddered in revulsion.

The plates returned, scummed with cooling gravies and littered with the unedible, unappetizing, unwanted fats and rinds, skins and gristles which Moseby scraped away into his own private bin. The washed plates were stacked within reach of the avid waitresses, eager for their tips, and they carried them quickly to the cook to repeat the sickening process of supply and demand.

He did not finish until after two and the bins had gone out for collection in the morning. These last wrestling moments as he half dragged half carried the weighty trash out to the back alley were the very worst of all. Clinging with sweat and his back sore from standing he bent low over Helen's tubs to

7

which were now added his own gleanings, and inhaling the rank odour of waste he felt each time that he would make this night his last. That he didn't, or hadn't so far, could be attributed to the walk back.

Once out, free of the restaurant, the perspiration drying on him and the streets growing empty and quiet, all this eased his mind and almost at peace he walked back to his room under the roof, observing certain phenomena of the night. A window from which a perfume of music and laughter exuded. A glimpse of more solitary proceedings under a lamp. Couples locked in the privets, shushing as he drew near, cats, of course, and metronomic policemen. A car's headlights stenciling swinging shadows. And somewhere, some train, somewhere bound.

Then in and up the stairs, over Mr. Schonfield's head, past Khan and Delussie, up to Geiger, Walters and Ormgood, then Steegmeyer, Yannick, Horst, and at last to the top floor where Moseby and Giffen lived. In and his pilferings upon the table. Now heavily, thickly tired, yet oddly clear-headed, again almost the feeling of well-being. Off with his food-smelling clothes, the trousers damp on the front from dishwater and into the paisley dressing-gown which Edna had borrowed money from her mother to buy out of Shannon's sale.

Outside the lurid hue of the London sky implied holocaust. Moseby watched it and tried to feel the distance between him and those he had left. He could not. A night's journey. A day's travelling. Eight hours. Four hundred miles. It did not add up to a realization. Only if he suddenly needed or wished to be with them would its actuality emerge. Otherwise he was permanently adjacent, perpetually removed.

What are you doing standing here? Looking out of this overpriced cabin at the London night? Must. Sort things out. Only way. Shit. You ran away because it was easier. Easier than going down and facing her. Too bloody true it was easier. She would have understood. You have to be joking. You don't understand being kicked in the parts. You feel it. Ran away out of cowardice. Ran away because of the weeks, months, years of recrimination, of the face that went blank when a radio voice mentioned "other woman," when the word "unfaithful" appeared in print, when the image of him and whoever she was burned on the retina of hindsight. That's why. You ran away little man because you didn't love your wife and your only begotten girl child enough.

All of which being true Moseby nodded to the orange sky then turned from his observation to bed and there perhaps sleep.

In the morning Sammy Giffen. A knock, face round the door, pink froth of stubble, the pale pale blue eyes, anaemic Van Gogh. "Morning, John, eh wake ye up did I, brought your mail, that bliggy Schonfield," and he was inside now, a letter in one hand and his kettle in the other, "on at me about the bliggy rent, he knows I'll pay, I'm just making a cup of tea, John, would you like a cup?" going towards the gas ring. When Sammy said he was making a cup of tea he meant he had filled the kettle and could he boil it and borrow milk, tea and sugar. Moseby sat up.

"The letter, Sammy." But he was behind the screen.

"I'll just put this kettle on," in the tone of someone disclosing a new, economic way of making tea, "that bliggy German Jew, God forgive me for saying it, at me in the hall, I got a letter from Father Anselm saying to go up for a week. Meditation. I'll have to hitch it up to Nottingham."

"My letter, Sammy."

"From your home town, John, Greenock, you're right across from the Polaris base, marched up there last year, never been to Greenock, though," and he came round the screen in his quick scurrying way.

"Give us the letter for godsake."

"Oh aye, right, there you are, John, aye Greenock, hope it's good news for you," and he handed over the letter then backed away to a chair, to re-open his own envelope and read it aloud to himself, nodding in concentrated ingestion, frowning over points of interpretation.

"Mr. Samuel Giffen. Dear Mr. Giffen, In reply to your welcome enquiries I have to inform you that the Abbey is open to those members of our faith who wish to engage in religious retreat and meditation." He looked up. "Meditation" he said, explaining much. Moseby nodded, unhearing. His letter was from Edna. The precise, unformed hand knotted his thoughts. "Please." "Never." Each equally terrifying. "The duration of the retreat is usually one week and is without charge. Applicants should obtain a letter of recommendation from their parish priest." Sammy smiled at this. "I can get Father Cassidy to write me a letter. He's a bliggy bog Irishman but he's not as bad as some of them fanatical Irish Catholics are, it's them that's holding the Church back."

"Make the tea, Sammy."

"Aye right, John, cup of tea," and up and round behind the screen with a little humming of tea-making earnestness. Moseby looked at the postmark. Greenock. 28th August. In the year of Their Lord. Open it Moseby you scab. After tea.

"Everything all right then, John?"

"Don't put too much milk in my tea."

"No, right John, not too much."

Sammy talked of the retreat and Father Cassidy and the evil influence of McQuade in Ireland and the problems Catholic C.N.D.s faced in being both Catholic and disarmers, the rapid stumbling talk with its tone of moral fervour constantly breaking into uneasy grins at his own hypocrisy. Moseby watched him, fascinated and aghast at the spectacle. Sammy was a semi-illiterate Catholic-convert Communist crypto-homosexual Scottish working-class playwright sort of guy in addition to being an inveterate beggar, borrower and reluctant returner. He had breath like an old dog and a tendency to psychosomatic skin ailments that had his hands constantly at one another or on his face, picking and scratching. He had improbable red hair, quite long but thin so that the scalp showed, flaky with dandruff. Moseby on occasions showed that he found him beyond all bearing, but a remarkable capacity to ignore snubs weathered these times and kept him in almost daily touch with his "fellow countryman" as he called Moseby.

48 Shore Street,
Gourock.

John,

I thought you would like to know that Carol and I have gone to live with my mother. I cannot bear to be in

10

that house any longer, the last few weeks I spent in it I was so unhappy. It is not very convenient for mother to have us here but she has insisted that we stay. I don't know what I would have done without her. She has been very good about everything and has not made things more difficult for me by criticizing you openly in front of Carol. I know she thinks what you have done is despicable as indeed it is. I suppose you will have had time by now to think up something in defence of what you have done but as far as I am concerned, John, there can be no defence.

At this time I am so miserable I can hardly think straight and I don't know what we will do. My mother says I should consider divorcing you but there is Carol to think of. I went up to Glasgow and saw Cathie Pollock and I think she is pathetic. She just said she was sorry for the trouble she had caused and asked me to forgive her. I felt sick after coming away and thought I was going to faint in the street. Now that I have seen her I am in no doubt as to what you wanted from her, it's sticking out a mile that she's a slut. She asked me not to tell her husband, I was so disgusted I wanted to hit her. I pity him wherever he is, of course he may be the kind who doesn't care. I wouldn't be surprised. What I am surprised at is you having anything to do with a common little slut like her. Surprised and disgusted.

I feel sure now that this is the fact that you were adopted coming out in some way. You are obviously mixed up very badly and I should have thought, although I'm no expert, that you are in need of help mentally. You said in your letter you have to sort things out. Do you think you can sort things out? I don't. All I do know is that I could never think of you in the same way after what you have done to Carol and me. We are telling her that you have gone for a special examination to London and won't be back for a long time. When you come back to start University again I suppose we will have to meet to discuss things but please don't come round to Shore Street for mother won't let you in and I don't want any scenes in front of Carol.

Just remember this is your problem, John, and that you have to solve it before there is any point in us meeting to discuss things. The only person who knows apart from mother is Mr. Maxwell who says he will be writing to you. I just hope you are as unhappy as I am then you may come to your senses a bit more quickly.

Yours, Edna

Oh Jesus Christ. Wasn't it all just there. He could just see Mrs. Davidson not openly criticizing. And she'd gone to see Cathie. What a meeting that must have been. He could see Edna every step of the way, doing it to make some sense out of her pain. Well at least she'd managed to feel superior. "You are obviously mixed up very badly." The Great Bartender had forgotten to shake well before pouring. "Gone to London for a special examination." Oh Edna, you stupid hard done by cow. He loved her though, didn't he? Don't know. How do you know? The only person he could be sure he loved was John Moseby. All the pain was probably that other people kept making it difficult to get on with it. Oh be quiet can't you, can't you just shut up your fucking little yap Moseby.

"Good news from home, John?"

"Marvellous. Mafeking's been relieved."

He went up with Sammy to see Father Cassidy. Sammy was full of the week's retreat.

"Be a wonderful experience, under vows of silence a lot o' them, canny talk. Silence. Reading their brevitaries," and he put his open palms under his face and dragged his feet, and all without a vestige of mockery, then skipped to catch up. "And the food's awful good, grow all their own vegetables, be awful good for you. Would you not like to come, I could get Father Cassidy to write you a letter."

"I'm not a Catholic, Sammy."

He thought about this for a moment then grinned and did the little sideways step that marked a switch of roles, "No but it would be a good experience for you, for your writing." He had seen some manuscript of Moseby's and assumed he was, like himself, a Scottish playwright. "And Father Cassidy wouldn't know, I could say you had just come down from Scotland and you wanted to go into retreat for a week."

For a week? Moseby smiled and shook his head. "No, Sammy, I don't feel the call," and something in his tone reached the prospective recluse and darked his view.

"No, no well maybe another time. I might not like it myself when I get there."

Across the street, with a large white handbag over her heavy arm, Helen stood, the other arm round the waist of a big man with an open-necked shirt and the wild, middle-parted hair of the Irish labourer. By the abandon of their laughter they seemed to have newly emerged from the Marylebone Arms behind them. Moseby stepped inside Sammy and lowered his head. The old jingle. Slowly, with feeling.

> "If ye see a big fat wummin
> Standin' on the corner bummin'
> That's ma mammy."

What if indeed. And not the pale, dark lady in the walled garden gathering peonies in a shallow cradle basket, whose eyes, as they first met his, would fill with knowing and all surrounding love, his mistress-mother-sister-friend who would spoon him egg and cradle his head on the soft rise of her breast.

With a red mad report a bus blundered by. A tree in the wind crashed itself on his sight and the sun emerged from cloud to smash in countless blazons of glister on sudden windows, spiky blinding sunflowers. Assaulted by the violence of the moment Moseby recoiled from his dream. But as he waited later for Sammy to get his letter he thought of his nostalgia, if nostalgia can be for what one has never known. "We sleep within the bosoms of our causes," awaiting the opportunity to be born. He presumed being born was something that went on endlessly. If it ever stopped you were dead. And if it never started you were worse than dead. Sammy came down the steps, his yellow smile wide with triumph, patting his breast pocket in self-congratulation. Into which category did Sammy fit, Moseby wondered, momentarily diverted from consideration of himself by the visible evidence of his good fortune as it came scampering across the street.

"I can take a drink," Helen was saying, "and I can leave it, but there's them that's not able for it and they shouldn't drink and it's the same with every other mortal thing, enough's as good as a feast and anything more than that is a sin against the living God, d'you understand me?" and Moseby nodded. Helen was peeling and dicing onions and her eyes watered and gave her words a certain air of contrition, although the tone remained unaltered, rancorous and wheedling at once. "I've seen all sorts, seen the gentry and seen them buggers," jerking a head out front, "and they're all about as bad as each other with their goings on, when you've been in service to some of these Protestant gentry there's not much that's left you to learn about the ways of the world, 'twas them filth that made me glad to be a Monsie, seeing the likes of their ways, shameless she was bringing down her clouts all stiff with the blood of her and handing them over to be washed like they were my lady's kerchief, the curtains of her master's pleasure no more and his big beefy hand up your knickers quick as you like when you were bent over a wash, filth the lot of them and all at church come Sunday, smiling like Jesus Christ himself owed them money, made me a Monsie for sure."

"What's a Monsie, Helen?"

"A Monsie Catholic. All Christ's leavings the lot of them."

There was a girl showing a lot of leg and Moseby read the paper of the man next to him to keep his eyes away. The provocativeness of skirts and stockings presented itself irresistibly. He longed to reach across and put his hand, better still his head, up under the canopy, to be swallowed into that fleshy dark. The man moved his paper so that it was hard to follow the print. There was a piece about crocodiles in the sewers of New York. People had bought them when they were small and flushed them down the toilet as they got bigger. They had adapted to a diet of human excrement and rats and multiplied enormously. The man got off and Moseby, his mind swarming with shite-eating crocodiles, was left to gaze up the skirt of the girl opposite.

Passing a furrier's he saw a small intent man trying to suck a bee out of the corner of the window with a vacuum cleaner. His face was rapt with the chase, the crippled bee inching along the bottom of the window, the awkward vacuum fitment following it. He caught Moseby's eye and held it a minute, then uneasily looked away. Briefly reprieved the bee made ineffective burrowings down into the felt. Moseby went on, but the thought of the bee went with him, trapped now in that dark tube, ingested with the dust and hair, crawling helplessly through the stifling, matted dirt, far from the vivid flower mouths of its sunlit delvings, taken down into the bowels to slowly choke, far from pollen and petals, honey and home.

The winds rush through the dark tunnels, hot seedless winds, smelling of greenless places. They ruffle the hair of the wan waiters and flap their clothes around their knees and fill noses with arid odours. The stale winds blow beneath the land and behind them come the red worming tubes to gather up the buried people. Moseby found himself sucked down, pulled down, ferried down to these unimaginable circuits and there transported at their will, round about and under below.

A spoon fell into the bin. He plunged his hand in after it, into the entrails of waste, into the dark tangle of rejected foods, and it came out smeared and slimy, having been where the eye could not go, having seen what was inaccessible to sight. As he dried it he looked carefully to see whether it had been affected by the experience. Pale crab, scuttling the rancid tub, what do you now know. The hand smelled a little sour but was not otherwise impressed.

Written on a toilet wall amid the anecdotes and boasts and assignations and depictions, in neat block capitals, printed in a box, the epithet "God is a maggot." Its manic certainty impressed Moseby and after he had finished deciphering the other graffiti he returned to this, wondering about its owner and his implacable convictions.

On his day off he went to a cinema. It was more to escape the people in the streets than to see the film which was a revival of one of the early Tarzan's. Inside was almost empty. There was that red colouring, that sarcoidal velveteen so much beloved of his youth. A man was playing an electric organ, one of the kind with coloured lights around it. Moseby hunched low into his seat, looking out across the sea of curved seat backs. Here and there the atolls of other castaways like himself. The organ sucked him down, into sunken caverns where drownded sailor sounds filled his ears, whorls of gaudiest submarine. Only the sight of it sinking, still lit up, rescued him, like some survivor of the *Titanic*, seeing its pantomime plunge beneath the motionless waves.

On Sunday they went to Hyde Park to the Speakers' Corner. There was a man with a beard proving that the yellow races were destined to rule the earth. A few impassive occidentals watched him. Beyond, in the midst of a dozen or so hecklers, a pacifist lady, smiling tolerantly at the interruptions and saying "I'm sure you did, my man, and your country thanks you for it, but. . . ."

The largest group was round a young, pale-faced woman, on a portable platform, wisping back her hair from a broad smooth forehead and drying the sweat from her palms on a very large cambric handkerchief. She represented the Catholic Truth Society and Sammy drew Moseby towards her.

"She's a wonderful speaker this lassie, you want to hear her, John, a working-class lassie, self-educated, listen tae that bliggy swine."

The bliggy swine was a small balding man who wanted to know how any rational being could believe that the Virgin Mary ascended into Heaven bodily. The woman spoke in a clear, slightly tremulous voice, explaining the process by which the dogma had been established. Once when she used the expression Papal Bull the little man interjected "bull shit" which drew a weary smile of recognition and an angry "sssh" from Sammy.

There were further questions, all of a hackingly sceptical sort, and the girl, incessantly wiping her hands and touching her hair, answered them, clear lucid textual answers learned in the past and brought out as required. Sammy's sympathy with her for the moment stilled the gingery ferretings of his face and he looked up devoutly out of his pallid blue eyes at the word made flesh. He finally asked a question himself, designed to ease the strain on the speaker, an open unbarbed query inviting rhetoric in response.

"Why do you think Catholicism is the answer to the world's needs?"

The very generosity of it caught her unprepared, her mind tense to receive blows, this sop unnerved her. She flicked away her hair and twisted her hands on the handkerchief. Her voice started, then faltered and someone "yaahed" and another called out "what about the Albigensians?" which phrase was caught up by several uncomprehending voices and a babel of requests rose as to the fate of the Albigensians. The girl gripped the rail of her platform and closed her eyes. An older thickset woman handed her up a glass of water which she held for a moment before drinking, her eyes still closed as she did. Then she said something inaudible and came down the few steps to the ground. The derisive calls lasted a moment and then the group drifted away, their interest evaporated. Only Sammy and Moseby, the girl and the older woman were left. The girl stood with her head down, resting against the platform, her lips moving in prayer. Sammy approached and congratulated her on her speaking. She nodded and walked off slowly towards the trees at the edge of the park. The woman began to dismantle the platform and Sammy, somewhat unnecessarily, helped. Moseby stood a moment and then followed the girl. She was standing against a tree and her face was away from him.

"Excuse me. . . ." Without turning she said,

"Not any more questions today please, not today," and turned her head even further though from her voice he could tell she was near to tears.

He looked around. Sammy and the woman were strapping up the platform. Pigeons clockworked about, their braque-bird shadows in close attendance. There was a spangly light

17

through the trees that fell at their feet in goldshoals of sunfish and across the park lovers lay prone and linked in the grass. He touched her shoulder and she stiffened away.

"Please keep your hands to yourself," cold and angry and she looked at him now, an unbalanced face, high above the brows, peaky and pressed in the features.

"I didn't mean to offend you. I just thought you looked a bit rough."

"I'm all right now thanks. Can I help you?" drawing upright and away from the tree.

"What are Monsie Catholics, do you know, is it a sect of some kind?"

"Monsie? Monsie Catholics? I've never heard of them."

"It doesn't matter. Just something I heard, curious. Sorry to have bothered you." He turned away. A rutting cock puffed and panached. It reminded him of one long ago Saturday morning, taking Carol down to feed the gulls. He looked back at the girl.

"It's very beautiful, in a godless sort of way," including with his hand the park and the courters and the pigeons and the quick sunlight in the trees, the sungold shoalfish. The girl returned his gaze.

"It is only an illusion of well-being, the easiest way of all is to think things are as they seem. But they are not."

"Jekyll and Hyde Park," Moseby said. The girl looked uncertain. He smiled politely and left, allowing Sammy to catch up with him.

His play was for radio and took the form of two voices, one speaking passages from Defoe's *Robinson Crusoe*, the other Moseby's meditations on island solitude. It seemed to him absurdly pretentious to be hacking up an English classic to make a thirty minute radio feature but now commenced on it he was determined to see it through to a submitted manuscript. Much of the early work had required him to read *Crusoe* over and over, extracting the likeliest sections for his use and planning the development of his own theme. He was only now commencing this contribution.

CASTAWAY VOICE:

Two shoes on the beach, derelicts,
nothing sadder than shoes filled with sand,
standing still.
Footless on the empty shore;
the sea sounding jumm-drum washes,
salt falling, sand sifting sea.
[*Pause and the sound of the sea.*]
Souse sea, souse; sift sand, sift.
So much sand, so much sea.
How many hour glasses have emptied out their grains,
how many chimes the sea has struck this beach,
bare as bone, bleached white by salt and sun and sea.
[*The sea tolls on the shore. Then a man weeping, terrible in its abandon.*]

DEFOE VOICE:

And this threw me into terrible agonies of mind. I resolved to sit all night and consider the next day what death I should die, for as yet I saw no prospect of life.

Moseby walked, thinking and piecing the thoughts together, seeing where he could the pattern, the design in it all, but the night and the city everywhere pierced the fabric, its lurid reality inescapable.

The girls on the posters, moustaches on the lips and crotches. A film star's finger wearing a solitaire of chewing gum. And the several coated tramps, drifting along the walls like blown hanks. Scrawled on a wall "white women love a black man's cock," and on a toilet door, "I take it up the back and in the mouth. This is not a joke. Make a date." Down in Euston a train sighed smoke up, like a sad whale in a salt sea.

Moseby waited on the parapet, watching his white spit spin down into the extinguishing dark. And again. How was he come to be here, hawking his sputum over a London bridge? Where was the meaning, the rhyme? The multiple lines of Euston webbed and wove, shining mazily in the last light.

Sitting down in the bath, shivering in the cold air, the hot water sudden in contrast, he had a sense, if that, an apprehension, nothing more, of his vulnerability. Yet vulnerable was not the word, the awareness posited no threats against which he might require to protect himself. It was all to do with the coldness that was the world without and the precarious warmth of his body maintained. The bath was but the metaphor of the many different warmths that comforted the heart. Of being asleep, or in the summer sun, the warmth of flesh sealing out the cold, in sex and, most comprehensively in the womb, "the bath of birth." He sat in his little pool, remembering Tarzan and Jane playing with Boy in the hot springs, how the absurdity of the actors and the synthetic backdrop faded and the little tableau became real, tender in its trite happiness so that he almost cried, his nostalgia for some undwelt-in Eden sweet and strong.

Sammy was being psychoanalyzed on the National Health and every Wednesday took the 31 bus over to St. Stephens Hospital at Chelsea. He derived great satisfaction out of having his case history elicited each week and related the findings to Moseby as though he'd never heard them until that very moment.

"My trauma was my bliggy fether, owl swine that he was, killed my mother with his drinking and always going on at her, wouldn't leave her alone."

"How many in your family, Sammy?"

"Oh, just me."

"He couldn't have got very close to her then if you're the only one."

"It wisnae for want o' tryin' I can tell you. And then after my mother died he merrit this right bitch. That's why I became a Catholic. I had to, John, honest, that was the only thing that saved me from a breakdown."

"The bosom of Mother Church."

"That's right. They ask me all about this you know."

"Sammy, you're no more a Catholic than I am."

"Oh I know I'm not a good Catholic, but I want to be."

"Well, what about this poovery then? How do you manage to get around that? I mean, do you confess about humping men?"

"Oh my God no," and a peal of excited pink laughter rent the upper deck.

"Do you actually hump them, Sammy, I mean do you actually do anything or do you just think about it?"

"Oh no, John, oh I do. I always keep the masculine role in my relations though."

"So what do you do, tell me how you go about it."

"Well," and he gave a quick little glance behind, "well you see a boy, you know, gay, and he sees you and you get talking and buy him a drink so that he knows you're the butch and then maybe you can take him back to his place or he'll come back with you."

"And then?"

"Oh, John, you don't want me to tell you that?"

"Come on."

"Well you just get in and, well, if he's game for it, you get into bed."

"What if he's not game?"

"Oh but he is if he's let you come back. Sometimes they like to be coaxed though."

"So what happens?" Moseby said, steeling himself for the perpetration.

"Well, you get into bed and, and then you embrace." And the kindly incongruous word choked Moseby with its horror and pity and Sammy's presence receded and he wanted to hear no more, confronted again as he was by the face of love, unsuspected under the mask.

While Sammy was being analyzed Moseby waited in the Fulham Road Cemetery, just inside the entrance, round the corner under some plane trees against a high brick wall. It was an unused, overgrown part where the gravestones were all of the same rough erosive pale stone and the names inscribed were all worn close to illegibility. To Moseby's casual scrutiny no one had been buried in this corner since the century began, time and distance had mellowed the edges of the cuts and in soft granular symbols they stated themselves and their age and the condolences and hopes of the then left alive.

One particular stone drew Moseby to it, the Rushton's; with

his back against a tree and the hush of the burial ground thickly everywhere, he let the names of these unknown people slip through his mind like a rosary of strange comfort, these curious human callings that had once summoned the quick, little lads and mothers, for which men had turned at the heads of stairs and girls had tossed their plaits and never looked back. And now such peace was theirs as Moseby perceived he had never known, beyond call or care, fallen to earth, shaken from the tree of life, they offered their appells to the random picker and gave no thought to the morrow.

Thomas Howard Rushton. Mary Alice Rushton. Fleur Rushton. Gilbert Rushton. Samuel Cabot Rushton. Philip Walter Rushton, Rebecca Rushton, Matthew Rushton, an infant of four months Moseby noted. Jonathan Adam Rushton, and he was ninety-two. The dead burying their dead. They all lay there in family repose and the roars from the adjacent football ground rolled over them silently. Moseby envied them their seeming affinities and close bond. He felt himself a nameless, faceless one, hung over the void. Into which plot would he fall, what towering tenement of names would rise above his head, where were his Mary Alices and Samuel Cabots, where was Rebecca and where was Matthew and where oh where was Fleur. . . .

The gravestones swooned in the grasses and the tree swept the tattered blue sky into the pyre of the sun and blinded him. He lay against the bole and watched his feet spin round.

[*A gun shot, close to, loud. A great outcry of birds held for a moment. Then in a reverential whisper.*]

DEFOE VOICE:

I believe it was the first gun that had been fired there since the beginning of the world.

[*End of the bird calls, quiet descends. The castaway voice, reflective.*]

CASTAWAY VOICE:

The first since creation, the first man to walk here, to crush with his foot these grasses, to smell these flowers, cut these trees.

[*And there commences the sound of chopping.*]

If a tree falls in a forest
[*Chopping*]
and nobody hears it
[*Chopping*]
is there any sound.
[*And the sound of a tree crashing down. When the castaway continues a ticking is heard in place of the chopping.*]
If a man dies alone
[*Ticking*]
and nobody knows
[*Ticking*]
did he ever live.
[*The ticking builds up into the whirring of a clock about to strike. Instead a tree crashes down. In panic the castaway,*]
I don't want to be alone,
please God make me not alone
not alone on my desert I-land.

Helen sat at the table and her blunt fingers bruised among the lettuce, plucking at the crisp hearts and discarding the exteriors. From time to time she took sips from a mug of tea and looked to Moseby with a nod that was nearly a wink. He speared and swallowed the little sachets of his ravioli, wondering if he had offended the cook somehow, seeing how beggarly the portion was. Helen released against her chair a barrage of farts, rapid blurtings which sent Moseby's head down over his ravioli and set her off talking. "I was with this mick last night and they have only the one thing in their mind and I had to hit him with my handbag at the wind up, who wants that sort of thing, all the one they're at and you knowing from the first it's to be up against some wall and that big tarrier under your skirt and he'd leave you there with his stuff running down your legs and bid you good night, anyhow I told him he was nothing but a hardon with a man stuck to it, filth the lot of them and him supposing to be a Catholic, from the south you see, and them's worse than Protestants for going on and I told him, not that the ignoramus knew the one half of what I said, but I told him if he looked at himself for longer than a minute he'd see he was nothing but the rakings of Our Lord, the dirt of him and his passing. . . ."

"I don't quite see what you mean by that, Helen, about . . ."

"What, now what's to understand to a young man like yourself out of college, what's to understand? Sure it's plain enough to see we're his leavings and filled up with our pride we are, that's all that keeps us from seeing it, pride, consumption of pride and you'll hear them saying this and that and in between but it's all pride talking not to face up to it. Because when you face up to it then there's only one thing you can do but that wouldn't suit them."

"What do you think happens when we die, Helen?"

"Aha, well then, that'll be the showing of them that thinks they know, eh," and here again released a blatter of farting and stood up as though cued, the thick soupy smell of it after her.

"But you won't want to be knowing about after you're dead," moving to the sink, "not a young mister like you, you'll be thinking on the other most nights and what you can get off a girl."

"Helen, what's a Monsie Catholic?"

"Well, you're not one by all accounts."

"Are you?" and at the question the woman turned, stricken.

"God knows and it's the truth I was and now sometimes I'm no better than the rest of them filth forgetting everything I was learnt, but I was and with His help I will be again," then she went back to the sink, the slump of her broad back prohibiting further enquiry.

It was like the jungle only it wasn't because it was dark and he felt his way along the walls and hurried home. When he got there they were all gone and he knew something must be wrong because all Carol's things were scattered everywhere and Edna's clothing and he ran off looking for them. The crocodiles were all sliding down into the water and he had to swim very fast and it wasn't like swimming at all, more like crawling along the surface of the water. There were two tunnels and he met Helen sitting on a trunk eating fish and chips and she told him that Edna was down one and Carol down the other. As he stood trying to make up his mind who he should try to save all the while more crocodiles were crawling down into the water and disappearing into the tunnel. It was impossible to choose which one and he found himself sitting down on the trunk with Helen and ate some of her chips. Everything changed and he was on the tube and he kept watching the stations to see where he got off, except all the stations were named after streets in Greenock. He got off at Dempster Street and it was all quiet and he hurried along knowing they must be in some danger and he noticed all the houses were empty and the windows broken and inside paper peeling off the walls and when he got to 48 it was the same and he ran up the stairs and his door was lying open and everything smelled of damp and on the walls was fungus and he went into the room where the green wallpaper had all mildewed. His books were on the floor and he sat down in the rubble and started to read one. It was about a man who was shipwrecked and who kept a fire lit so he would be rescued. Only he couldn't find enough wood to burn so Moseby broke up the chair and then the table and opened the window in the kitchen so that the smoke could get out. If Edna said anything he would tell her the furniture didn't mean a thing to him. It was only wood. The cat had been alive and she had destroyed it. The chair burned well and so did the table and his books and smoke poured out of the kitchen window but nobody seemed to see it and after a while there wasn't anything left to burn and when he looked out of the window he could see that the town was empty, still and silent. He looked for a long time but he could see no one. Perhaps the cat wasn't dead, the vet had made a mistake. If there was nobody left the grass would start to grow and weeds and moss and flowers and trees and all the street names would be lost to view. If he wanted to find Brougham Street and the vet's house he would have to go soon. The West Kirk clock started to strike and the alarm woke him out of sleep at once, assailed by the loneliness of his dream and the memories of his dead cat.

His dream remained, like a stale taste, in the morning and he was quite pleased when Sammy came, bending over a great parcel of newspapers. On the brown paper wrapping there was a label *Catholic Worker*.

"These are my *Catholic Workers*," in a tone that suggested he both wrote and printed them.

"What for?"

"I sell them."

"Where do you get them?"

"All the way from the United States. I get them sent."

"What for?"

"Oh it's a very intellectual Catholic paper, very left wing, very liberal ideas," and the yellow grin.

"How much do you sell it for?"

"I take it round all my committees."

"How much?"

"Aha John," and his mirth was almost infectious.

"How much?"

"Sixpence, that's not much for the size of it."

"And how much does it cost you?"

"Oho," almost dancing with glee, "penny a copy but I took the risk sending for it, didn't I?"

"You are a rogue, Giffen, and a bad Catholic, and a capitalist."

"Oh no, that's one thing, I'm no bliggy capitalist, I hate them buggers, I'm always true to my socialist principles," and this with mock vehemence.

"You mean you draw the N.A.B.," and Sammy gave out his yodelling laugh of capitulation and commenced making the tea. Moseby thought of the organization in America sending off their paper. Our man in N.W.6 Samuel Giffen. You had to laugh.

The Underground drew him down into it like a vortex. Down out of the light and time of day, down the hastening escalators down to the sunken routes, the great intestinal tracts of the city's system. He looked at the map of the network, the black and red and brown and green and magenta coils and loops, arterial threadings of this underworld empire, with its arid air, its arbitrary winds, drifting no seed and bending no bough, a land peopled by transients, ever eager to board and burrow on, save for those dark men and women who attend the stygian shores and sweep the passengers' droppings and know the rhythms of its thoroughfares.

He would escape from the daylight down into its depths and changing trains at random, twist and writhe through the innards of the earth, noting the station names less than the people who entered and exited, once seen wayfarers, carrying their secret lives off to secret destinations. Sometimes a moment of nearness approached, unbidden. He and another, moving for the same vacated newspaper, met and paused, offered each other what was not theirs, then retired uneasy at the imprudence until the next halt when Moseby got off.

A man in a grey pinstripe suit, striking match after futile match into the bowl of his extinct pipe and between each little failed flare, scowling at the other passengers and pointing to his face, transversed by a crumpled scar, between his brows to beneath his ear and informing them that They did it and that there were plenty of Them still about and They would get all those present in time and the matches kept spurting and dying and dropping around his feet like little bones. Moseby watched him until at one stop he bolted upright and ran out of the train. The rest of the travellers raised their heads and allowed themselves brief smiles of self-congratulation at having behaved so well.

For Moseby there was a kind of escape into limbo, a quiescence born of movement however purposeless, only when they broke surface and ran among houses and people walking did he feel the uselessness of it and turn back again into the caverns of his precarious content.

At night there were four regular waitresses. A tall impassive French girl called Martine, whose pancake makeup and pale eyes made her almost faceless. Two English girls, one married and making money in the evenings, the other at a Midland university. The fourth was a Greek girl who barely spoke the language and was becoming noticeably pregnant.

Their attitude to Moseby had changed over the weeks of his stay. Assuming him at first to be another one-week worker they hadn't troubled to learn his name. Then as he appeared night after night they began to smile and talk with him and discuss the management and previous dishwashers and Helen.

The one who went to university was called Angela and when she found out that he was at Glasgow doing History and English Lit. she became very chummy and told him of her boyfriend who only managed to come up from Exeter every two or three weeks.

It was the other English girl who found out he was married and had a child. She had a daughter somewhat younger than Carol and talking about her provoked a parental comment from Moseby. Quickly on the scent she soon elicited the fact of the separation and asked him whose fault it was.

Whose fault? How did evil first enter the world? What historical process had culminated in the manic digit, I, John Moseby? What cult of the individual was he but a highly specialized instance of? Whence sprung his black guilt and his lack of contrition? Question mark.

"Mine," he said, being the only possible answer for the time-served egomaniac.

"Do you love her, your wife? Surely you love your daughter?"

Love. Love is but Evol reversed as God is Dog. Who do you love, J.M., having had no parents proper nor a teddy and unlikely to have been breast-fed, and she, the wife, didn't understand me. As for my daughter, well, you love a child like you love ice cream. Do you not? Or do you?

"Oh yes, I love them," because anything else was too complex or involved censure.

"What are you going to do then?"

Ah well, that is the crucial issue of our time, is it not, is it rather more good to suffer the knives and forks of the bogging Montmartre or take offence and get the hell hence to whither we ken not.

"I don't know," wherein was contained a whole lifetime of experience.

Then lest any of these totally unconcerned females should disapprove of him he deemed it wise to prepare a speech in his own defence.

"Ladies, you see before you a poignant example of an important mid-twentieth century phenomenon, modern man in search of his hole. Edna was not so much my wife as my dugout where into I would retire when assailed by doubts as to my significance in the order of things, an oft-time uncertainty. Prised now from cockpit I am engaged upon a quest, a blind search for a holy braille which when found will decipher my question, or rather would if I but knew what the question was. While awaiting illumination on this point, I am assuming the guise of the suffering servant, in which connection the significance of this restaurant's name will not have escaped you, I'm sure, the Montmartre, the Calvary Caff, scouring the platters of the polloi, unlayering the onion of my soul and weeping mock tears at the insubstantiality of that item. For others maybe the matter is simpler, 'if at first you don't succeed, pull your foreskin o'er you heid' as the old saw cuts. Doubtless their desolation is more utter than mine, wrapped around by the prepuce of self-deception as they are, but at least they have the advantage of not knowing it to be so. When the Great Taxidermist comes he will find the stuffing of such a matter little moment, but for the spiritually circumcised like myself there will be needed sawdust by the cart load, nor will all his preservative arrest the stench of it." Which had it been delivered would doubtless have brought to a halt that barter of food for money which all there were dependent on for their very existence, and probably caused the Greek girl to bring forth before her time.

Once with Sammy at the hospital a roomful of women, sitting splay-legged and dull, causing him to think of mushroom growths in the stomach. Their eyes on him with dim resentment since he could not share their internal terrors, and was in his facsimile the cause of not a few of them. The smell of women brought together assailed him, rankling in the nose, festering in the mind and he saw women then with their sluttishness and the uncleanness of their ways and left with a quick male step.

Sammy was virtually living on Moseby now, eating with him in the morning and often in the afternoon, and sometimes when Moseby got home at night, limp and yawning, Sammy would be awake with his "Will I put the kettle on, can I have a wee slice of your bread, is that a cake?" and at any sign of resentment withdrawing into abject apology, "Oh I know I'm awful Johnny, it's this bliggy N.A.B., think it was their money, how's the script going?" And each anger passed as he thought on its trivial grounds. Did he not steal most of the food himself? Was not Sammy hungry? Did he not need Sammy for things too? In him was made clear that at least Moseby was not in the worst of predicaments, and for this reminder he was, as he should be, grateful.

"I haven't always been in the Mount Marty you know, oh I was in a big restaurant in the West End before this and good money earning and a decent place to work, clean overall every day and something to show for it, God forgive me for using his name but it was a palace compared with this."

"What happened?"

"Oh you might know, the filth got in and that was it started, there's one thing I cannot stand and that's working with filth and trash the likes of which you shouldn't be asked to work with."

"What do you mean, Helen?"

"Blacks, black women in beside us and I said how can you keep white clean when you let black in, and they couldn't answer me. I quoted Our Lord's words to them, not that they were any the wiser, that the sepulchres were white-washed without but were putrid bones within and they couldn't answer me, not the one of them. Filth, they love filth and don't see that's all they are, leavings the lot of them, these white women that have to do with blacks, letting filth inside them, and them blacks have terrible things on them it's well known, should be cut off their bodies when they're born."

And Moseby remembered the chalk scream on the wall and could see Helen smashing on the white words in powdery hatred.

The Manse,
Forsyth Street,
Greenock.

Dear John,
    I heard with great dismay of the way in which things

have gone with you and your life and I promised Edna that I would take time to write you. It is with very little feeling of confidence that I do so now. In the few meetings we have had I had the sense that you were struggling with things that might try you sorely before it was all out and sadly enough this seems to be the case.

Your wife seems to know nothing of this and we could not talk in any way that made sense to us both at once. I was required in my dealings with her to express my disapproval of your adultery, as indeed I feel it, but could not convey to her that this was, I am sure, but a symptom and not the disease. I have every sympathy with Edna for she has been placed in a position no less terrible for being so novellettish, but I feel she sees too little of what is at stake.

What is at stake I have already said to you on one of your visits to Forsyth Street. My deepest regret is that there is so little I can do about it. Also this is a case in which I must exercise very great care over my attitude to you. It is a great temptation for me to say that you are an extraordinary case, a soul *especially* worth the saving, but in doing this I would be wrong and would have fallen into most dangerous error. You are indeed an extraordinary person, but these are human qualities and a human assessment of them. But God's love is not primarily concerned with these features, He loves us for the very fact that we are at all, "God loves each and every one of us as though there were but one of us to love," to quote St. Augustine. He loves us all alike, impartially. Only in God's love can you attain that complete certainty as to your own worth and the meaning of your existence. All other love is but the shadow of that love. For me to concern myself with you more than with the very humblest of my congregation is a sin on my part of which would have to repent. So I ramble on about how I cannot help.

What of how I can? Well I can visit Edna regularly and try to talk with her. She is at the moment living with her mother, a good woman in many ways, but of a limited point of view. Also when you come back to

Greenock I can arrange your meetings with Edna to take place here when you will have peace and quiet to talk things out.

As to your present sojourn in London I cannot advise. I presume you will return to take up your University term and possibly living away from Greenock for this length of time may help to clear things in your mind. But, and I'm afraid I will sound like a country parson out of Thackeray now, London is a place where one can find almost every temptation, and every opportunity for indulging one's imagination. What the mind craves for can be irresistibly offered to it and I am not talking now of striptease shows or prostitutes, they are the caricatures of temptation. The things that will tempt you will be considerably less obvious and it is the sin of pride to think that one can resist all temptation. Temptation is to be shunned rather than defied. I can only hope you come back to Greenock more certain of yourself than when you went. My gravest criticism of you, John, is that you are possessed of a great arrogance of spirit, and as a fellow sufferer I can sympathize and warn. No matter how it seems to the contrary, you are not the centre of the universe, God is. Any time spent seeking God is well spent. All time spent seeking self is waste and unprofitable.

Yours in God's love,
James Maxwell

Well now, Moseby, that's you told. "God loves each and every one of us. . . ." Does he now? He thought of the handsome minister and his wife serving tea in the sunny garden and made an up-you sign across the room. Trouble with ministers is they never think the problem might be that there isn't any God. Still, it was a nice letter, very sympathetic. Made him sound about eighty though. "Arrogance of the spirit." "Fellow sufferer." See what he means. St. James's epistle to the Outcasts. "Come unto me, all ye that labour and are heavy laden, and I will give you rest." Some promiser.

Mr. Schonfield was burning his haulms and the fragrant blue smoke rose up past Moseby's window in the yellowing afternoons. It was reassuring somehow to see him, the tall stooped foreign man, making his little pyre of leaf and frond and its slow smoulder through the hours. Moseby, working, paused often to look at the scene and draw from its some analect of solace. Allotment Adam sending up into the tawny air the sweet melisma of his sweepings.

As the day drew itself out into its final blayke light and the silhouettes grew plum blue and the branches of the trees pleached with darkness his pain throbbed in him like an old honourable wound. The swallows made maw in the empty evening sky and here and there the chimney pots flowered. The swifts sickled harvest air and early lights were lit. The world hurt his eyes with its casual beauty. It was all so right and perfect, so holy in its chance perfection. An anonymous fiddle raised its voice and traced a thread through the night upon which the seconds hung like pearls, limpid empty moments of time, gratuities to the racked mind at the window. "God is good, it is a beautiful night," he said, and the enigmatic line eased his heart, said to no one against the pane.

CASTAWAY VOICE:
A bleached branch by an empty ocean edge watching the sea as it smashes its green smither on the prone concaves of the shore.
[*The sound of the sea.*]
Sound of the sea in a shell,
in the whorly coil of the ear,
a walking shell who hears all the seaside day
a brooding ponder of ocean thoughts,
until its meditation grows marine.
[*The sound of the sea.*]
Old lapidary, polishing clear an antique reflection,
in which can be discerned certain conclusions,
endlessly urged in the massy glasses of the swell.
From such glimpsings panic flights him.
[*The sound of the sea.*]
He runs until a smooth branch,

Boned bare by the tides,
raises its limb from the sand.
Leaves long since scoured away,
rubbed down to its final idea.

DEFOE VOICE:

Then I cried out "Lord be my help for I am in great
distress." For I had reason to consider it as a determination of heaven that in this desolate place and in this
desolate manner I should end my life.

CASTAWAY VOICE:

like this nurled timber,
a random sculpt,
a bleached branch by an empty ocean's edge.
[*The sound of the sea.*]

In the "Personal Column" of a paper picked up in the
tube.

Lady in early middle age hopes for companionship with
gentleman. Has travelled and read well. No religious bias.
Genuine relationship only. Box 2731
Widower, childless, seeks to meet widow or unmarried
lady. View to matrimony. Has small private income. Box
3962
Extensively travelled lady, refined tastes, excel. education, wishes equally stimulating male companionship.
Wide range of interests. Excel. bridge, fond of walking. Photo on request. Box 812
Superior gentleman seeks lady, matrimony in suitable
circumstances. Car. Income. All replies strictest confidence. Complete sincerity. Box 6233
Gentleman, intellectual disposition, seeks lady similar,
refined upbringing. Minor disability prevents socializing.
No help required. Box 1109
Lady wishes employment. Companion-housekeeper, to
gentleman. Small income, excellent cook, would require
no wages. Child. References. Box 136

And they went on down the page, with never a "need" and
nary a "want," little atolls of desperate choking print. Moseby

34

screamed inside his head and got out, finding himself at Oxford Circus, a circumstance which filled him with inexplicable terror.

"Where do you come from, Helen?"

"A little place outside Belfast, name of Drumkeera, lovely little spot, many's the time I wish I was back there and then again I don't."

"Why's that?"

"Oh it's no use you going back where you've been when you're younger because it's different all the time."

"Were you happy there?"

"Happiest days of my life and that's the God's truth, till I went into service, then it was all changed. Like the fall from the Garden of Eden that was, out of the garden into service and for nothing but filth."

"But before you went to service you were happy?"

"As the length of the day, well'n what child but isn't, it's the happy time isn't it, running about and not a filthy thought ever coming into your head till the likes of them start looking at your things and up your legs and then God's curse on women for tempting man starts and you're sent off into service not knowing the why of nothing and after that there's no going back, they're all at you and God help us but you learn willing enough and soon you're as bad as the rest wanting all sorts of filth. Oh there's no going back to what it was."

"How did you become a Monsie, Helen?"

"When I had a right realizing of myself that's when, what a dregs and a spittle I was, He didn't want the likes of us or He would have took us with Him. We're nothing but fit for burning. Leavings."

"But didn't he say he'd come again? He said that to the disciples."

"And so he did come again. After he had harrowed Hell he came again on the third day and went up into Heaven and sits on the right hand of God the Father. And we're what's left behind. Sure weren't they expecting His coming every minute of the day on account of what He said to them, and them not having the wit to know any better."

"What did he say?"

"Don't you know your Bible, and you with all your book learning, asking the likes of me. Don't you know that He told the disciples He'd come again before the generation that was had passed away."

"Yes, I know that."

"Well'n didn't He come and they wouldn't believe it and them thinking He was coming to save them all and not knowing Him when they saw Him. Leavings the lot of them."

"So he won't come again?"

"And why should He for the likes of us?"

"But we weren't there, why should we be punished?"

"We're punished for the sins of them that gave us life, don't you know that it says 'conceived in sin, born in iniquity' and that's the sin of them that laid down and coupled like beasts in the mud. How can you think any good can come out of that?" Moseby didn't know.

"And there is nothing to be done then, Helen?" She looked at him, the coiled mind sensing some sneer or trap. Moseby looked back, trying to make his narrow little face open and sympathetic, feeling unconfident of the outcome.

"What can filth do to make itself clean, eh, I ask you, all the rich and gentry and the priests and bishops even the Pope in Rome himself doesn't know, singing and chanting and blessing, it's filth blessing filth and what good is that, eh?"

"None," Moseby conceded.

The rhythm of the hours was now fixed. He worked from six in the evening until half past two in the morning and walked back, made the tea and sat up until the light came, writing or reading or just sitting, looking out and thinking, over and over, the facts and fancies of his lot. Then to sleep and his reflective, distorting dreams, and wake foul-mouthed and sticky about twelve. From then until he went to work included eating and getting cleaned and perhaps a pint of beer and maybe a matinee and more like than not Sammy and possibly a few more lines or revision on the play. Then the Montmartre caught him up again in its cockpit of greasy dishes and clamoured orders and meals with Helen and weariness and boredom and the decision, never implemented, to leave that night, or at the weekend when he found another job.

Of it all the ante-lucan hours most compelled him. He was tired from standing and the chair received him luxuriously. Despite the teas and coffees he'd been sipping all night the one he brewed then comforted most. He propped himself back against the window attic and cuddled his cup to his chin. Outside the city smouldered dull ochre, populous and smoky, and at the lanterns of windows black figures magicked back and forth. Far down in the gardens cats drew sooty trails through the growth and the occasional car revved and roared. There were no stars and the moon looked strange and contrived as it turniped along.

The sounds settled, like sediment in a jar. Chill grew up out of the earth like grey grass and the windows coffined themselves, swift unheralded extinctions. To Moseby, his tea cold and his shins aching, it seemed then that day might never again dawn and in perpetual dark the world would lie. If he was affrighted by the prospect it was scarcely greater than the shudder from the starting drab of sky away across eastern roofs, growing wearily more wan until certain silhouettes declared themselves and the spinning earth on old momentum thrust its denizens once more in the light, against which illumination they clenched their coverlets, and eyes, and each other, reluctant to give up the illusion of unbeing they had so briefly established.

Moseby, like the devout trogdyte he was, retired to his pit.

The anfractuous winds that blow beneath the city carried his thoughts into darkness, into inmost nigger. He travelled less now than he sat, on some long deserted curve, a shore of this plutonic river, there to watch the ferries come and go. It was not tedious to wait there, papers blew past, which when culled, gave news of surface events. On occasions there would be little gyrant dances of cellophane and silver paper, dying away as inexplicably as they had arisen. The castaway there was self-supporting, fruit and nuts might be plucked from the machines and his health estimated from his weight and his

37

tobacco cured and rolled. His mind was catered to by pictures of faraway places and people. Once there it seemed as though he might never wish to leave so long as he was content to sit and brood black thoughts. But always something came and goaded him onwards, inwards. A furtive skirter of the edges would impend him with scenes of suicide, or a glimpse in passing of some girl's face, a cool knowing face that promised much could it be but awakened, or a fat woman opening her legs for spidery glances. He would, for whatever, uproot and leave, jolting on, gibbetting from a strap.

Sometimes, for a moment, the lights would dim with an awful slow decease and in the pitch his mind would multiply atrocities, faceless wreakings on soft female flesh, whimperings for reprieve unheeded in the masterful dark until light would send them scurrying and his eyes would meet cryptic glances from his fellow subterraneans, assuming for all he was worth the guise of patient boredom worn by the others.

"I don't have it, Sammy. I just make enough from that sweat shop up there to keep me."

"Oh I know, Johnny, I know you'd give me it if you had it, I told him I'd get his money for him but the bliggy old Jew wants it right away."

"How much do you owe him?"

"Eh, oh about three or four weeks."

"How much do you get from the N.A.B.?"

"Eh, five pounds twelve."

"Your rent's only two ten isn't it?"

"Aye, but well you see I've been going over the score with this wee Scots lad I met, oh he was a lovely boy, Johnny, I was going to bring him round to meet you, he's a Scottish writer too, he writes, comes from Edinburgh. I've been, you know, spending a bit on him."

"Well, I don't know, Sammy. I've only got enough to get by on. You must owe Schonfield what, seven pounds odd?"

"Aye, maybe I'll get into this place in Essex."

"What place?"

"Oh maybe they'll get me in, it's a group you know, a group and you all discuss your problems and help to face reality by discussing things together. It's a sort of thepary you know."

"Therapy."

"Aye, that's right, well they might get me in there."

"What's your problem then, Sammy?"

"Aye well, that's right, I've got this problem. I mean when I was a boy I never mastrubated. No, never." And he gazed earnestly at Moseby to see what effect this revelation had.

"So?"

"So well I was repressing. Did you mastru . . . did you when you were a boy?"

"When I was a boy."

"Aye, well you see I didn't. And I was always nae use with the lassies."

"Have you ever been to bed with a woman, Sammy?"

"Once. Once I had an affair. With a nurse."

"And you went to bed with her?"

"Yes, with this nurse."

"How many times?"

"Once. But only I couldn't do anything. I couldn't come. I was no use when it came to the bit."

"And how about these lads you go after?"

"Oh, I'm all right with them. You should have seen this wee Scots lad, John, oh he really was lovely. He was a right bad wee bitch and all when it came to it. And I thought he was a virgin first time I saw him," and his laugh at this remembered misapprehension froze Moseby's mind with horror.

The water was that way he couldn't sink into it but remained on the surface no matter how hard he swam. After a while he grew tired of this and got out and there was a telephone box with a tree growing inside it. There was a lot of trees and he looked for the creepers to swing from. They weren't creepers really but bits of rope and old chains but whenever he swung on them they just lowered him down to the ground and he would roll over. He knew if he walked he would never find it, the grass was too high. If only he could see somewhere he knew, a landmark, then he could figure out how to get there but trees and weeds grew over everything and the street names were all up too high. The only thing was to find Mount Pleasant Street for he knew he'd recognize it by how steep it was. Then he could guess all the rest of the streets and find the house. He saw someone waiting outside the phone box and went over to tell them it was out of order. All the way across the street he thought it might be Edna and didn't allow himself to think about it until he got there so she wouldn't change into someone else but when she turned around it was Helen only she didn't look like Helen. He pushed her into the telephone box and tried to make love to her but there was so little room and he couldn't get her clothes off until she started to undress and then as she was getting off her brassière which was red the phone rang and he wouldn't answer it so Helen did and said it was for him but knowing it was sure to be Edna he woke up.

Sammy was on the slide. A constant jitter in his eyes and an inability to keep still, his face had gone a patchy flaking red and the corners of his mouth were crusted with small unhealing hacks. He walked on tender, unclean feet and swung his arms like an old retired soldier. The smile was engaged without relation to the words or the occasion. He smelled of dried tea leaves and socks and his tongue was brown. His hands scratched each other alternately. He said he hadn't moved his bowels in a week. Moseby could scarcely bear to look at him, and felt guilty at his failure to be compassionate towards one of the least of these his brethren.

"There's a big march on and I should be there because I was one of the committee when it started and they want me out because I'm not a bliggy yes man and I say what I've got to and a lot of them are bliggy Jews and they know I'm a Catholic and so they want me out and if I can't be on the march then they'll get me out of the committee."
"Why don't you go then?"
"Aye, aye I'll have to go."

"He thinks he can get me in all right, he says he wants to talk to my oldest friend. Oh my God, John, I don't know what I'll do if I don't get into this place, it's really getting me down with that bliggy bastard, forgive me for calling him that, but that's what he is, he knows I'm not well and he keeps at me and if any important phone calls come for me he won't take them, he'll not leave me alone until I have a break-up. So I said to him you'll come and speak to him, won't you, John, at the hospital?"

"But I haven't known you very long, Sammy."

"No, but you know how to put things, you'll be able to put it to him."

"Oh my God, John, I'm a swine, d'you know what I've done, oh I know it's wrong but I canny help it, he was that lovely, he had them long curly eyelashes and the skin he had and he said he had problems he didn't like girls and I said I could help him an we went to this party and it was all gay people there and we were dancing and he was touching me up, well he was drunk, and he kept saying he loved me, he did, he kept saying that and that he wanted to go to bed with me and he kept touching me and I came all inside my trousers and he was lovely, oh he was lovely, Johnny, and I'm a bliggy swine."

"Why Sammy?"

"I took him round to this man I know and he gave me a pound for bringing him over."

"They make you tell them everything about you, asking questions and making sure you're not keeping anything back and you begin to see what your problem is and then you can face it and not just find ways to avoid it and when you see it you can deal with it. If they get me into this place then they'll be able to deal with it there, won't they, John?"

"I'm sure they will, Sammy."

A quiet evening in the Montmartre. Several couples dining in the corners, Finchley Road going past outside the window like some inconsequential back projection, full of quiet cars and out of focus people. Moseby sat eating an unwanted boiled egg and picking his nose. What are you doing, John lad? Sitting here with your finger up your nostril. *Pourquoi*, as they say in France not speaking a lot of English. Doesn't make sense. Maybe Edna, at this very minute, is sitting in her mother's bog, thinking *pourquoi*. Well, it's easy for her. She knows why. Because I'm sitting down here that's why she's sitting up there. Can you see those two little Dutch figures? Sitting under the toothbrushes. Can you? Look at them, Edna. Do they not mean anything to you? Have a good look. Do they not frighten you? No, not you Edna. You've got your head firmly planted in the ground. You never wonder why. You know the answer. Because. Oh Edna I love you. You're all that's normal and stupid and lasting and sane. But it's why for me every day. I don't even know who my parents were. Why don't you look? Afraid I'll find out. She'll look like Helen and he'll wear a clip-on bow tie. But it's cheating. Looking at the answers at the back of the book. It's not that. It's your consumption of pride. Your arrogance of spirit. You want to find out who you are all alone. Then claim virgin birth. Who are you anyway? Me. I'm me. Frenzied applause from Western Hemisphere. John Moseby, long distance wanker and abernephy biscuit eater, for your services to Kilmacolm and environs I pronounce you man and wife. Very droll. Oh yes, give him a big hand, he's a local lad.

Dear Mr. Maxwell,

Thank you for your letter. It was kind of you to take the trouble. I feel you to be very, perhaps overly, sympathetic to me and somehow I feel undeserving of your concern. You see, Mr. Maxwell, it is exactly what you warn me against that I prize most highly in myself. My arrogance of spirit as you call it. Well I think on it as ego, an ego inherited from my parents, whoever they were, and from the whole process of European thought since our friend Martin Luther. It was my A. of S. which in the first place took me away from my wife and daughter. When I knew I had been found out in my adultery I knew also that there was a prescribed course of behaviour open to me. That I should go and be sorry, apologize, ask forgiveness, then say it wasn't of real importance, a moment or two on a couple of afternoons, sulk and allow life to go on. Edna would be hurt, indignant, angry, but finally forgiving. The event would recede and in a year or so we'd look back and wonder if it really happened. Occasionally Edna would blackmail me with it but for the most part it would be submerged.

That was one way and I wanted no part of it. It's not that it's a shabby solution to a shabby business although it's certainly that. But for me it's mainly a kind of denial of my identity. There was one moment in that little liaison when I knew what the world was about. I don't have that sense now and I didn't have it for very long then. But I did have it and it was mine and it came from all the things which are me and they are the things which led me into bed with Cathie Pollock. I'm not defending what I did. In a way it's so irrelevant as to make Edna's attitude ridiculous. But that doesn't matter either. My trouble is I don't know who I am and my sin is that I think it's important to find out. In fact I think it is the most important thing there is. Perhaps I'm like your version of the legless man throwing away his crutches. Arrogance of the spirit if ever I heard of it. Perhaps I do need Greenock and respectable society and an honourable profession to buttress me against the fact that I am nothing, zero. You will tell me how God loves me as though I was the only one. What you must find impossible to comprehend is that for me God is dead. I am surrounded and haunted by the memory of his existence, but he no longer lives in my life. And so I, John Moseby, assume the central role in the world drama. Moseby for God and Samuel Giffen for Jesus Christ. Forgive my blasphemy for I still think on it as such. That's the problem, about it being hard to kick against the pricks. I am saturated in guilt about my own unworthiness, my original sinfulness which I cannot throw off no matter how contemptuously I disprove it to my mind. I am not a pagan, Mr. Maxwell, for if I were I'd have no remorse at my failings. I'm a Christian for whom God is no longer a reality. Hell remains but Heaven is closed.

I love my wife, not because she's my wife but because she's Edna. I think that alone almost justifies me in saying I love her more than she loves me. She loves me for the good and dutiful husband she hoped I'd make. She doesn't have to try and love me for me, which I admit wouldn't be easy. Sometimes I think I'm just a little bloke who got caught cheating his wife and ran away like I'm apocryphally told my father did. Conceived in sin born in iniquity. And my daughter will grow up into a divided house, whether I return tomorrow or stay away forever. The inevitability of things sometimes seems indisputable. "All history is inevitable because it has gone to the trouble of happening." And if you're wondering who said that it was me. Not that it illuminates much. Thanks once more for your interest. Please give Edna my love in whatever form seems most digestible.

Yours gratefully,

John Moseby

P.S. The Samuel Giffen I irreverently proposed for the post of Second Person is only an acquaintance of mine and no one you know. I don't know why I mention this but reading the letter over it seemed rather esoteric.

Sammy's psychiatrist had a white coat and glasses. It was a not unfamiliar feeling to be sitting across the desk from him as he drummed his fingers while studying a manilla folder. He wondered who MacIndoe was procuring for his wife now. Or perhaps they had gone to Salford for the summer. The psychiatrist was youngish, short, and his frown knitted up the flesh between his eyes and at the top of his nose so that his glasses moved appreciably. His name was W. O. Elkin on the desk shingle.

He looked up, flashed Moseby a smile and looked back at the folder. Looking down, he said,

"You're Mr. Giffen's closest friend?"

"I believe so."

"How long have you known him?"

"About six weeks." The head did not come up.

"Would you say Mr. Giffen makes friends easily?"

"I wouldn't have thought so."

"How did you become friendly with Mr. Giffen?"

"He lives next door to me."

"Do you know any of his other friends?"

"No."

"You are, according to Sammy," and he looked up at this point, "a student and a writer."

"Yes."

"And Scottish obviously."

"Yes." He pursed his mouth and shook his head sagaciously.

"Sammy is rather a fascinating case." Moseby nodded politely at this assessment, feeling he had answered some sort of oral examination successfully.

"He will take anything, literally anything, in lieu of love. Have you noticed this yourself?" And again shaking his wise head.

"I don't quite know what you mean."

"Do you smoke?"

"No, I've given it up."

"Wise man. Neither does Sammy. But he always takes a cigarette when offered one. He does not wish to refuse anything offered. Cups of tea, extra helpings of sugar, the odd biscuit on the plate, an old biro. I once gave him a broad, red elastic band that was partially worn through, said, this might come in handy. Sammy seized upon it and racked his brains to produce a good purpose he might put it to."

"What does this mean then?"

"Well, in a pat little phrase, he wants to be loved, because he isn't," and he stood up with the air of a man who has said something weighty that had needed saying for some time. Moseby kept his face impartial. Elkin poured himself a glass of water and sat down again. Into the glass he tipped several little pods from a paper bag. They slowly expanded into flowers. He chuckled at his whimsy.

"Fascinating things. Relax the mind and the eyes. They're really a therapeutic device initially. We're only scratching the surface of things. What do you think of Sammy, Mr. Moseby?"

"I think he needs help. I don't think he knows who he is."

"Ah, do any of us?" staring down into the well of the glass.

"Perhaps not, but Sammy's doubts are beginning to congeal." Elkin looked up.

"What an interesting phrase. 'His doubts are beginning to

45

congeal.' Yes. Yes, that is to some extent correct. What do you think will happen to him?"

"Well, I think he's beginning to need other people to convince him he really exists. Being Sammy he's going to find those people harder and harder to come by."

"He thinks a great deal of you. Cigarette? Oh no, you've given them up. How did you manage that?"

"I stopped smoking." Elkin's furrowed look smoothed out for a moment as he examined Moseby's face and reply.

"What sort of sense of humour is that known as?" and when Moseby remained silent he brought it out of the air with a map of fingers: "Dead pan. George Burns."

"Chic Murray."

"Ah, the local variant. Yes, well what you say about Sammy is very true. Of course, it's not only people he turns to, it's institutions as well, the Catholic Church, are you Catholic, Mr. Moseby?" Moseby shook his head. "Socialism, Communism even, Nuclear Disarmament, Catholic Nuclear Disarmament, the homosexual institution."

"Is Sammy really homosexual?"

"Well, if you mean is he a classic invert, no. It's really all part of the same pattern. Homosexuals have a group identity which transcends in some ways personal identity. Also it's essentially an experiencing of personal relations however we choose to denigrate the relations. To this extent it's made to measure for Sammy. All he has to do is don the uniform."

"Yes, but does he really participate sexually? I never know whether or not to believe him." Elkin rose and took up the glass, looking into it as he spoke, "Well, to a certain extent he may be expressing fantasies. But yes, I'd say he has undoubtedly had homosexual relations. The interesting thing is that according to him he makes a great point of retaining what he calls the masculine part. This choice, the beefer, to use argot, is one which hints at reserve in our Samuel. Were he to allow himself to become invert in the homosexual relationship he could obtain for himself much more in the way of attention and much more materially from his actions. Yet he never seems to think in terms of being the passive partner and I'm fairly certain his homosexual experiences do not as yet include

46

an affair where the roles are interchangeable. No. He is simply joining the homosexual club as a heterosexual. He has no moral or aesthetic scruples about the act but is basically interested in the security so belonging confers on his identity. If Sammy has to seek external images to bolster his sense of reality then one must say that being homosexual is a more effective choice, potentially, than any of the others. There is more love likely in bed with a boy than on the road from Aldermaston." As though to clinch this contention Elkin dashed the glass of water and its flowering papers into the basin, filled it again and drank it this time, then stood looking at the empty glass.

"We don't have the time, not really the kind of time someone like Sammy needs. Sad but true. And Sammy is one of the reclaimable ones." He put the glass down, came and sat again. "Time, interest, concern. Another human being. An affair. But it's not likely, is it? No. Not probable. Right, next best is a love affair with himself. Such as we normal people conduct throughout our normal lives." And it was difficult to tell whether he was sneering at himself or at Moseby. "That's what psycho-analysis comes down to, helping people to fall in love with themselves. That's why we want to get Sammy into this place that's going in Essex. Perhaps you've heard of it. No. Well, it's very experimental. The man behind it is more or less theorizing his way. It's all fringe cases, social misfits not yet crystallized. Not yet congealed." And he smiled. "You see that's the next danger with Sammy. That he'll assume, under pressure, an identity which society terms as criminal. He's on the borderline as it is. What if this need for concrete instances of love becomes just a little more dynamic? What if he starts taking such pledges for himself? Kleptomania. This place that we want to get him into might avert that. They live in dormitories, virtually unrestricted and each day they talk in open groups about their thoughts and feelings, towards themselves, each other, the staff, the food, anything. The hope is that, guided by the doctors, they will develop a sufficient interest in themselves to withstand assuming some identity that falls within our classified list of do-nots."

"Sounds very bold."

"Oh it's bold enough. Bit too bold for my personal taste. But it takes all sorts. But the people aren't cranks. They aren't expecting miracles. They know the rest of the work has to be done outside." Elkin paused, long enough for Moseby to take the point. "He can't just be turned out to the same old world again, disinterestedly looking after number one. To some extent the interest shown in him and his problems has to be sustained. Not by me, because I'm overworked as it is, not by a formal group because for the most part they're useless. Not by any social body that is now in existence. . . ." He seemed prepared to go on listing these unsatisfactory parties.

"But by me," Moseby said.

"Well the Group Therapy place won't accept anyone who hasn't got the guarantee of someone to come out to. Someone approved by whoever is sending them in. That's why I had you along. What do you think?"

"So Sammy doesn't get into the bin if I don't lift the lid?"

"Well it's not as final as that."

"What do I have to do?"

"Well you go out with him. Meet the people out there. Write him. Visit when you can. Be at home when he comes out. It's a job for friends. You seem to be Sammy's number one man."

"Poor bastard."

"Yes. Well you can claim expenses for travelling through the Essex County Council." Great. Expenses for accompanying S. Giffen to laughing farm. He grimaced to himself and looked at Elkin, who read it as affirmation.

"Good, I'm glad. Well, if you'll excuse me now," and he stood up. He was all of twenty-four Moseby reckoned.

Sitting in the front upstairs nearside seat. Sunny. Two men, one telling the other in a middle-aged catarrhal London voice, "This cleaner woman gets in about five see, Bert's on his round and she's in the outsize section when he comes round, cleaner woman's got this hump on her back, Bert says good morning like, goes on then blessed if he knows why he said he went back quiet like and had a look and here's this thing stripped off trying on the dresses, couldn't get one to fit her no how and looking at herself in the mirror like she was Lizbeth Taylor or something. Bert said you never saw a pantomime like it in all your days."

"There were eight of us and the two youngest died God rest them. I was the oldest girl." He wanted to ask how old she was but didn't.

"Two brothers older than me. One of them killed in the war, right at the start. The other one's up in Scotland working, Glasgow, and my sisters all married young. What was that place right at the beginning of the war? Lot of them got killed."

"Dunkirk?"

"That's the place."

"Are you the only one that didn't get married, Helen?" She flashed him a look that he thought rebuked him for his temerity, but which he realized almost at once was not a reprimand but a kind of panic. The great, beefed woman was shy.

"Were you married then?"

"As much in God's eyes as any of them," with a flash of vehemence and she fell silent. Moseby looked at her anew, searching for the shape of a woman in her thick girth, at the bunches of stubs for fingers that might have made caresses, at the potato face to see how it might have mouthed its over and over yesses. All, all gone, untraceable in the sour dough of her unleavened presence. Lyricism gave way to the lickerish and this time the vision of the wide mottled thighs and the pendulous lip of her belly, dripping over the rank black muff opened in his mind and he could suddenly smell her, distinct from all the other kitchen odours. Black blooms in the dark glass of his mind.

He couldn't get to sleep now before dawn and there were times when he had nothing to do but could only wait, chill and cramped in his chair, enduring the final hours of darkness. He wrote mental letters and defended himself before imaginary tribunals until his head ached and his mouth grew tired from talking to itself. The winds were moving unseen in the trees, bringing down new leaves for Mr. Schonfield's fires. He sat on

49

and thought of those two squatters in his mother-in-law's toilet. They started it all. In a way. No, they just summed it up. They just put it so that it couldn't be ignored. The world is waiting to give birth to the mind. For each unborn thought somewhere a metaphor waits. A blind search for a holy braille. Where are you at, John Moseby, with your gaudy notions, the desert is everywhere and the tree gives no shelter. When the sun is high it will burn away all umbrage and leave you without a shadow. When you have no shadow how will you know you exist. You are wrong. You have sinned. Pride. Arrogance of the spirit. You must bow down and ask forgiveness. Of whom? Of that empty sky. Of these empty sands. Of that great brass burnish the sun. Of yourself. Ask forgiveness of yourself. I cannot. I am not truly sorry. Forgive me for I am not sorry.

In chill pity the dawn came, forgiving humankind one more morn, releasing him from the throes of his dream.

They took a tube and then a bus and after the bus they were in country of a sort and another bus took them to a long treesided lane and they walked up, Sammy carrying a small brown suitcase and Moseby some paperbacks held with a tie.

The Group premises were a set of disused looking ex-Army type buildings with rectangles of cracked concrete here and there between, where nissen huts had stood. There were a few people about but all seemingly at a distance of fifty yards. It had been raining and was beginning to do so once more. Neither of them had a raincoat, Sammy not possessing one and Moseby refraining from his out of sympathy. In a large tiled hall a girl was picking at a piano. Their footsteps cut across her efforts and she turned round, saw them and went off. They stood and looked at each other and around the hall. Sammy's usual frenetic manner had subsided on the journey and he now looked, in his brown corduroy jacket and wide bottomed flannels, desperately like what he was, someone awaiting admission to an institution.

"You'd think there would be somebody to meet us, wouldn't you, John?" he ventured. Moseby shrugged and walked towards the piano. Sammy stood, forlorn, holding his case.

"Put your case down anyway." And he did, just like that. The piano had keys like horse's teeth. The one Moseby struck caused no sound at all and stuck down, making an indent in the oppressively even grin. He started to work out the odds on his having tried the dead key first but his eye couldn't count the dozens of identicals. Behind him, Sammy stood, stranded in his shoes, a raw scruffy bird, peering around him for his keepers. Somewhere in the rest of the world a radio played a brass band. It was Saturday afternoon on the Home Service. Sickeningly strong, repellently powerful, memories of those dead, coral cumulant afternoons, piling up to this momentary apogee. Oh dear God, what is life, and crushed by the pressure of the sunken past he sank on to the piano stool. As by interdependence the jammed key came up making a dull baize bong. Time, dismembered time, that had once been present, now lurking in corridors of the mind, waiting for a brass band to stray across the compound of a dingy asylum and release it from obscurity. The hyper-tidy room, his foster father doing accounts, his wife knitting, and under the table in his tent, ignoring the Warrington Colliery Brass Band's selection from *Iolanthe*, his little embryo self. The rain rushed against the windows with a rattle of small beaks. He was near to tears, dry-eyed but close to weeping.

"Fuck them, where are they?" he said loudly and hit the piano with his fist. Thinking of his parents had unnerved him. The chord clamoured in the empty hall and he shivered. The memories threatened still to come tumbling back. Sammy was sitting on his case making the hall look like a railway station. Moseby, possessed of an intolerable wish to get away, stood up and said,

"Wait here, I'll get somebody," and went across the hall to a door that stood ajar. Sammy did not say anything nor look after him. Moseby wanted to run. Places made you so vulnerable. This bare unlovely site and the strains of a band had brought him to the edge of despair. It was Sammy really, the thought of leaving him here, but what could he do? Inasmuch as ye have done it unto the least of these my brethren. Get fucked. For Sammy there was nothing else. For him there was his warm little house, and forgiving Edna and his joy pod,

his love tickle, his only begotten daughter. He was upstairs on a landing and there were several large rooms with
beds along the wall and pieces of clothing, curiously genderless
to his glance. There were lockers beside the beds and on a
table in the middle of the floor was an electric iron wired to
the light fixture.

He went into the end room in which a number of large
chairs sat unoccupied and ping-pong table waited, bats and
balls present. Moseby struck the white celluloid viciously
across the table and heard it skitter about on the floor. From
the window he could see Sammy going across the open space
towards one of the farthest nissen huts. With him was a man
with a limp. Sammy kept looking round, carrying the paperbacks awkwardly so that they impeded his legs. Moseby
stepped back out of sight. The ping-pong ball came rolling
towards him. Sammy was nearly there now, a yard or two
behind his hirpling guide. At the door of the hut he made a last
survey before entering. Moseby trod the ball flat with a splin-
tering little crush. Then he left, quickly and with his head
down.

He didn't recognize her for a moment and then he did.
Seeing her walking among other people was a shock; since his
last sight of her in the open she had remained among the bins
and over the table peeling spuds, preaching her refuse religion.
In the light, among the other bodies, she looked neither so
gross nor so impressive. He stopped in front of her and she
nearly walked past him. For the first time he realized she was
short-sighted and her left eye was ever so slightly squint.
When she noticed him her greeting was more effusive than he
would have expected, with a hand on his arm and a flood of
hellos. They went across the street to a pub and in the worn
red plush of the saloon he ordered her a John Jameson's. He
wondered if the barmaid thought he was with his mother or
perhaps an aunt. Turning from the bar he caught her pinkie in
her nose and looked away to let it get out. She spoke differently it seemed, here in the outside world. He could scarcely
bring himself to commence topics that belonged to the back
kitchen of the Montmartre. She spoke of how good the
whisky was and how expensive things were in the shops. He

asked where she lived and recognized it as not many streets away from him. When she asked him when he would return to his studies his dubiety caused her to urge that he would not neglect his learning. Learning she said was the one thing that could get a poor lad on in this world. That and knowing the right people. Her fella she added had had neither and that was why he was where he was today. He asked where that was and she pointed to her feet. There was a pause and he prepared to enquire the circumstances but she went on without prompting.

Martin Birkett his name was and he had been more of a man in every way than any before or after. He had a terrible hungering after knowledge and taught himself reading and writing and tried to study to be a priest but the whole mockery of it put him off and he went back to farming his own land and she met him when she was still a girl and he a man of thirty-five and she'd never been with a man though God knows plenty had tried but she fell by the wayside to Martin Birkett for he was a real man and he told her about the falseness that the papishes were and he one himself mind you but he wasn't afraid of them for he had the Gospels and that was the one thing they couldn't contaminate with their ways and he read out of the Gospels to her and told her how Jesus would have spat on them that preached his word today. That was why they never got married in church because of them that married you weren't fit to speak the words and he married them himself at his farm with just the two of them there and she became a Monsie like him and promised she would never bring a life into this leavings of a world and have no child for didn't Jesus never have any dealings with a woman although it wasn't that he didn't like them for weren't there always women about Him, even the worst kind, only mortal men couldn't control themselves but still they could remember never to let another poor suffering soul join those already in this world and that was the cunning of the papishes for they encouraged the bearing of children so that this world could go on for ever, getting worse and worse and it was only when everybody became a Monsie then some day there wouldn't be any of us left and that would be the end of it.

And as she spoke Moseby could see it, see the grass growing

53

everywhere and trees and the wind making moan through the branches. He saw himself coming down Bank Street, the cobbles muffled by moss and ivy wreathing the columns of the Mid Kirk, while opposite, where the fountain had been a great tree grew, higher than the Town Hall tower and West Blackhall Street was a long leafy avenue. The mind was lulled by the monotony of green, no more words, no more guilt, only green upon green, Eden green.

Helen, a voice crying in the wilderness, unheeded prophet of the distant, ever receding millennium. The sense of countless as yet unborn lives oppressed him with their great chaotic potential. Suddenly he was aware of her leg, lying like a log against his, its pores exuding a hot ask. He rose to fetch her another whisky, receiving as he did so a bent but unmistakable eye.

He was seized now in the grip of rabid sexual fantasies. Women in the street throbbed under their diaphanous clothes. Masturbation had long since failed to relieve his aches, achieving only a dull boredom. Now the carnal images walked abroad, young wands of girls all downy bummed and tender cunted, with delicate scrolls in their oxters and merest bubs of breasts. Corseted matrons holding their poly rolls in rubber bands, bosoms ashudder in their cups. And secretarial birds showing hot panty lines under their skirts, scissorings of shining legs, jumbles of tit-elation. At night behind every locked door the women taken aback, legs aloft, receiving their cumuppance, dancing the thingummyjig. He was in the grip of those long warm ago afternoons of adolescence when the images dripped milky and miraged the deserts of longing. Now women and their parts and purposes drifted across the retina of his concupiscence, searing the erogenous tissue of the imagination so that he stalked, perpetually erect, like some little Fatty Arbuscle of pathetic phallusy, breaking the backs of women in a last despairing act of impossible penetration.

He lay with the half empty half full bottle of violently purple very precious virgin's pish studying the rise to fame of a small green-coloured greenfly up the spiring stalk among the smell of crushed grasses and the sound of the soughing wind in the boughing trees and the sickly sweet taste of the empire brand sherry-type slop he was gurging all mixed together to give an impression of not being where he was which was the Fulham Road Cemetery on a Wednesday weekday afternoon of windy summertime and the Rushtons all beneath him in tiered and tearless death but rather in some childhood happy hiding place with the adults out at the women's home league and at the shop and nothing to happen save he lying alone in the warm walled garden but beyond even that bliss further beyond unexperienced yet remembered before the cauliflower head destroyed the melonic bliss of gardenal secluse and Humpty had his seedenfall from fatherdize all now perilously reprieved by one bottle, 12 fluid ounces of lobotomic jungle juice made from the skin of the potato in our Barrow-in-Furness factory which does not really matter in the same way that nothing really matters in this state of disgrace to which we have deservingly fallen.

He drank lying on his side and spilled some from a lax lip down his cheek and into the grass, whence to sober earth it went. Down it went to his absent friends, his dear departeds, down among their thirsty bones to warm their clodded hearts, revive affections and hopes, here my bed-fellows have some more and the bottle let out a further spill of sweet red blood wine into the thirsty soil for your Lord was not against a small bevy remember and on the day of judgement when the Great Bibber spits out the last mouthful you will all be got stowshus on sacramental biddy then up will get Mary Alice and up will get Samuel Cabot and up oh up will get Fleur, but will I be there on the day, no, I'll be scouring the dishes of the damned that's where I'll be because I've been a naughty lad and didn't wash my hands when I did a number one who must be looked after at all costs else the job might have to be left to the Great Enema who is time and what a whoosh that would be my brethren the least of whom is as much as Himself as Helen would put it same inside as Queen Victoria of blessed memory who sat upon the po when you-all were covered in flesh and breathing air my not lost but gone before buddies in the days before little Johnny was a smear on his old woman's thigh, before daddy crutched his legless way up the Lyle Hill of lust before anything was for me and everything was for you my dust dreamers, my mouldy maid, my flowerless Fleur, at most a mole beats in your breast and grass is looking out of your once green eyes, the sweetmeats of your memory are wormy feed, did they all unwitting devour your day with Reggie Bothwick after the sunblazered regatta when you let him under the willows, green tresses trailing as the punt rocked to his bottomless poling and his straw boater crushed and his flannels creased and your underskirts starched and your once green eyes were hot as the sun through the droopy leaves of the weepy tree and the fish flick swim blims fell spangling you both on that far day in that dear departed world I never knew like you my Fleur know not this.

And in a drowse he let spill the wine, through his shirt into the waiting earth.

DEFOE VOICE:

I now looked upon the world as a thing remote, which I had nothing to do with, no expectation from, and indeed no desires about. In the first place I was removed from all the wickedness of the world here. I had neither the lusts of the flesh, the lusts of the eye, or the pride of life.

CASTAWAY VOICE:

No desires, no wickedness, no lusts.
Removed from all temptations, nothing to do
but watch the burly hurl of the waves on the supine shore,
the all night long salt kissings of the surf,
pale glamour of the moon on naked beachings.
Till day comes
and the grasses are filled with the stridulation of
myriad couplings.

DEFOE VOICE:

I descended a little way into a delicious vale, surveying it with a secret kind of pleasure, though mixed with my other afflicting thoughts, to think that this was all my own.

CASTAWAY VOICE:

A green cleft, a succulent fecundity,
where the mouth fills with juices
and abundance brings forth fertile imaginings.

DEFOE VOICE:

I found melons upon the ground and grapes upon the trees, and the clusters of grapes were now in their prime, very ripe and rich.

CASTAWAY VOICE:

Clustering grapes, clutches of purple bubs, soft and sunwarm, heavy in the hand, solace in the lolling fruit.

DEFOE VOICE:

I contemplated with great pleasure the fruitfulness of that valley, I was so enamoured of the place that I spent much of my time there.

CASTAWAY VOICE:

In the umbrage of some tree, whose leaves like tresses cover my thoughts and let me imagine moving shapes. Now in a green drowse words form like fleshes in the mind,
thouings and theeings, curved words tasting of fruit.

DEFOE VOICE:

I saw here an abundance of orange trees, and lemon and citron trees; so fresh, so green, so flourishing, everything being in such a constant verdure or flourish of spring that it looked like a planted garden.

CASTAWAY VOICE:

A secret garden thick with growth, sun stained,
green yellow goldgild,
a warm seclusion, a yielding plot in the mind,
where fruit rot and from their slimes breed birth.

DEFOE VOICE:

This thought ran in my head and I was exceedingly fond of it for some time, the pleasantness of the place tempting me. I was king and lord of all this country indefeasibly, and had a right of possession.

CASTAWAY VOICE:
Lordly kingly powerful possession,
To possess,
To go in into the green gardens.

Hello John,
It's wonderful to be here and getting treatment at last
feels as if helping me with my problem. We talk every
day nobody holds back I told about my dreaming and we
all open up everything nobody holds back asking me
about it and I analyzed it. The food here is good not a lot
though and there is a place in Burley where it's chips.
We come in and nobody says anything I really feel it's
helped me with my problems they say everyone has a
problem not just the ones in here. Hope you can get out
visiting to me on visiting day Saturday after dinner.
There is a Scottish lad here for going to bed with a
junior girl under age but I don't have much to do with
him. Mr. Maskell says I'm for a month maybe more but
if it helps me with my problem it's worth it in the end
for a bit to stay here. Any letters come to me send them
or if you are coming visiting day bring them with you. I
need toothpaste and toothbrush I can pay back we get
our National Benefit here thanks for your friendship and
hope to see your play in production see you soon,

                                                        Sammy

Now the journeys all merged into one, into one endless
odyssey and he bolted through the dark canals sharing his
thoughts with a racing reflection. It might have been a dream
and at night it often was as he whirled the dark corridors
beneath the metropolis of his mind, locked in holds of hateful
love with the night people, the phantoms that populated his
subways. He would ride the sparking rod and read the jiggling
print of discarded newspapers, write in his epileptic scrawl,
solving the puzzle of his life. Fourteen across. A four letter
word meaning come unto me all ye. But he needed it for
himself. He couldn't even spare some for Sammy. Who was
Sammy? Sammy was his personal leper. Not only was he a

leper but he wanted to be loved for being one. Fuck Sammy. Inasmuch as ye have done unto the least. Sammy and his problem. Sammy's problem was that he breathed. As long as he doesn't breathe on me. If he could love Sammy then he could love anyone. Even himself. Down here it seemed possible that he might manage that herculean labour. But above, in the light, the illusion corroded. He couldn't, not Sammy, not anyone, not Edna, not Carol bless her, not Mr. and Mrs. unloved Moseby, not his unknown unfound unlooked for mother or his unthought on father. He could not love. Not them or himself. Could he then live without love, unloved, unloving, loveless in Gaza. God is love and love is God. Which helped no end. Fuck God, what about me. Helen's right. Messrs. God and Son. Limited Company. What about us poor little stunted crippled arrogant pride-consumed guilt-edged shareholders? What about us when the Great Chairman puts us into involuntary liquidation? His blasphemous reflection as it flitted through the underworld of his searching seemingly knew no more than he did.

All green everywhere. Long grass growing in the back courts and the roads all cracked with flowers and weeds springing up. Grass grew out of crevices in the buildings and at the most unexpected places there were trees. All the street names were concealed but he could still recognize the streets in relation to one another. He walked along Roxburgh Street and turned up Bruce Street to the steps. Trees had grown over to form a green dark tunnel climbing steeply upwards. The stairs were longer than he remembered but he knew Dempster Street was at the top and as long as he kept going he couldn't miss it. Finally at the top he stopped to rest. There was a man in the telephone booth at the top of the stairs who beckoned him over. When he got to him he saw it was McGreevy the vet only dressed in a black suit that buttoned right up to the neck like a tunic. He opened the door and McGreevy said come in and although he really wanted to get on he did so.

"You won't find her," McGreevy said, "she's dead." He thought on Carol lying in the road and felt frightened but he didn't show it to McGreevy. "How do you know?" he asked.

"Listen here," McGreevy said, holding out the receiver, but he didn't want to and pushed the door open and stepped out. McGreevy tried to get out also but there was a lock on the door and he locked him in then ran away along Dempster Street. Just as he got to 48 he heard the voice and recognized it immediately and ran on to the corner where he could see him at the top of Mount Pleasant Street, standing with his arms outstretched. Although he could hear the voice he did not know what he was saying. When he saw Moseby he beckoned to him but he wanted to look in 48 to see if Edna and Carol were there for he remembered McGreevy saying that Carol was dead. He called out he wouldn't be a minute and ran back. The entrance was all overgrown with bramble and thorns and when he looked up at the windows he could see all the glass was broken. Then McGreevy's face appeared at Carol's bedroom window. "I told you she was dead," he said, and he held up the cat by the tail and when he saw this Moseby turned and ran back to where he had heard the voice for he knew McGreevy was going to throw the cat at him so he ran very fast but even so it hit him on back of the neck and he could tell it had been dead a long time it was so stiff and hard. He ran on wiping the back of his neck but he couldn't wipe away the feeling like the feeling after he had lifted Carol down from his shoulders but her weight was still there and as he turned the corner he looked back and she was lying where she had fallen but he did not stop but hurried on. When he got to the top of Mount Pleasant Street however there was no one there, the place was empty except for a telephone booth. He went in and in the little square mirror there was a photograph of Johnny Weissmuller only someone had drawn a moustache and a beard. He tried to rub it off but it only smudged his hand. When he tried to get out the door was locked and he could see McGreevy walking away down the hill. In a minute the phone would ring and he would be told she was dead, it would be the voice that tells you the time, at the third stroke and there would be no argument, he would have to accept what he was told. He lifted the receiver off the hook, if it was off they wouldn't be able to get through. Then as he stood there he heard the sound of the wind on the other end of the line and he listened to it with a terrible sense of dread. It made an empty tuneless song, cold and desolate as it blew in some wastes of his imagination, he recognized it as he had recognized the voice and it frightened him, this vacuum of his heart, if Mc-Greevy searched down into it with a catheter no red blood would spurt vivid in the air, only this wind, desiccated coils of arid air, would be freed to spiral round the cold cornices of the universe. He was dead, his cat was dead, his daughter. . . .

. . . A knocking on the door and a voice saying, "Mr. Moseby, you are wanted on the telephone," and it was still dark and he knew then it was Carol and she was dead or run over in the street and he got out of bed and now that it had happened he felt very empty and cold and knew his voice wouldn't come and please don't let it be Edna on the phone slapping me across the face with her tongue telling me it's my fault because it is, let it be the police or the doctor or Maxwell but not Edna, only he knew it would be and he put on his dressing-gown from Shannon's sale and Mr. Schonfield was going down the stairs slowly and Moseby came up behind him and said he was sorry to get him up. Schonfield said he had been reading anyway and it sounded very important, a man's voice asking for him, said it was urgent. At least it wasn't Edna, though it might be the operator with a person to person and on the next flight of stairs he could see Carol all bloody and broken limbed and he stopped, sick, where he stood. His only child with her pyjamas and sixpenny kisses and feeding the seagulls and how she said "must for to" and Mr. Schonfield was right behind him so he went down two steps at a time making a lot of noise trying to be quiet even as he slammed down hard and the light in the hall over the phone showing it lying black and bodeful and he tried to prepare himself, to say the confessional word in his heart that would cleanse him to receive this bereaving news but he couldn't and choked with terror and guilt and not yet woken from his dream he lifted the receiver and said hello.

"Oh hello, John, these bliggy swine, John, they've, oh my God John, the way they're treating me, I just had to speak to you, you're my only friend, and I just had to, oh they're bliggy bastids, not the doctors, it's these other ones that are in here, they're at me and I've just told them and I'm coming out, I'm discharging myself out of here because I'll just get worse in here, John, John do you hear me, are you there John?" and he was, seething with relief and angry near-tears helpless laughter and he was trembling and when he spoke his voice shuddered.

"Aye, I'm here, Sammy. You'd better come out if it's as bad as that."

"Oh it is, John, oh I'll never forget you John, you're my only friend in the world and I knew I could depend on you, it's these bliggy swine here, they're all hooligans and I told them just. . . ."

But Moseby wasn't listening, he stood against the wall with the receiver at his ear and like a stone in his chest breaking and his breath choking he wept, for his undead daughter and his pierced heart and the tears swelling hot in his eyes then spilling down his face while Sammy's voice keened in his ear.

After the phone was replaced he found he did not remember much of what Sammy had said, when he was coming out or anything about it. He was turning to go upstairs when Mr. Schonfield called up from the basement.

"Would you like a cup of coffee, Mr. Moseby?"

Moseby went down the narrow stairs and only at the bottom realized he was still sobbing. The knowledge that he was caused further tears, tears of gratitude that he could cry, that he had not completely left the land of the living. He wiped his face and went into the little kitchen where Mr. Schonfield was boiling water.

"Your news has upset you. I am sorry to have been the bringer of bad tidings."

"No. No you have beautiful feet really," and felt quite giddy at his abtruse little joke and was close once more to weeping. "No, it was good news really. Relief, it's relief." And he put his hand under the tap and wiped his face. "I'm sorry you were disturbed."

"No, I was reading. I'm glad it is not bad news. Here is a towel."

"Thank you," and he dried his face.

"Relief. Yes. It can be almost as shattering as disaster." He poured the milk and coffee simultaneously, then checked, "I'm sorry, perhaps you would prefer black?"

"No. No, that's fine."

"Let's go into my sitting-room, it is more social."

They went next door carrying their cups. Moseby had only glimpsed into the room when he first arrived and hadn't been in the basement since. It was a low room and had a great amount of furniture and many books.

"There are too many things," he said and waved Moseby to a seat. "I have come to that time of life when I cannot part with anything that has the past in it. In short, I am getting old," and as though to emphasize it he sat with elaborate deliberation in a deep chair. "All these things are places, places in my past. I managed to bring most of it from Germany." Moseby sipped his cup and felt warmer.

"I thought my daughter had been killed," and then regretted saying it, it seemed such a begging, Sammy-like remark. Mr. Schonfield nodded, deep in the chair a small assenting movement.

"Yes," he said, "terrible things can happen." The light fell on him from above and to the side and the heavy etched features recalled and nodded. Moseby looked around at the pictures and framed photographs on the walls.

"You have only the one child?"

"Yes."

"How is she called?"

"Carol."

"Ah, Carol. That is a lovely name," and nodding, the light catching the bay of bald that reached back into his greying hair. Moseby thought on the flowers opening in the glass and wondered why. He touched the knowledge that Carol was safe and felt himself relax. Mr. Schonfield reached his cup on to a small table and the cuff of his quilted robe slid up, showing his yellow arm and the heavy blue veins on the inside of his wrist.

"Where are your family?"

"In Scotland."

"Ah yes, you are Scottish. You must miss them so far away from you."

"Yes."

"I often wonder why we are so often parted from what we love."

Moseby nodded to the old man's thought. He looked at him, piercing the recesses of the chair to see him, the mouth a dry fold in his folded, dry face, the ears long and large.

"You are fond of gardening," he said in order not to think about Mr. Schonfield.

"I have become fond of gardening. I was not always. How old is your daughter?"

"Nearly four."

"Yes. When will you see her again?"

"Oh soon now."

"You are going back to Scotland soon?" and Moseby saw he was wondering about getting his attics let. Sammy's was still empty.

"I don't quite know when." Mr. Schonfield waved his hand.

"I have no wish to pry into your affairs. Please would you like another cup of coffee?"

"Thank you." As he turned to go Moseby saw the sunken occipital cavities, frailly hidden by the thin hair. The whole fragility of the head oppressed him, this thin shell around his old foreign thoughts. He could see it, quite against his will, crushed and broken, hair and blood and those little prisoning grey cells. He stood up and looked at one of the photographs, a woman with two children, girls, in a dull silver frame. They were in a garden. "Unterdenlinden," unbidden image phrase. The dark Jewish matronly face. The button-eyed little girls, summer-smocked years ago in the far garden.

"Yes, that is my wife and our children. They could not manage to leave Germany." Moseby took his coffee and sat down again, in one of the more fortunate chairs.

"You are a student?" Mr. Schonfield asked, the question of a man who has been thinking up questions.

"Yes."

"What are you studying?"

"English Literature and History."

"Ah now, history. I studied history as a young man. But of course most of the history that affects us hadn't been made then." He managed a smile, a dim affair that died away quickly. "Now there does not seem to be much point in reading history, what can one believe after what has happened?" Moseby didn't want to be in this basement talking to this scarred, memory racked old Jewish man. His daughter has just been given back to him, risen from the dead. This old man's daughters were doubtless dead these twenty odd years. He didn't want to know, there was nothing he could do. He thought of jackboots and atrocities and Edna and the egg vulnerable head all in one revulsive compelling image. Oh God but we're monstrous. Monstrous.

"When I was young we believed in progress, even after the Great War. It was still somehow possible to think of that war as a terrible warning, a mistake from which it would be possible to benefit. It was only a war, bigger, but the same as other wars. But not any longer." Now we knew didn't we. We knew now what we were. Don't we old man. Not just Heil Hitler and all those others. All of us.

"It was a terrible irony that the Nazis should use the Jewish people in the manner of the scapegoat, to release the sins of the German nation, I have often thought to myself that there is some deeper meaning to what has happened to us, my race, than we have thought to understand."

You're right, old man, there is. Now we know what we are capable of. Your Siggy started it and our Adolf finished it.

"I lost my family in the concentration camps." But you saved your furniture, didn't you. That wasn't fair he checked himself. Only don't go on. I don't want to know about them, which camp and what ages, and how long you spent trying to trace them. The coffee had grown a scum and it clung to his lips. He grued and wiped his mouth. Mr. Schonfield cleared his throat.

"But you will not be wishing to hear about that," and Moseby realized his silence could only be constructed as rudeness. "I'm sorry, it's just, well, it's all so hopeless, isn't it?" The old man nodded.

"Just so. Hopeless." And Moseby flooded with remorse. He needed to talk about them to keep them from utterly perishing. Flowers in the frail little pot of his head, watered by the tears of memory. Did he talk to them in this stuffy, crowded room. Converse behind the trundle of the mower. Soon he would be dead himself and his dreams stilled. He looked to see if his host could sense any of these thoughts but he was drawn in upon himself, his head nodding slightly and with long pauses in between. Moseby stood up.

"I've kept you up long enough, Mr. Schonfield. I'll let you get back to your bed."

"Oh well that is not very important. I do not sleep so very much now."

They stood a moment, facing, then Moseby said thanks and good night and went. As he closed the door he saw Mr. Schonfield settling down once more into his chair.

Upstairs it was getting light. He sat a moment on the edge of the bed. Sammy was coming back. Did that mean anything? Mr. Schonfield had lost his loved ones in the gas ovens. Did that mean anything? The world travelled around the sun at a speed of 26,000 miles an hour, revolving on its axis as it did so. Did that mean anything? Without propounding answers to all or any of these questions he got into bed. As he moved closer to sleep, keeping his mind still, almost empty, with a lot of space around the thoughts, there came, touched off by he knew not what, a still photograph memory of the Commandant of one of the camps, sitting with his family at Christmas, decorations, and a starry tree, at his feet an Alsatian dog. It brought Moseby back from sleep, this bizarre image of the evil immanent in the world, this symbol of Satan that burned the mind with the enormity of its reality. Evil was not an abstraction, not to be rationalized into cause and effect. Evil was still the anti-Christ even though Christ himself was but a shadowy hero, memorable only in the rhetoric of his gesture, leaving minds such as Moseby's to piece together a credo out of blasphemy and secularities, ever haunted by the nostalgia of past sureties, the ruins of righteousness.

Together with his dreams and his fears for Carol this awareness knotted itself in a despairing cramp. He felt himself to be assailed by forces against which he had no defence. There was nothing, nothing he could do, he was too weak and too selfish and too sinful. "Come unto me all ye . . ." He was heavy laden

God knows. This was where the drunkard opened his Bible at random and found a text that set his life aright. Some text. Anyway he didn't have a Bible. He must write his own Sermon on the Mount and preach it and become its disciple. He lay back, affrighted by the loneliness of such messianic pretension.

Sammy was waiting in the street for him on the following afternoon. He seemed to Moseby much improved. The facial scurf had gone and he did not look quite so twitchy. He had lost the hysterical tone of the phone call and seemed rather to possess the reserve of one who has been through it and would rather forget. Which was, of course, not so. He wished not to forget but to remember, and he did, in multitudinous, inchoate detail. Moseby, as he moved things about in the room to accommodate him, gathered the impression of an orgiastic borstal, staffed by dangerously lax scout masters, of boredom and high octane explosions between the inmates, and of a closed system of thought within which both patients and keepers saw themselves immune to either reality or common sense.

Sammy's failure to survive for longer than he had, seemed, in these circumstances, to augur well for his mental well-being. The trouble it appeared had been his determination to deal with his problem. Unlike almost anyone else there he believed implicitly that he had a problem and that he was there to do something about it. This naïveté marked him off from his companions and made his testimony the butt of later discussion. When in addition to his attempted honesties, he had contracted a passion for one of the youths there and proceeded, in the cause of therapy, to air it for the communal ear that he was attracted by the lad in question, he was punched in the stomach and called a dirty Scotch poof.

To Moseby's enquiry on the degree of success evident with other patients Sammy could only give one instance of total achievement, a girl who had entered lesbian and gone out pregnant. Moseby found himself pleased at the failure of the group, and at the larger failure of modern science to deal with this specific task. In part he knew it was a respite from the guilt he felt at not having gone to visit Sammy, and at having deserted him upon his admittance. But also it was because he felt in some way best fitted to look after the newly released leper himself, whose putrefaction had at last recommended itself as a possible means of expiation. As he made up a bed for Sammy on the mattress of his divan Moseby felt the flush of righteousness which is attendant upon good works. If he could love Sammy enough then surely he could love Edna enough, and if he could love Edna enough then all things would be given unto him. He washed Sammy's shirts with his own and lent him socks after his had disintegrated at an umpteenth rinsing, still exuding vile brown silt from the slippery soles. The three handkerchiefs he could do nothing with, sense and sight recoiled and the suffering servant in him gagged. In penance for this failure he gave Sammy two of his best white ones, unsullied since his cleanly wife had ironed them flat.

The rest of Sammy's belongings had, in some inexplicable fashion, come to be strewn across London, partly in the custody of the British Railways left luggage, partly with a friend, and the remainder in a locker of a room used by one of his committees. All the stored articles were declared by Sammy to be important in the extreme and his manner of going on about them caused Moseby to realize that in some way his identity was bound up with these few books and newspaper clippings with his name and the letters he had had published on one important topic or another, his manuscripts and the photographs showing him on his various protest marches. It was these items which gave his existence some density, lent conviction to his faltering assertion that he, Samuel Giffen, was truly alive.

The recovery of these credenda was complicated by the fact that he had lost the ticket to the left luggage office and could not remember the location of the hall in which the now disbanded committee had held its meetings. Sammy presented himself at the left luggage department and upon refusal of his property delivered himself of an impromptu rant on bureaucracy in nationalized industries. Moseby drew him away, apologizing and returned later, armed with a note of authorization and a list of contents. Resentment remained, however, and the man who had borne the brunt of Sammy's tirade sent his emissary out to Edgware to see the district station master. The journey, which took a million years, reduced Moseby to the size and consistency of a second-hand chiclet of chewing gum. The station master, an unctuous, utterly uninterested man listened distantly and finally left him, stuck to the edge of the counter, for some twenty minutes. After this hiatus a minion appeared and listened, with regard but defective intelligence, to a repetition of the plea. He, breathing laboriously, wrote out a chit authorizing the release of Sammy's zealously guarded belongings. Moseby searched himself for the energy and venom to scream an insult or commit an outrage but could discover nothing sufficiently powerful. He returned, via the moon, to collect his prize.

The second obstacle to Sammy being restored to his own lay in insufficient information regarding whereabouts. Bayswater, "a street with a funny name," and "a lovely big modern building," were the co-ordinates of his triangulation. He spoke on the phone to some of the ex-members who seemed to have as much difficulty recalling the existence of the committee as the scene of its meetings. Finally the street name was discovered, Chamberlain Street, which brought forth from Sammy the comment "that bliggy fascist." Moseby pondered this as he travelled on a damp afternoon in search of "the lovely big modern building," a description which, when the place was found, gave rise to as many doubts about Sammy's sense of architecture as his comment on Chamberlain aroused concerning his view of modern history.

An old, irascible man in a brown overall denied Moseby any right of admittance. To escape complications he claimed the items were his own and was subjected to many questions as to why he had left his bleeding things on these premises, which were, it was stated, some two dozen times, private. In addition it appeared that whoever had put these things in this locker had locked it and without authority had taken away the key and the locker had required to be forced, thus bleeding well ruining it. Moseby denied locking or removing the key and was finally and reluctantly allowed into the room. Somehow its bareness, and the nondescript chairs, and the smell and the thought of the ex-committee meeting here to utter words now unrecalled, all these cohered in Moseby's mind to summon up a sense of abortion, of waste and futility. He took Sammy's things and left, aching with sadness.

In the street a fitful wind tried unsuccessfully to lift some sodden newsprint from the gutter. Moseby kicked it in an attempt to get it airborne but it stupidly plastered round his foot and the face of a politician, promising wetly, smiled up at him.

"Fuck the Welsh Navy," he said, gaining some slight solace from the absurdity.

At night when Moseby returned from work Sammy would be asleep, snickering in his nose, mouth open, like a detail from "The Triumph of Death." He awoke shortly after the kettle boiled and accepted gratefully the bacon sandwich and cup of tea which Moseby had made and would talk of how tomorrow or next day, or some suitably future occasion, he must look about for a job and get a place of his own. Moseby said nothing to these protestations but sat looking out, trying to find some feeling of love for mankind that he might include himself in it.

The final salvaging was from a bed-sitter in Hampstead. A friend of Sammy's called Keith was reading some manuscripts. Moseby came along for the walk. He'd never really been in Hampstead village before and the plane trees and the sweaters and jeans and the gentle evening air were all ingredients of a mild, sedating euphoria. Keith was a very queer young man with a crow's wing hair swoop and menstrual eyes. They roved across Moseby's face on meeting and from time to time flicked over with that veiled but unmistakable implication of sympathy. With him Sammy verged on the outrageous, the slightest campery being met with exaggerated screams of recognition. After one peal Keith looked at Moseby and said, droll and flat, "Who's your friend?" Moseby smiled the smile of the tolerant keeper at the harmless lunatic. He looked at the prancing, rufus rogue beside him and felt fond and protective.

They went to the William IV, Keith declaring that he'd

spoken to a most marvellous Scotsman here only last week, the butchest thing you ever saw he promised Sammy who hooted. He was not there however but Keith regaled them with details of the encounter.

"I don't think the creature knew it himself but trust your instincts every time. I took one look at him and I thought," and here he managed a moue which set Sammy aquiver.

Moseby excused himself to go to the toilet. The pub was very full and pushing between some people he wanted, like a yawn, to leave. He came back and made excuses to Sammy and Keith. The latter's warm damp hand held his a moment. Outside he wiped it dry on his trousers. He walked up a narrow little lane breathing deeply, walking slowly, looking about him. There was a second-hand bookshop with a board of one shilling bargains. He glanced through their unwanted titles. Inside he could see dark round the wall shelves and remembered Bunce's and Glasgow and Greenock, distant silhouetted Greenock, the empty house on Dempster Street, overlooking the roofs and the chimneys and beyond the flowing river. He remembered and strangely the feelings that moved in him gentled and eased him. He walked on, slowly. Something he felt was happening to him, he was beginning at last to leave himself alone, let his mind free wheel, live by touch and taste and smell again instead of only through the agency of his overheated mind. The planes on Fitzjohn's Avenue had brown and yellow leaves around their feet and he picked several of them up and shredded along the delicate veins as he walked.

That Sunday he borrowed a pair of shears from Mr. Schonfield and wrapping them in the *Sunday Times* he took the 31 bus to the Fulham Road cemetery. He bought some sandwiches in a pub and a bottle of beer and sat against the wall opposite the Rushtons' plot and read the paper and ate his sandwiches and drank his beer. A number of people visited the cemetery but passed by his corner, going down to the middle part where the more recent burials were. The wall warmed his back. He looked at the light through the green bottle. Smaragd sun. Green. The colour of innocence. The little bits of green in his life. Their laundered garden, hemmed and bordered. Mr.

71

Moseby trimming and exterminating. Yet seen from the dark caverns of Mrs. Moseby's frustrated cleanth it shone, glowed emerald. He remembered Cathie Pollock's bed, set in, looking out, the tablecloth, hypnotic blue. That was his memory of the garden again, seen from within the house. Not actually being in the garden, but darkly, through glass, watching. He half closed his eyes and let the scene liquefy, swimming verdigo, white islanded by gravestones.

He rose and trampled slowly among the plots, scrutinizing names and dates. Two butterflies came past in erratic stagger. One of them landed on a spread of angelica growing against the wall. The other made a sudden white smut on the wall itself. Moseby moved towards them. As he got close they both rose and went off, bright whims of flight. The angelica stood waist high to him. He remembered them growing at the bottom of the garden, behind the shed, in a secret avenue of neglect and weed. Dwarf trees, high as his chin, their flowers prepuced in greenskin. How he would prise them open, into the seedy, sticky chamber in search of caterpillars. The memory assailed him, rank and vernal, the warm wood of the shed, and somehow he always needed the bathroom, the heavy pleasant pain of his laden bowel, denied as he searched, a composite excitement, the discovery of the little grub, personal somehow, meaningful within him as his waste was, as though in ransacking the house of the solitary maggot he revealed himself to himself. There was a guilt, and a furtiveness that wasn't only the contravention of toilet training, he looked round the corner of the shed lest he be come upon unawares in this act of indecent experience.

Afterwards the caterpillars always died, curled little tubers in their matchbox coffins, brought forth unready from their green wombs, unfit to make the transition, the second birth that leads into the world of light and air.

The butterflies danced their flimsy dance over the dolmen. Life choked him in the very moment of perceiving its inextinguishable sweetness. Taking up the shears he went upon his knees in penance and commenced trimming the Rushtons' grave.

Helen was being sacked from the Montmartre for arguing with the owner's wife. That lady had seen fit to comment unfavourably on the state of the kitchen.

"And I just let her have it, likes of her in here once a month and she has the brazen effrontery to come out with the likes of that. I know what they want though, they want to cut costs and get blacks in, they'd have a black washing only he's out where everybody can see him and they know customers don't like to see a black near their food but in here it'll be one of them and pay her less, oh those Jews don't miss a trick believe you me."

"Where will you go, Helen?"

"Go? Oh I'll not put myself out for a bit yet. I'll have a day or two taking it easy and then I'll get myself in down the West End, some of those places are palaces compared with this."

"Well, I won't be seeing you again then."

"Oh never's a long time, sure you know where I am, you come up and have a cup of tea and tell me all the tales about the kind of leavings they've got in my place. You mark my words on it."

He thought if he didn't ask her now then he'd never know.

"Helen, what is a Monsie Catholic? What does Monsie mean?"

Helen looked at him and a conspiratorial frown gathered between her eyes. "Ah, you've been thinking about what I said then?"

"Well, I've been wondering about this Monsie Catholic thing, nobody ever seems to have heard of them."

"No more they would and them thinking they know the right of it and what do they know, they don't know the first thing. Martin explained it all to me and he told me I'd find them all saying different things. A Monsie is them that know there can be no end to filth on this world till all them that causes filth are finished and done with."

"Yes, you told me about that, Helen, but where does the Monsie come from?"

"Was Martin that explained that too, from his reading and

studying, when it was safe not to start any more children if you couldn't control yourself, not like the Romans with their safe times, that's just a way to get more and more of his leavings born, sure isn't eight and nine they have, and more from them to live fat on, there's only the one time when it's not a sin and that's the monsies, and that's how a Monsie Catholic gets his name."

So there. The new religion that was at last to relieve humanity of all the terrors they were heir to. Out of ignorance shall come forth wisdom. When the Great Lexicographer looked through the classified index of his various denominations would not a fond smile be reserved for the name of Martin Birket, the thick as shit bog Irishman that he was.

All Sammy's things were gone and two shirts of Moseby's and the rent money which had been in the rent book and the *Shorter Oxford English Dictionary*. Moseby sat on the bed and disbelieved until anger made him stand up.

"Oh you bloody fucking get of hell, Giffen."

The city seemed suddenly deserted. He would notice figures at the end of long empty streets, crossing and disappearing, leaving a pale sunlit desolation behind. Across the road, on their crisp toes, rattish leaves scurried. Far away a dog yapped. Scraps of a torn letter fluttered along the gutter,

". . . nnot any mor . . .
. . . al must fin. . . ."

He reflected in the empty street on the rueful little fragment. An epitaph. His perhaps, were he dead. Looking about he thought that not unlikely. Only in the eyes of others do we live. And who would come along here whose look would not grant him life. He had needed Sammy almost as much as Sammy needed him. Judging by his departure, more. The empty street, mustering its fallen leaves. The piece of paper in his hand. Its cryptogram. He stopped, uncertain whether to go on or turn back, or in which direction "on" lay or which way "back" was. Must he not now return, to where eyes would light upon him, if not with love at least with recogni-

74

tion. To go on was directionless, towards no terminal. A Sammy or a Helen. He was in his way as desperate as they, he inhabited a wilderness commensurate to theirs, his fellow nomads. Here we sit, each in his own desert, under the shade of our illusions. Was it not now time to return, he had spent long enough here, go back, lest like Mr. Schonfield he also lost his dear ones, learn to tend his provincial plot, grow flowers in the borders, plant the seeds in their seasons. Let the mantle of Mr. Moseby descend, even if it did not fit. Let the scrap of paper butterfly off, let the enigma go. Say it Moseby, say it. Say you are sorry, sorry for your pride, your arrogance, your ego, say you are sorry for those you have wronged, for those you have failed to love enough. Say it, Moseby, say it. He looked around. The street was empty. Say it to whom. There is nobody here but me.

After work he walked up Fitzjohn's Avenue instead of going home. It was drizzling steadily, without wind. The black branches of the near bare plane trees caught the light from the street lamps and wore them in great concentric whorls. Moseby walked beneath them, thinking inwardly, ever inwardly.

If there is no God then there is only me. And only my will be done. And there is only now and here, then final black. And I must choose, and when I choose nothing is proved except that I have chosen. No right, no wrong. No good, no bad. But that is anarchy, final, utter chaos. Not one stone left upon another. An abomination of desolation. Inhabited only by hordes of self-seekers seeking self.

And above him the trees held their high still vortices as Moseby was drawn down to his inescapable fate.

Then nothing is to be saved. Save the self. But it will perish in isolation, for it will let no other near its sovereignty. For the great loneliness is upon us, like an unending night. Unless we love. But love is only the desire to escape solitude. It is a metaphysical assertion that cannot be maintained. Not in the face of the mind's solipsism. Did you hear about the lonely prisoner? He was in hi'sel. Then why do we want to leave? Why the ache for freedom?

And the wet nightwebs shone overhead as the spider of his

mind ran riot, spinning its mad gossamer, dangling above voids of unhuman space.

The biggest dwarf in the world. Me. Small i. Arrogant little strut. And all around the outer spaces of nothingness, the heartless stars, the cold moon, the barren sun and in the middle this iota, this one candle power wanderer, John Moseby, mannikin.

And in the branches the light spiralled and made the shape of a great uneaten fruit, an unreachable apple in the ruined trees.

CASTAWAY VOICE:
    One existence is very much like another
    when seen thus,
    a succession of marooned minutes,
    linked by the memory in an attempt
    to sustain identity.
    In island solitude is taught a truth,
    man's life is a point in time and space,
    a location without area,
    the smallest atoll.

DEFOE VOICE:
    I was a prisoner, locked up with the bolts and bars of the ocean, in an uninhabited wilderness, without redemption.

CASTAWAY VOICE:
    Once landed there is no leave,
    excepting in dreams when we fly to other lands
    and dwell there until mornings
    come up out of the sea
    and wake us to witness in splendid loneliness,
    the sun, old solitaire and image of our plight,
    commence the long largo of another day.
    Under the sun, at its middle height,
    in that time when all is light,
    for a brief noon of knowing we recognize
    our solitude for what it is and give thanks.

DEFOE VOICE:
    And with my heart as well as my hands lifted up to

heaven, in a kind of ecstasy of joy, I cried out aloud.

CASTAWAY VOICE:

I am myself alone, no other than,
I am my world and it is me,
across my eyes the sun goes
and in my mind the grass grows
and when I die night must fall
and darken all.
For each man this is a prayer
and the purest prayer he can make,
his homage to the mute mind
that uttered his word.
Around words a silence must.
A man is a word and in the silence
he may hear himself speak,
to and for himself
for as long as he lives.

DEFOE VOICE:

How long he might live I know not, though I know a
notion that they live a hundred years. Perhaps he may
be alive there still, calling after Crusoe until this day.
[*The sound of a parrot calling. The sound of the sea.*]

Out behind the Montmartre he stood, sallow from his la-
bours, breathing deep of the night air, breathing the rank
aroma of the bins and the odours of the subway escaping
below him and the tired drab air slowly turning, milling over
the roofs, the fumes and reeks and exhalations of countless
exhausted bodies. He breathed heavily from his toil, damp
from his sweat, drained of thought, drugged with routine
boredom and tiredness, alive in his aches and the cling of his
shirt, the faint loup of his healing thumb, one of the herd,
hoping soon for rest. He expanded to include the night and its
scents and saw a cat and smiled and yawned. The Montmartre's dishwasher was taking a breather.

Everything was running down, spinning slowly to a stand-
still, the air was full of falling, turning leaves, and the swallows
seemed to drop downward through the sky at evening to

merge with the dark below. He revised and tidied the play and Mr. Schonfield allowed him to use his typewriter, an old weighty machine that rattled like a stick on railings. He bought a manilla envelope and put the manuscript inside. He had titled it from a Stevens' poem and the dedication was, a little affectedly he felt, to the American poet. "The Place of the Solitaires," a montage for radio, by John Moseby. It fell into the pillar box and he waited as the postman came along and collected it. There, he thought, goes nothing.

But it was another instance of things coming to their end, a further portent of closure. Moseby found himself walking up into Hampstead village more than before and one overcast afternoon he found the Heath, like the sea behind a line of sand dunes, an unexpected oceanic green. It sedated him with its mock rurality, its contrived air of bucolic peace, with tweedy ladies and old spaniels and twenty-twos of tiny foot-ballers and nurses on afternoons off and the occasional self-contained harrier pumping along the paths.

He lay in the grass under the trees and felt almost nothing and heard high above the small severance of a leaf from its branch and then it came spiralling down, and then another and another and in a tree further off three came down together. He thought of all sorts of things long past and distant done, in his buried childhood, in his bitter youth, felt shadows of feel-ings move across the stretched screen of his mind, all falling through time and space to this moment on the grass, where he lay, bruised but unrepentant.

Seeing Sammy on the tube wasn't really a surprise. Seeing him at all was a bit improbable but if they were to meet again the tube had its own undeniable priority as venue. He was scanning a *Peace News* with an ostentatious avidity that de-nied comprehension. He was wearing a rather smart tweed jacket, that is to say, one which fitted him. He did not see Moseby and got out at Swiss Cottage. Moseby, who was only travelling, followed him. For a moment on the street he thought Sammy was hailing a taxi but it turned out to be a greeting to someone on the other side. He set off up Fitz-john's Avenue and Moseby, rather enjoying himself, brought up some fifty yards behind. Sammy walked the walk of someone importantly late, the *Peace News* batoned under his arm. He went along to the right, a long quiet stretch Moseby didn't know. As they reached some shops Sammy increased his pace to a fair old scuttle and Moseby was half-minded to call out to him, only he crossed over and went into a pub. After a moment Moseby followed. The bar was long and in the daytime darkish, and Sammy was sitting up at the back with an older man. Moseby sat at the bar and had a half of bitter. Now that he was here he felt a bit foolish. There wasn't much he could do short of bawling Sammy out. That was probably his money and dictionary he was wearing. There would be a tirade of "sorry John's" and how his problem made him do it. What was he doing in this pub? He was sick of living in Schonfield's attic and sick of the Montmartre. Term would start in a few days. If he had to live on his own he'd be better doing it in Dempster Street. He could get Edna back. He'd convince her there hadn't been any women all the time he was away. The thought of the kitchen and the bright light over the river and Ayrshire bacon and the outsider off the loaf dizzied him with nostalgia. He finished his drink and stood up to go and as he did Sammy came lunging down the bar.

"Oh my God, Johnny, it's good to see you, I meant to come round but I've been that busy, come away up, I want you to meet Paul Roland. I'm working for him, I'm his assistant, he's a friend of Keith's, you remember Keith, aye well Paul's a social worker for delinquent boys and he's opening a place down at Plymouth, very liberal in his ideas, a great socialist, he's a wonderful man to meet, maybe he could help you with your plays," bearing down on a rather small, plump man with a Van Dyck beard and a plum red bow tie. Moseby was introduced as a young working-class writer from Glasgow and bought half a pint of best, apparently by Sammy, who asked Paul what he was drinking and was reassured in a deep warm voice that nothing further was required at the moment. He went on to say to Moseby that he hadn't heard Sammy speak of a friend who wrote. Had he had anything published? Moseby said no, he'd only just submitted a first script. Mr. Roland deplored the state of the West End theatre as totally committed to satisfying bourgeois tastes and the only worthwhile people in it being Joan and Wesker. Moseby said his was a radio script and at that point Sammy came back with the half pint.

"Well, how's it going with you, John, how's the play, it's a play he's writing, Paul, it's all about the sea."

"A sea story," grasped Mr. Roland.

"Kind of," Moseby admitted. Sammy rattled on about their, his and Mr. Roland's, work, and how marvellous Mr. Roland was, to which the man felt obliged to say it was work that needed doing. During all this Moseby sat in a tensed expectancy for Sammy to commence apologizing or to refer, however obliquely, to his disappearance and theft, but gradually began to realize that it was not forthcoming. Sammy had either forgotten or had decided to call things even and not mention the matter. The audacity of it, after a moment's anger, began to tickle Moseby. He leaned over and pinched the lapel of his jacket.

"Bit of good stuff that."

"Oh it's real Harris tweed, John," the owner admitted with pride, the face open with pleasure. Moseby smiled and shook his head.

"Health to wear it, Samuel." He finished his drink. "I'll have to be getting along."

"Aye well right, I'll see you around then, John."

"I don't know about that, Sammy. I'm going back to Greenock."

"Oh are you going back to University?"

"Which university are you at?" Mr. Roland asked with new interest.

"Glasgow."

"Oh, and you're going back to take up your studies again?"

"That's right."

"Maybe you'd like to come to our party before you depart from among us. Tomorrow night. Sammy will give you the address."

"Oh aye, right, sure, Paul's giving a party tomorrow night for a lot of the people who're interested in the work we're doing, there might be somebody there who could help you with your play."

"Yes, do come if you feel like it."

"Thanks. I'll get along if I can." Sammy wrote the address down on a page in a small notebook and then tore it out and gave it to Moseby. The action surprised Moseby more than anything else about Sammy. It seemed alien to him, strangely self-assured. He said his thanks and left. Outside the door he stood and looked about him, not knowing whether to laugh or be impressed. Marvellous. Nobody has to worry about Sammy. That's the original asbestos kid.

They took his notice at the Montmartre calmly enough and despite himself he was a little annoyed. He came out of the swing doors unemployed and feeling somewhat insecure. Finchley Road milled up and down and he stood, curiously undecided, at the kerb. Decisions bristled around him, asking to be made. He could go now, pack his bag, catch the train, be in Greenock tomorrow morning. He could go to Tenby where he and Edna had honeymooned, see if it still looked the same from the headland. He could buy a bottle of V.P. and go visit the Rushtons. Or he could go to this party. Take Helen and pass her off as a Belfast working-class writer lassie. While pondering these alternatives he saw a dog being run over. It had started across from Moseby's side and halfway changed its mind, started back and then turned again. The lorry was over it front wheels and the rear wheels jammed and dragged, leaving a skid of blood behind. Its cry was immediate and piercing and faded in a series of diminished yelps until the traffic covered. Moseby turned and walked away, his choices for the moment invalidated.

The party was well attended when he got there, the people spread into several rooms. The flat was large and well furnished, there were Negro masks and a skin-covered drum and two samurai swords and against one white wall a spiky branch of blackthorn. Sammy was in seigneurial vein, greeting arrivals and calling out names to Paul. He met Moseby with less than his accustomed fervour and did not announce him. Moseby followed his finger to the drinks and wondered how anyone was taken in by him, and of what possible use he could be in this, or any other, undertaking.

It seemed to be the sort of affair where the music remained

undanced to and everybody clotted into small earnest groups. The drink was all red wine and a nasty vintage at that. As he grued he remembered the dog and it developed into a shudder. Sammy flitted past and suddenly the ingratiating manner and the furtive eyes made a new sense, a callid, crafty recognition. For the first time he resented Sammy and immediately felt depressed that he could. He looked at the other people. They didn't all look mentally retarded. Did none of them see that parasitic get for what he was? Didn't Paul Roland know he had an escaped lunatic on his premises? Still, maybe there was a bit of the vice versa there, if he was a friend of that shrieking queer Keith it was odds on. Home for delinquent boys. Sammy, bobbing his head in acquiescence, agreed without reservation with a man in a leather patched sports jacket. Moseby had a picture of Sammy under the lorry, his tongue stuck incredibly far out of his mouth, the eyes popping with the pressure of blood. How could he hate Sammy, derelict pathetic Sammy? How? Because Sammy at this minute didn't seem the derelict one. Because he, Moseby, was the out of work, purposeless creature. Sammy moved off and Moseby followed him. He went into a study room, with many books and a desk under the window. Several people were talking, sitting around a low table. Sammy was asking them if they wanted any drinks and then hustled back with their orders, bumping into Moseby.

"Sammy, I want a word with you."

"Oh aye, right then, but I've got to get these friends of Paul a drink," and he was gone. Moseby noted he hadn't been called John. His reaction balanced between the resentful and mirth. He went over to the desk. Lying on it, with several other books on top of it, was a Shorter Oxford English Dictionary. He hauled it out. His name had been clipped off the top of the fly leaf and in Sammy's hand the inscription, "To Paul Roland, for the fine work he is doing, from Samuel Giffen."

There was a point even as he read it when he could have laughed, could have hooted at the sheer impossible manic bravado of the whole thing, but he put it away and let his anger ride up. Sammy came in with a tray and drinks trembling on it, making it look like he was walking a tightrope.

Again at the sheer comedy of it he could have laughed and picked up his book and gone but he let Sammy start dispensing the wine and closed his mind into a fist. You scrofulous cunt, Giffen. Sammy came over and offered Moseby the last drink on the tray.

"I brought you a drink, John, there'll be some interesting people here later that might be able to help you with your play."

"Sammy, this is my book. You stole it," and he did know for at once an animal panic leaped and stared out of the reynard face and at this sign Moseby was contrite and wanted to ask "why did you do it to me?" but Sammy started backing away, his voice quivering, "For Godsake, John, don't you bliggy start on me, don't you start accusing me, you just want to see me back in that bliggy place, you just took me there and left me and you never came to see me, don't you start accusing me," and near tears now he turned away and Moseby couldn't let it rest, had to deny the truth of Sammy's words, and the resistance he was putting up and the clumsy ineffectiveness of his defence and guilt at his own behaviour and as antidote and solution and release he threw out his right, once, catching Sammy in the middle of his face and felt as he did so the small, distant break of his nose.

Sammy covered his face with his hands, from under which blood began to seep, and turning ran without sound from the room. Moseby stood aghast at the event till he noticed that no one seemed to have seen the incident and so slowly assembled his limbs into some semblance of social order. Then, leaving the book behind, still open at the inscription, he went in search of Sammy.

He was in the bathroom holding a wet towel to his face. When he saw Moseby he removed the towel to speak. The damage he had accomplished with one blow terrified and excited Moseby. Sammy's nose had swollen and was, as well, unmistakably askew, giving his whole face a botched almost obscene look. There was blood on his chin and on his shirt and his eyes were tear-red.

"Ya blithy bastig" was all he could manage. The bathroom was in lilac and white and Sammy was dropping his improbably dark blood on a candlewick bathmat and into the bath where the drops struck long vivid exclamation marks against the pastel sides.

"I think your nose is broken, Sammy." The door opened, bumping Moseby forward. It was the owner of the bathroom, aghast at the blood.

"What's happening, Sam, what's wrong with you?" and they were all in and the door closed. A drop of blood fell on Moseby's shoe and his foot within winced in revulsion.

"Oh Paul, Mr. Rolanth, it wath tha blithy, he say I, it wath him," and he began to cry, choking snorting sobs that blew blood out of his nose in spurts, peppering the bath and the tiles and the wash basin with a great number of small polka dots. Roland was incensed.

"Look at the mess. My God, how disgusting, can't you stop dripping blood everywhere?" He had quite ignored Moseby and for some reason this made him think on Sammy confessing about a man he'd taken a boy to and received a pound for it. Roland was trying to mop up some of the stains in the bath and Moseby stepped behind him, next to the door. Then another drop of Sammy's blood fell on Roland's wrist, he shuddered violently, a reaction Moseby could feel sympathy for, and straightening up shoved Sammy against the lavatory seat, so that he sat down and his head sank between his knees, cupped in his hands, weeping and dropping starry splatches between his feet. For the first time Roland spoke to Moseby.

"Get out, you hooligan, get out, out, get out." Moseby eased open the door and nodding mechanically at Roland's accusation escaped. The door was closed and the bolt pushed across.

The party knew nothing of these gory goings on. Moseby went through it to the study, took his dictionary and left. The bathroom door was still closed but he did not stop to determine what was happening within. He went down the stairs and across the street. There he sat on a wall and looked up at the lighted, animate windows of Paul Roland's flat. The evening was mild and there was a scent of roses from some garden. Cars ran up and down the hill and on Finchley Road the belishas bloomed in their regular seasons, soft orange bongs of light. After some ten minutes Sammy appeared, carrying a hold-all and pressing a handkerchief to his nose. He stood uncertain on the street until Moseby stood up and he saw him, then he came across.

"Is that you, John, that blithy swine, he's thrown me out, tolth me to pack up and go, blithy ow queen that he is."

"I think you'd better see about that nose, Sammy, it's broken I think."

"I know, I felt it break. Look at my coat, will these stains come out?" exhibiting some dark patches on his jacket.

"I think so. Best thing is to go up to the hospital now," and nodding in agreement Sammy turned with his new-found friend up the hill.

They sat in casualty, in the greenish light, in the Dettol air and Sammy made a wet fluttery noise in his damaged nose and kept rearranging the handkerchief to find a clean part. Moseby held the *Shorter Oxford English Dictionary* on his knees like a square blue baby, bouncing it up and down out of the tension that was threading knots in his stomach and made him want to go to the lavatory although he had only just been. He felt very strange, stretched and drawn, a little hysterical. There was a man in the room who had cut his hand on a car door handle, an improbable occurrence he felt compelled to explain. Each time he tried Sammy would start to weep, silently at first but growing in volume as the man went on, until he stopped. Sammy snuffled a few times more and let out a heavy sigh. Recognizing his cue, Moseby asked him what was wrong.

"Oh I'm sorry, John, but when I think on it, I was getting on that well, that job I had, and now I'm worse off than ever, I think maybe I should just do away with myself, I don't see what I can do."

"Oh come on now, Sammy, it's not as bad as that," although it was.

"I might as well John, I've nowhere to go, I've got no money, he didn't pay me anything you know, I don't know where to go." "But the Son of Man hath not where to lay his head." "Inasmuch." "Come unto me . . ." And it all led, by illogical, inescapable steps, to Sammy sleeping on the floor and his odours and scratchings and his whining relentless mock gratitude until he was ready to venture forth again. You owe him nothing. You owe him everything. Sammy is your cross and he has to be borne.

"And I don't want one of them attending to me," he said of a buxom Nigerian nurse who came in and beckoned to the man with the cut hand. Moseby looked at Sammy in weary disbelief.

"What do you mean?"

"I don't want one of the bliggy coloureds near me."

"Shut up."

"Oh no, the things I've heard about them, I want a white nurse or I'm not being treated here, aah John, John," and Moseby had his shirt and his tie and his throat and had him against the wall.

"You fucking bastard, Giffen, I should kill you, I should kick your rotting head into a mush, do you hear me?"

"Aye John, I'm sorry, I'm sorry, John, what did I do, I'm sorry."

He let him go. His hands were sweaty and he felt sick. He had bitten his bottom lip so that the blood came through the torn skin. The *Shorter Oxford* lay crumpled on its open pages where it had fallen. Sammy's face was a ghastly pallor in the green light, the eyes red and bloodshot, the nose ludicrously swollen and askew. In the nostrils the blood had dried in rings of shiny black. Through the dry flaky skin the itch of his beard pinked.

Behind them the nurse said, "Less noise out here, please, this is a hospital. If you're not waiting for treatment please wait outside." She stood a moment, then went back in. Sammy looked at Moseby, uncertain of his reaction.

"I'm sorry, John," he said to cover his general sins. Moseby picked up his book and stood up.

"Where are you going, John, you're not going?"

"I'm going, Sammy."

"Where, where are you going, what will I do, I've got no-where to go, can I come round after I get my nose fixed?"

"Don't come near me, Sammy, don't show your horrible face near me or I'll break your nose again, do you hear?"

"But what will I do, John, what am I going to do?"

"Kill yourself, Sammy, jump under an Edgware line train, hang yourself, cut your throat. Only don't do it near me, Sammy." The nurse had come out at some point without Moseby hearing, she stepped between them, black-faced and white-starched.

"You ought to be ashamed of yourself. What do you mean by saying that to anyone? Who are you anyway?"

"I'm the one who broke his nose. I'm his best friend. Next to yourself, that is." And he went out, into the warm humming hush of the sleeping sick house, down the corridor and out into the night.

He walked slowly carrying the book of words in his arms. It was downhill all the way. The street lights stained his face and hands yellow and the people he passed had great purple sockets for eyes. The streets fell in long silent falls and he fell with them, weighted down by the book. He walked at a peculiar, slight angle it seemed, tilted slightly to the side, slightly forward. In a garden some flower or other smouldered magenta black. He tried to pluck it but the petals flaked away, baring the ugly stub of the heart, the stem broken. He let it hang. He crossed Finchley Road without noticing if there was traffic or not and entered the long dark passage that ran alongside the railway, walls of warehouses on one side, the embankment on the other. It stretched inside him, this long dim canal, and he recognized its route as he walked, downwards to his compulsive nadir. For a long time one assumed the worst was to hand, assumed the comforts of the damned when damnation was yet afar off. This was not now a final pit, merely another station in a line that stretched from the obscurity of his beginnings to the obscurity of his ends. So he counselled himself as he walked.

He found the street, or the street found him, and the hall door was open, as it would be in a dream or in a particular kind of reality, and the stairs rose, wide and banistered into flights of darkness. He mounted them and looked for number nine. He knocked, his fist a bony knob. Within was silent and he knocked again. Looking through the letter box revealed nothing, only the smell of things he could not name but knew none the less. Then there was movement and some distant dim light and then he saw her, barefooted, with a coat over her slip.

"Who's that at this hour?"

"It's me, Helen. John from the Montmartre." A chain rattled and a bolt withdrew and he went into where she stood, every pore breathing sleep.

"My God, and what brings you here at this time?"

"Oh, I just wanted to see you. I was passing."

"Were you now? Well come in." Into a room that smelled of stewed tea and soup and herself. In the light he noticed the small crutches of dirt between her toes, the nails of which had sometime been silvered. He sat down, the book on his knee.

"That's some size of a book you have there, you for reading me a story?" He put it on the floor, and his feet on it, like a footstool.

"It's just a dictionary, just words."

"Oh you'll be a lad for the words. Would you like a cup of tea?"

"Please."

She went off on her bare padding feet to the scullery. He heard the gas pop and hiss. The room was full of things that his eyes saw and would not recognize. Things, furnitures and items, bits of pieces, all with names he could not recall or had never known. In the corner, rumpled from rising, the place where she slept itched at his mind. He felt numb in the head, the single certainty in his whole being, now that the book no longer pressed on it, grew firmer with each carnal second that passed.

When Helen came back she had two cups of orange tea and had put her teeth in. Moseby sipped his tea and set it by the book.

"Well and what's been happening at the Mountmarty? Did they get a black in after I left?"

"Yes," he said though it was not true.

"Helen knows the way their minds work."

"I've left."

"Have you, couldn't work beside them eh, like me, well

how can they imagine a white can, and them supposed to be white themselves, makes you wonder."

"When you take it back they're Arabs in the beginning though, aren't they?" Moseby said, closing his eyes.

"They are, though they make out they hate the Arabs. Are you tired?" He looked in time to see her legs cross and their great girths massed darkly in his sight.

"A bit."

"Time you were getting to your bed, eh?"

"I'm sorry for getting you up."

"Oh I'm glad you came by. I've been expecting maybe you would, but not at this time of night."

"As long as I didn't disturb you with anyone."

"Oh, and who would you be likely to disturb me with?"

"Oh, one of your boyfriends."

"As if I'd be having any of them up here."

"Well, you've got me up."

"Ah now, that's a different story, sure and you and me have known each other a while now."

"Where do you go with your boyfriends then, Helen?"

"Have a drink in the Marylebone."

"But when you want a bit?" and he thought for a moment that she was going to take offence. She uncrossed her legs and sat up, then she laughed and her body shook, the flesh loose upon the bones.

"Oh, so that's how you're feeling tonight, is it?"

He undressed in the dark and found her waiting, reaching out blindly feeling for the bed and the first touch of her, then finding her all, spongy, damp the flesh and without form, only extent, and the rounded masses of her legs and shoulders and the great loose udders of her and a wide soft midmost spread that he gathered in handfuls and kissed all the while she groaned endearments and her hand fastened on him in a painful pressure. Slowly he was engulfed, submerged in her smell and feel, in the legs and clamping arms and the darkness deepened as all centred in the stiff digit of his single-minded assertion.

Across the wastes of her and to her far side he went, across the sunless flesh of this great dark moon woman, this birth hudder of his heart's desire until with a muttering of warning she held him and hoicking up her great legs put him against the furled little hole and bade him, for safety's sake in the dangerous times, have her there.

And Moseby sent his seed into the darkness, his sons and daughters he sent heedlessly into the dark and he cried out against himself and lay, spread and utterly spent.

He scouted the streets cautiously on his return lest Sammy should be there but no ginger man lurked and the rows of houses lay in their long quiet curve, alike in their blinded witness as he passed between them, running the gauntlet of their disregard. In place of all the previous realities or unrealities there was now, like a committed act, the cold awareness that there was not, somewhere waiting, a simple solution to all this. The dream of a choice, once taken, the rightness of which would sustain him for ever, was gone. It was the last of his innocence and without it he felt exposed and frail.

He went in and on the telephone a message for him. "Mr. Moseby ring SWI 3903. Message from Mr. Gibbon." Harry Gibbon. The name rang a bell or struck a chord or whatever the musical image was. Well, that was something to do, save him making up his mind about anything. The thought of the room waiting above to receive his thoughts unnerved him. He turned back to the door. All along the street a wind had sprung and blew in every tree and each tree tossed and loosed its ready leaves. The wind was of a quality he had never felt, across what desolations it had blown he could scarcely begin to guess but it chilled him and as he watched he shivered to perceive that the whole street seemed full of ragged trees letting loose their ragged leaves. It frightened him, this dead wind in the dying trees. Against the vision he closed the door and went upstairs.

In the brief pre-dawn the city achieves its true sovereignty, the streets lead here and there, unfollowed; the buildings multiply their aphonies and a great cold emptiness exudes. It is a mortuary, a catastrophe of desolation. Silent empty corridors filled with the arid brood of mute existence. A silence which is not the mere absence of sound but a thunderous stone hush, a deafening cataract of empty noise falling upon no ear. It is the wilderness made manifest.

Like great brown scarves of sand the birds leave, spiralling out from the centre, radials in the centrifuge of exodus, countless grains of flight. Their going ushers the day and its denizens.

Two

Roots and Leaves

—Sometimes it seems as if there grew
In the dull garden of my mind
A tree like this, which, singing with delicate leaves,
Yet cracks the wall with cruel roots and blind
Sometimes, indeed, it appears to me
That I myself am such a tree—

CONRAD AIKEN: SENLIN—A BIOGRAPHY.
The Hogarth Press

The wind, moving in the tree, caused movement in the room and Ruth rose, from a mindless curiosity, to look. The gust had passed and the tremors were settling back into green peace. Outside her window, a slim tree and young, a pale bark ash whose fingering branches touched the pane at the prompting of the wind and some nights woke her, beckoned her out of sleep to stand and look, stand by the window watching the tree reach and reach and think of the wind, fractured from its city crossing, playing a moment in the small fountain of leaf. Back once more in bed, under the lee of Harry's sleeping back, she imagined the wind as a traveller, dusty and dispirited, bathing its weary feet, grateful for her tree, or thought of it as it travelled on, beyond London, across the country, regaining its sweetness, breaking in great waves on the chestnut trees in Knutsford, swaying the Scots pines on her little knoll. She thought of the wind and of the trees it blew in and snuggled down under her lover's bulk.

It was at night she seemed most alive. The days passed mainly indoors, with trips for shopping and the twice weekly calls to pick up her charges from the dancing lessons. Then there was a meal to prepare for Harry and Stolleman if he was coming in, and she did washings, Harry's heavy, work thick clothes, and ironing and a dress she was making herself, cut out and inching towards completion. The days passed in a monotone, trivial and full. It was in the night, with Harry in the quiet mass of his sleep that she sometimes came awake at the tree's touch and lay to think far thoughts and near and consider her life.

Harry she thought of, become so soon so permanent. Her life followed his rhythm and it surprised her that it should seem so natural to live with a man and make his meals and mend his clothes and share his bed. There was already a gloss of habit on their lives, the early morning cup of tea, brought to her bed, which she drank still more asleep than awake while Harry washed and dressed and came to kiss her before he left.

She would hear the door and his feet on the steps, then fainter on the street and then he was gone and at some unmarked point thereafter she was asleep.

Her second and proper awakening came about eleven when the sounds of Stolleman in the kitchen got her up. She sat in her brown robe and washed away the taste of tea with the flavour of coffee and talked gossip with Stolleman. The idea of their sharing his flat had proved a highly satisfactory one, making it possible for Harry's wage to support them un-augmented and providing Stolleman with exactly the backdrop of female companionship and convenience he liked, without involving him personally. She sometimes thought that all that was needed to make perfect her life was the presence of Cuffee, still her brother but now outside the pale of her need, but made once more accessible by her love for Harry, or by Harry's love for her. For the first time it was possible for her to know her brother as a person, free from the labyrinth of their past and its tangled emotions. It was the inability to enjoy this freedom to the full that caused her to dislike Gerda, since it was she who most effectively baulked her.

That Gerda loved her brother she had no doubt but there was something in the quality of Gerda's love which Ruth found improper. There was a weight, a solidity born of single-mindedness in it which seemed oppressive. It was not a simple possessiveness, it was as though Gerda's whole nature was ful-filled in the act of loving him and Ruth could not but feel that Peter must find this a barrier in time. At the moment, how-ever, he seemed content. The end room at the mews had been cleared and he was painting, new paintings with new colours, but of old things, fruit and vegetables, flowers and faces, bodies and branches, but seen simpler than Cuffee had seen before. He was painting and he seemed happy to be doing so and she had to admit that Gerda was in much responsible for this stability.

Yet she distrusted her, and with her Cuffee's well-being. There was something about Gerda that she felt to be false, a lie, a dissimulation. The nearest she had come to uncovering it had been on an afternoon visit to the mews when she had opened the door with the key on its string and come upstairs. Her entrance was masked by Gerda's bath water running and on coming to the top of the stairs she saw Gerda standing before the mirror in the bathroom, naked, posturing her large fleshy body, and all the while holding the bloody little mouse of a Tampax by the tail. Ruth had held her breath a moment then crept back downstairs, to return more ostentatiously announced. She thought often of that curious glimpse and what exactly she thought it essentialized, but never to any final conclusion.

If she was uncertain about Gerda she found her ex-husband even more baffling. She liked him but assumed his appeal lay in the polite hopelessness, the fastidious, dated appearance and the stutter that only several drinks or fast driving relieved. All else about him was unsure and disconcerting. He seemed to need Gerda still although their relations contained nothing that Ruth would have considered irreplaceable. They had lunch every fortnight or so and occasionally, but only occasionally, Terry would drop round in the evening for a drink.

He had taken to calling for Ruth on odd afternoons, saying things were slack at the showrooms and taking her for drives up through Hampstead and Highgate and among quiet countrified houses, driving with a rapt, loving expertise, talking eagerly about how the MG handled and saying she must learn to drive and that he would teach her. He never did though and she didn't press the point, seeing only too clearly the virility that resided in this accomplishment. Ruth always expected that at the end of these trips Terry would try to kiss her or put a hand on her leg. He never did and this further puzzled her since he presumably found her attractive. She mentioned it to Stolleman who expressed the opinion that Terry was impotent and had been ever since the end of his marriage to Gerda. Unfair though she knew it to be Ruth used this as extra leverage against Gerda, as though she might be held responsible for Terry's hypothetical incapacities.

She thought about them and about herself and her parents in Knutsford, of where they were all going and what would be their fates. Sleep would dim their faces and she would lose the thread of her speculations and her last thoughts would be of her tree, outside, close to the pane.

The dancing classes were held in a high bare hall with Arthur Rackham prints hung out of reaching distance and chairs along a wall for the mothers and escorts to sit on. There was an upright piano played by a small, owl-faced man in shirt sleeves, and there was the teacher Miss Rose and usually about twenty little girls between five and eight. Ruth collected three children twice a week and took them to the classes and then to their respective homes. Usually at this point, seated in a tubular canvassed chair between the mums and the *au pairs*, she wondered why she did it. Scarcely for the money, nor did she talk to any of the others, just sat, hands in her lap and watched Miss Rose's supple waist imitate the stem of a flower, revolving to follow the sun. "Slow, slow, slowly, children," and the simple piano, its notes like white pebbles into a well and the tubby slender clumsy poised pretty plain children danced around. Perhaps for this inconsequential peace she came, flecked with boredom and scratched with occasional embarrassment for a mother's child or a child's mother, but peace nevertheless, fragrant with all the little melodies she had forgotten. "Baa Baa Black Sheep," "Hickory Dickory Dock," "Ride a Cock Horse," "The Grand Old Duke of York," they all came back, children's songs, magical tunes, sacred words, fixed in the mind, the very pillars of identity in a way. It moved her strangely to hear them again, falling without adornment upon the ear. It made her feel strangely vulnerable and happy. She glanced about her lest it should be observed but no one seemed aware of her or her thoughts.

She found Miss Rose, whose dancing school it was, rather fascinating. Her voice, clear and honed on elocution to a razory timbre. The ordinary, unremarkable body in a cardigan and skirt that rippled and flowed in the exercises. She would point down with her toe and the calf made a lovely bevel. And the face, attractive and unembellished, not young but scarcely old, yet the flesh round the eyes like crêpe and the fine down of an incipient moustache upon the upper lip. Ruth wondered about her, about her age and her life and if she was happy and why.

There were also her charges and the walk home with them. By listening to their chatter and asking a few judicious questions it was possible to patch up an interesting impression of their lives and the lives of their parents. So interesting that Ruth forced herself to stop, neither to listen nor to ask questions, save in the case of Jessamyn, whom Ruth hated. Jessamyn was a tall pale blond child with remarkable composure and an icy way of speaking which came, almost undiluted, from her mother. She was a stretched ex-beauty of about forty-eight and Ruth imagined Jessamyn to have been a grudging concession on her part to the duties of good wifery. Ruth pried as far as she dared with Jessamyn, trying to dredge up the shards of domestic life, encouraged by occasional treasures such as the fact that Jessamyn's mother called her husband "floppy" when she was quarreling with him.

Walking home herself she realized that almost all of her waking hours were spent in wondering and pondering about other people. The world seemed now to fairly teem with them, after the near hermetic life of Manchester, London seemed densely overpopulated and she watched agog as they swam to and fro, up and down, all shimmering in their various guises.

In the room she put on the kettle and lit a cigarette and put on a record that Harry had bought her, a Beethoven Trio with an opening movement that always reminded her of when she was a child, a Royal Air Force band playing in some autumnal park, her father, not long returned from the war and still a stranger, sitting beside her mother and the music full of cinnamon leaves and clockwork pigeons.

The tree seemed to respond also to the music and Ruth watched its delicate accompaniment until the kettle hooted readiness.

Work agreed with Gibbon. It tightened him just that little bit, paring away the suggestion of sloth, giving his bulk a firmness. He always had some small cut or bruise on his hands and Ruth would wash them with a certain ritual, him sitting on the high stool and she would hold his hand over the plastic basin with the warm soapy water and she would scrub them gently and swab the cuts with Dettol. Harry talked about the job. He had a working man's love of lengthy narrative yet he was witting enough not to bore. The names of the men he worked with became familiar, their natures and mannerisms. They seemed, in Harry's telling, good men, men honest and kind, beyond their intolerance and pettiness they made her glad to hear of them and their existence.

She realized also that these recountings meant a great deal to Harry. It was in a way the subject on which he could talk best, the quiet affectionate observation of his fellows and the tasks he had himself to perform. On other subjects he was quick to withdraw into silence at the first sign of her disagreement. In some way she felt he thought of her as his intellectual superior and it was partially this which made him eager that she should not find a job in a library. He was in fact trying, amid all the trappings of the Hampstead affaire, to behave like a married man in Greenock.

Greenock was the only other thing he spoke of, Greenock and his friend who lived there. Ruth could form no real impression of either since Harry never indulged in descriptions but spoke as if the subject was already familiar. She sensed a romanticism in this, an almost deliberate obscurity, but it never concerned her enough to press him on it.

The only thing that did concern her in their relations was bed. Even this was the faintest of matters, not a dissatisfaction and barely a worry, more a kind of reservation. There was something about Harry, he did not seem somehow fully committed to the sexual act. He made love to her and she had pleasure and often satisfaction from it and he in turn seemed content, but nevertheless she felt incomplete, somehow disorientated. Occasionally she thought if just once his ever constant tenderness would desert him and he would take her, uncaring whether comfort was present, if she could feel herself beneath a mere maleness instead of always gentle Harry, perhaps that would supply the missing ingredient. Against that, however, she told herself she had a kink about crypto rape or, more serious, that she sought in Harry Gibbon some element of her brother, in which case she judged herself doomed to disappointment.

It did serve to remind her though that the question of her relation to Peter was still an ambiguous one, and not wholly free from danger. What he felt remained as remote a speculation as ever. The long, rapacious face would set empty, the eyes holding for long seconds, then switch devoid of interest to something else. If she hadn't seen him for several days he arrived almost as a stranger and it would take an hour or so before he thawed. Ruth assumed this to be the fact of living with Gerda but when she asked him about it he denied knowing what she meant.

When he did come over they went walking on Primrose Hill. She liked the decorous little park, with its view over the zoo to London town. They walked around and around its paths and she watched the young mothers and the dog owners and Cuffee talked about painting, more to himself than to her.

"See Stolleman's in a different position. He supplies his own imagery. He's painting these Pacific atolls or something. Never seen an atoll in his life. Out of here," tapping the side of his head. "I'm looking for things to paint, the right things. So I just paint what's to hand. They're not right, not the right things but I'm painting them better. But I'll have to strike my seam shortly. Trouble is I don't know what it is. This is when you wish there was still a series of fit subjects to paint, crucifixions, pietas, temptations, George and the Dragon."

"You bwute, look what you've done to Towser."

Cuffee smiled, "Yes, funny little painting that. Think I'll nick it from the National." She looked up into the high plane trees where the erosion of the year was already well advanced. A leaf fell, carrying out over the railings and across the road. She watched it the whole way, its ebbing, sidling fall, deeply relaxing like the breath released, long pent, from the body.

"What are you going to do, Peter?" she asked at the end of her sigh.

"What, with my life you mean?" smiling.

"Yes."

"What's wrong with my life I should do something with it?"

"Well you won't stay with Gerda for ever, will you?"

"Now that you whittle it into a point, no."

"What will you do then?"

"Oh come on, love, 'what will I do,' how do I know?"

"What about this Uta?"

"Ah, the bold Uta. The girl with the fibre-glass knickers."

"Harry thinks you were pretty involved with her."

"He'll rupture his head thinking away like that will your Harry."

"I take it you're not telling then."

"Look, Ruthie flower, I'm recuperating from a traumatic experience, don't nag me. I'm on my therapeutic art bit and if I'm very good I'll get a painting in the next nutter's exhibition. The night is yet a small dog," and he went on in that vein for a bit. She knew the style, it was the last remnants of his embarrassment at not sharing. It made her, under her exasperation, warm to him.

She asked Stolleman about Peter as a painter but he didn't say much.

"Can't tell. Talented of course but something's switched off. The toad on the spring. But I've seen it before when a painter was just getting ready to find out what he really wanted to paint."

Harry predictably enough, thought Cuffee was all right.

"Well I mean she's good for him, you know, I mean I know it's not love and maybe he will leave her but just now it's really ideal, isn't it?" Ruth could see his point but that did not make her agree.

"What was this Uta like?"

"Oh well, I didn't know her, only saw her once or twice."

"Did you like her?" Gibbon heaved his shoulders and lolled his head.

"Oh she was a meat eater. We weren't, you know, not alike." His big gentleness touched her and she put her face into his neck.

"Did you have many girls in Paris?"

"I didn't have any girls in Paris." She snuggled deeper.

After a moment he drew his head back and squinted down at her. "Do you mind?" She laughed, happy with his innocence.

"Oh Harry, you are a dear one, you are."

Gerda rang her in the morning and wanted to talk to her about Peter. "What about him?"

"I want your advice about something. Can you come over?" Ruth was reluctant. She didn't want to go over there. She had been drifting quietly about tidying and dusting, with the radio babbling dimly from Stolleman's room. She would have had a solitary afternoon in her high cool room with the Beethoven and a book to read. She didn't want to give Gerda advice about Peter. Not that Gerda wanted advice anyway. Whatever else she wanted it wasn't that. But she couldn't think of anything convincing enough so she said she would come over. She stood by the phone, caught for a moment in a little bubble of inertia. Quietly the radio spilled into the room, filling it up to the brim and she could see the tree, outside, wind-waved, tremble soundlessly against the glass. Feelings moved in her, moved and disturbed her, feelings far short of the density of emotions, feelings that had no other description save the place they occurred in, the time of day, the weather and such similar irrelevancies. Feelings in an empty room at eleven o'clock of a bright gusty morning, anonymous, pregnant feelings. She felt female and vulnerable and somehow threatened. They lasted almost all the way to Gerda's by which time she had convinced herself it was her period coming.

Gerda's sitting-room was quite small and in it she looked larger than she really was. She seemed in constant danger of bumping into things. The prospect of that ample smooth flesh chided by the corners and protrusions of inanimate objects was rather disconcerting. She had beautiful skin. For a woman so nearly fat she had rather a special quality about her body. And her subtle auburn rinse and the carefully done eyes. Ruth reluctantly granted that she was attractive and then smiled at herself.

"You said you wanted my advice."

"Yes, I do," and Gerda sat down opposite her. That's when she had to be careful, when she got herself settled, a lot of the appeal went when the flesh started rubbing against itself.

"Yes, I'm a bit worried about his painting."

"Oh."

"Yes, I want him to have an exhibition." Do you now, darling. Quite the little patroness getting.

"Oh. And does Peter not want an exhibition?"

"Well he says he's not ready for an exhibition but I've asked Michael and he says he doesn't see why he shouldn't have one." Ruth wondered if Stolleman buttered his bread both sides or whether it was just Gerda taking what she wanted out of a noncommittal reply.

"Well if Peter doesn't want an exhibition surely it's up to him?"

"Yes but I know someone who is part owner of a very good little gallery. I'm sure he'd be interested in seeing Peter's work. Do you think you could use your influence with him?"

"I don't have any influence with Peter, not about painting. And even if I had, knowing that he was against it would stop me from saying anything."

"But he isn't against it. He just needs to be convinced that his work is good enough." Ruth felt a superior smile curling up.

"I don't think Peter has to be convinced along those lines."

Gerda looked at her coolly for a moment.

"I don't think you know Peter as well as you imagine, Ruth."

A little silent jangle of the nervous system told her that Gerda had reached her real topic. For the moment she let her come on.

"Possibly not."

"I mean I know you were very close, still are, but I think maybe that closeness has blinded you to some things about him."

"And you not being so close can see these things." Gerda's expression of slight surprise told Ruth she had been a bit precipitate but she choked back the impulse to say something conciliatory.

"There's no need for us to quarrel about this, Ruth. I mean we both have Peter's interest at heart." Which made Ruth glad she hadn't apologized.

"Look, Gerda, it would probably be helpful if I told you just how I regard Peter's best interests. I think he is somebody you have to let look out for himself. I don't mean he knows what is best for himself but I think he's the kind of person who'd rather choose wrongly for himself than have anyone else choose right for him. So I don't think it's for me to say or do anything."

"Are you still in love with him?" She didn't want to be asked such questions by this woman whom she couldn't like or trust, trustworthy and likeable though she doubtless was. She should be able to say "no" to her, it didn't matter what she said here, aloud. Yet "no" was a cutting little word. Enough "no's" and the delicate threads of relation were hacked apart, without knowing, thinking as one did that words were not deeds, when they were the most damaging deeds of all.

"I don't know."

"I think you are, and that you resent me."

"That's possible." At this flatness Gerda shifted her tone.

"Look, Ruth, please, please be on my side."

"Against whom?"

"Against no one. I love Peter. I've never loved anyone before like I love him. It's not a girl's love. I'm forty-two and I won't love anyone again like this." Ruth was moved by the appeal, even against her will.

"What do you want me to do?"

"Help me to help Peter."

"How can I do that?"

"Look, Ruth, just because I'm in love with your brother I'm not gaga. I know Peter is going to go off, sooner or later, on trips, even after other women. But I want him, after each trip, to be able to come back. I want him to feel free to return and I want to help him to be a painter and have success."

"You want him to be indebted to you."

"All right, if you like. But I know what it's like to want somewhere to go, somewhere that was safe. Peter will need that. It's in his nature. He has to fight everything. And every now and then he'll take a beating, like last time. You ask Harry. When Harry brought him back here after they'd been to Paris, Peter was in a bad way. By the time you got down he'd really thrown it off, but for a couple of weeks he was ill, and I don't just mean physically. I don't know the whole story but whoever she is that girl really put him through it, or he really put himself through it. Well that wasn't the end, it'll happen again, and again. Is it asking so much that I should be the person he comes home to?"

Despite many reservations Ruth admired her, yet couldn't give her approval. Not because of the reservations, which were almost technical, but because she distrusted the basis of the exchange Gerda was planning. It seemed so generous on the surface but Ruth saw it differently. Even if the assessment of Cuffee was accurate and he would need somewhere to come back to time and time again, it wasn't right that she should help to manufacture the drug that he would come to crave. Gerda was trying to induce a special form of addiction, she was peddling solace this woman, the solace of those great bubs, those undemanding arms, the generous mouth. Like perhaps she had peddled it to Terry to his final destruction. Peter was no Terry, but there was no telling what Terry had once been.

"I'm sorry, Gerda. I can't be on your side. I don't know what would be good for Peter. Why don't you just take your chances. It probably will work out exactly as it would have even if I had been in complete agreement about everything you say." Gerda sat for a moment, silent. Then she got up.

"You're a cool little miss when you want to be, with your clipped voice and that 'this-is-the-way-it-is' manner. Would you like some coffee?" and went into the kitchen without waiting for an answer.

She thought about Gerda's description of her on the way back. "A cool little miss." She'd never thought of herself as being cool. It struck her that she had no very clear idea of what she was like, had no real image of herself. Perhaps, among other things this was what she had to cultivate, the days of being her brother's wan mooncast shadow were over and without needing to think about it she knew she would never be Harry's shadow. In a way this was one of the things she admired in Gerda, the image she projected, with her mannerisms, her makeup, her clothes, even before you heard her speak. It would do no harm to learn something from her.

Stolleman was in his room, lying on the bed listening to a record of a piano playing a slow blues. Ruth looked round the door and he raised a leg in greeting.

"Hi, Roosevelt, made any new deals recently?"

"Hello, Michael," and sat on the edge of the bed. "What's the record?"

"Jimmy Yancey being soulful. What you been at?"

"Michael, what am I like?"

"You're all right."

"Describe me."

"Describe you?"

"Yes."

"To a stranger?"

"Yes."

"Not very tall, good face, good eyes, not bad hair but wears it badly. Not a great body, bit short-legged."

"Thanks."

"It's nothing." Yancey made the spaces between the notes get wider and wider, stretching the music over a fragile framework until it threatened to break into silence. When the silence finally came Ruth had outlived her pique at Stolleman's forthrightness.

"You don't like my hair?"

"Well, low buns aren't exactly the rage." Ruth remembered the girl Merle Curvis saying something about how sisterly her hair looked.

"Do you think I should have it cut?"

"M'm." He turned the record over. Ruth rose to leave.

"Do you think Peter should have an exhibition?" Stolleman looked up.

"Been talking to Gerda?"

"Yes."

"Well she wants it. She's very determined Gerda. Puts all her weight behind things. I don't think Peter has either the quantity or the quality of work for a decent show. But if he treated it as a sort of starting point, well it would do no harm to have thirty odd canvases hung around."

"I think I will have it cut. And my legs stretched."

That night the tree woke her, or at any rate she woke and it was there, chinese black in the silver print of the moon. Harry slept on the threshold of a snore, hunched over on his side, his wide back warm and comforting. She kissed his shoulder and slipped away from him. The tree was motionless, holding itself so still and taut that she felt uneasy and shivered against the glass. She thought of her parents, coming into their random collusion, cohering and dividing and giving chance life to her, this now consciousness against the pane. The enormous triviality of the event touched her and poised between the ridiculous and the sublime her mind held a moment then jerked free.

The empty moon let its illusion of light fall on the land. The tree cut its sharp shapes on the window and solitude, casually sought, gripped; inescapable ordinary isolation. Here as she stood, musing briefly on her source, it came and the undemonstrative cruelty of its certainty did much to reconcile her to its rigours.

It seemed not unfitting that mortals, hazardous creations that they were, should be locked within themselves for ever. Not at this moment, against the glass, before the tree.

But then the wind upped and blew and as the leaves rearranged themselves, so her feelings were re-ordered from within and at their flux an exultancy rose, nameless, liberating happiness, unreasoning, unreasonable joy. She turned to her bed where the pale smear of Harry's back phosphored in the gloom. She wanted to tell him, express all this but knew there was no telling, not with words. All she might do would be to waken him with love touches, to penetrate his sleep with her warm body. Frustration at her female inadequacy in this direction irked her and she lay sulky under the slumber of his unwitting back. Her insights and awarenesses slowly crumbled until she was left thinking wearily on the sound of a car, interminably revving on Finchley Road.

Jessamyn was unwell it seemed and unable to attend her dancing class. The high bare hall and the little man watching the children as he played, the audience in constrained silence, Miss Rose fluting her voice up and down the scale of instruction. "Now reach up tall as tall, up up to the sun, lovely flowers reaching up with their petals, stretching up, very good Marion, very good Jacqueline, reaching up and following the sun as it travels across the sky, very good all of you." There was something about her, about her body. She looked so much like the mother of her pupils, only in her supple movements there was a certain eroticism as though the ordinariness was but a veil through which could be seen, albeit dimly, the woman. Ruth could imagine that in her way she presented more of a threat to these women than some more obviously attractive female. This was themselves minus the layers of fat, the stretch marks, the varicose veins. Ruth liked her without any real reason save this appearance she had. Also she always seemed particularly friendly to Ruth, often smiling between exercises as she came to the piano to inform the pianist of the next sequence of dances.

The piano was playing "The Grand Old Duke of York" and it reminded her of Stolleman's record somehow, despite the disparate idiom. The words went through her head unbidden and in the middle, "when they were up they were up" and half thinking of Jimmy Yancey and watching Miss Rose miming a soldier marching, she suddenly heard the song as being deeply sexual and the words almost baldly suggestive. She blushed and looked to see if she were observed but no one was looking at her. Ruth slipped out as quietly as she could and went to the washroom where she washed her hands and face and then walked up and down until the class finished. By the time she had got her two changed and ready almost everyone had gone and at the last minute one of them wanted the toilet. Ruth was still standing waiting when Miss Rose came out with the man who played the piano.

"Not gone yet?" Miss Rose said.

"No, Jennifer was taken sudden like."

"I'll be off then, Miss Rose," the pianist said and Ruth realized she had never seen him walking about before, only at the piano. He was slightly bow-legged and had an overall pear-shaped appearance. He chucked the second little girl under the chin and went off, leaving Ruth and Miss Rose standing together. Jennifer took her time in returning and Miss Rose looked after the figure of her piano player.

"Very fine pianist, Mr. Turshaw. Surprisingly good for

what he's doing here." Ruth watched the caliper figure go round the corner out of sight. Miss Rose went on. "Yes, it's rather a waste really. He has excellent qualifications but he doesn't make enough money from teaching to live on so he plays for me." In some way Ruth found that her thoughts about "The Grand Old Duke of York" were connected in her mind with Mr. Turshaw so that this totally innocent line of talk had an uneasy undertone. Fortunately at that moment Jennifer reappeared. Miss Rose locked up and they stepped out on to the street. It seemed that they were both going in the same direction. The children went on ahead and Ruth noticed that Miss Rose crossed over behind her to walk on the outside. In her low-heeled sensible shoes, sling bag and springy walk she struck Ruth as the epitome of the county woman, varied interests, fond of walking.

"Do you live in Hampstead yourself?" she asked Ruth.

"No, not really. King Henry's Road. Behind Swiss Cottage."

"Oh yes, I know it. On the way to Primrose Hill."

"That's right."

"Do you have a flat?"

"I share with friends."

"That's nice. It can be very lonely here on your own." Ruth checked on her hands again. Only a garnet on the right. Good hands, short well-kept nails, clear varnished. The clock on the church struck five and they stood a moment under the chimes, both of them silent and slightly awkward.

"Well, I have to go down this way," Miss Rose said.

"Oh, well, goodbye then." Before she could move off a 187 bus came trundling round and down the hill. The two children waited at the edge of the kerb, holding hands. "Say cheerio to Miss Rose then," Ruth called to them but they didn't hear as the bus meshed its gears. Ruth smiled apologetically, feeling foolishly embarrassed and on the point of blushing. The thought of the Grand Old Duke of York being up and down took this opportunity to re-enter her thoughts.

"Perhaps," Miss Rose said, and her voice was trembling, or was it just the need to cough, which she did immediately before going on, "perhaps you'd come and have tea with me one afternoon, when you don't have the children to take back." Ruth felt panic-stricken at the invitation and looked wildly up into the trees around the church. They swayed in the wind, high above the ground, remote from red buses and unwelcome invitations. Ruth had a longing to be there, looking down, an aloof eye. "Shall we say," bringing her down like one of the leaves that seemed always to be departing, spiralling earthwards, "Friday."

"Yes, yes, Friday, thank you, I'd love to."

"Good, I'm so glad you can manage. I'll see you on Thursday anyway. Goodbye, Ruth," and she was gone, her buoyant stride just this side of the vigorous, pitched between athleticism and elegance.

Ruth watched her for a moment before crossing the street. A leaf landed in front of her and turned over several times. She looked directly up into the branches. Their height was suddenly dizzying, or the angle at which she craned her neck made her vision swim, the trees and the sky rotated around her crazy axis and she nearly stumbled. It was all quite mad. She took control of herself and balanced firmly by a child in each hand she pressed on.

That night Harry was in one of his talking moods. He got to remembering his family, of whom there seemed to be hundreds. Soon she was lost in a maze of names and relations, of deaths and births and strange vivid images amid the blur of second-hand recollection. Like his anecdotes about work these researchings obviously fascinated him and she could see him as he talked allowing him the power of his narrative to carry him away. Her own firmest impressions were of his father, who sounded a strange, almost unbalanced man, and of some distant uncle who lived as a preacher. They seemed, even at this remote telling, remarkably unlike the large, slow young man who bore their name and who told their now finished tales.

It ended up making him sad, quite without his realizing it his anthology of past lives became funereal. He stopped speaking and there was a long silence. Then he looked at her.

"I go on a bit, don't I?"

"I like you to talk."

"It's all a bit, well it's pretty depressing in a way."

"You mean that people die."

" 'All the dead are dead and all the living are dying.' But not just dying. Just you wonder about, well when it's over it all might as well never have bothered."

"Oh I don't know. Life is good. There's a lot of things. . . ." and broke off because she felt that it was all a bit callow, talking pro and con life in the evening, after tea.

"All my folk were religious in one way or another. I was brought up to be religious only there isn't any religion that I can have. Sometimes when I think the most religious things in my life were just lying in bed when I was little on Sunday mornings and my mother and father having breakfast and me knowing they were just next door and feeling all safe or when my mother would wash her hair and dry it at the fire and she'd let me comb it for her, all hanging down and we'd roast apples on the hob and the smell of the apples and the sugar and my mother's hair drying, or when I used to take my father's tea up to the yard when he was working late and the smell of the wood in the sawmill. That's what's really most religious, not God or Jesus or anything and how can you believe in that, it's all in the past, just a memory."

After he spoke he sat a moment, then uncharacteristically rose and prepared for bed without another word.

Ruth found herself irritated, not by what he had said, but because all evening, stemming from the afternoon's experience, she had been growing progressively readier for sex. There had been a languorous period of almost an hour when she had let Harry's voice draw milky trails of concupiscence through her mind, just his voice and his presence and behind that the thrustful presence of the Grand Old Duke of York throbbed meaningfully. She felt female, distended, ready for taking. As Harry however showed no indication of wanting to take, the well-being passed and became a faint but pervasive frustration. In bed when his smooth quiet bulk gave no hint of desire she had an abrupt headache and a silent, twisting rage at her tormentor. Her plight seemed suddenly to be purely female, doomed to passivity, to await the male's approach. In her case that approach was seldom undertaken. Or was that fair. She had no idea how often men wanted their women, having never lived with anyone before. Yet she could not see Gerda lying silent beside her mate and suffering unsated appetence. She felt quite inadequate then and could not restrain herself from blaming Harry. She should get a job. It was doing nothing all day that brought this situation on. But beneath this rationalization was a more basic resentment, that without knowing what sexual satisfaction might be like, she knew herself to be unfulfilled and the knowledge rubbed at her mind until it was raw.

The aftermath was with her next day. She woke depressed, and lay on in bed until her headache returned. Angry with herself she rose and phoned Cuffee. Gerda answered. She said Peter wasn't in. Ruth disbelieved her. She made herself some coffee and burned her tongue drinking it. It was obviously a day for cutting thumbs while opening tins. She went, reluctantly, outdoors.

Slowly the day soothed her. It was tawny and bright and its colours freshened the eye as she walked. She was simply bored. It wasn't such a terrible admission. She wasn't used to doing nothing all day. Nor was there any need that she should. After all this was London. There were galleries and exhibitions and museums and shops. And she knew people. There was Miss Rose and Stolleman and Terry. She could pass each day in activity. She could even get a job.

By the time she got to Swiss Cottage she was almost cheerful. Terry's car showrooms were a bit further along. She'd go along and see him, maybe find out some scandal about Gerda. Feeling more in humour with herself she stepped out, catching sight of herself in the shop windows. Just beyond Finchley Road tube station there was a café. It was large and almost empty. Its wide front windows had sketches of can-can dancers done on to the glass. Despite the hideousness of these and the general tattiness, it looked inviting somehow in the mid-morning, quiet and spacious inside. She sat at a table and watched out on to Finchley Road, content to eddy here for the moment. The only other person apart from the waitress and herself was a large woman in a green overall who stood at the back with heavy arms folded across her chest. Once she came forward and went to the door, gazing across the street at someone. As she watched her Ruth could feel relief rise. At least she didn't look like that. The whole nature of the world would be totally altered should she have happened by some parental misfortune to look like that. This proof of the inevitability of one's nature, however superficial it might be, made a strong impression on her. She was her parents' child, as was her brother. Their mark was upon them both. If it carried its privileges, inasmuch as she had a certain intelligence and some measure of appearance, surely it must carry its penalties. She, and Peter, must be like Mr. and Mrs. Cuffee in other ways. With Peter she could see it, despite his antagonism towards his father, they were in so much alike. Did that mean she was like Mrs. Cuffee? It made her realize that even if that were so she was not much the wiser as to her nature. Mrs. Cuffee seemed quite featureless at that moment and in contrast the dark passionate personages of Gibbon's forebears came back to her, disturbing with their power to survive in her mind. They were all tied into the pattern of things by these knots, they were what they were and what they were to become and they were also what one struggled not to be. Perhaps there was no formal unpicking of them, they must needs be cut or ignored. To some extent Cuffee and she represented these respective courses. At this stage it was impossible to say who was having the greater success.

Terry was in the office at the back of the showrooms. He got up in surprised pleasure.

"Well, hello there, wh-what do I owe this honour t-to?"

"Just thought I'd drop over see how you were."

"Yes, glad you did. L-look, s-sit down, I'll get my man to see to things, then we can go for a spin. Would you like that?"

"Lovely." He went out and she sat in his office. There was a calendar with naked women flaunting considerable amounts of charm for each month of the year. August was a honey blonde with nipples like pink saucers. Someone had drawn a little potato man at her feet looking up in awe. It was rather a deft little doodle and made Ruth smile. She was looking at it when Terry came back. His sallow face flushed.

"B-bloody things, g-get sent them you know, f-firms send them."

"Did you draw the little man?"

"B-bloody silly of me, really," he admitted and tore August off although there were still a few days left in the month. Then he held the door open for her and they went out.

He drove the MG along and up the hill into Hampstead, then up through the village to Whitestone Pond. The Heath stretched away, undulant and still thick with summer green although the gutters already ran rust with leaves. They turned right and drove towards Highgate. Terry had been silent ever since leaving the showroom and Ruth asked him what was wrong.

"Nothing. Why?"

"You're very quiet."

"Really nothing."

"It's not that calendar that's bothering you?" He glanced at her swiftly.

"N-no, of course not."

"Oh I just thought you might have been embarrassed."

"No, j-just b-bloody silly thing to have done."

Ruth said no more but remembered what Stolleman had implied about Gerda and Terry and bed. But when had Terry last been to bed, even in impotence, with his ex-wife? He wasn't still in love with the woman surely. She glanced at him, the pale, almost handsome face, yet weak, somehow lifeless. Fair fine eyebrows, darker hair. Eyes the colour of which evaded her. Greyish, bluey, indeterminate. She wanted to ask questions but felt the association would be too obvious. Instead she relaxed and watched his driving, the most purposeful thing about him, until after a time she felt it safe.

"How did you meet Gerda? I know it was during the war, but how did it happen?"

"We were both stationed at the same place. Down in Sussex. Lovely part of the world Sussex. D'you know it?"

"No, I've never been."

"Bloody marvellous. Not so far from London really. Could take a spin down sometime."

"That'd be lovely."

"Yes, best county of them all. I'm from Suffolk myself but you can't beat Sussex," and he drove on for a bit in silence, rapt in the remembered beauties of the English landscape, then: "Yes, stationed there we were, that's when we met. Funny place to fight a war really. Didn't make sense. I mean war's usually a bit like school. You go away for a term and come back at vacation. This was like going to war each day and coming home in the evening." He shook his head. "Funny business. I can remember, coming in one evening, sun just gone down, everything looks so bloody marvellous from up there," lifting his chin to indicate, "little houses and cows and people. Used to be a French convent school, evacuee kids, all in those smock things French kids wear, going through the lanes like a white snake, everything at three thousand feet so bloody perfect. Only you'd just shot down some poor German bugger into the splash and he probably thought things looked just as marvellous when he was coming in to land, only not any more he didn't. Funny bloody game."

"Was Gerda there when you arrived, or did she come after?"

"Oh, a bit after. I'd been there a while. Battle of Britain and that. Then they sent some WAAFS down, Gerda was with the first batch."

"And did you start going out together right away?"

"No," he said and was silent for a moment, bending the little car around the curves. "No, not right away." Ruth sensed delicate ground and switched her line.

"Has she changed much since then, in appearance?"

"Oh yes," and for the first time since leaving he smiled, a wan affectionate smile. "Scrawny little piece she was then, thin as a match. Oh she's not the same girl at all. She changed a lot after her illness."

"Oh, what illness was that?"

"She had tuberculosis, they didn't find out until nearly the end of the war. Sent her off to a sanatorium. She was there nearly a year and a half."

"Were you married then?"

"Lord yes, we'd been married four years when she came out of hospital. Put on about six stone she had. Like a barrage balloon. Got a lot of it off mind you but she never went back to what she was. Suits her much better actually, a bit of weight. She didn't suit being thin."

"Were you in love with her?"

He was giving all his attention to the road for a moment and she was going to repeat the question when he said, with a small shrug, "I don't know. Love. It was a funny time. Things were all a bit mixed up in those days. There was quite a lot of love about." He glanced over, "I'm not being whatsit, it's just difficult to explain what it was like, the atmosphere. Gertie was in bad shape. Parents got killed in the bombing. Southampton. Bad show really. I felt sorry for her. In a way. But I wasn't in such very good nick myself." And his lips pulled away from his teeth in the bones of a grin. "I was in love though, not with Gert . . ." and he checked himself and looked at Ruth in some alarm. "Oh, you m-mustn't say, n-not that I m-mentioned . . ."

"What?"

"Gertie. Gertrude Phillips. She called herself Gerda after she came out of the sanatorium. Can't b-blame her really, can you?" and they both laughed.

"Who was this you were in love with?"

"Oh, Suzanne. Suzanne Duval. She was eight years old. Went to this convent school. French. Just learning to speak English she was. I taught her the names of flowers. Used to know a lot about that sort of thing. You never realize how many flowers there are until you start naming them."

"What happened?"

"To Suzanne? Oh she went back to France after the war. I got posted but I went down again in forty-six and the school was closed. They'd all gone home. She'd have quite grown up by then," Ruth could see them, the slight, pale-faced man in his RAF uniform and a little white-smocked girl reciting a litany of English wild flowers. Then marrying his Gertie Phillips out of habit and need and pity.

They had come to a halt at traffic lights. Terry looked over. "Funny business really. Never know how things are going to turn out. Just as well maybe, what?" and Ruth nodded, still immersed in his past and for the moment not catching the self-derision in his voice. When she did and looked up, the lights had changed and Terry was once more attending to his machine.

Miss Rose's Christian name was Meriel. She lived in a first floor flat on Christchurch Hill, looking on to a sort of annexe of the Heath, planted with several languorous willows. Ruth was very impressed by the flat. It gave that sense of having grown organically, the plates on the wall in their wire clips and the soft fade of the velour on the settee, the little pieces of silver and china and on the mantelshelf a black and gilt clock that struck long oval chimes on the hour. Everything had belonged for a long time, seemed domiciled, content to be where it was. It was this harmony as much as the articles themselves that pleased her, that made the mellow tastefulness that soothed her inordinately. It pleased her beyond expressing to sit in the dull, brown, leather chair and select a discreetly toasted macaroon from the pale gold plate and recognize the blending of these disparate items, the unity they possessed in their colouring. The tea ambered out from the swannecked pot and a diminuendo of tinkles accompanied their stirrings. It reminded Ruth more than anything of the few, dim visits she had made as a child to her mother's parents in Devon and it caused her to reflect just how far short of such impeccable rightness their house in Knutsford fell. It made her wonder, almost for the first time, if her mother regretted the loss of such gentility. To avoid the subject she asked Miss Rose about her name.

"Meriel is an unusual name, isn't it?"

"Yes. Rather dated. My mother was called Meriel. She rather regretted giving it to me I think. Her maiden name was Malory so it had rather a ring to it."

"Meriel Malory."

"Mother was an actress. Rather bad actually but terribly statuesque and beautiful. She used to say she was really meant for tableaux and not the stage proper. That's her there." A long pale face with great dark eyes and vivid brows, her hair tumbled on her shoulders.

"She was very beautiful," Ruth said, impressed.

"Yes. So they say. I really just remember her as being very tall and very difficult to disturb."

"Is she dead?"

"No. But she and my father separated when I was still quite

young. They separated and divided everything between them. Furniture, money, property, children, cars. My mother had my brother Gerald and my father had me. I'm not sorry. I would have hated living with my mother."

"Is your father dead?"

"Yes, poor dear. He was very tired of life towards the end. He was a very simple man at heart and I think he had long since ceased to understand the world and what had happened to him. He left me quite a lot of money and among the property this flat which I took because it was the least like my mother of all the places."

"How did you come to teach dancing?"

"Oh I had had ballet lessons when I was a child, had dreams I suppose of Sadler's Wells, but it was possible for me to get a teaching diploma after father died and I decided to open a class. It was as much to give me something to do as anything."

For the occasion of Ruth's visit she was wearing a dark blue blouse, cut like a shirt, with French cuffs and rather long peaks. The colour suited her better than her pastel cardigan and she looked stronger, more handsome than pretty, sitting straight back on the settee, her cup and saucer on her lap.

"Do you ever see your mother now?"

"Oh every so often she comes up to town and we have tea at Fortnum and Mason's. She's rather pathetic now, persists in thinking she sees people she recognizes and I have to keep telling her she's wrong and that the person she imagines it is is dead and buried." Ruth had a quick little picture of Miss Rose driving the nails into her mother's coffin amid the debris of Fortnum and Mason's high tea.

"How old is your mother?"

"Seventy, maybe a little more. I suppose she's remarkably alert for her age." She opened a bureau drawer and took out a large, immaculately compiled album of snapshots.

"These are all my childhood holidays. Before mother went off."

They were of the Rose family in the various watering places of the period. Deauville. Le Touquet. The Brittany coast and some of the more exclusive English south coast resorts. Ruth noticed Tenby among them and remembered she'd heard Harry speak of it. In the photographs Mrs. Rose was always central, always posed to reveal the face bright and empty with surprise that a photographer had been within a hundred yards. Mr. Rose was a stubby little dark man who usually seemed to be on the outside edge of any group. Meriel was almost unrecognizable, tow haired and with exaggeratedly thin arms and legs. Her brother was very handsome, dark like his father, delicately carved like his mother. The little square segments of the past, countless cul-de-sacs. Ruth flicked the pages over.

"Where does it all go," she said, meaning no question, but seeing Meriel Rose look at her she nodded down at the book, "the past, I mean."

"Oh it just runs away," the older woman said, almost wearily and making Ruth suddenly aware just how much more of the past had run away for this woman opposite her than for herself. It made age and time seem uncomfortably comprehensible. In a twitch of anxiety she pointed, almost at random, to a photograph of a tall man with a black moustache who stood close behind Mrs. Rose on several of the snaps.

"Who's that?"

"That, oh that's a man, he was a professional golfer, Jack Teesdale I think his name was." Her voice had a fluttery, quick tone and made Ruth look up.

"Let me get some more hot water for the tea," Meriel said and stood up, leaving Ruth to scrutinize the face of Jack Teesdale, which, from its impregnable position in the past, stared her down.

Cuffee came around one morning just after Harry had gone to work. Ruth had gone back to bed and he got her up.

"Idle bitch," he said, coming in past her smelling of outside and himself and cigarettes and paint.

"Did you see Harry?"

"Yonder peasant who is he," shading his eyes and gazing afar.

"You're early up. Not to mention a stranger."

"Haven't been down. Been covering canvas, lass."

"Any good?"

120

"Looked all right when I left but there's no knowing. Cup of tea on the go, is there?"

"Sure. Put the kettle on."

She went to the bathroom and considered her pouches and several threatening spots. Her skin wasn't really one of her assets. A bit on the open-pored side. Her gums bled as she brushed her teeth. She pledged herself to a softer toothbrush. Cuffee was out on the verandah behind the kitchen when she got back coughing heavily.

"You all right?"

"Who needs two lungs?"

"You should have a check up," suddenly remembering Gerda.

"Why stretch your luck?"

"How ill were you that time in France?"

"I was quite unwell."

"Harry says you nearly died."

"Rectum? Just about killed him."

"There's a bit of the little Georgie Woods in you this morning."

"Yes I was rather under the weather. Pulled through by three dozen nuns praying for me night and day for a week. Prayer is a wonderful thing. You may mock, you may jeer, but I know. I was there."

"Seriously. What were the nuns like?"

"There was one nice one, had a very well cared for beard. Nice girl. Sister Therese. Spoke the Old English. Not a bad looking girl under all that kit. She should have divested herself of some of her bad habits. Joke."

Ruth made the tea and since he showed no signs of coming in, took the cups out. In her loose brown robe the cool morning sheathed her, making her flesh firm and grainy. Her breasts, unsupported, hung quite heavily.

"Peter, what do you really feel about this Uta?" looking down into her cup as she spoke, warm expanding thought in her bosom. Instead of the anticipated flippancy there was a pause, then he said.

"I don't know. It's all tied up with other things. Like painting for instance. I mean, just now I'm painting, quite a bit, and some of it is quite good. The paint's well put on. Not great, but good. Except I've got nothing to paint. The subjects are useless, meaningless. They have no meaning. It's a bit like I think it might have been with Uta, or what she made me realize was wrong. Her holding me off like she did gave me a chance to see that I needed a new, well excusing the expression, a new sort of relationship, not just bed and, well, not what we had. Like now I need new things to paint, things which are mine, before they are natural objects they are my personal images, but also they are real, not figments. Uta has something, I don't know quite what, to do with that."

"And this is different from how you feel about Gerda?"

"Well now, Gerda is something else again. She's made for men to use. I don't mean that cuntishly. Her life is men, or a man. She's not really alive when there's no man about. She asks of you that you use her and hopes that as you do you'll come to think you can't do without it or be stricken with remorse if you try. Her generosity is tainted with latent blackmail it always seems to me."

Oh you keen boy, you scathy lad. She forgot sometimes just how beautifully clean and exact he could be. How could they ever touch him, cage him or tame him. Seeing out of his narrow, one-sided eyes and not pretending anything other. In him sometimes arrogance was beautiful, untainted.

"I love you, Peter." He hooked her head on to his chest and spoke into her hair.

"And I loved you, Ruth. I won't love like that again. I might not love like anything again if the blood of our illustrious father is anything to go by. Come on, get yourself clad and we'll take the air."

They walked on Primrose Hill. It reminded her of Meriel Rose's flat, its self-contained urban charm, not trying for the Heath's bucolic swagger, content to be pathed and lamped, hemmed and overlooked by buildings. Walking with her brother in it was a kind of exhilaration, it was self-evidently too small for him, like a hawk in a canary cage. He seemed unaware of its confines, however, the knavish face looking almost serene, occasionally glancing down in half-mock tenderness. Ruth was happy and it surprised her how different happiness felt from what she had as quotidian. In time her surprise turned to concern. Thus she asked:

"Peter, what was Harry like, in Paris?"

"The last of the provincials, bless him."

"I mean, with women." Cuffee looked at her, almost amused.

"Burny, burny."

"No, I'm not trying to catch him out or anything. I just want to know."

"He didn't bother. Not to the best of my knowledge. Most of the time he went around with this American poet chap called Kimber, a faggot."

"A queer you mean?"

"Yes, nice enough chap for a poove, I mean he didn't lisp or let his wrists flop."

"And Harry was friendly with him?"

"M'mm."

"Harry's never mentioned him."

"Dare say not. Ask him."

"What, were you friendly with a homosexual in Paris and was that why you didn't bother with women?"

"It's what you're thinking."

"Not exactly."

"Well, inexactly then. Is he not poking you or something?" It was a shock to know that he could so simply objectify the sexual act in relation to herself. It let her see that he was further away than she was. She looked at her feet while answering.

"Oh yes, it's not that. It's, oh I don't know. Harry's so gentle," and stopped herself, remindful that she had an allegiance to Harry and that to put words to her cloudy apprehensions was to betray him, even if the betrayal were only to Peter. Or perhaps especially if it were to Peter. The day was suddenly not so fine and Primrose Hill a trifle arch in its prettiness. There were layers upon layers and she was uncertain what kernel waited uncovering. She tugged at Cuffee's sleeve to make him run and then launched forth into private descent.

Her visits to Meriel Rose were as much for the pleasure of sitting in her front room and savouring the velvety persuasiveness of order, of the mundane hallowed by ritual, as for the actual meeting with its custodian. It was indeed almost a feeling of church Ruth derived from her afternoons, from the slow repetition of trivial observances. Making the tea and setting out the tray, sugar cubes and milk, side plates and the slicing of Dundee cake, and the buttering of cream crackers. Scalding the pot and the smell of tea dust. Then she and Meriel sat and sipped and moved by ordered stages into proximity, a relationship of nuance and ellipsis, the words left unsaid having the more weight for that restraint.

Yet when she left and returned to her own high, empty chamber it was with a feeling near to relief. Once out of hermetic cozenage she had twinges of agnosticism. Back and forth in her mind she moved on the low rocker, between Meriel's landscape and her own, watching from unfocused eyes her tree reveal the notions of the wind, thoughts coming and going, achieving articulation against the transparence of her consciousness, or dissembling in a soft bother of leaves, occasionally to stand stock still, empty of movement, like a picture in an album of the past.

Somehow with Meriel Rose it was the past which seemed to matter most. Her room honoured the past more than the present, forced the present and its inhabitants to admit the existence of time for ever gone. Ruth would flick over the faces in the albums and each face was a small cypher, an unopened door behind which stretched a tunnel, down and back to birth. In her own room no breath of yester stirred. Her present devoured itself, leaving her stationary despite the velocity of her fall through time. She could not measure its passage on the finely calibrated scale that was Meriel Rose's, instead of frail teacups and the spandrels of clocks, she had to recall childhood, adolescence and other such enormous circas. It made her feel rootless, without possessions, some species of refugee. Yet the cloisters of Christchurch Hill did not wholly seduce her. Meriel Rose's present seemed less than totally desirable and it was, after its unfathomable fashion, the present which held them all prisoner, both living and dying at one and the same time.

Meriel was almost forty and had never been married. She

was reticent about her emotional life but Ruth had the impression that there had been, somewhere in her past, an unhappy love affair. The crucial themes of her life, this shadowy episode aside, were her mother and her father, together, apart, in relation both to each other and herself. Meril was now the end product of a process neither distinguished nor unusual, yet for all that quite unique.

Her father had contracted a slightly suspect marriage with a well-bred but temperamental woman some ten years younger than him who refused to give up an unexceptional theatrical career or, at various points throughout their married life, a number of lovers. Meriel was the second child of a marriage which, even when she was born, was no longer a valid one. She grew up without any real sense of this, adoring her beautiful aloof mother, fond of her reticent, bewildered father until shortly after her tenth birthday they parted never to live together again. She went to stay with her father, and from then on her mother was an occasional visitor whom she slowly and obscurely grew to hate, an emotion which even now she could not give a name to, but which never failed to animate her voice when she spoke of her. She had, from shortly after her parents' separation, been farmed out to various institutions by her father; boarding school, evacuee during the first years of the war, holidays abroad, college and university. Only when her father's eyesight began to fail did she return to him for any length of time, finally becoming his nurse and housekeeper while he accumulated the defects necessary for exit from this world. Meriel was part grieved, part relieved and part released from bondage to her origins. By which time it was long since too late to matter.

There were a thousand questions Ruth wanted to ask. She was surprised how much there was to know about another person. She had an insatiable appetite for such information it seemed and one that with Meriel Rose could never be fully gratified. So many of the questions were prying or indelicate and had to be built up from many smaller, less forthright enquiries. Ruth had wanted to ask her had she ever had a lover, despite not being married, but could not bring herself to do so.

She was also apprehensive lest no romantic involvement whatever had befallen. So, tacking carefully, she asked when Meriel had been most happy.

"Oh, when I was a child. We lived in a nice house. I was happy then."

"Mmm. I don't think I was. We had a pretty knotted childhood, Peter and I. We were happy sometimes, of course. Were you ever as happy as that again?" She seemed to know the answer to that and replied without hesitation.

"Yes. Once."

"When was that?"

"During the war. I was evacuated. Into the country. I was happy then."

"What age were you?"

"Oh, in my early teens. I think I was just turned twelve when I went away at first."

"Where did you go?"

"Wiltshire. It's lovely there. Beautiful county."

"Did you like the country?"

"I did then. I don't think I do now so much, or have done since."

"How long were you there, I mean evacuated for?"

"Oh well, father was very busy, he was in one of the ministries in London and mother, God knows what she was in, but she was busy too, I was evacuated for about two and a half years all told."

"Weren't you lonely, sad to be away from them?"

"Yes. But it was all right after a while. Then I was happy."

"Did you have many friends?"

"Oh, some friends. I became friendly with a German prisoner of war. There was an internment camp near where we were. They used to work for the farmers."

"Did he speak English?"

"Yes, some. I taught him English and he taught me German."

"How old was he?"

"Oh, I don't know. Quite old. Well, twenty-five, he might have been thirty."

"What happened?"

"Well he was, what do you call it, sent home, repatriated, when the war was coming to an end. Actually that's not true, he wasn't repatriated. He was sent to Italy. I don't know why. You don't know anything when you're that age. I never really understood why he was there, in Wiltshire, speaking German in the funny clothes they made them wear. There was a sign up in the school we went to. Fraternization with P.O.W.'s is prohibited. Imagine the mentality of whoever had that put up in a school where children of that age were. They explained what it meant but just looking at it never seemed to mean that I shouldn't see Werner. The words just never made sense."

It was about then, from her tone, that Ruth perceived that they might now be talking about the most important romantic attachment in Meriel's life. Afraid to go further, lest this be confirmed, Ruth refrained from her inquisition.

"It must have been a strange time, the war I mean. I don't know anything about it, not really."

"Yes, it was curious. You forget so much," she said, looking out on to the Heath, remembering.

She woke up thinking about Meriel Rose next morning. Harry was still asleep and Ruth reached out and pressed in the stud of the alarm clock. Somehow she couldn't face the prospect of spending the day alone. Meriel Rose had made her mark. Ruth was angry where she lay, a thin bitter wrath at the unavoidable shape of it, growing out of the past, out of parents pre-moulded in their turn, fixed catena of cause and effect. Did she hang by such a chain, here in her seeming emancipation, was she as helplessly suspended over a predictable pit. It caused her to think of her parents, and of Peter, to plot herself from this triangulation. Still her location remained imprecise, and her plight depressed her.

Gibbon slept on steadily past his appointed rising. His bland back mocked her. She had an urge to wake him with her nails, she-trails of resentment. His bluff broad maleness offended. He had no problems, no complexities. He needed so little to make him happy. He was still a child, unspoiled, direct, lovable. At that moment his virtues rankled and she drew away from him. The movement disturbed him and he woke.

"Jesus Christ, is that the time. Did the alarm not go off?"

"I don't know, I didn't hear it." He was starting to get up but she held him, suggestively, with her legs. While he made love to her she felt cunning and somehow immoral. Afterwards she lay, pleased with her trivial deceptions while Harry made the breakfast.

He didn't go to work and they lay late and talked. As always when given his head he talked about Greenock. She asked him about his parents. Without being evasive he was vague. They were both dead. He had been young when his mother died. He remembered it though. He had been much older when his father died. He remembered his grandfather also. He still had his open razor. That's who he had been called for. Harold. He remembered him shaving at the kitchen window, the sound of the razor on his beard and how he'd wipe it on a small piece of newspaper so that it looked like waves, the kind they call white horses. They always reminded him of his grandfather. And his shaving brush, all mopped out with soap, like a snowy oak. He used to feel his chin after he had finished to see if he had missed any, and if he had his grandfather would let him dab the place where it was still rough with the brush and he would shave it again.

"Did you love your father?" Gibbon looked a little disturbed.

"That was my grandfather I was telling you about."

"I know."

"Oh. Yes, well yes, I loved him. He was a bit strange in some ways. Took after his uncle more. I've told you about him."

"Yes. Did you cry when he died?"

"I suppose so, I mean I'm sure I did. Why?"

"I just wondered. I don't know if I'll cry when my father dies."

"He died at twenty-five to five in the morning. I was with him. I was glad, that it was over. He took quite a long time to die. The doctor said he might last until the morning. But he didn't. I was with him. I didn't cry right away though. Not until after the funeral. I hated the funeral. It was all so false. Looking at him and saying how fine an appearance he had, how peaceful. Somebody said, I heard them say it, 'he looks awful like himself.' I wanted to choke them. I tried to get him a greenheart coffin. Undertaker said there was no such wood. Funny name when you think on it. Undertaker. The man who takes you under." Stupidly she was near tears herself now but she got up without saying anything and he didn't notice, lying as he was on his back looking at the ceiling.

Harry took the day off and they went to the zoo in the afternoon. The entrance, with trees trained over into a canopy and the noise the turnstile made as they passed through, caused her to feel very young and she held Harry's hand tightly. They walked slowly along the front of the monkey house, past the wrinkled sloth of the orang-utang and the raucous vulgarities of the chimpanzees, slowly and with a slight shudder past the stony brood of the gorilla. Cages abound with capuchins and rhesus and tiny marmosets until at the end in a large quiet cage two gibbons, one on its back with its arms behind its head, the other on a perch at the back of the cage. As they approached the reclining gibbon looked up, a movement accomplished with a slight frown of effort between the eyes, awkwardly held a moment before the head settled back in comfort. It was an action so trivially human that it caught her breath. Harry's hand squeezed hers. They stood by the fence. The gibbon arose, a laconic up-getting and stood a moment holding the cage meshing, then turned and walked towards the back of the cage, with the manner of a bather going over a stony beach to the sea, a gingerish toddle, arms spread for balance until suddenly it swept upwards and in two swift loops settled by its partner.

She heard Harry's breath leave him in a long sigh. His face was open, incredulous as it gazed into the cage. She disengaged her hand without his noticing. The gibbon came back to the front of the cage in a series of fluent linked swings. Ruth could almost feel Harry trying to reach the creature, the intensity of his awareness. She wanted to say something, something to let him know she sensed his mood, then as he showed no sign of requiring such recognition she wanted to say something that would break the exclusive concentration. The gibbon stood by the front grille. Erect it was three feet tall, long armed and deep chested, very slender in the nethers.

"Built a bit like Peter," she said and almost choked on the

words at the moment of utterance, only then perceiving how venomously complex the remark was. But Gibbon showed no signs of having heard, remaining stationary before his name-sake, enthralled by kinship.

After a moment Ruth suggested she walk on and meet him later back at the cage. He made some half-hearted protests of accompaniment but she brushed them aside and moved on, disturbed by her reaction to Harry's childlike response to the gibbons. There were several layers to it she knew; which was the most important was uncertain. At one level she was faintly irritated by the naïveté of it, his delight with these apes of all apes, bearing his name, most delicate, most human. But beyond a distaste for what she considered sentimentality there was a further dissatisfaction with Harry himself. It had been present this morning as she lay awake, a resentment of his very person that could find no reasonable outlet. Also she had some notion that its roots were sexual for certainly the remark about Peter in front of the gibbon cage had been made with a sexual ambience, a desire to hurt and un-man.

Her mind aprowl with such thoughts she found herself at the lion house. Feeding time had turned almost all the inmates into sandy sleeping sacks. She walked around the outside and back down the arcade inside. In the first cage on the right one of the tigers was awake, multiplying a figure of eight inter-minably, locked as much within the bars of his skin as those of his cage. It disquieted Ruth further as he turned in and through upon himself and drawn in by this hypnotic weaving she became aware of how large, how enormously big this crea-ture was. It was not simply the bigness of bulk but the vastness of functional perfection. This was a complete and total in-strument of violence, the essence of destructive force made manifest. Her mind widened and her heart recoiled and at that moment the beast chose to halt and roar, and the sudden stench of his entrails broke on her face. She jerked back and hurried on without another look, back into the open air.

From a distance she could see Harry, still with the lissom gibbons, swinging the frondy aerials. In her mind the tiger stalked, all stripèd and of lurid eye, great padding augur of savagery. Even as she hurried towards him it was with an intuition that the distance between them was not susceptible to so simple a bridging.

After the revelations of the afternoon their evening was deceptively mild. Harry, rather to her surprise, showed no inclination to rhapsodize on his apes but applied himself to fitting sliding doors to the cabinet in the kitchen. Ruth sat in the rocker and read in a desultory fashion, the sound of Harry working both soothing and irritating at one and the same time. Soothing because it was domestic, humdrum, speaking of order and rightness. Its irritation lay in the fact that she could not, in her present mood feel such order was permanent, or even real. Not for the first time she forced herself to think why she was here with Harry and where this would lead them. She knew that beyond her direct feelings for him she was moving aimlessly along on a current of circumstance. She should, for a start, get herself a job. There was something in Harry's insistence on her not working a little underhand. It was as though he was trying to inculcate in her a sense of being a house woman, dependent on the male for support and sustenance. It was, in a way, the masculine equivalent of Gerda's overall permissiveness. The most important thing about it was that it worked. Although she was often bored by having nothing to do all day nevertheless the thought of going back to work in a library was an unpalatable one, she had to some extent become addicted to possessing her days. Disturbed by this she wondered how far Gerda had managed to erode Cuffee's independence. It made her suddenly wish to see him, to hear in his unmistakable terms the self-possession that he commanded, as though by right of blood she might share his confidence.

Next day she was depressed and irritable and her period had come, in full spate from the word go. It bothered her with its pervasive sense of uncleanth and the attendant loss of energy. Women, in bondage to the phases of the moon. They could never escape the vegetable side of their nature like men could. Each month, bloodily reminded of their subservience to the impersonal ways of fertility. While they danced and talked, played the unconditioned creature, deep inside them another little potential life had presented itself for impregnation, waited its appointed wait, set in motion a process of assumption that, finally disillusioned, resulted in jettison.

The room seemed cramped and restrictive and the tree a mere irritation as it scuffed against the glass. Yet she had no wish to go out, or possibly it was that she knew she couldn't go out; as with the tiger the confining bars were those of her own. She read fitfully and half heard a record then wandered, distraught, around the room. The purposelessness of her life suddenly frightened her. Here in London, moping indoors, while the world, or what passed for it waited outside. Yet she seemed cut off from any sense of loss, she could not even feel that she was missing something. It frightened her even more that perhaps she wasn't, that this was life in its fullness.

In an impulse to act against the smothering intuition she opened the window, surprised to hear her own voice, pitched on a high, unreal key say, "Oh, it's so hot in here." The absurdity made her want to laugh but she refrained knowing that tears lay behind her eyes and would undoubtedly follow her weak mirth. As antidote and distraction she let her handkerchief fall, fluttering blue scrap. It lay there, surprisingly permanent-looking for an item that had so recently been damply crushed in her hand. Her mind, febrile and stretched, ran a riot of utterly trivial fantasies. What did the handkerchief feel as it was released from her grasp, did it think it was free from its repellent duties once and for all? Dropping softly down to the grass. How do things happen? What makes a handkerchief below her window seem so final, and what did that mean, so final? At one point things are one way and at another point they're another. What happens in between? Is it always as fleeting as the fall of a handkerchief? Could she jump like that, slowly down to earth, floating falling down? Did death feel like that or like nothing?

Against the window frame she leaned, aswoon with hydra thoughts, her mind possessed by them and wishing respite. With an effort, both physical and mental, she pushed herself away from the window and went to fetch her handkerchief.

The tree looked different seen close-to and from below. It wasn't quite as delicate or as slender. Her two hands couldn't quite encompass the trunk. And the roots, she hadn't seen them before. They knotted up through the bare earth, more like talons, gripping, clutching. Not the dovey silver grey of the bark but like the leathery toes of some great hen. She took one of the very small ones and pulled on it. The earth ripped up in a line to the wall under which its end seemed to have gained purchase. There was dirt on her hand and she brushed it off roughly. The bared root looked obscene. It asked all the questions her handkerchief had asked and more. She felt slightly dizzy and a little nauseous, the sun was hot and she had a sweaty feeling from having come downstairs quickly and the effort of pulling the root and behind that, the origin of all this, the knowledge that she was bleeding and leaking into her double soluble. In a weak little gout of rage and humiliation she wrenched on the protruding root and it snapped off at the point where it went under the wall, the broken end staring up from its crevice like a small white eye. Ruth cried, leaning against the tree.

That night she went with Harry and Stolleman and Gerda and Cuffee for a drink in Hampstead. She did not really want company, or at any rate not this company, but she wanted out, out of their room and out of Harry's comfortable presence. They sat out in the back garden of the William IV and Gerda looked majestic and female in a way Ruth could not remotely feel. Seated, with the pale pink prism of a gin and Campari in her hand, she composed a voluptuous landscape of curve and colour, the soft theatrical light of the evening soothing away her crow's-feet and the little lines at the corners of her mouth. In the dull cinnamon of her dress her bosoms bloomed green-white, melon shapes and when she laughed her throat swelled full of sound and her head fell back, shaking her hair into momentary autumns of auburn. Cuffee sat beside her, detached yet unmistakably hers, for her hands fell upon him at their whim, touching an arm, a thigh, a knee. Several men came and said hello to her and she knew their names and spoke to them with a secure, easy flippancy. Some of them had been her lovers Ruth felt sure and envied her the poise of her greetings, looking so regal with her latest, greatest consort on her arm.

She thought of skinny Gertie of the Sussex WAAF and tried to see what lay between the poles of then and now. Did she herself think back to then, down the years like a handkerchief falling back to when she knew Terry and how many more like him, see herself without all her reassuring flesh? Or was she now only her present, the past a remote set of blurry pictures, inhabited by everyone but herself? Pasts and presents, teasing the mind with their proximity, a proximity that troubled more than it reassured. Her own past, sitting on the other side of the table, inaccessibly near. At that moment she hated him, and her, and certainly herself.

In this mood she drank quickly, whisky and ginger ale going down without heed of her limited capacity. Only when the scene had achieved a sufficiently underwater feel to it did she slow up. Now everything was contained, sealed inside the gelatine of intoxication. Everything happened very slowly and she could focus on it single-mindedly, or very fast, in which case she paid it no heed. Thus she saw cigarette ash and hands and mouths listening and noticed an insect many miles below and heard words, all vivid and close and on the threshold of meaning. Beyond her comprehensions everything else went on, Gerda fondling Cuffee and Gibbon telling how someone inside had tried to pick him up and a new voice of a friend of Gerda's and the smell of Stolleman's cigars.

They went at closing time to a party. She remembered the stairs and noticed the wallpaper and then the room burst open and music and many people. Somewhere behind her eye she told herself that it would be best if she were sick. The bathroom was in interminable use. Twice Gibbon asked her if she was all right. When she got in sickness refused to come. Strangely sober she returned. The people she had come with were all crowded out on the stairs. There had been a fight someone said.

"Did he win?" she asked, assuming without thought the fight had been between Cuffee and Gibbon but having no clear idea of who she meant by "he." On the stairs Stolleman put his arm round her shoulder.

"Best let them sort it out." "Them" were Cuffee and Gerda's friend, a thick-set man in a cardigan. Ruth could hear his voice, loud and browbeating telling Cuffee he was an arrogant young thug and typical and bloody asking for trouble. All she could hear Cuffee say was "fuck off." When she got down the stairs the fight was over, only its curious epilogue remained to be witnessed which frightened her more than any fight could have done. The man was on his knees and holding his face and his voice said muffled, wet words calling Cuffee a bastard and Cuffee was walking towards him from the other side of the street drinking out of a milk bottle. When he reached the man he poured the remaining milk over his head, jumping back to avoid being splashed on. It was strange and made her shiver, the supplicant beaten figure and the white splashing milk and Cuffee, dexterously arched clear, ritualistic and horrible yet intensely real, the reallest thing of the unreal evening.

They went then, except Stolleman. Gerda walked with Cuffee and she walked behind with Harry, very tired and heavily drunk. They got a taxi and it dropped the others first. She heard Gerda talking about the fight and Gibbon, slightly disapproving saying Cuffee had kicked the man whose name now came to light as Tom. When she got in she found it quite simple to be sick in the sink with the dishes in it. The room spun round the bed for a time but by holding the pillow it was possible to stay on until she went to sleep.

She felt very bad in the morning and lay on after Gibbon had gone out. She was still there at half past ten when Stolleman came in.

"Hello, got a head?"

"A head? I've got everything."

"Yes, you were planting them past last night, I'll give you that."

"You been tiling?"

"Yes. Little girl there, amazing today's girls. Couldn't have been more than sixteen. Knew it all. And expected it. Too much like work really. Technique can disguise a lot but there's no substitute for quantity. That was the gist of her attitude."

"Michael, is Peter painting much?"

"M'mm. Yes, he is."

"What's it like? Is it good?"

"Quantity can disguise a lot but there's no substitute for technique."

"It's not good?"

"Well, he's painting things he can paint without painting them a lot better than he's always been able to paint them. He could sell them though. Particularly the nudes."

"Nudes?"

"Yes, he's done about six biggish nudes. Not original but who's that. Good solid paintings."

"Of Gerda?" Stolleman looked a little blank.

"Well, yes. I think she sat for them."

They were of Gerda. She took Ruth through to see them with a slightly elaborate casualness. Big opalescent nudes, painted in pale pinks and paler blues, yet achieving weight by the monumental quality of the line, so that they sat and lay around, frail in their massiveness, enormous in their delicacy. Despite herself Ruth liked them. They looked accomplished and achieved if something in the nature of an exercise. Looking among the canvases for something more personal she found a smallish painting, obviously done some time ago, a row of iron railings and behind them a cemetery, the gravestones slabbed in with a palette knife dead blues and thick greys, sullen reds, while on the spike of one of the railings was stuck a glove, a yellow glove with one finger, the middle, pointing up and the others flopped emptily down. It touched her immediately and she stared at it greedily, drinking up its implications. She looked at the back and saw it was called "Lost Glove." She didn't want Gerda to notice her interest so she put it down and looked at some others, then went through again with Gerda to have some coffee.

"I think those nudes are the best thing he's done." Yes, you would. That's just how she sees herself Ruth thought vehemently, a big odalisque sustaining the young painter's erratic talent by her body and soul. She sipped her coffee and said nothing.

"Did you want to see Peter specially?"

"No, just wanted to ask him what happened last night."

"Oh, that was Tom's fault. He started to argue with Peter."

"Mind you that doesn't take much doing sometimes."

"What do you mean?"

"Well, he's just naturally violent. I mean his violence is part of him. He'd just as soon pick a fight as . . ." and she stopped in mid-sentence, bored by describing Cuffee to someone else. Gerda obviously misunderstood her pause.

"As what? What are you trying to say?"

"Nothing. Just that Peter can be a bit violent. He's like his father," thinking of that distant relative for the first time in years it seemed.

"I don't think he's like his father, not from what he's told me." Ruth felt resentful of this woman for venturing such a remark and resentful of Cuffee for discussing Mr. Cuffee with her.

"Well he'd be the last to know, wouldn't he," and her tone was tart. Gerda smiled, a broad expansive smile of insight and tolerance.

"You're a funny girl, Ruth."

"Hilarious."

"No, you are. I mean you take offence so quickly." Ruth couldn't think of anything to say so she thought of the painting "Lost Glove." Gerda waited a moment to make sure there was no retort coming. "Why do you resent Peter and I?" You have to admire her Ruth thought and put her coffee cup down with great care. Then she stood up.

"I'm off. I'm going to take that little glove painting. I know him, he'll just paint over it next time he's short of a canvas."

"Hadn't you better tell him first?"

"No, I'll just tell you and you can communicate it to him telepathetically, wherever he may be."

"He's out buying material, he'll be back shortly. Why don't you wait for him?"

"I won't bother. I really don't want another discussion about you and Peter and my attitude to it." To her surprise Gerda caught her arm.

"Can't you see, Ruth, you still want him for yourself."

She felt the desire to say "How dare you," to own complete and unqualified indignation. Instead she could only manage a shrug out of Gerda's grasp and a "I don't think that's really any concern of yours, one way or the other," and found herself wondering why she had said "one way or the other." It was a meaningless piece of padding to make what you say sound more substantial, like "as it were," or "so it seems to me."

"As it were, or so it seems to me," she said and laughed foolishly.

Gerda remained serious. "Ruth, can't you see it's best over? I mean what would have happened if you'd become pregnant? It could only have destroyed everything." And of course with you little earth mother it'll be just hunky dory. "Hunky dory." She must be going out of her mind and at the same moment as she thought that she realized that Gerda either was, or was trying to become, pregnant by Peter. The rightness of the sense was irresistible. She looked at her and then, pointedly, at her waist. "Are you in the family way?" She didn't actually blush, or do anything really. She just looked blankly back. Ruth went along to Peter's room and picked up the painting. When she came back Gerda was at the top of the stairs. Before she could say anything Ruth went past her.

"It won't hold him you know. Not if he decides he's for off."

"But it might bring him back. All I want is for him to come back." The nakedness of the appeal embarrassed Ruth. She hated Gerda for her large fleshy vulnerability.

"You're mad, he'll only come back to where he's free. Anyway, I don't know why we're standing here talking about him, you know, it's a bit pathetic."

"But it's only you he wants to get away from." It was like a blow, a sickening blow. She was astonished at how it hurt her. She had thought it didn't matter, was over and past and now these words hitting her across the face.

"Why, why does he want to get away from me?" and hated herself for the ingenuous question but she had to know.

"Because you're the past, like your parents and anywhere you were brought up and Manchester. It's the past Peter's running away from and in you it follows him, can't you see that?"

She could really. It was all very probable. Ruth wanted to be gone. Away. Somewhere else where these people didn't exist, Peter and Gerda and Harry and the others. An island, a hole in the ground. She held her painting tightly and left, saying nothing, not meeting Gerda's eyes. On the street she felt like crying but instead she ran.

Meriel Rose asked her if she would come for tea after she had taken Jessamyn home. Harry was working until seven-thirty and rather than sit in the flat alone she agreed. With her money from Jessamyn's mother she took a taxi and rolled up early to the house on Christchurch Hill. It was a warm, rather thick day, the pressure of the sun like a headache behind the heavy grey clouds. The willows across from Meriel's windows trailed languidly in the slow air. Ruth wanted to lie on the grass and sleep. The green invited her to oblivion, she felt tired and frail, for moments at a time rather dizzy, or rather she felt herself to be standing at an angle and everything looked very clear and precise but somehow odd. To end this curious malaise she rang the bell and had Meriel come and take her inside.

They chatted about the dancing class and some of the mothers. Ruth described Jessamyn's mother and Meriel said she had met her.

"Actually she looks not unlike my mother, more the style than anything."

"You don't really like your mother now, do you?"

"No. It's only these last few years it's been at all simple to say it. I don't even feel bad about not going to see her. She comes up to London about three or four times a year. We have tea at Fortnum and Mason's. That's rather her style, sort of a genteel baroque." And Meriel smiled at her malice.

"Does she live alone?"

"Oh well, there's always house guests, mother keeps up with people very industriously. All her old lovers and their wives come to visit her."

"Was Jack Teesdale one of your mother's lovers?" Ruth asked, suppressing an instinct against the question. Meriel looked surprised and almost alarmed.

"How do you know about Jack Teesdale?"

"You showed me his photograph. In one of your albums."

"Oh yes. So I did. Yes, I remember now. For a minute I wondered how you could possibly know Jack Teesdale. He was quite a well-known golfer but that was a long time ago. Professional at one of the large clubs."

"The name's almost familiar. But it can't be from golf."

"There was a bit of scandal about him just before the war, something about him cheating, moving his ball or his opponent's ball or something, and it got publicity and he had to leave the club he was with. Mother employed him for quite a time until it all died down. He was a revolting man," and her voice was very matter of fact but she did not look at Ruth as she spoke. "He died just quite recently. Mother went to his funeral. She's a very loyal person in some ways. Loyal about strange things. Sometimes I just think she was common. I know that sounds awful but it was something like that about her. There's a kind of vulgarity about her. He was vulgar, Jack Teesdale, and most of her men were. Flashy, bold, oh I don't know, maybe I'm just jealous. I'm so refined sometimes I'm afraid I'm not there at all," and Ruth saw, quite without warning, a tear drop and splash on her blouse. She tried to blink them back but couldn't and one large perfect one fell on her upper lip where Ruth could see a hair, magnified by its convexity. Meriel wiped it away quickly.

"I'm sorry, I don't know what caused that."

"It's me, asking all those stupid questions."

"No really, I don't mind that. I'm just being silly. I suppose I can never quite forget when I loved her and thought everything was just wonderful. It's when the two come together that upsets me."

"I don't think I can ever remember really loving my mother, not really loving."

"Oh I loved her all right. She was so wonderful. I can remember her playing badminton on a lawn at someone's house in the country and it was a lovely summer's day and she had on a white blouse and the bow on it swung all over the place and every time she hit the shuttle-cock she would laugh. I was just a little girl but I remember that."

Ruth could see it herself, the green lawn, the players laughing easily in their game, the white bird of summer flying cease-lessly, gracefully across the net. A little girl in love with her lovely mother. It seemed so perfect, even its sadness had a quality about it. But the appearances meant nothing. They would be of no consolation to Meriel as she looked back, the tableau would seem as it was, the charade in which she grew up believing until one day it was destroyed and she found herself alone. Once that happened the appearances could only be most cruel irony, the pictures of a paradise she never dwelt in.

Perhaps she was fortunate to have no such idyll to harken after, except a memory of the countryside round Knutsford and a deep pool under trees and the sight of a hawk.

> "As hawks in their cages
> dream of hills in the morning
> so the mind, implacable imaginer,
> yearns for freedom."

The fragment rose again in her mind and its meaning deep-ened within her. For Meriel the cage was so cunningly con-structed that she thought it was life. Her tiger was a spayed tabby, its jungles the long grass across the road. Ruth for the moment could almost envy her her landscape with its pastel hues and minuscule appetites. A glance at Meriel, however, showed that she was in no way assuaged by the pettiness of her plight.

Harry was home when she got back. He seemed preoccu-pied and she thought perhaps he was angry that she hadn't been in when he returned.

"What's wrong?"

"I got a letter from Edna, Moseby's wife. He's left her and is living down here."

"Where, in London?"

"Not very far away actually, over the other side of the Finchley Road. Edna opened the letter I wrote him and she says she is worried that if I go and see him he might never come back to Greenock."

"You were quite a good friend of his, weren't you?" and she

noticed an almost involuntary spasm of annoyance on his face. My God, aren't men touchy, she thought, recollecting what Gibbon had told her about Moseby.

"Yes, we were quite friendly," he said and remarkably his voice held no sarcasm.

"Does she want him back?"

"Edna's asked me to talk to him and tell him he'd better go back."

"Better go back?"

"Well, his next term at University is going to start soon. She doesn't say anything about going back to her."

"Does she want him back?"

"Oh yes." In his offhand answer there was a kind of vicarious smugness which Ruth found extremely irritating. Just because the woman was in the provinces and had a child it was assumed she couldn't do without the creep who'd run off and left her.

"What do you think I should do?" he asked.

"What do you mean, what should you do?"

"I mean, should I tell him to go back?" Ruth laughed and Harry looked puzzled.

"What's it matter? Do you think he'll do it if you tell him to?"

"No, no I don't suppose he will."

"I'm bloody sure he won't. Who takes advice?" Harry thought about that, then he said,

"Me," so innocently that her resentment melted and she laughed and kissed him.

"Oh Harry, you are a child, really you are."

He phoned the number Edna had sent but Moseby wasn't in so he left a message. The letter and their conversation seemed to have depressed him and Ruth left him sitting in the rocker while she made a meal. After a moment he came and leaned against the door. "What do you think will happen to us?" he said. Ruth was surprised. Harry never ever talked in a speculative way about their relations. Sometimes she thought he just assumed they were married and expected them to go on for ever.

"I don't know. Either we'll stay together or we'll split up."

"Pretty deep thinking that," he said and the gentleness of the mockery made her suddenly want to cry and laugh together.

"Oh, stop being such a big kinda nice guy," she shouted, without thought but containing one of her deepest instincts about him. Harry looked discomfited.

"I'm sorry. It's just not very illuminating what you said."

"What do you want me to be, a flash lamp?" and the absurdity of the remark had them in instant laughter. Harry folded her in his arms and they laughed on, uncontrollably. Ruth realized as the mirth bubbled and rose in her that it had been a long time since she had really laughed, empty of everything but the act of laughter.

When they had stopped laughing Gibbon asked her again what she thought would happen to them, which made her think that her first remark had been an instinctive cutting off from the question. There wasn't much she could say.

"Why do you ask?" was the best she could manage.

"Do you think maybe we should get married?" She wasn't angry, or even annoyed, but the underlying assumptions to his question irked her.

"I think that would be very foolish."

"Why?"

"What would we have being married that we can't have now?"

"Children."

"Children. Marriage, children, prams, cod liver oil, telly, the whole bit."

Harry looked steadily at her.

"Well, when you do get married will you want any less than that?"

"Whatever I want I don't want it now."

"You're not ready for it?"

"No."

"Why's that, do you think?" and she saw she was being cross-questioned. It certainly was Harry's night for asserting himself.

"I'm not ready, and neither are you. You want another half

a dozen women under your belt at least before you think of settling down with one," knowing as she said it that nothing could be less what Harry needed and wondering if perhaps she wasn't stating her own requirements. Harry looked serious.

"I don't think I need to know more women. I don't want to have to count. Is that a bit odd?" Ruth was touched, lightly, with the finger of remorse.

"No it's not. It's a good thing. I'm being all flippant about it."

"Well don't," and his voice was intense. He stared at her for a moment with open hostility and then turned and left her in the kitchen.

For the first time since she had known him he was in a bad mood. It lasted the rest of the night and into bed. As he turned over on to his side Ruth touched his shoulder.

"Look, Harry. I'm sorry. I don't quite know what for but I'm sorry." He lay as he was, half turned away.

"If you don't know what for then I don't see how you can be sorry. But anyway, that's not necessary, you don't have to be sorry. Just try taking me seriously sometimes," and then he completed his turn and left her looking into his wide, impassive back.

Cuffee came round next morning.

"How are you?"

"Fine."

"Oh yes, I see. Fine is it. I used to know the code, 'fine' meant bloody rotten I think. What's up? You in the club?" She had the swift malicious urge to tell him he was but turned it away.

"No. I'm all right. How are you? Been painting?"

"Yes. Gerda said you took a canvas. Which one?"

"Lost Glove, the one with the glove on the railings." Cuffee made a face.

"Yuchh."

"You don't like it?"

"It's a refugee from another of the internment camps in my life."

"When did you paint it?"

"Oh, in Manchester."

"I like it."

"All right. Only don't say it's mine. If anybody asks say it's from an aunt in Chester who does painting by numbers."

"I like it."

"Your taste's in your mouth. Never mind, it's always a sale. Can I have my hundred and fifty guineas in luncheon vouchers?"

"You prefer the nudes I suppose."

"That's an old, badly painted picture. I mean, look at it. There's nothing there you couldn't have done yourself."

"Maybe that's why I like it."

"You'd be better starting up then. We can have a joint exhibition."

"Any chance of you having one?" Cuffee shook his head, breathing cigarette smoke down his nostrils as he did so.

"Why not? I thought Gerda could fix somewhere, a gallery." Cuffee rose, walked out on to the verandah.

"I've got nothing to show. I'm not nearly ready. Those pictures you saw, the nudes, they're not bad, in their way, but it's only one little technical problem they're about. They're just compositions really, trying to achieve mass through form. That's why I painted them in the colours I did. I mean, any silly cunt can suggest weight and density with cobalt and earth browns and magenta. That little painting you took. Well it's a nice little idea, idea you understand, the kind of literary idea of it is evocative. But it's painted like a nail getting hammered into your head. It's cheap, sentimental, because of the technique finally, because I didn't know a better way of painting it."

"But it exists for me as something quite real. I like it. That's not just me defying your assessment. That's what I feel. Where do my feelings come into it?" Cuffee smiled and nodded his head in mock agreement.

"Ah well now, that's it. Where you are standing they are all objects. Paintings are only special kinds of objects, like flowers and chairs, and buildings. You look at them and you have feelings. That's the basic response between you and the world of objects. And that's right. Like I can't say you shouldn't like a flower I can't say you shouldn't like a painting. Once it's painted it becomes an object and unless I choose to destroy it, it belongs to the person looking at it. But I bet you God is sitting up there looking down at the Lake District or gladiolas or Holland and thinking 'Christ, I made a right shambles there.' But then he had an excuse. He had this exhibition on and he had to rush everything to meet the opening date. Probably Gerda arranged it for him," and he smiled quickly at Ruth making her heart quicken and her breath catch. It didn't really matter how you went around it you always came back to the same place. She loved him, perhaps not so vulnerably as of yore, but still and yet, loved, him, her brother. In a way she was glad to be able to say it and not avoid the fact. She knew she couldn't have him so there was no question of the situation being dangerous. It was simply better to know. The more you know, the simpler it is, even if it's harder. She turned away to make tea.

"I think I'll get the glove painting framed."

"Yes, you do that," and he came in at her back. She rather wished he would have stayed outside. It wasn't that she wanted him physically. In a way that didn't come into it at all. Just if she had a bit of space around her. Things pressed very close at times.

"Why did you have that fight with the man at the party?" Cuffee shrugged.

"Stupid business. He was one of Gerda's pokes and he was pushing it a bit. Just chancing his luck, harmless really, I didn't have to bother. I mean I don't care who's been up her or who's going to be. I wouldn't even mind if she was having somebody else at the same time so I don't know why I didn't just walk off and leave him to get on with it, but I suppose I could sense that Gerda wanted me to, well sort of be her man, take up the old attitude," he laughed and shook his head, "amazing, isn't it? Anyway, I did and he did and then I began suddenly to hate him. And before we knew where we were it happened. Good for me in a way. Clears the mind a bit of the old Marquis of Queensberry."

"Didn't look much like the Marquis of Queensberry to me what I saw."

"True. It got a bit out of hand." She scalded the teapot and then as she was making the tea she asked,

"Does Gerda know you feel so, well casual about her?"

"Casual? You mean about not minding her having other men?"

"Well, obviously you're not as madly in love with her as she is with you." For some reason this annoyed Cuffee and he swore a single violent word.

"Love. That's all you hear, everybody's hitting everybody over the head with love, it's the original blunt instrument."

"That's a very Peter Cuffee type attitude."

"Balls. I used to think Gerda had it all worked out, knew the score, could look after herself. Now all I can hear is love."

"Don't you want her to love you, really? Wouldn't you be a bit mortified if she really was in control?"

"You have to be mad. What do I need with somebody like Gerda being in love with me. I mean she knows it's only a question of time before I go." Ruth realized that the sinking feeling in her was not for herself but for Gerda. The bond of being female tightened on her sympathies and she found herself resenting Cuffee's brutal masculinity.

"I don't think she does."

"Well she bloody well ought to."

"She's trying to get pregnant." And she said it deliberately without thinking out the implications of her disclosure. Cuffee had a cup at his mouth and it stopped a moment then he drank and put the cup back on the table. He shook his head.

"What the Christly fuck does she think she's at?"

"She's trying to keep you."

"And does she imagine getting in the club will do that?"

"Probably she wants the baby for itself."

"That'll be right."

"Oh you smug bastard. She could just have decided that it was time she had a child and was using you for stud." Cuffee grinned.

"Sure."

"Anyway, I wish I'd kept my mouth shut." The phone rang. "I want you to promise you won't say I told you."

"She'll know. She knows you don't like her."

"What do you mean? Who says I don't like her?"

"I do. You better answer the phone." She went, upset and almost trembling with the emotions and Cuffee's arrogance. It was a voice she didn't know at the other end.

"Can I speak to Harry Gibbon please?"

"Oh he's not in. He won't be back until six. Can I give him a message?"

"Just tell him I phoned. My name's John Moseby."

"Oh yes, of course. Hello. Harry phoned you last night but you weren't in."

"No, I work at nights, well I used to."

"Are you working tonight?"

"No."

"Why don't you come over and have a meal with us. I'm sure Harry can't wait to see you."

"How did he get my phone number?"

"He wrote to you in Greenock and, eh, well your wife didn't send it on or something."

"Very possible. Tonight, what time?"

"About sevenish."

"About sevenish," and his repetition seemed faintly mocking. "All right, thanks. I'll see you. What's your address?"

"Eleven King Henry's Road. Do you know it?"

"I'll find it."

"All right, see you tonight then."

Cuffee looked up without interest as she came back but she told him who the caller was just the same.

"Yes, big buddy of Harry's from his Greenock days."

"You say that as if you thought they were behind him."

"Well he's out now. That's what it's all about, getting out."

"And what do you do once you are out?" Cuffee lifted his hands.

"Run amuck, how do I know." She had a vivid image of the tiger padding through Meriel Rose's sitting-room, incongruous and terrible.

"Well I must be getting back." The phrase "getting back" touched at her memory.

"Do you never think you might end up in Knutsford?"

"On a slab."

"You don't care if you never see either of them again, do you?"

"I do a lot more than don't care."

"Were they that bad, Peter, were they so exceptionally bad?"

"I don't know. I've got nothing to judge them by. They seemed pretty grim at the time. Anyway, it's not their badness that prevents me from going back."

"What is it then?"

"It's our closeness. I mean that's what we are, Ruthie. Him. Her. And Knutsford. I mean I even look like him. You don't have that cross to carry. And I'm a lot like him. Maybe I'm exactly like him. Sometimes I think we've got the same kind of talent, the same kind of minds. I don't need to go back there. There's mirrors in all the gents lavatories nowadays."

"I think I'll go up for the weekend," meaning it to be a defiance of him but he only grinned.

"You think Gerda will be hunting you down. Don't worry. I won't let her know how I guessed."

"Oh the hell with you and Gerda. You think I'd be going up to Knutsford just to keep out of that old boot's road?" And at this outburst Cuffee laughed, loud and delighted.

It was curious to see Gibbon with his friend. Moseby was quite short with dark close hair and a pale face and grey, rather cold eyes that remained empty when he smiled. She didn't like his appearance. He had a quiet way of talking and not talking and he made Harry seem very big and voluble. She noticed that Harry's accent thickened immediately and at times their conversation was almost impenetrable. Harry laughed a lot at what Moseby said although Ruth found very little she thought funny. It was not that his jokes were unfunny, they scarcely seemed jokes at all, anecdotes that tailed off without punch-lines or climaxes. She felt a slight twinge of jealousy for their instantly established intimacy but since she had no real desire to be included anyway it was gone almost at once.

When Gibbon went to the pub to get beer Moseby helped her with the washing up. He explained that he had only recently left a post of a similar nature. She asked him, somewhat vacuously, what it had been like.

"Very nice," he said and for some reason this made her want to laugh.

"I'm sorry, I don't know why I asked such a stupid question. I can imagine only too well what it must have been like."

"Well there's not much point in being a servant if you don't intend to suffer," to which she had no response.

When Harry came back they sat in the kitchen and after half a glass of tepid beer Ruth decided to retire. She had arranged with Terry that he would drive her to Knutsford next morning and she made this an excuse to leave them alone. Their voices slowly dimmed in her mind as she lay watching the dance of her tree, many-handed, moving to the music of the night wind, its gestures full of unshaped meaning, inarticulate thoughts in her mind, trying to be born against the glass. As often happened under its spell she felt, with almost an ache, aware of things, things so acute as to resist knowing, needling, threshold things, whose near revelation filled her with a kind of breathlessness. Why was it she wondered that these moments never expanded into the comprehension, that this promise never bloomed wide and royal, became fullest sense. Why did she not know, beyond all imagining, what her mind held captive. When they achieved their freedom they seemed much more mundane, theories, insights, assumptions, not the incandescent knowledge, incarnate, that moments such as these hinted at.

Through the door the men braided their voics in a monotony of talk, the tree dwindled into smallest peace and Ruth scarcely awake, heard, or thought she heard, a chime or a teacup tinkle or a laugh or a door in a small sweetshop with the large bottles around the walls all filled with the jewelled lights of childhood treasures. The attempt to determine which sound it was proved too exhausting and she gave up to sleep with a sigh of abandon.

It was a beautiful run. Terry drove very fast but always safely and after the first few glances at the speedometer she stopped thinking about it and let the sensations carry her.

The country stood still in the full grasp of summer, the trees piled yet with leaf, scarcely tinted with yellow. They passed rookeries still raucous with rearing and across the fields lapwings tumbled, pied and piping. The corn had attained burnish and sat in great brassy blocks. There was a sense of richness from the running land, a sense the more powerful for its impending sack. Soon ambers and umbers and cinnamon browns would come and fullness would topple into ruin, the trees would wreck upon the winter reefs and the shapes of things, bony and stark, would reappear. Was golden summer then but illusion and were the truths of winter irrefutable? Had there to come in everything a declension, a counting down to some zero, the final total and greatest sum. Thinking so she saw the fecund land trembling in its transience, its beauty the more glorious in the imminence of perish. Along her eye a stream of verge poppies rippled, blood-shotting her sight in their brief pass. She closed her eyes and saw them, red kisses in yellow rain.

"Do you go home often?" Terry's voice.

"Home? Oh well I'm not long away." Home. Was that what it was? Scarcely. Yet what else? Back among the familiar strangers. In a way John Moseby was no more of a stranger than her parents, nor Gerda nor Terry nor Meriel Rose. In which case what was "home" about Knutsford? Just that on a number of nights from the same window she had seen the harvest moon hang enormously in the sky above the chestnut trees? Was home a habit, an accretion of memory? A graveyard where childhood was buried? And the caretakers of this persepolis, Mr. and Mrs. Cuffee, were they, in any sense that was meaningful, her parents? With a little tremble of apprehension she saw that these were questions her visit asked. The possibility of answer was not wholly comforting.

Terry drove into the square and pulled up.

"Won't you come home and have something to eat?"

"No. W-won't bother, really, thanks j-just the s-same. Get back now."

"Thanks very much for driving me up, Terry. It was very kind of you."

"N-not k-kind. Pleasure. Would you like me to come and f-f-fetch you?"

"Oh no, I'll come back by train."

"I'd like to. Really. G-give me a ring d-day before. Come up and c-collect you. Pleasure."

"Well, if you'd like to."

"L-love to."

"All right. I'll phone you at the office. Monday probably."

"F-fine. Have a nice time."

"Thanks. Drive carefully on the way back."

"Always do." She kissed him lightly on the cheek and slipped out. He moved the car off and swung it round the square. The white face, a brief wave, and he was gone.

Knutsford sat as always, quiet in the sun, hushed by lunch-hour closing. A bell beat in the temple of the church, a throb of brass, one gong. Sunny early afternoon September Friday. One o'clock at the centre of the world. Apprehensions and hopes mingled, heralded by the chime, summoned from the great unexplored hinterland of the self. She picked up her case and went on into the interior.

The house, when she opened the door, was warm. The warmth of warmed things. Windows and curtains and sun-struck chairs. A clock tocked, far and near in the torpid air. The smell of Mansion Polish and the old mac on the stand, dry and sour. The school photograph. She kissed a finger and placed it upon Cuffee's small, years-distant face. The knot in the mirror and the faded Axminster with its cords showing. All waiting, patient as the objects in a museum. "Anybody home?"

Mrs. Cuffee was in the garden and came through at the second call. There was a little fluster of greeting and nearly-given, half-avoided kisses. They went through and sat in the sun porch, sitting on the edge of striped canvas chairs, sur-rounded by her mother's potted ramblers and the vivid mouths of geraniums. A fly blundered around knocking against the glass. Down in the garden the old tree hunched heavily on its crutch and behind it the rhododendrons massed their leathery green leaves, here and there the remnants of their blooms re-lieving the sullen luxuriance. It was all as it had been, all as it would be, the fixed centre of the turning world. Mrs. Cuffee talked while Ruth sat, sipping her pale tea, talked and occasionally glanced up at the erratic fly, of who'd spoken at the Guild and new paper for the sitting-room and the people who'd moved in next but one, an architect and his wife, completely converting the place and Merle Curvis was dead, terrible business . . .

"What, Merle Curvis, the girl who was at school with Peter and me?"

"That's right. Killed herself with sleeping pills."

"When, when did this happen?"

"Oh not long ago, last month, no July, yes, not long after you went to London. Inquest said while the balance of the mind was disturbed. Poor girl, she was pregnant."

"How do you know?"

"It was all brought out at the inquest. Killed herself in her flat."

"Why did she do it? Just because she was having a baby?"

"Well she had to give up work."

"Oh yes, she was a model. But you'd have thought she'd know somebody who could have helped her."

"Well, it seems she'd been to someone because the medical evidence said there were signs of an unsuccessful you know."

"Was all this in the paper?"

"No, but Myra Lee, you know Lee the grocer's wife, well she went up to Manchester with Mrs. Curvis for the inquest. She was terribly upset Mrs. Lee said."

"Poor girl." The tall elegant poor girl with the good legs and the careful makeup. She tried to remember their conversation in Coleman's. It seemed like years ago. She must have been pregnant then. Had she said anything that might have hinted? Something about wanting to leave. But Ruth couldn't remember, only the picture of her sitting there, poised and worldly and all the while the unwanted child growing inside her. Oh it was all so bloody unfair. The fly rattled frantically against the glass, matching her sudden panic at the thought of Merle Curvis with her end drawing closer, carrying her death around with her. "Oh it's all so bloody unfair."

"What is, dear?" her mother asked.

"Women and babies."

"Yes. Well you must take care it doesn't happen to you."

Ruth was surprised at the remark and the assumptions that lay behind it. But she reminded herself that this mild woman pouring tea in the back garden was committing adultery with her husband's best friend. In the light of that perhaps her comment was not too extraordinary.

"How is father?"

"Fine. He's a bit busy this weather what with the new term coming up."

"And Robert?" checking herself from saying "Robert Eldman."

"Oh he's fine too." And no expression registered to indicate they shared a knowledge that were it public would bring her mother's life to swift disaster.

"Are you happy, Mum," she asked, without giving herself warning of the enquiry. Mrs. Cuffee looked up, bland-faced.

"Yes, I'm very pleased you could come. You should have dropped me a line though and I'd have had your bed aired." Ruth shook her head and refused another cup of tea.

She had a bath. There was something soothing about pushing the bolt over and letting the steam clamber up the walls, feeling its damp breath on her as she undressed. She lay and soaked, in water a trifle overhot, perspiring and wiping her face with the sponge, melting at the joints. She remembered the country she had travelled through to come here and how Merle Curvis had waited for her, dead and forgotten. Almost nothing of their last meeting remained. Except something she said about needing someone to help you get away. Which had been a true enough observation. She had needed Harry, who in turn had needed Cuffee. Who had Cuffee needed? Perhaps Mr. Cuffee. Her brother was possibly more in debt to his father than he knew. But then perhaps he did know. On the last occasion they talked he had spoken of the ties that bound him to his origins. And hadn't he spoken of "getting out." "Well he's out now, that's what it's all about, getting out." So perhaps he knew it all. The image of his painting came to her and as she saw it in her mind so the thought of Merle Curvis adhered to it with a sudden, inseparable insistence. "Lost Glove." The composite awareness beat heavily for a moment until she roused herself and set about soaping her legs, during which operation she had occasion to recall her envy of the dead girl's. A swift pleasure took her as the soap slipped over her warm living flesh. To be alive was in itself the primary source of optimism. For reminding her of this truism she felt a gratitude for the poor, cold creature now gone to earth out of the joys of soap and sun.

Mr. Cuffee seemed rather withdrawn over tea and almost immediately after he said something to himself about work and went upstairs. Ruth helped her mother to wash up.

"Has he always been moody?"

"Who dear?"

"My father."

"Moody, well I don't know, is he moody?"

"Oh come on, Mother, he has diabolical moods."

"Yes, I suppose he is a bit morose sometimes."

"Was he always?"

"Well he always was sort of, I don't know, romantic, if you know what I mean."

"Not quite."

"Well he was a lot like our Peter is now." The casual possessive pronoun somehow made Ruth's breath catch. "Looked a lot the same."

"Did you love him?"

"I still do . . ." then she paused and re-washed a plate. "Love's not what you expect," and Ruth felt she was talking about Robert Eldman, explaining something, "there turns out not to be enough of it after all." Ruth wanted to ask what "after all" meant but she waited for her mother to finish. She emptied out the dish water with a quick dismissive slush and dried her hands.

"Friday's a terrible night on the television," she said, untying her apron.

They sat watching the aching blue box for some two hours. It gave Ruth a headachy feeling. It was something about the size of the screen, the faces were too near normality to totally capture the eye. The light from the set made her mother's face look drawn and ill. Ruth said she was going to bed. Her mother nodded without looking up which surprised Ruth who had somehow imagined that her mother had been as bored as she was.

There was a light from under Mr. Cuffee's study door. She stood a moment and then knocked, half hoping the light had been left on by mistake.

"Yes?"

"It's me, I just wanted to say good night."

"Come in, Ruth, come in."

The room was smoky and warm. The adjustable lamp shone on the chess board which was set in a middle game position. Above the board blue bands of smoke hung, wreathed round Mr. Cuffee's head.

"Sit down, sit down." She pulled a chair up opposite him. "Wonderful game. Emmrich and Moritz at Bad Oenyhausen, 1922. Marvellous stuff. Cavalry charges, sabres shining. Not like your seventy movers today. See it's just poised. White's almost ready to break through on to the back rank. Black to play." He moved the queen down into the corner. "Queen sacrifice. Then . . ." and the two knights came in a trio of intermeshing checks to give mate. Even Ruth's elementary chess sense could see it, the little explosion of energy on the board, the splendid panache of it. It was very much as her father would want to play chess, possibly as he would have wanted to live his life.

"It's a wonderful finish." Mr. Cuffee puffed smoke and set the pieces back.

"Actually Moritz didn't see it. He played bishop to queen four and lost." His voice was almost rueful, considering this long lost opportunity for glory. "Must have been terrible for him afterwards, playing the game over."

"Perhaps he never ever noticed it." Mr. Cuffee smiled and looked up from the board.

"Aha, he wouldn't be that lucky. If you're good enough to get into that kind of position you wouldn't be stupid enough not to see the mess you'd made of it. No, he'd have seen it all right," and he played the move over again, savouring its perfection.

"I taught you and your brother to play. Do you ever have a game?"

"No. I haven't played chess in years."

"Pity, it's a wonderful game. Always wanted to be good. Really good, you know," and in the same breath, "Do you see much of him?"

"Who, Peter? Oh yes. He's living not far from me."

"How is he?"

"He's fine. Painting a lot. I think there's some hope of an exhibition soon," saying this because she felt somehow it might please him to hear it.

"Is he a good painter? I mean, does he have a genuine talent?" Ruth tried to decide if what Peter had was talent, genuine or otherwise.

"I don't know. I think so. I mean he certainly can paint." Mr. Cuffee played the final moves over again, the felt-bottomed pieces making only the faintest sound.

"Strange, I don't think I've ever seen a painting of Peter's. He never brought any work home," and he was suddenly sweeping the pieces off the board, clearing his mind of their implications. Ruth stood up disconcerted by the abruptness of his gesture and the starkness of the empty board.

In the morning, when she woke, there was a bird singing in the garden. She lay hearing it, hearing other birds songs from other mornings, waking in this room in this bed. Going to the window she knew where to look, hidden in the splice of the crab apple, a blackbird, motionless, and the sweet whistle of it ringing invisibly through the garden as though the tree itself were singing. Poor old crab apple, bent on its crutch, not like her straight young ash, slender and firm. Yet she remembered its roots, talons in the earth. The multiple aspects of reality assailed her, still dizzy with sleep and forced her to rub the images away with her knuckles. The blackbird swept to the end of the garden, its notes stilled. The cat made a token rush then stopped and strolled to the foot of the tree. It reached up and sharpened its claws on the bark. The blackbird rattled among the rhododendrons and was gone, over the wall. Ruth went back to bed.

They went shopping after breakfast. Knutsford had a villagy air on a Saturday morning, the women crooking their wicker baskets and trundling their shopping prams, a constant

157

flickering of smiles and hellos and little tangles of talkers, un-ravelling and moving on. Not having done it for so long it was quite pleasant. The sun was bright and the sight of the well-provisioned shops and the ready purchasing and the movement made a certain impact of rightness and well-being. The world seemed in good hands and reasonably managed this morning.

After the shopping was completed Ruth asked her mother if she would like a drink. Mrs. Cuffee made a great to-do of such a departure from routine and they went, rather fussily, into the Royal George. There were stained oak tables and hogs-heads cut as seats and garnishings of brass on the walls. Ruth had a whisky and ginger ale and her mother a sweet Martini. For the first time, sipping her drink, she thought on London and Harry and rather missed them. It was a pleasant little twinge and she celebrated it by downing her whisky. Mrs. Cuffee looked askance as she rose to get another. Ruth winked and smiled.

There were two young men at the bar and one of them turned as she reached it and said.

"Hello, there," smiling at her momentary blank, "you don't remember me?"

"Oh yes, of course I do. Colin Farley," the name just pop-ping out at the last minute.

"That's right, and you're Ruth Cuffee. You've not been seen around in a long time."

"Around where?"

"Well around anywhere I've been around." She knew him from a rugby club dance. He hadn't gone to their school but he lived in Knutsford. The only other definite occasion on which she remembered seeing him had been at a rugby match itself. Passing the edge of the field on her way home, stopping to watch the muddy crab of men lumber and brawl, she saw him suddenly snatch the ball out from among their feet and snap it away at full stretch to another player. She had been rather impressed by the swift shape he made and tried to do it in the garden with a cushion but winded herself.

"What are you drinking?"

"Well thanks, but I'm with my mother actually."

"Well what's your mother drinking?"

"Martini, sweet."

"And yourself?"

"Whisky and ginger ale."

"What a thing to do to good Scotch," he said and called the barman down. She half expected to be introduced to the other young man whom she didn't know at all but Farley kept his back to him and went on with the usual questions about how she was and where and did she like it. Her drinks came and she said thanks.

"Yes, well, cheers."

"Cheers."

"You're just up for the weekend?"

"Yes."

"Look, if you've nothing fixed would you care to come out for a drink tonight. We could drive over to Leigh or some such, fancy that?" She could think of no reason why not so she said "yes."

"Great. I'll pick you up at, half-seven do?"

"Fine, do you know the address?"

"I know the street."

"It's sixteen."

"Okay, I'll find it."

"Half-seven then, cheerio."

"Marvellous."

She went back to her mother. Mrs. Cuffee looked at her. "That's Colin Farley, isn't it?"

"Yes, do you know him?"

"Did he ask you out?"

"How did you know?"

"Oh, I noticed he didn't introduce you to his friend. That usually means something. Very good-looking young man."

He was, in a large, tweedy sort of way, bold and beefy, this side of fat, good teeth and well cut hair. But her tastes in men had long since been predetermined. Where did that put Harry then? She shrugged this query off and finished her drink. Her mother expressed disapproval at her air of long practice and left a lady-like dreg of Martini behind. She said cheerio to Colin Farley as they went out.

Outside was bright, sudden light coating the eye. The two

whiskys warmed, floated inside her. She felt her heels, hard little clacks under her upright walking body. She was alive, this trivial Saturday morning, her blood beat in her wrists, her heels marked out the brisk rhythm of normality. It seemed reasonable, life, eminently straightforward. They turned into their road, it dozed, fat with sunlight. Her mother walked slightly ahead, talking of she knew not what. Ruth saw something on her shoulder and quickened her step to look. A caterpillar, the kind that live on privets, pale, bare little tuber, erect and waving its head and trunk in search of some further purchase, a horrible blindness in the movement, and yet a terrible determination, the all-consuming wish to live. Ruth swept it off with a shuddering revulsion, thinking all manner of things, of the soft squashy thing itself, its vulnerability, of Harry and the painting of the yellow glove and the baby inside Merle Curvis and the stuff in which the fertilized egg embedded, corpus luteum wasn't it called, and the ruin of that body in the ground with the rains seeping through to it and waste, the endless waste of things irreplaceable, caterpillars and babies and lovehope. Mrs. Cuffee was looking at her.

"Oh, there was something on your shoulder. I just brushed it off."

Robert Eldman arrived after lunch to go with Mr. Cuffee to a local cricket match. He sat in the easy chair and talked to Ruth about London. It was so easy, seeing his familiarity here to think it was all right, normal. A triangle. Eternal in its simplicity. Three fragmented sets of needs, solacing themselves and each other as best they could. Who was harmed, what wrong was there in it? But Mr. Cuffee was deceived, he didn't know. Surely he didn't know. She could hear him upstairs, selecting a pipe. Did it matter that he was deceived, was it more of a deception than the one he practiced on himself? Robert Eldman asked her where she stayed in London.

"Near Primrose Hill. Do you know it?"

"No, when I lived in London it was in Fulham, near the Chelsea football ground. Used to watch Chelsea quite a bit." He sat, a quiet brown man, brown-eyed, brown-jacketed, brown-voiced. Mrs. Cuffee came in.

"I'm going over to Cilla Thompson for an hour, she's not

keeping too well, leave the dishes and I'll do them when I get back."

"It's all right. I'll do them." Robert Eldman said cheerio but that was all, didn't get up, didn't look, made no attempt to communicate. What sort of relationship could this be when your lover treated you as comfortably and casually as your husband? What was the difference? She wanted to ask him. What do you give her that he doesn't? Why does she need two of the same kind? Does she need them, either of them? Robert Eldman looked as though he might even have answered, sitting so comfortable, so content in his cuckolding chair. Yet he rose to meet Mr. Cuffee, rose and said.

"Ah, so you've chosen the meerschaum, thought you might," and Mr. Cuffee heard no irony in the words and explained why and she watched them through the front room curtains, walking side by side, talking, sharing their Saturday afternoon, friends.

After she washed the dishes she wandered abstractedly about the house and in the garden amid the smell of roses and cut grass and the drone of the traffic bypassing the village. Walking, absorbed in her thoughts, she bumped into the tree. It jarred her shoulder and she stopped, looking about the garden as though she had just woken up. It seemed vast. The emptiness of a place is the absence of meaning. This garden was utterly meaningless to her. Memories and associations drained out of it as she watched, the soft red walls, the heavy green shrubs, the old, twisted tree, all words she could not read, meanings she could not comprehend. Behind appearances lay reality, the lost glove in a dead girl's belly, the life dance of a grub, an appleless tree in an empty garden. Her mind expanded with incomprehension, threatening to know everything at once, make a cumulative sense of it all but to her relief the telephone summoned her indoors. Gladly she hurried towards its insistence.

It was Harry sounding drunk and very close. For a moment she thought he had hitchhiked up to see her and felt a swift flicker of resentment but he was phoning from the flat. How was she. He missed her. He was drunk. They were all drunk. All, Peter, John, Stolleman, him. Did she want to speak to them. He loved her. They all loved her but he loved her most. Was she all right. When was she coming back. Not until Monday. What time. If she told him the time he'd get off work and come to meet her. It was all right, he wanted to. Did she want to speak to Peter. Cuffee came on.

"Well, how goes it in Eugene O'Neill country?"

"All right. And with you?"

"Fine. Been drinking."

"The four of you?"

"Yes, Stoll and this friend of Harry's."

"What's he like?"

"Little get."

"Oh, why's that because?"

"Cocky little bastard. He's all right."

"Knutsford looks nice."

"Oh yes."

"I wouldn't mind being able to live here."

"Harry'll move, get a job anywhere our Harry will."

"I don't mean Knutsford really, well I'd like to come back to Cheshire."

"Oh you mean 'return to your origins,' and all that sort of shit."

"That's right, Peter, all that sort of shit you don't believe in."

"There's the pips, I'll hand you back to Harry."

"How's the wife?"

"Have I annoyed you or something?"

"Oh go away." There was a pause and then he called Harry.

"Don't be angry Ruth, no offence meant."

"All right, I'm sorry." Harry came on. He said he loved her very much. She said she loved him and as she said it knew she didn't. She said it again to make sure Harry didn't detect it in her voice. The circuit was broken, the phone replaced, the illusion of communication ceased. Solitary once more a panic threatened. Everything was so far away. An expanding universe. Ruth sat down, surrounded by distances.

Colin Farley came just after seven, driving a dark blue Rover with a soft top and whitewall tyres. Ruth, despite herself, was impressed by the dressage and his confident, door-opening manner. She was ready so that he didn't have to be brought in. She settled down and let the car take her. He drove competently, not with Terry's dedication, but purposefully, aware of the car and its market price and his gold cufflinks that caught the late sun as he rolled them round the corners and safe in the knowledge that in a good car a pretty girl looks beautiful, especially at speeds over fifty. Ruth counselled herself that his driving might not be so good with drink taken and regarded her knees which were generously exposed in the soft sloping seat. It wasn't that her legs were thick. They were just a little too short. Between knee and ankle. And the calves were a little too shapely. Be better this weather to have them straight and wear your skirts at the high port. The term reminded her of Cuffee from his Army days. That first leave he had they spent in this countryside that she passed through now, casual passenger. Cross purposes met and mingled, little knots of nostalgia and awareness. If emptiness is the absence of meaning then a landscape such as this, so redolent of recall, must needs be least lonely of all places, these green savannahs of the heart's desiring. The questions she had asked herself in Terry's car on the way up seemed a little closer to being answerable, watching the hedgerows brush past and the evening fields fill with dusk. Home is where the heart has been happy.

Through her preoccupations her companion chatted easily, picking up the threads of their unmutual past and implying parallels and relations. She asked him about his work. He was an architect, junior in his father's firm. They'd just got the contract for a housing development outside Altrincham. Could be very exciting. His father was a bit on the conservative side, good architect but basically he just didn't understand the new possibilities of the materials available today. Thought Le Corbusier and Frank Lloyd Wright were eccentrics and hadn't even heard of Gaudi. Since she hadn't heard of him either she asked. He seemed quite committed, involved, as he spoke. She smiled and listened, approving of his earnestness. In a way he was her intended goal in the ordinary course of things. It was to someone like Colin Farley that she might have expected to find herself married had she been in her youth a more social creature, less the pale shadow of her dark brother. Thus it was interesting to be with him now, this purposeful young architect chap, in circumstances close to normality, driving out for an evening's drinking.

The Wheatsheaf was already quite full. They went to a group in the corner of the saloon and she was introduced. Some of the faces were familiar in an out-of-focus way, many were alike. There were leather buttons on the tweeds and camel waistcoats and the girls had suede jackets and lots of eye makeup. Ruth felt pleased with herself for having judged it so accurately. Her black needlecord dress, slightly mannish with its epaulettes and pockets, didn't clash but set her apart. Which, with a little smirk of self-satisfaction into her first whisky and ginger, was as it should be.

The talk was rather clubby. Work and personalities at work. Parties been to and heard of. Some talk of next season's rugby. It wasn't boring at first, not looking at the faces and guessing things about them, not sipping her drink and sensing the girls sizing her up. But there were too many male tones, too many self-conscious half-stifled oaths, too much braying laughter, too many arguments as to whose round. She found to her pained amusement that she had a headache. Some calculations implied an impending period. "Once more into the breech clout" and smiled at her wit. One of them, a bullish young man who was probably younger than his thirty-year-old appearance, spotted it.

"What's amusing our silent friend?" Ruth smiled with her mouth at him.

"Something somebody said, not here, somewhere else," and realized halfway through how it could be construed but couldn't be bothered to mitigate the implied snub.

"I hope it's not boring you then, all this chat," quite aggressive.

"No, really. I could listen to you go on and on all night." There was some laughter at this.

"Got yourself a quick one there, Col," he said.

"Wouldn't have to be all that quick to get past you, Ben," and there was more laughter, firmer, surer because Col had kidded Ben and it was among themselves. Ben caught Col by the back of the neck and made to press his head into his pint. Another young man said it was no use trying to drown Farley in beer, he had a fifty pint capacity. This met with unbridled mirth.

Ruth sat back and surveyed her fate. The young man who had driven her here had gone, in his place a rather loud, slightly beery person laughed and quaffed. At that moment his hand dropped upon her knee and pressed, firmly. He was talking to one of the other girls at the time and he didn't look at Ruth as he squeezed her knee. It amused her in a way, this casual assumptive laying on of hands. She extricated herself and went off to the ladies.

When she returned they were talking of Merle Curvis. It didn't surprise her although she hadn't thought about her all evening. But her presence had been with Ruth almost from the minute she arrived in Knutsford, she was in some way part of her visit home, a feature of the landscape.

"She was nothing more than a call girl," Ben was saying.

"You don't really know that," somebody else said.

"I know it. Bloody well know somebody who called an' all."

"Who?"

"No names no bloody pack drill. But it's a fact. She was a posh whore."

"What is it you have against that?" Ruth heard herself ask, suddenly abruptly angry. Ben looked at her belligerently.

"What's wrong with whores? Is that what you're asking me?" trying to back her down with his tone. Ruth found it surprisingly easy to stare him out.

"Yes."

"That's what's wrong with this bloody country. There's too many tarts bloody kipping up with people and making too much money out of it. A call girl makes more money than a qualified architect, more than a doctor, more than a bloody member of Parliament. That's what's wrong with it."

"You're envious in fact." His neck, which bore the marks of extinct boils, was red.

"Envious nothing." He leaned towards her vehemently. "They're letting anybody fuck them who has the money, that's what's wrong with it." There was a sort of protest, a gasp from the girls at this outspokenness.

"And you don't have the money, is that it?" Ben swallowed hard and sat back, still staring at Ruth he said:

"I think maybe you picked a right one here, Col." Ruth smiled and stood up.

"I don't think the money would have helped you with Merle Curvis, Ben, she wouldn't have let that poxy neck of yours within yards of her," and then she left, feeling suddenly rather unsteady. The night was welcoming and cool. She walked across the road and stood a moment, breathing deeply. Colin Farley appeared beside her.

"Are you all right?"

"Fine thanks. You go back. I'll get a bus."

"Don't be silly. I'm sorry about Ben, you just got under his skin."

"What a repellent thought."

"Yes, well, you shouldn't have said that about his neck, he's . . ."

"Sensitive about it, is he? If he is it's the only thing he's sensitive about."

"I'm sorry, I didn't know you were a friend of Merle's. Did you know her up in Manchester?"

"I wasn't a friend. I don't know her. She's dead." And all at once she was near to tears. Merle Curvis was dead in a cold field somewhere. She wanted to be long since asleep.

"Will you please take me home?"

The drive calming, she sat deep down in her seat and saw the black countryside slip past, comfortable in the little cock-pit with the radio surging and fading. Farley looked over from time to time. She reassured him she was all right and that she was not about to be sick. Then in the darkness under some trees he pulled up.

"Excuse me, I won't be a moment," and he got out and the door slammed and his feet went back up the road a bit. It was quiet and warm and she felt almost at peace, briefly stopped by the roadside. She watched the dark shapeless movings of the trees out of the window. It was cold out there and the wind blew chill in the branches. She sunk into her seat and savoured her remove from such elements. He came back and got in. She waited for him to start the car but he sat a moment and the radio played away on another dimension of reality. His hand caught her shoulder and pulled her over and he was kissing her. She let him, his mouth trying to open hers and his tongue pressing against her teeth. She didn't hold him off, not even when his hand started to cup her breast. It was because he was quite unreal, she didn't know him, didn't know why he was doing this. Only as his hand went under her skirt and with a shock she realized that it was her thigh that was cold and his fingers that were warm, only then did she know that he was quite prepared to take her like this, in his car, at their first meeting, without words or overture. Scorn, then fear, then an excitement which she could not suppress rose in her. She despised his blind randiness but it frightened and titillated her. It made her feel curiously attractive, anonymously female, she could almost imagine the cramped struggle and the harsh yielding and to shut such images out she brought her knees up awkwardly, forcing his hand out and leaving her kneeling on the seat. He stopped and sat back, looking unsure of himself. Once physical contact was broken she hated him, quite simply and easily. He tried to reach for her once more but as his hand came over she knocked it away.

"You won't expect your wife to do this sort of thing, will you Colin? I mean, you'll expect to marry a virgin, won't you?" He said nothing, but sat looking baffled and angry. "Not that virginity means anything to you just as long as your little missis hasn't had somebody else up there before you. Only one owner. You really make me want to spit."

"Oh shut up, nothing happened to you."

"No, that's right, nothing, just somebody about three times as strong as me whom I don't know started pawing all over me in a dark country lane. Do you ever, ever, try to think what it's like to be a woman?" and in a way she knew she was teasing him, trying to tell him of the polarities of rape, inflame him with the potential of their situation. But he sat sullen, except for a swift twist to turn the radio off. The mood left her and she sank back, cold suddenly and depressed.

"I'm sorry," he said.

"What are you sorry about. That you wasted your night, that you didn't get to poke me? Why don't you make me walk back? You're sorry you won't be able to tell poxy Ben tomorrow what a good time you had." For a moment he looked at her, his face angry and a muscle in his jaw ticking away, then he set about those things over which he had control, switching on the engine and putting his car into gear. Ruth closed her eyes and didn't open them until she was home. As soon as the car stopped she opened the door and got out.

"Good night," she said, and closed the door quietly. She didn't look back and heard the car rev away down the street, making a noise of cornering and speeding up. Its sound hung a long time in the quiet air. Ruth stood by the door, all manner of feelings moving her. She could not hope, there and now, to still them long enough to examine their nature and cause. She turned the Yale and went in.

Her mother was still up, washing the supper dishes, in her monstrous dressing-gown. She offered to make a cup of tea and at the suggestion Ruth craved the taste, the clean, pungent taste of sane tea.

"Yes, let's have some tea." She went upstairs and washed her face and brushed her teeth and examined her face in the mirror. It told her nothing, her mind sat behind the mask of her features and received no sign of recognition. This could be the face of anybody. Dissatisfied she went downstairs. Her mother had carried the tray into the sitting-room.

"Cosier," she explained. There was a little silence while the tea was poured and sugared and stirred and tasted. Then there was a pause and then Mrs. Cuffee asked her what sort of a night she'd had. Ruth could not begin to think of talking to her about it.

"Do you mind if I ask you something, Mother?"

"What's that, dear?"

"Do you ever regret having married . . ." she almost said Mr. Cuffee but checked ". . . Father."

"Regret?" as though such an emotion had never entered her ken. "No I don't think I ever regret it." She sipped her tea in punctuation and made Ruth think of Meriel Rose spacing her thoughts out.

"Not now. It's a bit late for regrets now, isn't it?"

"Was there a time when you did regret it?"

"Oh dear, well now, I suppose there's always a time when you regret anything. But it passes. Unless you do something about it." She recrossed her legs and Ruth noticed, almost as though she had never seen them before, that her mother had long slender legs, not at all like her own.

"But you didn't do anything about it, when you did regret it?"

"No. But it was too late then anyway. Much too late."

"Why?"

"Oh, lots of things. We were married. Peter and you were born, well Peter was anyway, your father was in the Army, overseas. It wasn't possible." She paused and thought back to them, those days without possibilities. Then almost with a sigh of relief she went on, "You see I always thought I would marry Robert. Almost from when I met him I think I knew that he was the man I would eventually marry."

"Why?"

"Oh well, if you only know him now that doesn't seem very likely, but he was different then. He was a very purposeful person was Robert. Very sincere and intense. Pity he was short. If he'd been a bit bigger he would possibly have been quite an important man. I've always believed that, trivial things like being short or fat or bald are terribly important. Anyway, when I met him he was an important man, in his own world. He was president of the university debating society, prominent in the Fabians, captain of the soccer team. He was quite a prize."

"Why didn't you marry him, then? Didn't he ask you?"

"Oh yes, we were engaged."

"And then you met Father." Mrs. Cuffee blinked a moment and looked into the teapot.

"Do you want some more?" Ruth waved her hand. Mrs. Cuffee poured herself the last of the tea.

"Well he was really running parallel to all this. He was in the same year as Robert but he was quite different. For one thing he had no political interests whatsoever. I mean this was in the mid-'thirties when everybody was passionately worked up about Hitler and Appeasement and Spain. Peter was quite apart from all that. Had a kind of aloofness which was rather attractive I suppose. Sneered at Robert and the earnestness with which they did everything. His poems were always about feeling and shadows that reminded you of things you couldn't really remember. I can see him sitting listening to Robert talking about politics and at the end of it you'd realize he hadn't been listening at all but he'd have been watching the smoke from his cigarette. It was all a big pretence really but he was very good at it."

"Why did you marry him?"

"It all sounds rather terrible actually when you say it. Robert went to Spain soon after it started. I didn't want him to go but I didn't try to stop him. Not that it would have made any difference. And while he was in Spain I went on a walking holiday with Peter. It was all rather idyllic, we went to Scotland and he was looking very Byronic, he wore his hair rather long and it was a change after all the meetings and protests and I just let myself be carried along by it all."

"And you broke it off with Robert?"

"Well not while he was away. Not until he came back. I told him about Peter and me and he just said if that was how I wanted it he hoped I would be happy."

"Doesn't sound as though he was all that keen," Ruth said, ridiculously resentful of this long-past apathy.

"He was a bit strange after he came back from Spain. I think he was very disillusioned in Spain. I never really understood what happened in the Spanish War, did you? Anyway, Robert just left Manchester and took a teaching job in London for a while and then the war came. We were married by then and Peter was on the way."

"But why did you get married, I mean did you love him?"

"Oh yes, I loved him. I don't know if that was why we got married, sometimes I think it was more because Peter was coming. Anyway, when the war came and Mr. Cuffee was called up he was sent to London and I got a two-room flat in Urmston and that was that."

"What do you mean, that was that?"

"That was that. Life stopped really for about five years,

except that at the end of it I was twenty-seven and had two children and a husband I didn't know very well."

"Was it then, during the war, that you regretted it?"

"Yes. Urmston would make you regret anything. I loathed that place. Still do. Just to see a bus going there makes me shudder."

"Were you there all during the war?"

"Except for visits to London to see Peter, and they stopped in '42 when he went abroad and one week I spent in Scotland in the last year of the war. We tried to get somewhere to stay in London but they were all too expensive."

"And I was born in Urmston?"

"No, actually you were born somewhere quite nice, in Bideford, down in Devon."

"How was that?"

"Oh when your time was near I thought I'd go mad if I didn't get away so I went down to Bideford and got into the hospital there."

"Why Bideford?"

"Oh we used to go on holiday there when I was a child. My parents had a cottage there. I had a very happy childhood, so I thought you might like to be born somewhere that meant something to me." Ruth felt a near tears feeling behind her eyes and in her throat although she knew it was not all to do with her mother's words.

"That was nice of you. It must have been rotten for you."

"It was," Mrs. Cuffee said simply. "Those years were the unhappiest years of my life. Everything was so ugly, the clothes and the furniture and the films they made and all the queuing and not enough food and the spirit everyone was supposed to have and that terrible man Churchill and all the lies on the radio. Oh my God, I did hate it," and her mother was crying, head down, not making any noise but her shoulders moved in little jerks as she swallowed and once or twice she sniffed. After a moment she looked up, blinking her wet eyelids. "Oh, I shouldn't have started talking about it. It's all over and done with. Silly woman crying like that," and she stood up. "I've got a head now, and serves me right. I'm going to bed, dear. Are you coming?"

"Yes, in a minute."

Mrs. Cuffee went and Ruth sat on. Other people's lives. Ask a question, ask another, open the door, walk in. Behind the privet and the roughcast and the floral curtains there is a wilderness, a landscape you have never travelled in. Enter at your own risk, other people's lives are strange places, none more so than your parents', those lifelong strangers. She went upstairs past the room where Mrs. Cuffee was stretching out parallel to her un-meeting partner, past the empty room of the prodigal Peter, to her own cell. In its dark she stood behind the door, like women did in films, leaning back on it, strangely comfortable. Her mother and her father, their past, Merle Curvis and Colin Farley, her present, they all moved among each other, dead and alive after their various fashions. Out of them and their interaction could she not recognize the nature of her origins, the true address of home. She recalled seeing the countryside from the car and thinking of her childhood, when, despite its terrors, identity had never been more certain. She had been Ruth, Peter's sister. Such a description no longer met her requirements, yet its nostalgia moved her to longings, wild impossible longings in which she was once again as she had been, coming from the fields of evening, close on his heels, her arms trailing with flowers and grasses, safe in his shadow, heading for home.

She lay on her bed and remembered the knoll where she waited while Peter went foraging, the tall grey pines standing around, moving their high branches in the summer winds, how she would look, head back, up into their unattainable cradles. She had been happy then, or heedless of unhappiness, her gatherings around her, couched on sweet vernal, her mind ashimmer like the panicles of Yorkshire Fog, looking into the secret hearts of her pluckings, telling the rosary of their names over and over to herself, calyx and sepal, anthers, pistils, stigma, carpels and pollen; flower names, dream names. And telling the dandelion time, puffing the hours away over the countryside till the clock told zero. Breaking the stems and making the milky rings on her forearm, watching them grow black and indelible, eating the seedy little sacs of shepherd's purse or nibbling the acorns of rats tail, pulling the alternate spikelets from the darnel, crunching the sweet stems of the foxtail grass till he came, in his own time, to fetch her. Those monumental trivia, still with the power to move her, move her all these years later to tears, unshed but waiting, tremulous behind her eyes.

In the morning she awoke with the desire to leave already in her mind. There was no longer any need for her to stay. In some fashion her questions were answered or had ceased to be asked. Home was no longer here, she had no wish to go to the hill, that was no home, only homage. Home was where you could take your ease. Here things had become too real, her parents were growing into people before her unbelieving eyes. Mr. Cuffee mourning chances lost, Mrs. Cuffee exposing the nerve ends of her memory. It was strange that their anonymity in childhood should have been one of the indispensable qualities of the happiness of the era. Not without reason do children imagine themselves to be orphans, of unknown parentage, alone in the midst of father and motherdom. Consciousness alternates between the certainty of its own identity and the fear of losing it. In childhood this oscillation is best catered to. Home resides, numbered, in a street, inhabited by symbols of security. The fields of the imagination lie outside the door, the child shuttles swiftly between, weaving the special fabric of that unique freedom. She could see only too well that growing up was a slow retarding of that fluency as parents became more irksome, more real, and the areas of imagination were whittled down by knowledge.

Lying in her bed, looking at the ceiling, she knew now why home could never be here, Knutsford. Not for Cuffee's brutal dismissive reasons but because here she could never establish that dual world across the threshold of which she might flit unencumbered by remorse or scepticism. Where that kingdom might be set up was beyond her rarest guess. Only that it would not be here was certain.

She told her mother at breakfast that she was going back that day. Mrs. Cuffee seemed somewhat disturbed but said nothing beyond asking if she had the money for her train fare. Ruth helped her prepare the lunch, "Family Favourites" ping-ponging banalities back and forth across the English Channel.

173

The slow ritual of food being prepared, its odours, the lists of unknown names sending and receiving love and affection, the whole aura of normality enveloped her, stilled her disquiet, eased the tensions of her mind. Standing over the sink, a potato slicing cleanly white in her hands, fingers grown accustomed to the cold tap water, a pleasant ache in her back, she felt happy, momentarily content.

To her surprise Mr. Cuffee seemed rather upset by the news that she was going back that day. He insisted on driving her to Manchester to catch the train. For a moment she thought of staying on till Monday and having Terry come up for her but the thought of the train, travelling by a window, seemed a most agreeable notion and she remained firm in her resolve.

Sunday lunch was a well-rehearsed event. Robert Eldman arrived just on two and produced a bottle of Côte de Beaune which sparked off some opinions from Mr. Cuffee to which he gave an attentive ear. Ruth watched Eldman with more than usual interest. The knowledge that he had fought in Spain during the Civil War added a dimension to his character. She tried to imagine him with the butt of a rifle against his cheek, eye puckered along the sight. Had he ever shot anyone, this subfusc little man in their living-room, had he caused another human to exit? That he might have seemed ludicrously improbable, yet made his near obsequiousness faintly menacing.

So it was with more interest than usual that she found herself alone with him after lunch. Mr. Cuffee had taken her mother in the car to visit someone and when Ruth finished washing and stacking the dishes she found Eldman amid the Sunday papers. She picked up the *Observer* and turned to the book reviews, not that she would ever read any of the books listed, not that she would ever read anything again. Irritated by the sense of her intellectual sloth she put the paper down.

"I hate the Sunday papers. They're so full of people being clever and incisive and knowing things. Makes me feel very stupid."

"M'm. I only ever read the sports pages," Eldman said.

"I don't know, I never really seem to read anything any more. And I've got plenty of time."

174

"Well, bit like coals to Newcastle for you." For some reason she decided to confide.

"That's the point, I'm not working." His response was bland with unsurprise.

"Oh I see."

"No, I'm a lady of leisure."

"Lovely," and she felt annoyed that he should not ask the obvious question.

"They think I am, of course, but I'd rather not have them know. They'd just worry." Would they, was that why she didn't tell them? "You won't mention it," and felt stupid for having created the situation out of nothing. Eldman shook his head reassuringly.

"No, no, I won't say anything," and with that the conversation seemed at an end. Ruth went back to reading the paper and thinking irritably on her lapse. It made her realize just how much she prized her composure, superficial though it might be.

"How old are you now, Ruth?" Eldman asked, hidden behind the pages of small print. For a moment she deliberated, then, without lowering the paper said.

"Twenty-three."

"That's next birthday?"

"Yes, in November."

"Yes. November." When she looked at him he was sitting gazing not at her but into the unlit fire.

"Why do you ask?" He looked up.

"Oh, time, you know, you mark it in anniversaries of one sort or another. Have to, otherwise you'd never notice it slipping past." His tone touched her, reminded her of her mother.

"Are you unhappy?" Again he glanced up, but again without surprise.

"No. Not hardly at all."

"Were you unhappy when you were younger?"

"Oh yes, quite a different thing, of course, happiness then and now. Takes quite an effort to remember what happiness actually felt like."

"Can you?"

"Yes. Just about. Once or twice."

"I don't really know whether I'm happy or not. Not most of the time. I always think you should, know I mean."

"Maybe you're neither," Eldman suggested.

"I don't like to think that, it seems rather vegetable." Eldman smiled, an event which made him seem, not so much younger, as suddenly physically much closer. To her wonderment he began to sing, a light, clear voice, quite unlike what she would have imagined,

> "Life is but a
> Life is but a
> Melancholy flower
> Melancholy flower
> Life is but a melon
> Life is but a melon
> Cauliflower,
> Cauliflower"

to the tune of "Frère Jacques." At the end he coughed once, smiled again, and looked away.

"What a lovely song. Where did you learn that?"

"Oh, one of those silly things from university. Just came into my mind when you said vegetable."

"Oh I like that," she said, genuinely delighted. It was a little piece of trove, one of those discoveries which are instantaneously colonized by the mind so that within minutes she could hardly remember a time when it had not been part of her personal folklore empire. She looked at Eldman gratefully, for his undemanding donation.

"Sing it again," she asked him.

"If you'll sing it with me."

"All right," and they did, seated opposite each other in the empty house, sang the little hymn, both poignant and absurd at one and the same time, their voices twined among the words, mingling so that Ruth felt quite breathless with the improbable intimacy of it. When they finished a certain constraint fell on them both, Ruth tried to think of something she could ask him but they were all either prying or formal so in the end she relapsed into uneasy reading of the paper and then, as though they had never been gone, Mr. and Mrs. Cuffee returned and Ruth realizing that the moment of intimacy was over, went upstairs to pack.

Mr. Cuffee drove sedately along without talking. Ruth sat, hunched down into herself, perversely sorry to be leaving and eager to be on the train. She had come back home for the weekend and was returning. Her visit to her origins was over. She knew what? Nothing. Everything. Some gossip, and insight into another's life, a glimpse of what she had avoided, the recollection of time past, a sad little song. This melange was her gleanings, it wouldn't be until she was back beside her tree, in her chair, that it might chance to make sense, if then.

"I'm sorry you're going back so soon. We never really had the chance to speak to each other." Mr. Cuffee spoke without looking from the road. "Strange how we find we miss you. I mean strange because we never really saw a great deal of you. I've been thinking we might come down to London some weekend. You could show us around. Course I used to know London very well during the war. I was stationed there, just outside actually. But it was a different city then," he reflected, bringing the car to a halt at traffic lights. They changed. He let the clutch out and moved forward, "different world. Used to stand in the streets after the all-clear and all around the skyline was red. Red with flames. People were different, had to be. The war. Changes things. People."

"Did it change you?" He looked at her, exactly as Peter would have, the face long and expressionless except for the heavy lids drooping malevolently.

"Yes, I suppose it did. One is so sheltered really, from life. War isn't necessarily real life but some of its ingredients are. Do you know what I mean?"

"Death, you mean?" He nodded, as though pleased with her awareness.

"A lot of people were very happy during the war. It was their most sympathetic climate. Not mine. Didn't suit me. But then I'm not an anarchist."

"How do you mean, anarchist?"

"Well, wars are a kind of anarchy, under all the regimentation everything really goes. Morals, standards, beliefs. You only have to look at the birth-rate figures to see that. It's even got itself statistical respectability. The post-war bulge. Directly traceable to a great many during the war bulges." Ruth felt slightly embarrassed but as her father seemed, as was his way, to be addressing a general audience she allowed herself to remain an anonymous ear. Mr. Cuffee, however, had stopped, whether because he too was embarrassed or because he had nothing further to say she could not tell.

"You were in Egypt, weren't you, when you went overseas?"

"Partly. Middle East. Various places. Terrible country."

"Why?"

"It's difficult to say. It's an affront to the European consciousness I think. I mean you could see that at the time of Suez. There was a terrible resentment of the Egyptians in this country. Of course, it was partly the 'wogs begin at Calais' thing but every man I served with out there hated and despised them. It's something I thought about quite a lot at one time. Used to keep a notebook out there. Gave it to Peter, don't really know why, thought it might interest him. Lot of things in it about out there, the country and the people."

"Peter never mentioned it."

"No. Well it's nothing really. Just it fascinated me in a way, particularly the country. The desert. Terrible, frightening land. Sometimes think I'd like to go back."

"Why don't you?"

"M'm. Too late. Don't really care to go as a tourist and it's too late to go as anything else." Too late, too late. Little motif of despair beating like a migraine in the temple. Throughout this weekend it had sounded until its insistence was almost deafening. In an attempt to wrench herself and the conversation into the present she asked.

"Why are Peter and I so different, from you and mother," and without quite knowing why, "and Robert Eldman?"

"I don't think that you are. Not really. You live in different worlds but you yourselves are not different. Peter for instance despises me." Ruth must have made some twitch of denial for Mr. Cuffee looked at her and frowned. "No it's true. I know it is. He told me so. But I know why he despises me. He doesn't. That's really why I gave him the notebook I kept. Help him to see."

"See what?"

"That I'm him and he is me. And he despises me because I threaten him with failure."

"Why do you threaten him with failure?" one of those questions whose answer is self-evident at the moment of asking.

"Because I'm a failure."

"Oh I wouldn't say that."

"Then you'd be wrong. That's why Peter has made a point of rebelling against me and everything he thinks I stand for. But it's a waste of time. He has to face that our natures are the same and that nature he will have to come to terms with at some point. It's too easy now for him to see me as a kind of caricature. I hoped maybe if he read this notebook he'd see I was like him and he is like me and it wouldn't be so easy for him to disassociate from the fact of his relation to me. And it's only if he recognizes his own nature for what it is that he'll be able to control it. Otherwise it will control him. Everybody is like that. All failures of one sort or another."

"I don't believe that."

"It's true though. Everybody fails at some point. A lot of people don't know it, never let themselves know it. Some become reconciled, even become strong, find a credo which includes failure as being livable with, part of the nature of things. But there are some who want to win and will take no substitute. For them failure is not to be endured or explained away. They are the real failures. Failure is the cancer of their lives. I'm one of those." They turned into the station car park and there was silence while he parked the car. Then there was further silence while Mr. Cuffee took his pipe from the dashboard.

"Seven-thirty. You've got plenty of time," and Ruth felt he regretted having spoken so openly. She sat as he lit up, puffing, sucking, the smoke sworling in the small enclosed bubble of the car.

"You can see what I mean if you compare me with Robert. I mean on the face of things you could say he was a bigger failure than I am. I'm the head of the department, we both wanted the same girl and I got her, I can beat him at chess. All along the line. But it's not so. Robert has come to terms with it. I think he did so a long time ago, when he came back from Spain. He never really wanted to win anything, so he's quite content to be second. That way he avoids having his life eaten up by a sense of remorse."

"But remorse for what?" Mr. Cuffee seemed genuinely puzzled. He shook his head and looked into the bowl of his pipe as if conceivably the answer might be there.

"I don't know. It has often taxed me that question. The nearest I ever came to it was during the war. Not the answer, the question. Sometimes out there in the desert you'd take a little walk and just over the first rise you'd be on the edge of the wilderness, the original wilderness. I mean it must mean something that the prophets and saints went off into the desert to meditate. T. E. Lawrence says somewhere that in those silences they heard the word they carried within them. I suppose somewhere, very feebly inside me the word must have been calling out, hoping to be heard. And on one or two occasions out there I almost thought I heard it. But your heart beats too loud so you end up listening to that."

Ruth wanted him to stop telling her these things, exposing himself to her. She had suddenly had enough, heard enough, thought enough. The pipe smoke was choking her. She opened the door abruptly on the end of his words.

"Do you mind if we get out, it's a bit stuffy for me."

"Of course, I'm sorry. I forget what a fug talking and smoking gets up."

He came up to the ticket office with her and before she could protest he bought her ticket, first class, and gave it to her with a hasty, rather embarrassed comment about buying herself something pretty with the money she saved. Then,

"I won't wait, Ruth. Get back before the light goes."

She kissed his cheek and he went, a tall stooped man she didn't really know. As she watched him, the first genuine stirrings of regret at the omission touched her and made her eyes crinkle with those facile tears she was beginning to hate herself for.

It was good to be back. Harry had been in when she arrived, with John Moseby who went almost immediately. Harry fussed about making tea, coming to kiss her several times. She sat out on the verandah among a row of flapping shirts listening to the surf of the traffic. She felt herself unwind as she sipped her tea and made answers up for Harry's questions. It was behind her now. She had gone and now she was back. It doubtless had done her good. What good she couldn't imagine but nevertheless.

In bed Harry was all around her with his arms. She made love without much thought and simulated an orgasm to let Harry get to sleep. She felt very tired but not quite ready for sleep. Determinedly she kept her mind from following any of the many paths back into the weekend. Robert Eldman's song kept turning over and over in her mind. She sang it, silent at first and then in the quietest of whispers. She was in the middle of it when sleep swallowed her whole.

In the morning she phoned Peter and arranged to walk over and meet him. She met him turning off Belsize Lane and they walked up Fitzjohn's Avenue, talking.

"Glad to be back in the land of the living?"

"Yes, I am, though I wouldn't take such pleasure in it as you do."

"Find what you were looking for?" which made her look at him.

"What do you mean?"

"Weren't you seeking out your source or something?"

"Oh you're such a bloody smarty pants, aren't you?"

"And you're a touchy little cow," making them both laugh.

"Tell you what I heard."

"Yes."

"Remember Jane Curvis? Merle she called herself."

"M'mm."

"She killed herself. Overdose. She was pretty." Cuffee fished out some cigarettes and offered her one.

"Silly bitch."

"You'd think she'd have known somebody who would have helped her."

"Not a bad looking girl," Cuffee said.

"Lovely legs."

"M'mm, so she had. 'All flesh is hay, come drink tobacco.' " Ruth looked up at him. He was frowning and looking ahead, smoke flooding from his nostrils. He looked a lot like his father. They walked on in silence, under the tall disrobing trees.

Harry reckoned that Moseby had changed a lot. The thing with his wife was really eating him up. Ruth asked why he didn't go back to her.

"Well what would have changed?"

"What does he want to change?"

"It wasn't any use for him."

"What about the child?"

"Yes, well, as I say, it's eating him up."

He didn't seem particularly eaten-up to Ruth. He seemed quiet yet without inhibitions about talking. He made her feel quite excluded when he talked to Harry though what he said was not particularly esoteric. Except perhaps about Greenock. They talked of that with a kind of topographic obsessiveness, mentioning street names and pubs and churches more than she could conceive to be necessary in ordinary conversation.

She asked Harry why Cuffee hadn't liked him but Gibbon seemed unaware of any such feeling.

"Still, it's not too surprising."

"Why?"

"Well, they're a bit alike, in a way," which was something else she couldn't see but the mere positing of it caused her to look more closely at the dark little Scotsman, listen more intently to his rapid close-lipped talk. She wasn't all that sure she liked him herself then.

She went to see Meriel, picking up the strands. Christchurch Hill was rusty with leaves. Meriel was delighted to see her. The room was unchanged. Ruth sat down and looked on to the Heath. Knutsford seemed far away.

"Well, tell me all about your visit." The vivacious, ever so slightly sad face, poised above the delicate cup. Not to her

Ruth thought. There could be no untangling the tale here, in this room. She chatted away until it was time to leave.

Crossing over at the Playhouse she met John Moseby coming out.

"Been to the matinee then?"

"Yes. Takes you back, it does."

"Not working?"

"No. Can't seem to manage the effort."

"Couldn't Harry get you a start where he is?"

"He's offered. I suppose I'm not sure whether I'm going home or not."

"Do you really think of Greenock as being home?"

"Yes. Where else?"

"I don't know. Why there?"

"It's where I come from."

"Well I come from Knutsford but I don't think of that as home."

"Yes I know, but Greenock's the only place I know. Anyway, let's not stand here talking. Do you want a cup of tea?" Although she did for some perverse reason she said no. Perhaps she knew that she was due any time now to start talking and thinking about her visit to Knutsford. She could not imagine why it should be with John Moseby.

Gerda phoned. She was worried about Peter. Had Ruth said something to him.

"Like what?"

"I don't know. He'd been in a depression ever since he saw you."

"He often gets moods."

"Yes, but why?"

"I don't know. Ask him."

"I have."

"And?"

"He won't tell me."

"Well that sounds clean-cut enough."

"Ruth, what did you say to him?"

She thought. Nothing. Trivia. Hardly even mentioned Gerda.

"Nothing."

"You didn't tell him about me?" Ruth felt a flush of guilt but she choked it down. After all Cuffee had known for some time. If his depression stemmed from her return it couldn't be that. But thinking of Gerda being pregnant brought Merle Curvis to mind. In a sort of appeasement she said.

"Well I told him about someone he used to know who died. A girl he was at school with. Maybe that's depressed him. She killed herself." For some obscure reason of tact she said nothing about her having been pregnant. Gerda seemed somehow reassured by this. She sounded quite friendly as she hung up.

There was a clear winy tang to the mornings. The leaves were coming down. Her tree seemed intact but all around other older trees let fall their foliage. Ruth could see her visit to Knutsford recede, shrink into historic perspective. She was glad she had gone and she was glad she was back. The whole event seemed compact now, neater. Only the odd excresence scratched the mind. That caterpillar, groping upward. Robert Eldman's voice in his strange little song. The sudden claustrophobia of Mr. Cuffee's intimacy.

But these too in time would be smoothed down. The quality which caused them to disturb her would leak away. They would be pasted flat into the album of her memory. She comforted herself with this yet later in the day caught herself mindlessly singing the evocative images over and over. For some reason this lapse angered her.

She found Mr. Cuffee's notebook without too much trouble. It was in a drawer along with brushes and some palette knives. It had a soft cover and the pages were dog-eared. The writing was neat and stretched between the lines without touching them. Cuffee and Gerda were in the front room and she felt somehow as though she oughtn't be doing this. There was a large number of entries. Each one was dated. She flicked through the pages until one caught her attention. It was about a girl called Bibette or Bibby. There was quite a lot about her. She seemed to have been a singer and had been Mr. Cuffee's mistress. She read quickly, skipping bits. There were a great many entries about the desert and about the light and a lot about the Arabs and what he thought of them. There was also a lot of bits about the other officers. She was reading and flipping over quickly when she heard Cuffee coming along the passage. For a moment she thought of asking him if she could borrow it then all at once panicked. She threw the notebook back into the drawer and turned to face him, concealing her prying behind her back.

"You going to work?"

"Later." He crossed quickly and started looking through a desk. Ruth watched him for a moment, sliding the drawer shut.

"You all right?" Cuffee looked round.

"Yes, why?" Ruth shrugged elaborately.

"Just thought you were a bit strange this weather," which wasn't something she had thought at all but just said it for something to say.

"You women sicken me," he said and left, abruptly.

John Moseby came around just about tea time, before Harry got back. He sat in the kitchen watching her peel potatoes. Stolleman was through in the other room, she could hear his high off-pitch singing. Moseby seemed quite content to sit and say nothing. After a time it grew slightly irksome.

"Have you decided what you're going to do?"

"What, about my life?"

"About your life, and your wife's life?" It was an unnecessarily cruel retort but Moseby gave her no chance to apologize.

"Well I'd like to have settled some things before I decided what I'm going to do about Edna."

"Like what?"

"The problem between my wife and me is that the life we led was quite satisfactory for her, I mean it made sense to her, it was a reasonable mode of existence. . . ."

"But it wasn't to you." He paused as though reflecting.

"No. It wasn't. If I knew some other mode of life then I might have some idea of what was wrong with the one Edna and I had."

"Haven't you had another mode of existence since you've been down here?"

"Yes, but it's one which flatters the previous more than somewhat. I mean, three months of bed-sitters and I'd almost fancy living with Mrs. Davidson."

"Is that your in-law?"

"My outlaw. No, It's not a reasonable comparison."

"What do you want then?" Moseby looked at her, and she noticed for the first time how alert the face was, the eyes quick with thought.

"To find out who I am. Don't we all?"

"Do we?" she asked, refusing to be enrolled so simply. Moseby held her gaze until she looked to the potatoes.

"Perhaps not," he said. "Upon reflection perhaps you are right."

Stolleman came in wearing a string vest. "Perhaps who's right?" he asked going out on to the verandah for a shirt.

"John was just saying we all want to find out who we are." Stolleman came in holding the shirt against his cheek to see if it was dry.

"Do we?" he asked.

"Perhaps not," Moseby said, and smiled. It made her rather like him, the ability to mock himself.

There was a letter from her mother which she put in her pocket on the way out to the launderette. She had let the washing mount up and the plastic bag was heavy and kept stretching and tearing in her fingers. When she got there all the machines were full but one of the large load ones at the top was on its third rinse cycle. She stood by it until it stopped. No one came forward to take the clothes out. She asked whose it was but they weren't in the launderette. After a moment Ruth unloaded them into one of the baskets. She was just taking the last things out when a coloured woman in slacks, the kind that go under the instep, came up.

"What do you think you are doing?" she asked in a deep resonant voice that could be heard throughout the launderette.

"Oh I was just taking your things out."

"I can see that. You have no right to."

"I just wanted the machine."

"The machine has not been stopped for very long. I use this machine regularly. I know exactly how long my wash takes."

Despite herself Ruth was surprised that a coloured woman could talk so arrogantly to her. It made her resent the situation bitterly, yet with a certain uneasiness because of the woman's colour.

"I'm sorry. I didn't do your wash any harm."

"I don't think you quite appreciate the point," she said and with a quick glance into the machine to see that there was nothing left the woman picked up her basket and went off.

Feeling somewhat flattened Ruth loaded up and inserted her coins. She sat looking into the machine, the close soapy warmth of the launderette closing around her. It was only after some time that she remembered the letter and discontinued the fantasies in which she was subtly insulting the coloured woman without ever quite mentioning that she was black. Her mother's fine wavy hand straggled across the envelope. As she opened it it crossed her mind that it felt rather bulky.

Dear Ruth,

It is very difficult for me to write this letter to you and I am not at all sure it is a good thing that I should. I have decided however to write it and then decide later whether or not to send it after I have re-read it. So in fact you may not ever read this, in which case, well, in which case there won't be anything to say. Silly when you think of it like that.

All the time you were with us at the weekend I had the strongest desire to talk to you about something which even now seems a terrible thing, something which all my instincts tell me to conceal and hide. But seeing you at the weekend made me think again and after having thought I decided to write this letter and try to explain.

Thinking about how to say it I felt that it would almost need for me to tell you the story of my whole life, that only such a way would explain properly what happened and why. However you will be relieved to know that will not be necessary!! It will probably suffice if I tell you about during the war. Everything since the war has been very much like it is now. Before the war was unreal, like a dream. During the war was when it all happened so if I tell you about then you may understand, although I doubt if I could ever really tell you what those six years were like.

I was just twenty-two when the war started and I was still only a girl, married and with a child but younger than you are now and when the war ended I was twenty-eight and my life was over and it had never really begun. I know that plenty of women had to wait and bring up children with their husbands away from them and that they did it with little complaint. I admired them enormously, but I'm afraid one of the things I have always been cowardly about is being on my own.

When Peter went away to the Army I could only think of his leaves and to write to him every day. I was, although you may not have got this impression from me, very much in love with him and frightened to be without him. He did come home on leave as often as he could but it still wasn't very frequently. Peter, your brother, was a very difficult baby. He was very strong-willed and cried a lot of the time, especially at night and I got terribly tired and irritable and sometimes when I couldn't stop him crying I'd cry myself and we'd be there the both of us in that horrid pokey flat in Urmston, weeping and shrieking. I used to want to kill him, or myself.

Robert Eldman didn't get into any of the services, he had a wound from the Spanish War and they wouldn't take him. He had a job in the Ministry of Supply in Manchester and he was one of the only people I saw that I liked.

The only excuse I can make for being unfaithful to Peter is that I was so lonely. Robert never tried to talk me into it, he's not that type, it just got that I couldn't let him go away at night I was so lonely. For a long time he just stayed the night and nothing happened, but eventually it did although I cannot now really think why. It just did. I was terribly guilty and ashamed but once it had started it couldn't stop, it was the only thing that kept me going. Not love, because I didn't love Robert and it wasn't for the sexual part of it which never mattered so very much but so that he would be there in the morning or if I had to get up in the middle of the night with the baby crying.

I have told you all this and I am no nearer telling you what I started out to. In the end I suppose it has to be said straight out. Robert is your father. He does not know and Peter does not know. I had never intended that it should be otherwise but after you left on Sunday to go to the station Robert was talking to me and he said how he had always felt very close to you and liked you and he told me how you had sung that silly song he made up about the melancholy flower and it was a song he used to sing to Peter to try and get him to go to sleep and it made me remember the times I had gone off to sleep hearing Robert shaking the pram and singing that song and how grateful I had been. Sometimes I think gratitude is the decentest emotion there is. Well when he told me about that and he said something about you trying to find yourself I wondered if perhaps I had not done wrong in keeping this knowledge from you all these years. The more I thought about it the less convinced I became. So I started this letter, without committing myself to sending it.

When I found I was pregnant I left Peter with a woman who lived nearby. I told her my husband was embarking for overseas, and I went down and stayed in London in a hotel in Bayswater, the Elgin Court Hotel it was called. The funny, or unfunny, thing was that almost immediately afterwards he did get posted overseas. I felt all terrible about everything, I stopped seeing Robert, I told him I was too guilty, which I was, and he of course agreed, as he always did. We used to meet occasionally to go for walks in the park but he never came back to the house. Predictably enough I had a terrible time with you, being dreadfully sick and having awful indigestion. I just longed for a bomb to come down through the ceiling and blow me away. When your time had come I went down to Bideford. Peter stayed with the neighbour and I had about a week down there before they took me into hospital. It was nice and remote and I enjoyed being away from Urmston and Peter even though I was like a barrage balloon.

You were a very good child and although I was sure everybody must know from looking at you that you weren't Peter's I began to forget about it all and then Robert went away to work in London and the weeks and months went on and apart from the dreadful monotony of it, things were almost normal. I used to wonder that Robert never suspected but it's not so surprising really.

Then the war was over and Peter came home and after a while he got this job in Knutsford and we moved there. Everything was all right, Peter had changed a lot of course, but that was the war and nothing to do with you. I never ever tried to pretend to myself that you were his daughter but I suppose a lot of the time I must just have assumed it in a way. It doesn't mean very much to say he wasn't close to you for as I am sure you remember he wasn't very close to Peter either.

Then of all things to happen Robert applied for a job at the same school and Peter helped him get it and some-how there was nothing could prevent it happening that he came to visit us quite regularly. It was a long time afterwards that things started up again between us and then it was because, one day when we were talking, he just began to cry. He said his life was so empty, he would never marry now and he would never have children and he would have loved to have. I almost told him about you then but I didn't, I was too selfish or too frightened, probably both, so I just went to bed with him which was small enough consolation for the loss of a daughter.

I should really try to tell you how good a person Robert is but I don't really suppose he is all that good. He is weak, like I am and like Peter is, and he has his good qualities too. He is not a bad person, of that I'm sure. In a strange way I never got to know him well.

I wish there had been some way in which I might have told you this without it being a terrible shock to you. Perhaps you will be angry that I have told you at all. I did it because I think you are a stronger, better person than I am, or than Robert or Peter is, and that you want to be yourself and live your own life. If I was such a person I feel that I would want to know. If I am wrong please try to forgive me.

With love, your Mother

The machine was still on its wash cycle. Behind the sudsy eye, tumbling and churning, the clothes mimicked her turmoil, the feelings swilling helplessly about, unable to focus long enough to achieve the definition of emotion. She was a little girl again, helpless against the inflictions of the world, at the mercy of uncontrollable powers. Then, at the point where she was ready to break, to be overwhelmed by these enormous, destructive revelations, something in her clenched, tightened, split with a high cracking noise that was almost a pain and everything began to spin round very very fast blurring together then slowly clarifying, becoming empty with an intense lucid emptiness in the midst of which she knew everything and felt nothing, with an exhilaration akin to nausea. She got up and left the machine hurtling through its first rinse cycle.

She woke in the middle of the night and couldn't find her arm. It lay somewhere on the pillow beside her head but her fingers couldn't detect it and her arm couldn't detect the fingers. At last she traced it from her shoulder, a loose putty limb, flopping uselessly as she shook it up and down to restore the circulation. She could hear a baby crying. Her dead arm lolled in her lap as she sat up. Where was she? Where was she? Whose baby was that dead in her lap? She shook it frenziedly and it stopped crying. Pains and needs crept down her mind. Where am I? In the middle of the dark night. Oh Mother, whose baby was that? She lay down with her newborn arm and went to sleep.

Peter sat in the rocker. Ruth ironed a shirt of Harry's, even after the launderette it still smelled a little of work. He was waiting to be asked. She was waiting to be told. For the first time in her entire life she saw him as another, different human being, without the uncertainty of knowing where he commenced and she ended. She leaned firmly on the iron, smoothing the material down into a dull glaze.

"I'm going away," he said.

"When?"

"In a day or two."

"For good?"

"Well, I don't know when I'll be back."

"Have you told Gerda?"

"Not yet."

"Worried about telling her?" He tried to look as though that were a ridiculous idea but didn't appear too convincing.

"What did she say when you told her you knew she was pregnant?"

"I didn't tell her."

"Where are you going?"

"Germany. Then Spain."

"Well, don't forget to write." He seemed puzzled.

"Are you angry with me?" She folded Harry's shirt, feeling obscurely hateful, hateful of him and of Harry and of herself.

"No. Why should I be?"

"I don't know. I thought you might blame me."

"What, for leaving Gerda? Why should I?"

"Oh I don't know, because she's a woman and so are you."

"So is this Uta, or have I been misinformed?"

"Well in a way. She won't use any of the old ruses."

"You mean like getting pregnant."

"Not necessarily." Something touched her mind, lightly, a faintest prompting.

"Why have you decided to go now, so abruptly?"

"It would always have been abrupt."

"Yes, but why now? Has it something to do with Merle Curvis?"

"Why don't you fuck off," and he got up and went out

without looking at her. Ruth stood by the ironing board for a very long time, comfortable almost, in her cold despond.

She knew that she should talk to someone about it but could not think to whom. She had grown almost to hate Harry, with his large bumbling openness. He was from another planet almost, his niceness irritated terribly. And at her little spats his face would assume a hurt, rebuked expression which exasperated her more than anything else.

In many ways Stolleman seemed the most probable person, except that his detachment bordered almost on insult. It would be like pouring out one's troubles to somebody met on a tube. She had tried to sort it out in her head, alone, but it was curiously easy and deeply unsatisfying to reduce her mother's confession to a schematic. So Mr. Cuffee is not my father. But I never felt close to him anyway. So I have exchanged one stranger for another. So Peter is my half-brother which makes us no less close because our closeness was in growing up together. So nothing really has altered. But that was it. That was what finally choked her. That in her twenty-third year she could find out that her lifelong father was not and nothing really had altered. How could that be? In her letter to her mother she had said almost nothing, only that she was glad she knew and would take some time to absorb it, in the meantime for her not to worry.

But there was no way in which she could bring it to make sense. It remained an enormous, trivial fact and with its triviality went an awareness of the world as being an absurd and meaningless place. All at once the nature of home was delineated in the exquisite lines of deprivation. She did not belong to those two ill-assorted people she had always assumed as parents. She had passed her real father by a thousand times and never even sensed the faintest vibration of kinship. Home was what she had never known, home was a truth of which she had only heard a fraudulent version. Home was nowhere.

She knew Gerda would call and wasn't looking forward to it. When she did her appearance rather frightened Ruth. There was about the eyes, despite care in the makeup, a certain nakedness, a desperation which caused her not to meet their gaze.

"You know he's going?" Gerda said, once she was seated. It was a bright day and the coffee smelled good and Gerda was trying to keep her voice crisp.

"Yes," Ruth said.

"You did tell him, didn't you? About me getting pregnant." Ruth stilled her panic by the cold act of will she found so instinctive now.

"I did, some time ago." Gerda nodded and sipped her coffee. Ruth watched the falling leaves, feeling remote from all that this woman was about to say.

"It wasn't that which made up his mind. It was something else. I don't think he knows quite what himself. He's going to see this girl in Germany. You don't know her, what she's like?" No, except that she's not like you, you poor cow, not vulnerable and frightened and trying to keep calm when you want to fall down on your knees and say "Don't, please God, don't go." She's nothing whatever like you Gerda with the great buttery pats of your breasts and the overwhelming need to cling. Just take a good long look and imagine the opposite of everything you see. That's your rival, if rival you must have, if you need something more than that men and women want different things.

"No," Ruth said, "I know nothing about her," in a tone fit to end any conversation. But it didn't end this one, not by about two hours.

Harry seemed to be the last to accept the fact that Cuffee was going.

"I thought he was quite happy," he said, looking puzzled.

"It wouldn't need to be unhappiness that made him go."

"Well, I mean, he's painting and everything."

"And everything?"

"You know. He's got what he needs."

"That's a pretty feeble remark. He's got nothing that he wants. Painting for Peter is just a form of distraction. Keeps his mind off his real preoccupation."

"What's that?" And to her surprise, but only her faint surprise, she knew.

"Being his father's son."

"I don't understand."

"Say you hated your father and yet thought you were a lot like him. Would that bother you?"

"I suppose it would."

"Well it bothers our Peter all right." Gibbon thought about that for a bit.

"He'd be better off being like John."

"Why?"

"Well being adopted, he could invent his own parents."

"I didn't know he was adopted."

"I told you before, I'm sure I did," but Ruth was certain he hadn't, for it didn't seem feasible that such a fact would not have stuck. It made her think afresh of him, that taut little face, brooding on its origins. They were all of them in the same boat it seemed, except perhaps Harry, dear land-lubbery Harry.

With Cuffee's departure so imminent Ruth forced herself to think about telling him of her mother's letter and the realignment of relations it mooted. But she could see Peter, absorbing the information impassively, implying "so what" and making only token comment. Then he would be gone and she wouldn't have the chance to pry his true reaction out. And if he was, as it seemed she assumed, fleeing from the fetters of heredity it would only emphasize his condition the more to know that his nearest kin did not share his plight. These reasons recommended her silence and were of themselves honourable. But behind them lurked other reasons, and these, being less reputable, seemed to Ruth more likely to be the stronger ones. It was becoming increasingly difficult to credit oneself with decent attributes. The mind constantly sought the canker in the rose. So it was that she regarded the fact that in the last week she had come, quite clearly, to hate him. It was of course a feeling that left room for fondness, concern and love, but it was nevertheless hate. All the irritations, the reservations, the frustrations and resentments were canalized and she could, coldly and venomously, dislike her brother. Her half-brother.

This new dimension came from her sense of being female. She had joined the lists, taken sides in the great civil war of the sexes. At some point in the last months, and culminating in her visit to Knutsford, she had become enfranchised. Gerda had begun it. Her dislike of Gerda was less personal than a resentment at the particular sort of female position she was placing herself in. And Meriel Rose had heightened her awareness of being a woman although she was not an especially fulfilled or happy one. But it was Knutsford and Merle Curvis and the rugby friends of Colin Farley and her mother, that had brought the matter to its articulation. Before she was Peter's sister or anybody's child or Harry's mistress she was a woman, female. That was the exactest definition of her existence and the one with which she would most recurringly have to deal.

In relation to this commitment there was a way now in which she could focus Cuffee quite objectively, as a man, a male being. As such she disliked him, disliked his parody of masculinity, his dogmatism and brutishness. In a way he complemented Gerda and she fostered him. There is, Ruth thought, inherent in a supine will, the temptation of dominance. She could find it in herself in relation to Harry and perhaps if this Uta were some creature of spirit and egotism then Cuffee's quest of her was no mere romantic beckoner. It might well be that he knew that to escape himself as mirrored in his father he needed more from a woman than a slavish conformity. His journey might thus be a meaningful one, a thought which further bolstered her conviction that she should say nothing about her knowledge.

Yet even further back lay a single coiled question, which if answered aright would have let her rest easy about this decision. Had it, by any remote or remarkable chance, been Peter Cuffee who had deserted Merle Curvis, left her to distend and warp, to find her clothes unable to fasten and the taste of bile under her tongue in the mornings, left her to exit down the waste pipe, to be found and photographed and cut open and analyzed and sewn back and buried and left to rot in the autumn rains? If it were he then she hated him finally and for good. What was it Merle had said that day, long ago in Coleman's, "You always need someone to help you get out." Ruth could only hope that the someone she had needed hadn't been Cuffee. She could not be certain whether the unlikelihood of ever knowing pleased her or not.

The night before Cuffee left he came over for a meal. Gerda was to have come with him in a pantomime of normality but at the last moment she rebelled and caused a scene. Cuffee came alone and in a bad mood, obviously intent on getting drunk from the word go. Stolleman and John Moseby were there and Harry had bought a bottle of whisky. The four men drank it while Ruth was in the kitchen preparing the meal. They had wine with the spaghetti and then Stolleman went for another bottle of whisky. Everybody, excluding herself, was quite drunk. She took a certain pleasure from her detachment, sitting listening to them bandy back and forth.

Cuffee was in a hectoring mood and he had, almost single-handed, hoisted an argument about the importance of choice, of proper existential choice, as the only valid mode of self-expression. Harry listened in his usual disciplined silence, Stolleman made occasional deflationary remarks but it was primarily between Moseby and Cuffee that the dissension existed.

"Choice is fine but to mean anything it must be a choice of something, a real choice. What I want to know is what do you choose, how do you decide what choice to make?"

"You choose what you want. That's your yardstick."

"But the problem is knowing what you want, and a lot of the things you want are costly. You have to pay for what you get and often it's too much. So how does your choice work then?"

"You choose and you take the consequences."

"Take the consequences, the pain, of yourself and others, the fragmentation, the guilt. What if you can't?"

"Then you can't choose and then you're fucked."

"How do you avoid getting fucked then?"

"Like I say, make the act of choosing the really important thing, not the quality of the choices."

"M'mm, well it sounds a bit un-nourishing to me, a sequence of sterile choices made to demonstrate the biceps of your will."

"What's your solution then?"

"Don't have a solution. Try and make order."

"How?"

"Don't know. Find what is essential. Adhere to it, respect it."

"Believe in God you mean?"

"Well, if you're lucky, yes. Otherwise believe in something else. Where you come from, the seasons, natural beauty, whatever."

"Choice, can't you believe in choice?"

"Yes, yes I suppose you could make the act of choosing the reason for being alive, the proof even. I choose therefore I am. But that's only if you have some doubts as to whether you exist or not. That's never been one of my problems. I am, therefore I choose, although it's not very exalted makes me a lot happier. Happiest of all though is the simplest. I am therefore I am."

"Is that how you think?" Moseby poured himself some whisky, smiled ruefully at its pungency.

"Well, I must confess I convince myself of my existence on a rather less cerebral plane, I feel things, I want, I get hungry."

"What's your problem then?" Moseby looked up at him, at his sat-back, sour arrogance.

"My problem is that I have left my wife and my daughter whom I love because I can't make them happy and myself happy at the same time." The density of this was too much for the flimsy fabric of the argument. It fell through with a deafening hush. Everybody was sobered momentarily, except Ruth who found this little nugget of the genuine curiously intoxicating among the ersatz of the evening's talk.

Harry stayed off work in the morning to accompany Cuffee to Dover. He got out his sleeping-bag and rolled it up.

"You expecting to be out overnight?" Ruth asked.

"No, I'm giving it to Peter." Ruth remembered a long time

ago when before another of Peter's journeys she had slept in that bag. She touched its softness with her palm. A long time ago.

"Is the squire to accompany the knight on the first stage of his quest?"

"Something like that," folding the bag into its container.

"Wish you were going?" Gibbon looked up.

"No, do you?"

"What, wish I was going or you were?" deliberately misunderstanding. Gibbon knew he was being baited. He held her eyes a moment, then went on with his task.

"You've changed about him, Peter."

"Have I?"

"Yes. Why is that?"

"I don't know. I'm not sure that I have."

"I am."

"Big kind of positive guy," and walked away from him to the window as she said it. Her tree. It took her rather by surprise to see how much it had changed. The glossy spear-shaped leaves had almost all gone, the smooth grey bark seemed rougher, darker. Where the leaves had come away were little unhealed-looking indentations. The bareness offended her, she turned from it, finding her lower lip bitten between her teeth.

"Harry."

"Yes?"

"Has Peter ever spoken to you about someone called Merle Curvis, not necessarily recently, on your last trip, did he ever mention that name?"

"Merle Curvis? No. Doesn't mean anything. I might have forgotten it but I don't think so. Why?"

"Nothing, just wondered. Don't tell him I asked you."

"All right."

He came about ten o'clock carrying a small duffle bag. Ruth wanted to be able to say something meaningful but the secret she kept from him sat, toad-like, on the spring of her affections.

"Have you got money?" she asked.

"Gerda said she could sell some paintings, she gave me some."

Despite her wish not to quarrel with him she was angered, "And you took it?"

"I took it."

"Didn't it seem a bit sick, taking her money in order to leave her?" Cuffee hated her no less than she hated him at that moment, or so it seemed from the look he gave her.

"Where there is a wall someone has to go to it." The callowness of the remark made her want to hit him.

"God, but you're a right little *Reader's Digest* cynic," she said. Cuffee looked at her, face long and cold. Then he smiled and was suddenly near laughter.

"Coming out of the tunnel. Been given the kiss of life have you my little sleeping sister. It's different out here but you'll like it," and he kissed her forehead and put his lips to her ear. "Took you fucking long enough," he said.

Not long after they had gone John Moseby phoned.

"Harry's gone with Peter to Dover."

"Oh. It was just that I need a job rather badly. Rent and all that class of machine. I wanted to know where Harry was working. I could have gone up to see him."

"Do you really want to work as a labourer?"

"No, but I don't have a lot of pick, as the midget nanny said."

"Maybe I could get you a job."

"Where?"

"Friend of mine has a car saleroom. Do you know anything about cars?"

"Everything."

"No really."

"Well I can drive and I can tell the makes apart."

"Look, I'll go and see him, can't promise but if you give me a call tonight I'll let you know how I get on."

"Thanks. When will Harry be back."

"Well, he's hiking to Dover and up again. Tonight some time."

"You upset about Peter going away?"

"Not really. Are you?" Moseby laughed and Ruth felt a little twinge of disloyalty.

"I don't think Peter and I are compatible."

"So I noticed last night."

"Yes, I'm sorry about that, it was all a bit puerile."

"I don't know that it was, you were both a bit drunk though, but I thought your disagreement was reasonable enough."

"Well he can choose and choose and choose again because his feelings are always subordinate to his mind, he doesn't get into the sort of situation where his feelings are going one way and his mind the other. Mind you, that's good. I suppose I'm envious, really." She suddenly had a vivid awareness of his face, his mouth.

"You're guilty about choosing, aren't you?"

"Very. All choices are made for the self, no matter how you twist away from it."

"Is that so bad?"

"If you are as sick of yourself as I am it's not so good." There was silence for a moment.

"You still there?" although she knew he was.

"Yes, that was all very deep end talk. I'm sorry. I'll call you tonight, and thanks," and he put the phone down.

When she phoned Terry up he invited her to lunch. He came over and picked her up and they drove over to Highgate. It was a close, still day, heavy with diffuse sunlight, buttery among the privets, scarcely casting shadows but seeping everywhere, moist old gold light. Terry brought up the subject of Cuffee and said he was glad he had left as obviously it could have come to nothing with Gerda and she had behaved rather foolishly.

"Well she is in love with him."

"Oh it's n-not that, n-not the love. B-but this b-business about having a child. Damn silly."

"It's not such a weird thing for a woman to want."

"Can't have any. D-damn well knows it too."

"What do you mean, Gerda can't have children?"

"Oughtn't really to say but I know you'll be discreet. Gerda had, you know, the operation thing, oh five years ago. Got herself into a bit of trouble. Anyway something, I don't know, to do with tubes or something, infection, long shot of it is she can't. Not without another operation."

"Then why did she say, I mean she let me believe, and acted outraged that I might have told him. Why?"

"That's what I mean, damn silly business."

Ruth couldn't begin to fathom Gerda's reasons and so gave up. Everything but everything was getting too complicated. Over lunch Terry produced some photographs taken during the war, mainly of himself and other airmen in uniform. He hadn't changed much since then, darker perhaps, younger of course, but still Terry of the wan smile, the slightly remote gaze.

"That's me with Eddie Cobbs. Got shot down just after that was taken. I saw him go down, dropped right in front of my nose, like a stone. Damn good flyer he was. Bloody nice fellow." And there was one of Terry standing beside an aeroplane crashed in a field.

"Was that your plane?"

"Yes. Put her down in a field I did. I was on photo recce then, came back from Holland at about a hundred feet all the way. Thought I was being damn smart. Couldn't get the bloody undercarriage down when the tank dried up. Put her down in that field. Bloody luck. Oh, and that's my little French girl." A slender dark child in a short smock, holding a bunch of flowers in one arm and Terry's hand with hers. Terry looked quite different from the other photos. He was in shirt sleeves and was smiling happily.

"That's a nice one."

"Yes. That was a lovely day. Wonder where she is now."

"It's a bit sad when you think of it."

"Yes. I don't think I ever got over those days." Ruth remembered something that Mr. Cuffee had said while driving her to the station. "A lot of people were happy during the war. It was their most sympathetic climate." She flicked on through the snaps, thinking of Terry, still bound to his past, to those days of speed and purpose and comradeship.

"That's Gerda." Ruth had to look again to detect a resemblance. A scrawny, pudgy-faced girl with the dreadful frizzedout hair of the times, the long skirt, the heavy shoes, awkwardly posed in front of a nissen hut. Ruth felt guilty at having seen this. She bunched the photographs together and asked some question that took the subject away from the war and the past. She was aware of sympathy for Gerda welling up in her and had no wish to indulge the emotion at that moment.

Terry agreed to give Moseby a job, washing down the cars. Ruth, somewhat doubtful, said that would suit him perfectly. She also had to accept an invitation to go for a trip to Tring where a friend of Terry's had an antique shop. Ruth reflected that it had been a hard-bought favour and hoped Moseby wouldn't throw up his hands at the idea of being a car shampoo-er.

It turned out he was quite pleased.

"Well, I was washing dishes before. I mean cars must be a step up. Be elephants or buses next." Stolleman was in for a time but had to meet someone. They were all sitting in the kitchen.

"You know, girls today are remarkable. I've seen this child in her gymslip and school blouse, you'd never believe it was the same creature I picked up in a café."

"What age?" Ruth asked.

"Fourteen, but no jury would convict. Body like glass. Lives on pills and rum babas. Been going to bed nearly two years. Pregnant once already, brought herself on by posting two hours a day on Hampstead Heath. In two years she'll be bored with sex for the rest of her life. In about a week she'll be bored with me."

"What do you get out of it?" Moseby asked. Stolleman looked at him as though he had spoken in a foreign language.

"What do I get out of it? An experience. A singular, sealed in, foil wrapped experience. That's how an old man like me wants them. Smaller and more concentrated and shorter. It's like being with a wild animal, a randy gazelle."

"Don't you want to get to know her? Doesn't that come into it?" Stolleman smiled and tugged his cuffs out of his sleeves.

"That's for the young at heart all that trying to figure out what's going on behind the eyes. With my little Jewish pearl I know what's going on. Nothing."

"Sounds a bit pointless," Ruth said, feeling rather stuffy. Stolleman grinned.

"Don't blame me when your head caves in," and went.

"There goes a happy man," Moseby said.

"Michael has it all worked out. But then he's not really like us in the first place."

"Us?"

"Well, our, I don't know, our kind of people."

"Why, what are our kind of people like?" She wasn't sure if he was teasing her but as his face was earnest she went on.

"I'm not sure. They don't trust themselves, I think that's what it is." Moseby made a pursing grimace.

"That doesn't cover Harry, for one."

"No," she admitted.

"I don't know either. There is something, I suppose each generation has some distinguishing feature. But I'm sure ours isn't the same as Stolleman's little dolly. It takes me all my time to pinpont my own personal identity without attempting to describe that of my age."

Ruth felt as though she had been lectured for her presumption. She sat quiet a moment as though she were considering what he had said. After a reasonable time had elapsed she said,

"Do you know anything about your real parents?" He looked at her and blinked.

"No. Nothing."

"Is there nothing you could do to find out?" Again that facial pucker, as though belittling what he was about to say.

"Yes. Go to Edinburgh, look in the National Register under my date of birth, see how many male children were born in Johnstone that day whose parents weren't married. Then see where I can go from there."

"Why haven't you?"

"Fear. Fear of what I'll discover."

"What do you want to discover?"

"It's not so much that. I want to get to the stage where I am prepared for anything. I want to be, to some extent, past caring."

"That sounds, well it doesn't sound right."

"No, I admit it doesn't. But the alternative is to go looking for one's identity in strangers. I suppose it's the egotism of the orphan, I want to find out who I am from me. So when I go I don't want to be on some romantic search, only a fact-finding mission."

"You think Peter has gone on a romance, don't you?"

"It's all right for him, he's a romantic, the romantic gesture becomes him. It wouldn't suit me at all." She wanted to tell him then, to exchange confidences on their common bond when it crossed her mind that to some extent it was a bond which included the others, Peter and Harry both.

"Maybe that's what we have, people like us, we don't really know who our parents are, even the ones that do."

"Could be," Moseby said, "you might very well have a point there," making her feel she had been pretentious but without laughing at her. She liked John Moseby then.

Harry got back about nine o'clock. Moseby had left early in order to do some washing. She had wanted him to stay but said nothing. For the time she was on her own she thought quite a lot about him, and his wife and what their life must have been like. Harry was tired and rather depressed. He didn't vouchsafe any information, which was uncharacteristic and rather annoying.

"Did he get off then?"

"Yes."

"Was he all right?" Gibbon shrugged.

"I don't know." She felt sorry for him, somehow he seemed ill-equipped, a fruit eater among the carnivores. She sat beside him on the bed.

"John was over. John Moseby." Gibbon recalled him, seemingly with an effort.

"John. Yes, he's not in the best of nick, John."

"He seemed all right tonight."

"Yes. Well I don't know when we'll see Peter again. What was it he said, 'all problems are problems of geography.'"

"Yes, that sounds a bit like him."

"Why don't you like him any more, you used to love him?" accusingly the broad open face puzzled and hurt. Love, wielded like a weapon.

"That's your answer, Harry, I suppose. I used to love him, now I don't."

"Is it because of this thing you believe about the girl in Manchester?"

"No, not really. No it isn't."

"Because it wasn't him."

"How do you know?"

"I asked him. I asked him to tell me the truth. I said if he told me I wouldn't tell you. He told me it had nothing to do with him. I believe him." And he wanted that she should believe him also.

"I never really thought it was Peter. It was just something I got into my head." Harry put his arms around her waist and his face against her breasts. She kissed the back of his neck.

"You used to love him," he repeated. "I hate to think of it passing, coming to an end. Does it have to, is that what happens?" She clapped his back, as one would a child. Dear Harry with his childlike questions. Knowing no childlike answers she ignored his asking and continued to clap, gently, closing her eyes.

She didn't know who went off first but when she woke again Harry was certainly asleep, snoring into the pillow. There was a wash of a moon in the room. She stole silently to the window to observe the source. It hung, into the third quarter, some inches above the trees. Its light made her tree a black black thing, menacing in its bareness. The slender fountain which had played its green spray against her pane now threatened a tattoo of dry sticks. The memory of its roots below in the darkness gripped her thoughts. Things are not as they seem. Behind appearances, below surfaces, the other starker shapes. She was coming to know some of them better now, well enough not to be fooled by façades. Somehow she had always imagined that such awareness brought a sense of security. Looking out on this lunar paraphrase however she felt no such comfort.

It seemed like years since she had been to see Meriel Rose. There had been a phone call and then a little blue note asking her to come round. On the way up the hill she thought on Harry and his yearning that everyone should love everyone else. Where had he inherited his notions about that emotion, that mysterious explosion in the heart, like the spots they detected with their telescopes on the surface of the sun and reckoned to be intense storms of energy. They couldn't explain why they happened. Perhaps it was the sun falling in love with some flinder far star, travelling away from its warmth at terrifying speed in the ever expanding universe they said we were in. Everything moving away from everything else at ever increasing speeds. Cuffee gone and every second going further until he would be but the remotest speck. Like Harry she winced at the prospect of such diminution and looked aloft to dispel the notion. The sun seemed at its heart's ease today, beneficent above the Heath, unblemished by solar emotion.

There was a vase of peonies on the table in the sitting-room. Looking over Meriel's shoulder as she kissed her she saw them, heavy headed mass. There were a few petals on the table-top and even as she looked another joined them. Meriel told her all about the dancing class and how many new pupils she had and how tired it was making her. She did look tired Ruth thought, her eyes had a crumpled dark look and around her mouth there was a certain swollen edge, almost an outline.

"You don't look too well. Why don't you have a holiday?"

"Well, actually I was thinking of that. Only I'd hate to go on my own." Ruth was imagining just how dull it would be for her on her own when, startling in the arrested glory of the flower heads, a petal made an abrupt, soft departure, falling to the table-top as to still brown water, making a faintest sound on impact. The sight produced as corollary an intuition that Meriel Rose was about to ask her to go with her. She watched the vase of peonies, falling apart in the quiet room.

"I was thinking of taking a cottage somewhere, before the winter comes, Cornwall or somewhere like that. Just for a few weeks, just for the rest really, to get away from all those graceless little creatures for a bit." There was a pause in which

Ruth ached with the anticipation of petal fall, until Meriel went on.

"Couldn't you make a bit of time and come as well? It wouldn't do you any harm to get away for a bit either. You wouldn't have to worry about, well, the cost. I mean that wouldn't matter." Ruth made some non-committal reply and let the subject run down. Meriel did not broach it again throughout the urbane afternoon but the vase of peonies, dropping its thoughts like petals, would not let Ruth forget the request and its implications.

John Moseby was there at night and he and Harry talked of their past and of Greenock. It didn't irritate her this time, nor did it seem so strange. Perhaps she understood their preoccupation with home and friends of childhood. They were the co-ordinates by which they plotted themselves, found their location.

"Man my father used to work with," Gibbon said, "called Archie Knowles. Had bad eyesight, wore those very thick glasses, know the thick kind? My father said they were playing cards this day in the close, a Sunday, this is when they were boys, and the polis came along and spotted them. Seems then the cops were more interested in picking up the money than they were in catching the card players, so they would stand at the entrance and call out 'Right you lads, stay where you are,' so of course they'd all get off their marks through the close and across the back greens, all except Archie, he stopped to pick up the winnings and the cards, and the two big slops came running in to nab him so Archie puts the money in his pocket and away he goes and so he can run faster he takes his specs off and here he didn't see this clothes rope hanging across the green and it caught him under the chin and up in the air he went and my father says as he was falling he shouted out 'Run on, boys, the bastards have lassooed me.' "

Ruth laughed with them, completely spelled by the little fable and Harry's whole-hearted telling. Moseby chuckled on, thinking and smiling.

"Talking about clothes lines and back greens. When I was a boy I used to think the words in the first verse of the twenty-third psalm were 'in past oor green he leadeth me' and I had this picture in my mind of Jesus ducking under the washing."

"Jesus," Gibbon said, as thought a forgotten friend had been recalled to him. "Remember all those coloured pictures in the Bible of Jesus with the little children and coming into Jerusalem on a white donkey and that one where he's preaching on the mountain."

"Come unto me all ye that labour and are heavy laden and I will give you rest," Moseby intoned, his arms spread in an all-welcoming embrace. "That's the thing I remember best. Some promiser that boy. I mean that's not just 'how's it going?' or 'I'll see what I can do for you.' That's the big time stuff. Come unto me."

"Do you never think it might be true, John, somehow?" Moseby regarded his friend with a quizzical sadness as if touched that such innocence remained at large.

"Harry I'd give what I've got worth giving to believe it, lie or no lie. I'd love to think he was up there on the right hand of God the Father awaiting the second coming or Armageddon or whatever. But it's not on. We're going to have to find our own way home."

"But there has to be a God somewhere, I mean there has to be."

"Well, if there is I feel a bit sorry for him. He gets this plaything of his all stocked up with beasts of the field and fishes and fowls of the air and us and it's all smashing and great only he can't resist the final little touch, he puts in this thing that will make the whole thing go scrunch. I mean he couldn't leave well alone, it's in the book, Genesis, near the beginning 'for God doth know that in the day ye eat thereof your eyes shall be opened and ye shall know good and evil as gods.' And now he's sitting there looking at it, the great big shambles of it and wondering what he did wrong."

"But he just gave us free will, that's all." Harry's naïve insistence seemed to harden Moseby. His banter dropped and he leaned forward.

"It's all a big trick, lad, haven't you seen that? They've taken the holy things, the really holy things about birth and death and love and order and they've made a guilt machine out of it. Christianity is based on guilt. I don't mean anything as simple as the legal guilt of the convicted criminal but the existential guilt of the unworthy. And Christ's much published sacrifice that was supposed to set us free of all this guilt we have, it just found us even more guilty for having caused his suffering." Gibbon obviously had no answer for this. Moseby sank back and looked at his knuckles.

"If you know all this why do you go on being guilty?" Ruth asked him, irritated yet curious for his answer. He said nothing for a moment then unlaced his hands.

"It's what they do to you, how they cripple you and teach you to cripple yourself, the pressures on the infant mind, the thou shalt nots they tie in you until they make it impossible for the light to pass through without getting all fractured, nothing is simple, not love nor hate nor desire nor despair. There was always a contrary feeling you should have, or you had a feeling where no feeling was supposed to grow. They're bloody butchers the lot of them."

"Who, who are these terrible they's that have done all this to poor little John?" She thought he was going to lose his temper for a moment but it passed and he smiled, a baring of bone in his pale face.

"Years since I got that het up. They, who are they? Well I can only give you my they, you'll have to supply your own. Mr. & Mrs. Moseby, a long line of nameless faceless Sunday School teachers and ministers, a dozen or so teachers, almost all the adults I met before I was sixteen, most of the literature I had access to in my early youth and a general atmosphere known as the twilight of sabbatarianism. If you want to get historical I suppose you can blame it all on Martin Luther, you talk about Archie Knowles being short-sighted, Harry, he wasn't half as blind as Martin, the clothes rope he didn't see was a lovely logical one plaited by our friend Jim Calvin, not to mention Knox Knox who's there, consumption; consumption what, consumption not be done about that wee bloke trying to get away across the back green. The bastards have lassooed me is right." They were both silent now and Moseby grinned in near embarrassment.

"Of course," he said, "I could be wrong."

"But you don't think so," Ruth said, not quite managing sarcasm.

"No, I'm afraid I don't," lowering his eyes and his voice so that she realized, unexpectedly, that he was quite completely sincere and that his vision of the world afforded him no comfort, was reluctantly held. She wanted to reach out and touch his hand, tell him it would come all right in the end, whenever that singular event should chance.

The antique shop was in Tring and was owned by a friend of Terry's called Claud. He looked unlike his name, a short squat man with a puckered, young old face wreathed in beard and dull, once fair hair. He greeted Terry with a muscular friendliness, shaking his head and holding the elbow as he did. To Ruth he extended an encircling arm and there held he ignored her while he talked to Terry. He showed them around the shop, pointing to things and denigrating them by passing on immediately. There was, she sensed, a certain contempt in him for the things he sold.

They went upstairs to his living-room. There was scarcely any difference between it and the shop itself in regard to the amount of obviously valuable objects on display. Claud talked on, a catalogue of items interspersed with remarks like "all a deception, beauty, a deceit," and "quite worthless, in terms of what matters, man," the "man" being tagged on to most of his declamations.

He took out a decanter and poured them overly large drinks. Ruth asked if she could have some ginger ale. "That's malt, man. Don't go fucking up malt whisky with ginger ale. Bloody sacrilege."

It made her think on Colin Farley for some reason and the recollection surprised her so that she didn't answer Claud, who satisfied that his point was taken, turned to Terry.

"And how is she, man?"

"Who?"

"Your woman."

"Oh Gerda. She's all right. I'd h-hardly call her my woman though."

"Course she is, bloody course she is. Always will be. No

matter how many men she takes between her legs, always be yours." Terry looked embarrassed at this, glanced at Ruth, drank some of the whisky. "Don't you be discouraged, man. Woman like that's worth waiting for, suffering for. Real, that's what Gerda is, real. She's got her roots in the earth that one. Suffer for her, man, it'll be worth it."

Terry looked as though he were suffering acutely for her at that moment. Ruth, to avoid witnessing it, stood up and turned to the mantelshelf, as though to examine its display. Looking directly at her was a photograph. It caught her attention because it was not in a silver frame, or indeed framed at all. It lay against the wall, convexed and dusty, a snapshot of four people in a garden under some apple trees. Two men, two women, one of the women, the elder, sitting in a wicker chair and stretching out a bandaged ankle, while at her feet a sharp featured man in a high white collar looked into the grass, an amused malicious face, turned away from the camera. The other two were a pair, Ruth saw, though not close, he dark and sullen, big and aloof; the girl smiling, the only one who was, yet with a face made for tears and tragic silences, a small, delicately ravaged face, old and resigned behind its young smile. Who were they, this quartet of strangers, sealed in the swift blink of the camera. She wanted to know and turned impulsively to ask. Claud received the question without stopping his talk to Terry, which was still about Gerda, but he moved to the mantelpiece and picked up the photo. His arm went round Ruth's waist and his fingers pressed up under her breast. He looked intently at the photo as he continued to speak.

"Too big for us, us little men, can't take it, can't accept she belongs to the world, want private rights, trespassers prosecuted, all the old property-owning shibboleths. Can't with Gerda," and his hand, calm, audacious and firm cupped her breast. Ruth twisted free and he let her slip partially away, then looking at her, smiling at her, he crumpled the photograph, throwing it on to the set fire.

"Nobody you would know," he said and freed her, returning to his chair. Ruth sat down and tried not to hear Claud's voice as it lectured on.

After some time he went to collect what they had come for. Terry sat in silence a moment, then cleared his throat.

"B-bit overpowering, eh?"

"He doesn't exactly merge into the background."

"No, n-no he doesn't. Friend of Gerda's. Wartime. He was RAF too, bombers. Flew daylight missions over the Ruhr. Had a lot of trouble since, wife left him, went a bit potty. Gerda looked after him. He says she saved his life."

"She likes her men well assorted does Gerda."

"Oh n-no, there wasn't anything between Gerda and Claud. That's why he respects her so much. No, it wasn't like that."

"Oh, I'm sorry. I didn't mean anything."

"N-no, it's all right. Just I know for a fact." For a fact Ruth thought. She was surprised it meant so much to him but from his bright, insistent tone it obviously did.

Claud came back carrying a glass case with a stuffed bird in it.

"It's a hawk," Ruth said, "who's it for?"

"No, it's a falcon," corrected Claud, "peregrine falcon. Hawks are long-winged birds, get their prey by hovering, stalking it. Falcons have short wings, they stoop on their game. Just about covers us all, eh man?" Ruth could hardly quite see where Terry fitted in but only asked again,

"Who is it for?" to Terry.

"Gerda. Can't see why she wants the thing actually. Hate stuffed things, give me the creeps." But Ruth could see only too clearly the reason for it. How Gerda would have hated Ruth to be here, witnessing her symbolic acquisition. She looked through the glass at it, fierce-eyed atrophy of un-requited love. 'The fawcon has borne my luv away.' True enough. The bright lifeless eyes held hers, a meaningless battle of wills. He was gone, her halved brother, her unholy love, her broken link with childhood and its illusions of certainty. Her life was now to be spent with the others, the strangers who looked out of photographs, pass in the street, live upstairs. There was no comfort to the prospect but, as the falcon made clear, it was a choice made on this side of life and its multiple realities.

When they got back Terry stopped in at the car showrooms

and she saw Moseby, in a white overall too long for him, washing down a red sportscar. She went over to talk to him. Terry came out to run her home but she said she was going to wait for Moseby. All the way back Terry had talked of Claud and his way with women and how knowledgeable he was in his profession and how much he admired Gerda. There was an obsessive tone to the whole subject which disquieted her and she was glad to be able to escape it.

After Moseby stopped work they walked along Finchley Road.

"Let's go in here," Moseby said. "This is where I used to wash dishes. It gives me considerable, if juvenile, satisfaction to leave a dirty cup behind." They sat in, by the window. Ruth had been there once before, a long time ago now it seemed. Must have been on her way to see Terry. Moseby must have worked here then.

"So this is where you worked."

"Yes, the Mount Marty, as Helen used to call it."

"Who was Helen?"

"Oh, an Irish woman who used to work here." They both had tea and Moseby pressed the tea bag against the side of the glass to make it as strong as possible.

"Strange thing happened today, well, strange isn't quite the word," not looking at her as he spoke, stirring his tea. "Woman came into the showroom. Not bad-looking, in her thirties. She had on a black leather jacket and a white sort of plastic skirt, you know the stuff, shiny. And nylons." He looked up at her, frowning with concentration, remembering. "She was standing talking to Terry and I had this urge, desire, to run my finger tips down the jacket, down the skirt, up the stocking, over the double bit at the top and on to her thigh, on the inside. Almost did it. Had to walk away. Suddenly the textures sort of seduced me, the soft slightly granular, dry thing of the leather and then the slippy smooth white skirt, wiping your fingers of all sensation, then the stocking, polished, frictive, and the momentary blandness of the bit at the top and then the flesh, clinging, slightly damp. Almost had to do it, it was a very intense awareness." He looked at her again. "Dear Patience Strong is this satori or sexual insanity?"

Ruth laughed, but behind her laughter was a certain quaver of nervousness. His voice, intent on its description, devoid of the salacious, had quickened in her things that she scarcely recognized, flickerish wants, trembles of response, desire, formless and rank. She made herself talk.

"Yes, well I suppose all these things, leather and P.V.C. and suede too, they're all sort of flesh substitutes, aren't they?" Moseby almost brushed her words aside, so intent was he upon his experience.

"But it wasn't just a desire to touch her leg. I mean it wasn't really sexual, sexual's too specific. It was purely, purely in both senses, a sensual desire. If she'd had on a wool suit it wouldn't have crossed my mind, it was this, this, I don't know the musical term, but it was tonal, or a chord sequence, a tactile chord sequence. I don't know, something like that."

Everything was at an angle, an odd breathless feeling and her eyes felt hot, as though from staring. She lowered her mouth to the cup, drank. She could see Moseby's tea bag inside his glass. It showed an instant, black, amid the brown-blond tea, disappeared. She knew what she felt but would not pull up the string, bring her knowledge up to where it could not subsequently be disguised.

Now, for the first time since coming back from Knutsford, she was really unhappy. It had taken all this time to come together in the one place but now that it had she ached with the misery of it. Out of love and sorts with Harry, Cuffee gone, her relationships at home hopelessly jumbled, sexually attracted to John Moseby, quite without direction she found the days drifting by, filled with leaves and sudden gusts of tearful wind. She was all coming apart, the past was remote, the future not yet formed. She waited in her interim, uncertain of everything.

Stolleman noticed it and asked, in his flippant way what was wrong. Several times she made the conventional parries but once when he found her in the kitchen sitting over a mug of cold tea he was more persistent.

"What's wrong, Ruth. You pregnant or some such? This amused her for some reason.

"God no. No I'm just a bit of a drip this weather."

"I'm going down to the studio, why don't you come, you can clear up for me, make a cup of coffee." Reluctantly she went with him.

The studio was in a back garden behind a large house in Elsworthy Road. Ruth had never been there before. It was high-roofed with part of the roof and all the front glassed and a stove with a long thin chimney in the middle of the floor. There were canvases stretched around three walls and a large table with paints and brushes and jam jars and bottles of turpentine. Stolleman raked the stove, threw in some wood, splashed it with turps and threw a match on. It roared loudly up the chimney. He sat down in front of it and began to feed it coal.

"What's the problem, Harry?"

"Well, not Harry. Me. Harry's a nice person."

"Nice guys finish well back in the race. Harry's niceness is not in question. What's wrong with you and him?"

"I don't love him."

"Did you ever?"

"No, I don't think I ever did."

"Why the problem now then?"

"Oh, I don't know. Peter's gone. I'm all confused about things."

"What things?" He was pushing her and she had the impression he knew.

"John Moseby."

"What about him?"

"I fancy him," which sounded a ridiculous way to put it.

"And you don't fancy Harry."

"It's all a bit strange. I don't really think Harry fancies me. I mean he never seems very interested in bed."

"Maybe he sees you're not interested."

"No. Well maybe. I don't know." Stolleman put a shovelful of coal on and the coal dust crackled briskly in the flames.

"What are you going to do about Moseby?"

"What can I do?"

"Go to bed with him."

"I can't, how can I, I mean, he's Harry's friend."

"That didn't stop you fancying him."

"I couldn't help that. But that doesn't mean I have to do something about it."

"Ruth, it's a bit early in life for the unconsummated passion. You'll have to get it out in the open with Harry anyway. You will go to bed with other men anyway." Ruth had an idea of that distant happening, strangers out of photographs in her bed.

"Surely I should finish with Harry first though. Surely that's the least messy way."

"Child, child, there is no least messy way. There are only varying degrees of cruelty. Your brother, godspeed his feet, has a nice little aphorism which you should bear in mind 'where there is a wall someone has to go to it.' There's a wall here. You don't love Harry. If you don't put him to it, he'll put you to it."

"How do you mean?"

"You don't think Harry will suddenly snap his fingers one morning and say 'of course, Ruth doesn't love me. I'm awa'.' He'll stick it out to the bitter bloody end. And that means he'll make you leave, or hurt him because you're guilty. And I don't have to tell you about guilt."

"No, you don't. Why aren't you guilty, Michael?"

"Me? You've got it upside down. I'm the one people are guilty about. My friends and I are fulfilling a long felt want for the rest of humanity. Why else do you think we got into those comfortable cattle trucks so willingly. We know our place we do."

"I never think of you as Jewish."

"Oh it's been confirmed. Nothing they can do."

"I think I may be Jewish," thinking of it then for the first time.

"You've got the look, course in a sort of way so has the bold Pierre but it's too romantic in him, it's a Celtic thing, the narrow head, the colouring. Pity he won't paint, that boy. In some things he's got the required single-mindedness." Ruth had somehow been expecting him to return to the subject of herself and Harry. She realized now that he wasn't going to. The fire was giving out a lot of heat. She felt almost drowsy.

The song almost sang itself. "Life is but a, life is but a." It comforted her. It made the merest moment of sense, of order, moments threaded on a tune, moulded by words, absurd and exact. A song taught her by her father, while she was but a little childer.

The trees were almost bereft of leaf now, everywhere they piled their yellow and golds, were brushed brown into mounds, filled the air with a kind of music, innumerable descending scales, repeated into an ecstasy of monotony until her thoughts were deafened by this great chorale, these many hued hallelujahs of the fall.

Through a basement window a music more personal, specific of her lot. A girl, straight-backed on a chair, bowing a cello between her knees, its rich movings touching chords within Ruth herself, so that she envied the girl her partner, her music-making friend, together in the low room.

She wandered, distraught by so much melody, so much antithesis, aware of enormities and minutiae, on the brink of laughter, near to tears. Feelings within her burst and exploded, yet muted and obscure, never reaching the light of knowing, an inner chaos out of which the unreasonable emotions spurge and flare. Half thoughts prompted by semi-memories, flickers of feeling provoking uncomprehended images, a turmoil of being, feeding endlessly upon its own inexhaustible resources, that world within a world the thinking human is.

Harry was explaining about overtime.

"I don't like it but if I did about six weeks of it we could go away for a holiday. Go to the sun somewhere."

"Why don't I get a job, be just the same thing as you working overtime?"

"You don't have to get a job. I can get three nights a week and Saturday afternoons and maybe even Sunday. Only take a week or two."

"Yes, but won't a lot of it go on tax?"

"Yes, but when I'm unemployed I get it back again. Or else I get a rebate when I'm married."

"Thinking of getting married? Anybody I know?"

"Don't think so, just a friend of a friend. That was the great thing up the road. Getting married at April for the tax rebate. There's a shop in Westburn Street where they show the wedding photos. Never saw anything like it. Great some of them."

"Do you never want to go back to Greenock?"

"Well, some time. But not just yet."

"But when you settle down, get married, you'll go back?" Gibbon looked slightly discomfited. "What's wrong?" she asked, knowing.

"Just the way you talk about me settling down, getting married, as though it had nothing to do with you." This was the time to tell him, if not all, part, to insert the cruel wedges of words, tap it home. Gibbon looked at her, a child's face, open to hurt. Oh fuck you, Harry Gibbon, and your big Scottish niceness. And thinking that remembering Stolleman's warning.

"It's a long way off, Harry. We don't know what's going to happen to us," loathing herself and her trite, evasive tongue.

"Well, this holiday wouldn't be a long way off. What do you think?" What did she think. God how people beg to be shot close up. What did she think.

"Be fine, only I don't see why I can't get a job. I don't do anything all day as it is."

"You should be pregnant," Harry said, and for an instant Ruth felt panic. If she were then everything would be just that much more out of control. Somehow when Stolleman asked her it had been amusing. But when the suggestion came from its possible implementor it became a sudden dire possibility. With more venom than Harry could have expected she said,

"Like bloody hell I should," which brought to an end that particular conversation.

In a second-hand bookshop she found a small book with a ribbed leather spine. *One Hundred English Chess Problems*. She flicked through it, her eye pleased with the decorative position plates. She thought she might put some of them in frames for the wall, then decided she would send it to Mr. Cuffee. He was bound to do problems. She bought it from an abstracted man in a trench coat and carpet slippers who was reading a book with a magnifying glass.

Harry had started his working late and feeling both at a loose end and yet let out of school early she walked slowly down the hill to Finchley Road and along to Terry's showroom.

Moseby wasn't there. Neith r was Terry. Before he could come back she got Moseby's address from a man in the office and walked along. It was a long, sloping street down to the right from Finchley Road. It had lines of trees and lots of fallen leaves and parked cars. Moseby's house looked somewhat more decrepit than the others. She rang the bell with Moseby on it, and then again. She was turning away and just beginning to savour her disappointment when he came up from the basement area with a plastic bucket in his hand.

"Hello there. To what do I owe, etcetera?"

"Called in at the showroom, thought you might be down with the mumps or something."

"No, no, congenital bone disease laid me low, quite incurable. Coming up?"

"Thanks, love to."

"Up" was to the top, an attic that looked to the back, over some sycamores and a plane tree, down into the leaf-littered garden where a small flameless fire released the thick, liquid smoke of haulm burning.

There was very little in the room of a personal nature. Half a dozen books, a photograph of a child she assumed to be his daughter, a box of typewriting paper but no typewriter. It was dark in the room because of the way the roof sloped and boxed in the window. There was a gas fire and it was lit, glowing with that artificial clay brightness old gas fires have.

"Why did you take the day off? You're not ill are you?"

"No. Got a letter from the BBC, they might, just might, be interested in a play I sent them."

"A play? I didn't know you wrote."

"Secretive chap I am. Anyroads it's not definite but it was enough encouragement to take the day off."

"What were you going to do?"

"Visit some friends of mine, the Rushtons. Like to come?"

"Won't they mind?"

"Not at all, most equable. They're used to people being dropped in on them," and he grinned at her so that she felt very happy and smiled back.

They walked along Finchley Road and Moseby bought a bottle of wine, a cheap port type which he carried under his arm with one hand on the neck lest it should slip away from him. They got a 31 bus and went upstairs to sit at the front. Moseby uncorked the bottle.

"Get some of that down you, this is one of the worst journeys known to man, to the world's end this bus goes." The wine was a thick sweet syrupy drink which almost made her gag. Moseby tutted sympathetically. "If you're not used," he said and swigged away himself. "Doesn't do the teeth a lot of good but it has a certain insouciance, especially about the third bottle. Travels well too," putting his feet up on the ledge at the front.

"It's a lovely day," Ruth said, thinking as she said it that it was.

"Great Greenock weather."

"Why Greenock?"

"The light. Marvellous light Greenock. Fierce. Great. Town's all silhouettes come about half six. See right across it to the hills on the other side." He passed the bottle. She gulped and grued. "Horrible, isn't it?"

"It's very sweet," she agreed.

"Pub in Greenock call the Rowan Tree, sells the wine to all the old men. Good pub."

"Did you drink a lot in Greenock?"

"No. Not to get drunk. It's a working-class escape. My sort go to adult education classes. Philosophy from Plato to Wittgenstein one evening a week during the winter months. And in the summer there are the dances. Great dancers the middle classes. Dance like dervishes given half a chance."

"What are your parents like?" He took the bottle away from his mouth, waved a finger.

"No talking allowed upstairs about my parents. What are yours like?"

"I don't really know."

"Well, that's our parents taken care of. Have a drink."

"Actually, I've just found out that the man I thought was my father isn't." Moseby nodded and Ruth looked out of the window of her odd little travelling confessional, wondering how it came to be here and with him she unburdened herself.

"Funny thing is, I'd just started to like him."

"Who, your father or your non-father?"

"Mr. Cuffee, the man I thought was my father."

"Irony. Dead full of irony life is."

"Ever heard of a man called Moritz?"

"Moritz Chevalier?"

"A chess player, he made a terrible mistake in 1922."

"Oh yes, he bet on the Rangers in the Scottish Cup."

"No. He could have won with a cavalry charge but he didn't see it."

"Used to call it the calvary when I was a boy. When the bugle sounded and the beleaguered wagon train couldn't believe their lousy luck we used to stand up and scream, ehhhh, it's the calvary. Religious instruction for the young is a two-edged sword," taking the bottle from her and sighting its contents.

"Not doing too badly. Getting used to it are you?"

"I like it," she said in a flushed manner that made them both laugh.

"I may be part Jewish. I don't know. My real father's name is Eldman."

"Not Swahili, not by the sound."

"I don't know anything about him yet I've seen him almost every week for years and years. He's a friend of the family," she added as explanation.

"Well, it's nicer that way."

"I think I'm drunk."

"Talking about Calvary, my father who shall be nameless told me about a woman who passed your man on his way up the hill and he was having a rest and this woman saw the nails they were going to use and she stole one of them. Didn't think it would do a lot of good but she reckoned that one nail less was always one nail less as they say in the trade. My father told me this story to show that every little thing you do for Jesus is appreciated because God, who was watching from his box, saw this woman and was dead pleased with her." He drank and some spilled out of the corner of his mouth and Ruth, without thought, reached across and wiped it.

"Never believed that story until yesterday. Always thought it was one of my father's apocrypha."

"Why until yesterday?"

"Man in the showroom told a story about the Roman soldier saying to Jesus, would you mind crossing your legs I seem to have misplaced one of my nails." There was sour, caustic quality to his mirth that disconcerted her.

"Why are you so obsessed with Jesus?" He glanced at her, then stood up.

"I object, your honour. Counsel is leading the witness. Objection overruled." He sat down, drank and passed the bottle. "Well, he's our man isn't he, I mean the man in god, the god in man. He's what we can and should be. He's the lily of the valley, the bright and shining star. So to speak."

"Why aren't you a Christian then if you believe that?"

"Well I am. But fallen from grace. Fallen from the state of unblinking belief which is the happiest condition known to man, beast or three-legged lurgy."

"Don't mock me."

" 'Tis not thee I mock. 'Tis myself. To be caught taking oneself seriously would never do."

"But you take yourself seriously."

"It wasn't meant to notice." The words constantly being placed between them, like plates of glass, preventing touch or nearness. She felt angry with him.

"You love the sound of your own voice, don't you?" He reflected, seemed about to make yet another retort, then changed his mind and sat silent the rest of the way. Ruth felt apprehensive but said nothing, except "thanks" when he passed her the bottle which he did until it was empty.

They got off on the Fulham Road and walked to the right. "Do your friends live far away?"

"No, no," said Moseby. "Just along here." After a moment they turned in through the gates of a cemetery. Moseby quickened his step and she followed him. They turned left when they entered the graveyard proper, under some trees, in long unkempt grasses. Moseby went to a stone, of a rough white texture in which the legends were merely mossy cyphers.

"Here lie the Rushtons, father and daughter, mother and son. Absent friends." She could detect some names and dates now, Matthew, Samuel Cabot, Mary Alice and Fleur.

"Fleur. That's a nice name."

"Ah yes, dear Fleur. We were to have been married but for an unkind providence which placed some ninety years and four hundred miles between us. A lovely girl. Dark-haired, dark-eyed, gathering peonies in the walled garden she waited. And waited. But I did not come."

"And now she's dead."

"When I was a lad people used to die of galloping consumption. I'd lie at night and imagine somebody, Death I suppose, come galloping up on a big white horse and he'd lean down out of his saddle and grab the consumptives up. If you had to go it was the only way."

"Is that what happened to Fleur?"

"I don't know. She's snuffsies now anyway."

Ruth felt dizzy, felt the trees and the sky revolve. Put a hand out to steady her on the gravestone, found Moseby's arm. Held it, turned into him, he into her, his chin against her cheek, a hand stroking her hair until her legs began to melt and she sank taking him with her down into the grass, crinkly with dry leaves, back until she rested against the Rushtons' stone, and he was above her, his face blotting out the trees and the sky.

"Won't they mind?" she asked. He smiled very gently at her.

"No no, they won't mind."

In the cemetery, under the emptying trees, they made what love they could, a quilt of kisses and hand held flesh, of dark words and sighs and spread it over the old, cold dead in lieu of all the love that never would be theirs. When they finally rose they found several leaves had settled upon them.

There was a message from Meriel Rose when she got back. Such was her state of mind that she scarcely bothered to recall who Meriel Rose was. She sat in the rocker and wagged herself violently back and forth, shaking her thoughts into infinite kaleidoscopes of sameness. Her, John Moseby, to tell Harry, love. John Moseby, love, her. Harry. Harry, her, love Moseby. John, Ruth, love, love Ruth, John, to tell Harry. In these patterns Meriel Rose could not hope to fit.

When the telephone rang and she answered it, the fact that it was not John created a vacuum at the other end which it took Meriel Rose some moments to fill.

"Oh Meriel."

"Did you get my message? The man said he would leave it."

"Your message, oh I'm just this minute in. How are you?"

"Ruth, you must come round at once, please."

"What's wrong?"

"I can't tell you on the phone, you must come over now, say you can please, take a taxi. I'll pay for it."

"But what's wrong, Meriel, are you ill?"

"No, please, I'll tell you when you arrive. Please say you'll come."

"Well yes, but I'll have to wait for Harry, he's been working late tonight."

"Please be as quick as you can. I'm depending on you."

On second thoughts she decided not to wait for Harry but wrote him a note explaining Meriel's insistence. It might be as well if she had some topic to discuss when she saw him other than how she had passed the afternoon.

For a moment after she rang the bell there was no reply, and Ruth was beginning to conjure with lurid visions of Meriel in a pink bath of blood when she opened the door dressed in a housecoat and looking ill and tearful.

"Oh Ruth, I'm so glad to see you," and pulled her in by the sleeve then in one encircling motion clasped her close and put her head on Ruth's shoulder and began to weep. After a moment standing like this inside the door she allowed herself to be drawn into the sitting-room and coaxed into relative quiet. Seen close to she looked rather rough. Her face seemed thinner, the eyes had a bare look and there was a fine spray of lines at the outside corner and deeper ones by the edges of her mouth. On her chin an angry mark where she had pressed out a pustule.

"Now tell me what's wrong, Meriel."

"I've closed the dancing class."

"Yes, you told me you might."

"No, not for those reasons, for something else entirely. Something terrible," and she prepared to lose control again, her lower jaw trembling. Ruth could not bear the terrible ruin it caused to the older woman's face so in the guise of comforting she placed her hand against her cheek to stop it quivering. Meriel put her own hand over Ruth's, the palm surprisingly hot and dry.

"Oh Ruth, now that you're here it will be all right."

"Please tell me what happened, Meriel."

"Oh it's too horrible," and she put her face in her hands for a moment, but not long enough for Ruth to be able to withdraw her hand. "It's Mr. Turshaw, the man who plays the piano," and her throat worked convulsively as though she would choke before she could get out. "He, I saw him, oh I hate him, he interfered with that little girl, you used to take her home."

"Jessamyn?"

"Yes."

"You actually caught him?"

"Yes. I was absolutely shocked. Oh I thought I was going to faint." Ruth tried to remember Mr. Turshaw but all she could see was the piano and hear the tinkling tunes.

"Where did you find them?"

"In the toilet."

"Did Jessamyn scream?"

"No."

"No?"

"No, I'm afraid he seduced the poor child into, oh I don't know what."

"Look Meriel, what did you see? What actually happened?" Meriel took a deep breath and closed her eyes before going on.

"Everyone had gone, or so I thought. I knew he was still there but I thought all the children were gone and I was just leaving and I called out to him to lock up when I heard Jessamyn giggling. . . ."

"Giggling?"

"Yes, and I said who's there and I heard the toilet door open and when I looked into the changing room he was coming out of the toilet and Jessamyn was behind him, giggling."

"And what did he say?"

"He said Jessamyn had asked him to do up her dress. It was a lie. I knew by the way he said it and by the way the child was acting."

"What did you do?"

"I told him he was a filthy pervert and I was going to the police. He said I was mad and that he'd done nothing and to ask Jessamyn."

"And did you?"

"Yes, but she was lying as well so I made her get her coat and I took her home in a taxi. I questioned her on the way home but she denied it. Then when I told her mother she took it all very coolly. She asked Jessamyn and that little minx just trotted out her story, word perfect, that she'd been in the toilet and her zipper had got stuck and she'd asked Mr. Turshaw to fix it. I asked her why she hadn't come out of the toilet and she said she'd stood on the seat so that Mr. Turshaw wouldn't have to bend down."

"The cool little bitch. But Meriel you didn't actually see anything."

"I did, I did," and she was almost screaming. "I knew he was, he was excited, the swine." For a moment Ruth didn't know what she meant then did and was, unreasonably, embarrassed.

"Yes, well Jessamyn was obviously not unwilling."

"Ruth, you forget you are talking of a man of forty and a child of ten," making Ruth feel as though she were in some way a partner to Mr. Turshaw's alleged excesses.

"What happened then?" was all she could say.

"Well, Mrs. Somerfield wouldn't believe anything had happened. She said I was suffering from an overwrought imagination and didn't I realize I was accusing her daughter of lying and heaven knows what else. I said that wasn't Jessamyn's fault, she had been corrupted and that men like Turshaw were a menace and something had to be done and I must go to the police. Then she said she didn't want any publicity or bother for Jessamyn and as far as they were concerned, and she knew Mr. Somerfield would feel the same way, the matter was closed and then she actually said I'd better be careful or else Mr. Turshaw might sue me for slander. So I left. And when I thought about it I knew that I couldn't go to the police for they would all just deny it so I did the only thing I could. I closed the school down and notified all the parents and sent them their money back."

"You didn't say anything in the letters about Mr. Turshaw?"

"No, why?"

"I just don't want him suing you."

"He wouldn't dare. He phoned me up and said that if I was closing the school down I should have to give him a month's wages in lieu of notice and a reference."

"What did you say?"

"I told him he was lucky I didn't have him taken to court."

"What did he say to that?"

"That's why I wanted you to be here. He said he was coming round here to demand his rights."

"Here? When?"

"Tonight. And I was desperate that I might not be able to get hold of you. I couldn't trust myself to speak to him."

"But what do you want me to say to him?"

"Nothing. I just want you to be with me when he comes."

Ruth didn't know what to believe. From Mr. Turshaw's point of view it sounded only too like the sort of thing that might happen to a little man like him, completely innocent yet hopelessly compromised. The only thing which made her think that Meriel might be right was her distrust of Jessamyn. She could see her being that sort of child somehow. But Meriel's story sounded highly emotional and presumptive.

"Meriel, are you quite certain in your own mind that something happened?"

"I know, Ruth, I tell you, I know."

"Yes but, and I know this is difficult, but how do you know? What makes you believe it?"

"I just know what men are like, that sort of man, they're foul creatures, they want their own degraded pleasures so much that they'd make use of a child."

"Yes I know all that, but you still haven't told me what you know about Mr. Turshaw and Jessamyn."

"I've told you, he was excited, I could see."

"All right, let's admit he was, but he still needn't have done anything to the child and she might not have known a thing."

"Oh no, Ruth, I tell you I know all the signs, I could sense it, it's evil, you can sense it. I can."

The door bell rang. Meriel grabbed at her shoulder. "That's him. That's him. I can't see him, I won't. You see him for me Ruth. Tell him I'm ill. Tell him to go away. Please, Ruth." She loosened her grasp and stood up.

"What about his money?"

"I'll pay him a fortnight in lieu of notice."

"And the reference?"

"No, I won't give him a reference. Nothing can make me." The bell rang again. "Please, Ruth."

"All right, Meriel. I'll talk to him."

Mr. Turshaw stood with his back to the door. He swung round obviously with a rehearsed line at the ready. Seeing Ruth put him off somewhat.

"Oh, I was, eh, is Miss Rose at home?"

"She's not keeping very well. She asked me to speak to you."

"Oh well, it's really Miss Rose, my business is with Miss Rose."

"She has instructed me to tell you that she is prepared to pay you a fortnight's wages in lieu of notice."

"What about the reference?"

"I'm afraid she won't give you a reference." He blinked at that, several times, rapidly. Please God, don't let him cry, not out here on the doorstep. But he pulled himself together.

"It's not fair. I've done nothing. She has no right . . ."

"You should have been more discreet, Mr. Turshaw. It was

rather foolish of you to go into a toilet with a little girl and close the door."

"But I didn't close the door, she did."

"Who?"

"The little girl. She closed the door behind us."

"Why did she do that?"

"So help me, miss, I don't know."

"And you got her zip unstuck?" and his eyes which until that moment had been devoid of anything except plea altered somehow, he didn't look away, nor did he quite blink but the focus changed, he looked through her or in front of her.

"Yes, I tried to get it unstuck."

"Was it a plastic zip or a metal one?" This time he did blink, genuine puzzlement.

"I don't know. I wouldn't know the difference."

"What sort of skirt was it?" and he had to think.

"A tartan skirt, with pleats."

"And you never touched her?" and the eyes did that hardening again.

"No, I never, never laid a finger on her." It was almost in Ruth's mouth to say "and did she touch you" but she checked it. He would never admit to it if it were so and anyway it wasn't a simple matter of a man taking a child behind a door and touching her up. There were layers and under-meanings, behind the appearances the realities were complex. She could not probe any further out of mere curiosity. No good could come of it.

"I'm sorry, Mr. Turshaw, but that's all I can do for you." He stood, a small oval figure, half guilty, half innocent, torn between indignation and fear. His fear dominated him in the end.

"She won't go to the police, will she?"

"No, Mr. Turshaw, she won't do that." He stood a moment more, then turned and went. At the foot of the steps he turned and said good night. Ruth replied then closed the door.

Meriel made her stay the night. Ruth didn't want to but she had very little choice. It was absurd really, she thought, as she lay in the spare bedroom between the crisp, unslept-in sheets. Phoning Harry to tell him she wouldn't be back when she didn't want to be with him anyway but with little dark John Moseby in his attic among the trees. Next door Meriel Rose lay longing for her, terrified of her own memories and appetites. Harry, work-weary and sick with love, in his heavy sleep. Gerda sharing the night with her dead love; Peter peregrine upon the roads of Europe. All of them in a ceaseless flux of desire. Could not two of them come somehow together, and make common bond, love and be loved, before love and life itself passed them by and they took their place with the Rushtons beyond the reach of everything save the slow seeping rain. "All the dead are dead, and all the living are dying." Who said that, apart, that was, from Ruth Cuffee lying alone in the night?

Twice that week she told Harry she had to stay at Meriel's, and spent the night at John Moseby's. She lay on in the morning after he had gone, or sat at the window in Moseby's dressing-gown looking down into the back gardens. It was a busier scene than her own, yet more distant, further away from things. The trees couldn't be reached but she observed their movements in the hasty wind, how they surged and swept their baring branches and showered down their leaves in sudden concert. Later in the morning a man, whom she took to be Moseby's landlord, came out and started to sweep the leaves up. He seemed discouraged by his task for he moved slowly and paused often to wipe his nose on a coloured handkerchief. Ruth watched and the trees lurched violently in the wind over the stooping figure. It seemed some kind of contest between them, he brushing up the leaves they so violently cast away. Old man counting the dead leaves, the trees ranting overhead, old man lost in his tawny blizzard.

She was equally enclosed in her own storm of emotion. The trees did not assault her human frailty as they did the figure below, but made equal inroads upon her consciousness. As their shapes became daily more stark so Ruth came nearer to a definition of herself, as a heart and a mind and as a woman. These revelations were made to her through the agency of Moseby and their sexual union. He, in some way that was not as yet clear, caused her to know more acutely than ever before her sexual identity. In her relations with Peter there had been so overwhelming a sense of proximity that the sexual act had never achieved objectivity in her mind. With Harry the overall cocooning of his affection and gentleness prevented equally a true sense of carnal pleasure. But here, in this room, on this racketing bed had been made known to her the polarity of sexual life.

Ruth had no way of assessing Moseby as a lover, and between them existed no notions of technique or erotic skills. There was an anonymity in his desire that in its urgency provoked an equal anonymity of response. For the moments of their lovemaking her mind was cleared of all save images of their bodies and intense, vivid sensations in the centre of her mind that she could not get behind and "know." Subject and object were momentarily obliterated, only a luminous present obtained, a single stretching now whose end, when it came, filled her with plangent regret and a great expanding well-being.

Outside the wanton strip trees danced, autumn ecdysiasts, celebrating that most prosaic of the mysteries, the necessity of things to end for the sake of beginnings.

A letter came from Mr. Cuffee.

Knutsford. Oct. 19th.

My dear Ruth,

Thank you for the book. I've never really considered myself a problem man, their appeal is to rather a different sort of mind. Problems are something of a closed world, a world of absolutes in which white always wins and wins brilliantly, no attrition or fatigue, only the irresistible, the elegant and the subtle. It's the arena of the solipsist par excellence, he need not possess a chess board or pieces and that other awkward factor, an opponent, can be dispensed with entirely.

I have always thought myself too much in contact with the realities of life to find this a suitable form of mental activity. Yet the best of them do possess a considerable strength and aesthetic satisfaction for the solver. I will labour on with them and see if their blandishments woo my late middle age more effectively than they did my earlier years.

I was very pleased to have the chance of a talk when you were with us last and hope perhaps the next occasion will not be too far distant.

Your mother is well and sends her love, to Peter also of course. I doubt if he will be greatly interested in either of his parents' regards so I will not press you to convey them.

With thanks once more, your Father

The dignified, unreal tone of it depressed her. "I have always thought myself too much in contact with the realities of life." Like writing to your non-daughter, passing on the love of your adulterous wife, playing chess with your cuckolder, several millenniums removed from your only-begotten. He seemed tragic somehow, a king in his ruin, walking between the cracked columns, the grass growing in the courtyard, while around his feet at meals the wind blew dead leaves and played monotonously on the lattice. She thought of Mr. Schonfield and his sad, sacramental smoke, and almost understood what it was she knew.

All day the sense was with her, something waiting its moment before it came to mind, impending revelation. She could not stay indoors yet knew should she go out her steps would take her only one way and for the moment it seemed wrong that she should find solace with Moseby. What she knew was personal, was distilled from her own experience and should not have the imprint of that dark, vigorous mind on it. His world she had discovered was almost completely obsessive, shut in behind walls of guilt and distorted Christian imagery, soured through with his bitter self-abusive wit and sweetened by the soft centre of his nostalgia for Greenock and Victorian stability. He had the remarkable effect on Ruth of causing her to chain smoke when they were together. His presence produced the spontaneous need for sedation. Listening to the electric crackle of his talk, the sudden sharp rips of laughter, the face miming the mood of his words, all this was an exhilaration too real to be borne without the insulation of either alcohol or nicotine. The other insulation, or more accurately, the discarding of all defence against shock, was to love him. This she would not let herself do and was surprised that she could make and manage such a decision with such apparent ease.

As for Harry the whole thing had become a husk. There were moments when love, or compassion, leapt up in her but there was no continuum. What they had had, and she was uncertain what it had been, was over. She found innumerable excuses and reasons for not being home when he came home, for going to bed early, for sleeping at once, for not wakening when he went out. She knew she was hurting him, the face sometimes set in lines of childlike stoicism, sometimes blinked away its puzzled hurt, on one or two occasions his body hardened as if to rebel against his deprivation, but always slackened. Ruth knew that there was part of her enjoyed this cruelty, this slow unmanning. It was not a pleasant thought but since it could not be denied she accepted it as of her nature. This acceptance let her see something more important, that Harry's passivity fostered such feelings. Masochists breed sadists, theirs is a compulsive search for authority. Such a relationship, if projected into the future, could shape her in ways that would never be alterable. It was one of the boundaries she must in future recognize. She was no Gerda, it was in her to dominate, and in order for that instinct to remain a reasonable one it was necessary to escape those peculiar satisfactions that hurting Harry Gibbon afforded.

She went to the launderette. It was empty save for a pregnant woman in a pale blue smock. They sat in the warm noise and watched their machines. Ruth thought of her mother's letter and Robert Eldman. She could see him vividly, napkining his moustache. He was her father. In the cloisters of this cleansing chapel that did not seem a very relevant fact. She looked at her companion penitent who seemed lost in midmost thoughts. Is he turning inside you, making ripples on the pond of your belly? That must feel like nothing else in this world feels. She felt sorrow for those barren wombs, Gerda willing herself to conceive, Merle Curvis willing herself to a final sterility, the genteel aridity of Meriel Rose. She closed her eyes and amid the soft hubbub let her thoughts spin, seeking some solace that might reconcile her to the fate of being female.

That night Harry asked her if something was wrong. She had no inclination to talk to him about it and simply said she felt a bit rough. He seemed disinclined to believe her but she fobbed him off with some generalized evasions. He asked her if she had any idea where she would like to spend this holiday. Ruth knew there was going to be no holiday and felt bad at her deception. There was a silence during which she felt he might have said something that would not bear evading. Instead he rose and went to run himself a bath.

She didn't sleep well and awoke several times in the night. On the last occasion she got up and had a cigarette and made some coffee. After that she was awake and went out for a walk on Primrose Hill. It was scarcely light and the park was still zoned with yellow pools of lamp-wet. She walked through them, kicking the leaves and coughing every now and then from the raw air in her smoky lungs. On the grass the first blackbirds were plundering worms, running rapidly to and fro. From the zoo came the deep, throaty grunt of the predators against the dawn. It was all a further dimension of irony, the murderous songbirds and the impotent carnivores. Terror among the dewy grasses of Primrose Hill as the hapless worms twanged up from the earth. The world is not as it seems, its malevolence lies behind innumerable masks. A little girl asking for her zip to be unstuck, the mildness of someone like herself, the smile of a friend. Until it is exposed it seems a truth, is trusted, relied upon. It seemed to Ruth at that moment that illusion might be total and that everything was a deceit, even those things she held as truths might only be undetected lies. She stood, cold, in the early morning park amid the brisk butcheries of the blackbirds, shivering at the uncertainty of it all. Something has to be found that is beyond dubiety, does not present a different face to every question asked of it. But this something, this still centre in a moving world, would not be found outside of herself. Without being aware of it a process of profound scepticism had taken place so that she found herself, that had known so little of life, possessed by an ennui that threatened to swallow her whole. The ordinary happinesses seemed remote, the expectation of them had almost passed from her thoughts. She was in thrall and to what she knew not. Prisoned in her tower awaiting her knight, kept captive by the dragon. "You bwute, look what you've done to Towser." It was beginning to look like dragon-slaying was a do-it-your-self task, an awareness that brought little comfort seeing as how she had no notion of how to set about any part of the bloody business.

She found herself soliciting advice. Except it wasn't really that. Somehow to admit aloud to other people was to make it more inevitable, more an undeniable event, one that she could point to if Harry tried to deny it.

Stolleman said,

"Tell him. Don't make it into a big guilt thing. You didn't contract to love him for three years, did you?"

Gerda said, "He's got a right to know. Why does it have to happen to someone like Harry?" meaning herself.

Terry blinked rapidly several times, hurt and surprised. "Well, I w-wouldn't s-say, I m-mean, w-why hurt him, I mean?"

Meriel busied herself with teacups and warming the pot. "Yes," she said, "it's very difficult."

Ruth asked Moseby while they were in bed. "Well, you can pick the time to ask. I don't know what you should do. Tell him if you want."

"Thanks."

"What do you want me to say, 'Dear Perplexed'?"

"Oh shut up."

They lay for a moment, Ruth angry with herself for asking. Not so much for asking him but the others whose responses were but the distortions of their own desires. Even Stolleman's seeming rationality was but his manifesto of non-responsibility writ small.

"Did I ever tell you about my cat?" Moseby said.

"No."

"Yes. Called Boots she was."

"Boots? As in feet?"

236

"As on feet, yes. Got her from Boots the Chemist. Their cat had kittens. Anyway, I had this cat. We had this cat. Female. And Edna didn't like it. Said it tore the furniture, scratched the wallpaper, things like that."

"Did it?"

"M'mm, oh yes, it did. Well they do, don't they?" Ruth couldn't remember if their cat had or not. "I used to say it would settle down. You know, when it got older. But it didn't. Well not to Edna it didn't. We used to have terrible rows. I suppose they were really about other things but we hung them on the cat. They sort of made up my mind about a lot of things those rows over Boots. I mean like whether I wanted a nice home, or didn't I value possessions. Anyway, to pacify her I said we would have the cat neutered, that would definitely quieten it down, so we had and it didn't. After she got over the operation she was the same as before. Edna said it was the feeding it on raw meat that did it. To be fair, she got that one from her mother. So in the end we had her put down. Not Mrs. Davidson unfortunately—the cat." He was looking up at the ceiling and his face didn't invite comment. "I took it down to the vet after work, along Brougham Street it was, in a shopping bag. He said it wouldn't take a minute, did I want to wait. I said yes. Poor old Boots just sat on my lap looking around. I explained all the reasons why we had to put the cat down. He said yes they could be, a terrible pity though, and a lot about how it wouldn't feel a thing."

"Didn't you want to just take it home and tell her, I don't know, tell her you couldn't do it?"

"Aha, yes, well that's where the sin comes in."

"The sin?"

"Yes, I think I was killing the cat so that I could hate Edna for it. Never mind that. He gave Boots the needle. Said he calculated the dosage by pounds weight and he'd given her enough to kill a boxer. I presume he meant dog. Anyway Boots didn't show a sign of going snuffsies. Just sat on my lap and purred when I stroked her. Only thing was her hair seemed to come out an awful lot. But she just sat on and the vet said he couldn't understand it but it would certainly take effect and if I wanted I could leave her and go home but I wouldn't. He went out because he had a call to make and left me and Boots to it and very slowly she started to get drowsy and when I saw that, with the true indulgence of the self-piteous, I started to cry. I was still crying when the vet came back and by that time Boots had passed into a coma and her eyes had dried so that they looked all dusty. I wanted to confess to the vet what I had done to ask him to forgive me but he said it was all over now and that I could go, he would dispose of the body. But she was still breathing, ever so lightly, and I was afraid that if I left her with him he might just incinerate her there and then so I said I would stay until it stopped breathing. He must have been a bit fed up, or maybe he hadn't had his tea or something, because he said that the cat was well and truly snuffsies and couldn't feel a thing. But I wasn't convinced so he said he would prove it and he took her, all limp and still warm, and put her on the table, and he got a long catheter out of a drawer. I didn't have a notion what he was going to do, I just sat there watching. He slid this catheter under a rib and searched about for a minute. Although her heart was still beating he said she was dead and then he found it and pushed the catheter in and the blood out of her heart came spurting up the catheter, once, twice and then once more weakly this time, like two and a half red flowers and that was that. I had seen the whole bit. I gave him his ten bob and went, back to Edna and my daughter and my never-to-be-molested-again furniture." There was a long pause until Ruth said uneasily,

"Did you tell me all that for some reason?"

"You must remember Our Lord taught in parables also. It seemed relevant to something at the time."

When she told Harry he knew. He had known for some time. He didn't know how but he had. Just sensed it. Did she love Moseby? Ruth gestured emptily. Gibbon nodded as though he understood something. He would leave. Stay at Gerda's, work a week's notice. That made her angry. His large, passive pain. His knowingness, his working a week's notice. She wanted to hurt him, whip him with accusations. She confined herself to saying "I don't think you ever really wanted me." He looked at her puzzled, hurt.

"You're mad, I love you, how could I not want you?" Cruellest of cruel she didn't answer, looking beyond him to the skeleton of her tree.

Harry left and she got a job in the library at Swiss Cottage. It was only part time. She stayed at Moseby's most nights but didn't move her things in. He never asked her to and she didn't invite herself. She was smoking a lot and to her disbelief found nicotine stains on her fingers, faint but undeniable. She lost some weight and at the end of the month her period was late but came on the fifth day. Stolleman told her that Gibbon had gone away, he thought to France, and several days later she met Gerda who pretended not to see her. She went one afternoon to the National Gallery and stood before the little Uccello painting for about twenty minutes. In the foyer she bought a copy. Trafalgar Square was bright with sunlight on water and wings. Many couples kissed. She noticed and felt plain and unloved. Perhaps the Princess in the painting did not want to be free of her captor, was frightened to be released from bondage. Ruth could find it easy to sympathize. There was a certain security in captivity. She felt these last few days a quickening in her towards Moseby, a desire to hear him say, not love exactly, but something, some claiming phrase, some proof of ownership. He did not though, merely talked his rapid febrile talk, laughed his private mirth and traced all over her body patterns of furious phosphor that burned in her mind, sorting the just-returneds, folding her washing, looking across Trafalgar Square she felt them and his adamance. It brought no solace, his way with her, and she could long for its baldness to be hung with words, spangly sounds of desire and darling. But there was a stony reality in it. He wanted her, though others might have sufficed, she pleased him, as doubtless his wife had, and gave her orgasms so devoid of ornament as to seem like never-before experiences. To love him, she knew, would destroy this and put in its place the minarets and domes of longing. In their heart of hearts all women crave the east and its mirages. Ruth, in some way aware of this, held tight to the tatters of her emotions.

When Robert Eldman phoned and asked her to have lunch with him as he had to come to London on business she said yes, she would love to. She knew he knew but since he said nothing neither did she. He was coming on a Monday. The receiver replaced, she sat for a time waiting to feel whatever was to be felt. When it became apparent no feeling was forthcoming she rose and went out, although she had not intended to that night. Moseby came down in his very large dressing-gown. He had been writing. She could not tell if he was angry at being disturbed. She lay in bed watching him bent over the page. She wanted to talk to him but didn't dare. After she smoked three cigarettes she fell asleep and dreamt of how all the people hurried around the just-returned trolley as she wheeled it ahead of her, eager to sample what other anonymous readers had thought worthwhile. She felt, in her dream, an obscure loathing for their susceptibility.

"What did you do when you were a child, I mean what were your hobbies?" as they walked on Hampstead Heath.

"I had no hobbies. I was a solitary child. I spent long hours in conversation with myself and lying under the table with the fringed tablecloth hanging around me and picking my nose and eating it."

"What a horrible thing." Moseby disagreed.

"I have always considered those delicate tactile explorations instances of genuine aesthetic awareness. I may of course have been deluding myself."

"You didn't just pick your nose."

"No, I kept caterpillars in matchboxes."

"Did they become butterflies?"

"Never. They invariably died overnight."

"What did you feed them on?"

"Kippers and ginger snaps."

"No wonder they died."

"I have it on considerable authority that God is a maggot. I feel it my bounden duty to inform you of this fascinating fact."

"What difference does it make to me?"

240

"You forget, do you not, that God has made us in his own image?"

"So you think we're all maggots crawling about in a corpse or something."

"Or settling down to a last supper of kippers and chocolate biscuits."

"You said ginger snaps."

"She did have a nasty temper, yes."

With these absurdities acrid in her mind Ruth watched down into the opaque water of the pond where the feet of the ducks opened like little red flowers, submarine blooms, soothing to the eye, filling her with a brief peace.

The extravagance of autumn was almost at an end, the gutters were clogged with leaves and the rains made the burning slower and sadder than ever. In the trees the rain beaded twigs and made dark stains on the bark. The birds sat disconsolate among the unsheltering sticks. Ruth knew she had Robert Eldman to see on the following day and kept watch on the cyclamen blossoms, spannishing and vanishing in seasons less harrowing than this interminable declension around her. If she could stay leaning on this rail for ever, ambered in time. The future was altogether too much upon her, pressing, demanding. She looked at Moseby, several feet away, calling the ducks to him "che-che, pss wss."

"That's not how you call ducks."

"So I've been told. What do you suggest, 'here ducks'?"

"John what are you going to do? About Edna and University and everything?" He only glanced up, as though uncertain where she was, but he stopped calling to the ducks and leaned on the rail. She came closer to him.

"I mean you're just, well killing time, waiting to hear from the BBC about your play, what difference will that make whether they take it or not, as far as Edna's concerned?"

"Don't call her Edna, call her my wife if you have to talk about her."

"All right. I'm sorry, I don't mean to interfere." He straightened up, turned to walk away. She stood by the rail. He looked back, held out his hand.

"Come," he said. "Me Tarzan. You Jane," which made her laugh.

"You are a fool," taking hold.

"Did you ever see the very first Tarzan film. Called *Tarzan Serves his Time?*"

"Was he in prison?"

"No, when he was an apprentice in the jungle. He hears this blonde huntress screaming because she's fallen into the lion pit dug by the unscrupulous German slave trader and he looks up and goes aaaheeyaw and runs up a tree and grabs hold of a creeper and swings off in the direction of the cry, but the creeper isn't tied on and he comes right down on his arse and there's a wee guy walking through the jungle eating a fish supper and he says to Tarzan 'howdye get on?' "

"Is that true?"

"No," said Moseby, "I very much doubt it."

She met Robert Eldman at Baker Street Station. On the 74 bus going there she sat upstairs so that she could smoke. There was no use thinking any more about it, her mind had reached a condition of impenetrable numbness. She sat up at the front of the bus taking deep draws on her fag and looking out at the canal and the trees. At Lords roundabout she noticed St. George and the Dragon. She was aware that it was in some manner symbolical of something but had not the energy to determine what. It didn't really matter.

Eldman took her to a steak house not far from the station. She had decided to get over the initial meeting by shaking hands brusquely and not looking into his eyes. Thus they found themselves seated opposite each other looking at menus without a meaningful word having been spoken. A silence grew between them like ice on a pond. Ruth put the menu down and faced him.

"How did you find out?" His expression did not change and for one sudden suffocating moment she thought that after all he did not know. As her panic rose he said,

"Your mother told me."

"Did it come as a surprise?" He touched his moustache, as if to reassure himself that it was he.

"Yes, and then no. When Dorothy told me, at the very moment she said it, I was absolutely shocked, but immediately after that it all just fell into place, it seemed, well as if I'd always known. Which of course I didn't. Ever." Ruth nodded. It was, in a way, not unlike her own reaction.

"Am I Jewish, part Jewish?" she asked, surprised at herself.

"Well, I'm partly Jewish, so you're, for what it's worth, partially partly."

"There's a man, he's the landlord of a friend of mine. He's a German Jew. My friend says he lost all his family in Germany. Anyway, that's got nothing to do with anything. What do you feel about all this?" Eldman smiled. She was looking at her father for the first time. When he smiled his eyes puckered at the outside corners. She tried to detect his upper lip under his moustache. Was it like hers?

"It's more what you want to do about it. I mean I can't be anything but pleased. You, well, you could be a lot of things."

"I am. I'm a great number of things all at once. I've just taken it as a fact. It's there, it's so. I've tried not to think about it too much. It's not a thinking thing." That she could see her fingers breaking up a bread stick into inch-long lengths made her realize that she had stopped looking at him. She forced her eyes up. "I don't know what I feel. I don't know what we can do. It is maybe all too late for it to really mean anything." He wanted to protest against such an assessment but he kept it back, swallowed, nodded.

"Possibly. But we will have to wait and see for that, won't we?"

"Don't you know how difficult it will be?" almost an accusation.

"Don't you know how it feels to have a child, all at once, out of the blue?" and at that moment, blindingly brief, she felt he was her father. It was gone before there was time to experience it properly, before she knew whether or not it was a feeling she would welcome should it return. Eldman seemed intimidated by his own audacity, his eyes were cast down. The waiter placed their soup before them, offered them bread. They ate, allowing their food to come for the moment between them, aware as they did so that they were father and daughter, having lunch normal among the midday millions. Ruth thought on the duck's petal feet. Red. Like poppies. Melancholy flowers. Nothing was settled, perhaps nothing ever would be settled. The flux of feeling would go on, tossing them like corks, helpless iotas. If that was so it would have to be borne. She asked Robert Eldman some question of rare idiocy and received reply of matching hue.

After he had gone back to Manchester she went home. The flat was empty. She wanted to run to Moseby but stopped herself. Sat in the rocker. Played the Beethoven. It cut patterns and pictures in her mind. She felt lonely. Where were those people who had surrounded her, where had all these desolate wastes come from? Beethoven reached deep into himself for an answer, yet though she heard it she did not understand, these sonorities were not yet hers. Although it was only half past four she was tired. Sleep however was not involved in it. She got up after about half an hour of twitching back and forth. Go to him, tell him you love him. Even if he says he doesn't love you, something will be clear. Stolleman had sleeping pills. She knew them and took two. Made a cup of tea. It burned her tongue because she could not bring herself to wait. Not yet. She would tell him some other time when need did not press on her so heavily. She lay, waiting for the pills to spill out their black oblivious scent, to douse her mind. While she waited her thoughts kept crashing into each other until the noise made her moan, ever so softly, to herself.

When she woke again the moon was almost full. From the bed she could see it, creeping up the sky, cold emblem, queen of the night, madonna of moods, regina of the tidal flow, yet lifeless without the loving look of the sun. Its pallor lay in the room, silvered the surface of her mind, numbed her feelings into a frail peace, a lacuna of looking into the moon's milky eye. As well as being who one was there was being a woman too. She hadn't known that before, not as she had come to, woman in her bondage to men and menses, to the great dragon of fecundity. She hated other women for their refusal to see it, to admit and accept it, Gerda's earth mother myth, and distorted, thwarted Meriel Rose, her mother's pallid plight and Merle Curvis' useless gesture of defiance. She hated them all for not succeeding, for not overcoming their female fate. Would she in turn fail, choose the illusion, shirk the reality, make the compromise, deny the meaning. In the selenotropics she languished, an amazon seeking her own source.

Three

The Unalterable Animals

—It may be that one life is a punishment
For another, as the son's life for the father's.
But that concerns the secondary characters,
It is a fragmentary tragedy
Within the universal whole. The son
And the father alike are equally spent,
Each one, by the necessity of being
Himself, the unalterable necessity
Of being this unalterable animal.—

WALLACE STEVENS: *Esthetique Du Mal*
from COLLECTED POEMS. Faber & Faber

THE JOURNEY

In end September they went, along the roads that led to Dover. The swallows sat upon the wires, assembling for austral flight. In the woods the leaves were falling silently, cutting sideways through the damp autumnal air, sawing down soundlessly to meet the accumulate mulch of last year and the year before and the piled upon years of yore. The woods reeked of time running down, of end things. Cuffee as he walked sensed this without knowing quite what he knew. He saw the woods and their dank interiors, and memories of childhood woods, ominous with trespass, came to trouble him with their scent.

To Gibbon, hunched in his thoughts several paces behind, they signified nothing. He thought only of Cuffee and the noose into which his life was tightening.

Cuffee remembered the way rotten wood broke, the branch seemingly whole, then cracking, snapping away from the parent stem. He remembered high in a tree gathering chestnuts and a foothold that treacherously broke. The abrupt astonishing fall through the green foliage and the stunned moment as he looked up into the high perch, dizzy above him, rushing with a noise of wind that was the breath being driven out of his body as he fainted. It made him wonder why anyone should sing "Hushabye baby in the tree top" as a lullaby. He had never liked chestnut trees since.

In Dover they had a meal and watched the grey channel as they ate. It shifted and chopped and stretched to foreign lands. It had a rough unkempt appearance, like a cat whose fur has been rubbed the wrong way. Cuffee watched its sullen slop, thinking only of distance and time and the energy needed to overcome them.

"Must you go?" Gibbon asked, unable to hold silence any longer.

"Needs must," and gestured at the sea as though it explained.

"I wish I could go with you." Cuffee had nothing he wished to say in reply to this. He did not look at Gibbon. "Are you in love with her?" The coarse grey water chafed at the shore,

249

chopped against the harbour wall. It had no music, only insistence. In the watcher there was no music, only the urge to be gone and on.

"Love is not the issue here."

"What is?" Cuffee was angry then. He looked at his inquisitor.

"Harry, you overdo the innocent, you really do. Love is not the divine esperanto you would make it. For all you know your love, your compassionate Ruth is taking advantage of your being down here with me to be tearing off a strip."

"Why do you say that? You don't believe it. You love her."

"Get your head out of your arse, Harry. That was a long time ago, the golden days before the fall. Things cannot be like that any more, we stretched it out Ruth and I, further than it was ever meant to go, and after I stopped pretending she went on. It's not so long since she stopped. She doesn't want to hear that old song again, so soon. She wants a bit of room, a bit of cool. People who love make me laugh, they never notice themselves ramming their love down the beloved's throat, and all with that selfless look of reluctance. I don't love Ruth. I don't love Gerda. I don't love you. I don't love my mother or father. I didn't love Merle Curvis and she poor cow is dead. And for what it is worth I don't love Uta."

"Then why are you going? I don't understand."

"Let me tell you something my father said. He meant it to be a wise saying so listen carefully. He said, and I quote, 'The mark of the solitary man is his capacity to choose, not so much the quality of his choices.' I had to choose to do something and if you think about it there wasn't really much else I could have done."

Gibbon nodded, finally convinced by the single-mindedness of the argument. Not that he understood, but he knew that Cuffee was well beyond his reach.

Down on the front there was a wind and it bore the gulls along it, watching, gliding. They walked beneath the white carrion birds, the wet wind blusting against them.

"Ruth asked me something about Merle Curvis," Gibbon said.

"M'mm, she suspects it was me."

"I won't say anything." Cuffee looked at him, amused.

"It doesn't matter. She was having a child. She's dead now. It doesn't matter whether you tell Ruth or not." This also being beyond his comprehension Gibbon kept quiet.

At the customs sheds Cuffee would let him come no further. Gibbon gave him the sleeping bag he had been carrying.

"I won't be needing it for a while."

"Thanks. It's a good bag."

"All the best, Peter. Take care of yourself." They shook hands and then Cuffee was gone, lost behind crates and the figures of other passengers. Gibbon waited but did not see him again, except perhaps once but he didn't turn round.

Cuffee didn't come on deck until the ship had started to move. He stood and watched the receding land. The gulls swept and yawked, plunging to the grey coiled water for scraps. Those passengers who had faces on shore waved, the others fed the gulls and saw the port shrink into itself, lose perspective, fuse into a quartz of cubes and planes. As they moved further out the chalk cliffs drew in on either side of the town. Cuffee watched them, great white bastions of sanity, until even they lost their authority.

It was getting dark when the ship reached Ostend. Cuffee walked quickly into the city and found somewhere to eat. He sat afterwards, smoking, his bag beneath his feet, watching the reflection he made in the window. Beyond the glass the foreign people walked their foreign streets. It was a special flavour, the isolation it bestowed, an intimation of that severer solitude he sought. When his cigarette was finished he went out and into the night.

His walking was random, choosing only a dark street before a well-lit one, a narrow rather than a wide, but in this way he came to where he wanted to be, in a poor, dim district where few people were. After a time he came upon a bicycle leaning against a wall. The street was empty and the only light was some dozen yards away. There was a chain through the front wheel and around the frame. He took a pair of pliers and set the cutting edge to the link. It bit but would not cut. He squeezed until his wrists ached. Looking along the chain he saw a link that seemed thinner than the others. He set the pliers again and this time it sheared after he had applied pressure. He cut it again and freed the wheel. The chain he put in his bag. Then he strapped his belongings to the platform above the back wheel. There was no front lamp but the back one worked. He mounted and rode away, seeking the roads that lead out into the country.

It took him about two hours to clear the outskirts and find the flat dark land stretching out around him. He dismounted by a gate and went into the field. The bicycle he propped against the wall and then, taking off only his boots, he got into the sleeping bag. His friend's generous warmth surrounded him. Even as he luxuriated in it however he thought with relief of his freedom from that fondness, that claiming affection. In the breast pocket of his jerkin he could feel the little book of words his father had written so many years before. It lay square and flat against his heart. When he was far enough away he could really read it, consider it without the fear that had nagged him ever since his father had given it to him, the fear that within it was evidence, indisputable proof that he and his parent were one flesh. He had never been able to read it before because to discover such a thing while actually in the same country as Mr. Cuffee seemed almost indecent. Were he to be faced with such a revelation then it would be when he was alone, away from the claims of love. Where he was bound love would not come in that guise, was perhaps not really love. But it was life and enough life is love. Life is a pure flame fed by the invisible sun that lies within us. The people who do not know of that sun must seek reflected light, moon people. Women are moon people, all but a few. Perhaps Ruth would be one of them, but that was not something he could help her discover. Fusc disc in the clouds of uncertainty, pale partner, far and near, long lost sister love, drifting on the tides of night. Things pass and are changed and are no more. Once he could have told Ruth of his complicity in that girl's death. That and that alone concerned him about his journey. It was the news of it that decided him to leave, it was a trigger, the push which released his momentum. And yet he could have wished it something else, something less mordant. But it was done and could not be reversed. Things happen as they did because no possible alternative presented itself. That was why guilt about Merle Curvis or anybody else was futile. Inevitability was its own justification. He drew down into his sac and buried remorse under his arm. The journey waited on the far side of his dreams and he had an urge to be on with it.

In the morning there was a wind, steady and hard across the flat land. He rose and chewed his teeth to take the taste away. Then he pushed his bicycle out on to the early road. It ran well, big, solid, upright, comfortable to sit and easy to control. He sat back and let his legs pedal away beneath him, one hand on a rising falling knee, the other touching the handlebar lightly. Occasionally the wind lay against him and he had to hunch to and push. But mostly it came behind his shoulder and ran him on. Only his hands were cold. He stopped long enough in Bruges to buy gloves and a tin can for tea and a front lamp. Then he pushed on again, sparing no time for the old turreted town, driving the bicycle out along the canal flat land, pieced and patched, assiduously under cultivation. It filled him with a kind of scorn, this allotment paradise, as he pushed on over its unresisting level, the scorn hill people feel for the monotones of the plain. There were no vistas, no craggy heights or banked forests. No ravines or rapid rivers. Only the flat passive land, longing to be crossed.

He made tea in a field, down behind a hedge. He gathered sticks and found two stones. The flame ran among the small wood for a moment in a panic of extinction and Cuffee shielded it with his body, encouraging and blowing, feeding its feeble mouths with special tindery twigs until it bit and crackled and its first warm breath fanned against his cheek. When it was ready he put on the sticks and on top of those the can, new bright. Cuffee sat back and watched the smoke blacken the tinshine, huddling down out of the wind. It came in gusts that threatened his fire, so he propped the bicycle up and spread the sleeping bag across it as a wind break. Smoking a cigarette he remembered fires lit in the open, sitting around waiting for the potatoes to roast and they were never done right through but with a hard centre and a black crackled jacket that burned the fingers and tasted of ash. Ruth sitting devotedly waiting for hers, the intent small face, the eyes opening in anguish with the mouthful of hot potato. She had been just a little girl then, no older than Patsy, whom he thought on at odd moments. Was she still feeding the cats, looking up out of her rare violet eyes. Like Ruth, that was behind, past beyond recall.

The water in the can was beginning to thicken, turn grey and tremble. He undid his package of tea and when the bubbles started to burst on the surface he put two small heaped palmfuls in and stirred it with a twig. Then he squeezed in some milk from a tube and let it sit a while. Twenty yards away a bird sat against the sky to sing. The stone he threw missed but sent it scolding away down the hedge. When the tea had cooled somewhat he sat sipping it, wearing his gloves so that he could hold the can, eating a bar of chocolate with it, a delicious brown mud in the mouth. It all felt as it had when he was a boy, when everything was invested with significance, that intense awareness of the world around one, a kind of pre-pubertal pantheism. Stones, trees, tastes, smells, the feel of earth in the hand, the fascination of dead things, the transports of the imagination once freed from that house and the black brooding rages of his father. Those who spoke of the joys of childhood were never clear enough that it was a joy which was not concerned with happiness but with the fullest savouring of life. His childhood had not been happy but it had often been joyous. Sitting under his Belgian hedge he could almost reconcile himself to the inevitable role his father had played in those forefall days. He was the force that opposed life, he had made the scarecrows of childhood unnecessary, the sandmen and the bogies with which his mother had sought to curb him became as nothing once he had returned.

Perhaps now it was time for that role to be reconsidered. It was no longer possible to think on Mr. Cuffee as satanic, if Satan were needed he must be confronted afresh. The mind will not survive without its metaphors of evil, the imagination will not function on history alone. Being as he was, reborn by the roadside, his search must be for a new set of such metaphors since the old had ceased to serve.

When he rose the wind it seemed was stronger, the land cowered beneath it like a cur, remembering previous whippings. It seemed now to be blowing against him and he pushed into it, anger and exhilaration in him at the first combat.

By night it was a gale, dry still but with a hard muscular body to it into which he forced himself and his machine, standing on the pedals, thrusting their weight down, step by step ascending the wind.

He stopped well after dark at an inn. A sudden rush of fatigue smote him as he stepped into the lee of the wall. His legs trembled as he leaned against the rough, cold stone until they quieted. There had been a wall at the bottom of the garden, behind the rhododendrons where he used to wait out his father's anger, face pressed in presentiment of punishment against the stone, seeing only out of one eye and only the bleak surface of their wall at the end of the garden. It had been one of the limits of his universe that wall and he still heeded its warning. Where there was a wall someone had to go to it. He had tried to tell Ruth before he left but it was like everything else, it meant nothing because she had not come to it yet, the wall of no choice.

His sweat drying on him caused him to shiver and he propped the bicycle and went inside. It was warm and smoky and had an open fire. The people looked at him as he came to warm himself, the pale face, the black hair, the collar of his denim jerkin turned up under his ears. He stood and warmed the backs of his legs and the numb lumps of his buttocks. He drank a cognac and ordered something from the menu. No one spoke to him as he ate, ravenously silent, but a dog came and sniffed his feet to see from where he had come. He sat and smoked two cigarettes, letting the warmth soften his bones, torturing himself with the thought of going out again. His mind held no thoughts save the polarities of within and without. He would go when his second cigarette was finished. He watched it burn its last shards with the dull contentment of a man under orders. He had not much longer but what he had was indisputably his.

The country was prostrate under the wind. It rushed and tore among the houses and bent the trees and flattened the grass. He walked slowly with the bicycle until in the ragged light from the moon he saw an outhouse near the road. It wasn't open but it provided a sheltered corner where it met the dyke and here he got into his bag. The wind ripped above him. The moon hacked through the clouds like a dull knife. He thought neither before nor behind. Sleep rose up out of the ground like long dark grass, growing swiftly over his head.

When he woke the sun was shining brightly and it had been raining. His hair was wet and everything glistered in the bright, wet light. In the hedge an old man was cutting brush with a sickle. It made a silver shine in the air as he hacked. He had only one arm. The other, his right, was cut off at the elbow and wore a red stocking on the stump. At first, just woken, in the lustrous enamel light, with the steely blur of the sickle cleaving his sight, Cuffee had the sense of a vivid dream and that in it the arm was but newly severed and that it still bled and further back the presentiment that in the dream the man was his father. He lay for a time with only his eyes awake pondering dimly on the meaning of the scene until the old man went to the other side of the hedge out of sight. Then he got up and made tea.

The wind returned by midday and grew steadily stronger. It lay against him like a hand, contesting his progress, giving up no step without struggle. But the more it blew the harder he pushed, head down, thrusting on, flesh and sinew against the forces of the inhuman air. It scoured his face and reddened his neck at the cuff of his jerkin and his eyes were sore from its day long rubbing. Before dusk he was tired, and although dissatisfied with his progress he stopped near a little copse and took the bicycle up among the trees. He squatted down against a trunk and let his chin lie on his chest. He had not imagined it would be so hard. His whole body felt fatigue in the form of a dull pain. There was no respite from pedalling, no hills down whose far side he could career, only the flat enervating road and the small neat gatherings of houses at cross roads, the endless vistas of pollarded trees and the road going on ahead.

When he jerked awake he was cold and his teeth jumped together in his mouth. He could hear a stream somewhere close by and he rose stiffly and took his can in search of water. It took him further into the copse and then over to the right through some brush and down a slope. In the half light he almost didn't see the birds, wood pigeons, sat side by side on a low branch, looking towards him. Out of the corner of his eye he saw a stone, half buried in the earth, to his right hand. But they would see him throw and be well out of it. He moved closer, quietly. One of the birds hopped sideways and as it did its companion's wing flopped loose in a broken slouch. Cuffee straightened up and then clapped his hands. The uninjured bird flew off with a rattle of escaping wings. The other lurched wildly forward and fell from the branch. A feverish pursuit commenced, the large ungainly bird scrabbling along the ground, Cuffee blundering behind being whipped across the face and chest by twigs and once bouncing his head off a low branch. He caught it between some roots and lifted its warm living softness into his chest, smoothing down its roughed plumage, placing its wing carefully by its side. The bird sat still, looking at him with its head pointed forward, away from him. Cuffee stroked its beak and after a moment it made a peck at his finger. Its heart beat against his wrist. He stood for a moment breathing heavily, the light suddenly very faint among the trees. There was nothing to be said, the bird was right to fear the worst. It did not struggle as he took its neck. All manner of doubts assailed him, not only about the bird, but about why he was here and what he was going to do when he met Uta again. He had a longing to be at home, by a fire, with someone. Against these seductions he wrenched hard, the bird leapt in his hand and its blood flushed against his fingers. He threw the head away and carried it by the feet to the stream where he washed his hands.

After he filled his can he scooped out some mud from the bank and plastered it around the still warm body. Then more until it was completely cased, a large muddy ball. Then he went back to the bicycle and started to build a fire. By the time he was ready it was completely dark and around him the tree trunks lurched and leapt as the flames grew longer. The bird he placed in the middle of the fire and built sticks around it. With the bicycle lamp he went looking for fuel. Looking behind him he could see his camp, an orange grotto among the dark trees.

When he had gathered enough he got into his bag and lay

down beside the fire. The water in the can was nearly boiling. He kept turning the clay ball round and round in the fire. It was strange about that man this morning, cutting in the hedge. He thought he was dreaming, and the stump of the arm still bleeding. He examined his fingers to see if any of the bird's blood was still there. In the light from the fire both his hands might have been bloodied so he tucked them away, out of sight. And why had he thought it was his father? He remembered Mr. Cuffee punishing him, holding out his hands, palms uppermost, asking him to choose which hand he should be struck by. It didn't make him angry any more, just sad to think about it. He brought out Mr. Cuffee's book from his shirt pocket. It was written in brown ink on soft, yellowing war-time paper. He knew the entry he was looking for.

> 4th Dec.
> It is the hallmark of the solitary
> man that he can choose and his prime
> virtue. It does not matter so much
> the quality or the direction of one's
> choices, only that there is the energy
> to choose. Denied that he is left hanging,
> suspended on his inertia.

Like he had been in that hospital. A prisoner of time. That is when one suffers. Pain is not suffering. Suffering is a special state those denied choice have to endure. He could never allow himself to be denied choice again, even if the only choice were to destroy himself he would make it. Once you had made up your mind on that you were freed. It only took the courage to admit solitude, not casual loneliness, but final isolation, and everything else was added unto you. That was why he had to flee their love, all of them, it sought to convince him that in this world another human might be as important as he, tried to ameliorate the ache of being alone by holding out the illusion of togetherness. Their voices drowned his, his quiet interior voice, speaking softly, telling him who he was. He had left them behind with their clamour and when next he returned he would not let them start again.

The dark was all about and his little fire blintered in its midst. He reached his meal out of the embers with a stick and broke it open with a stone. The feathers came away with the shell leaving the bird whole and baked. The entrails had helped to keep the flesh juicy and came away in a little knot of stringy cords. The meat melted from the bones and he ate it in succulent gobbets, washing it down with sweet tea. Afterwards he got up to wipe his hands and make water, standing in the dark, shivering as the warmth left him. Up through the trees were stars and somewhere the moon was rising, a faint scad of pale light behind branches. The wind had dropped and came only in long sighs. He lay and watched the fire ebb away, thinking of the terrors the dark once held, of long breathless moments under blankets listening for what waited outside to make a move, reveal its dread presence. The agonies that parents visit upon their children out of the most casual malice. The red of the fire was filmed over with a bluey ash. It trembled most exquisitely and pulsed like a heart. Cuffee watched it until his eyes closed, and even then he saw it, slowly dimming down into sleep.

Rain woke him just before dawn. The woods were haggard with drizzle. The wheel of his bicycle dripped countless crystal drops. Between the roots of the tree the grey scar of his fire. He rose and bundled the bag up and racked by shuddering yawns trundled down on to the road and wobbling wildly went on, pedalling fast to get warm. This early in the morning in the steady sideways sift of the rain the land seemed a featureless flat, empty of colour or sound. He longed for a hill he might fight against, for the wind even, but the straight road across the low land swallowed his attempts at speed, made his progress as monotonous as the landscape.

Then as he travelled he came upon a strange sight. Across a bare brown field, coming towards the road, a man, pulling behind him a dog on a piece of rope. The dog resisted, sitting down on its haunches but the man never looked back, kept walking, towards the edge of the field. Cuffee cycled slowly alongside watching them, the stolid man, dressed in blue overalls and a short coat with a beret on his head, and the whimpering captive dog. Some thirty yards along there was a small mound of earth and a spade beside a hole. The man stopped at the hole and wiped the rain from his face with a blue handkerchief. He seemed not to notice his spectator, but stood as though alone in his landscape, in the early rain in the grey light. Then taking up the spade he pulled the dog towards him and aimed a blow at the creature's head. The dog jerked away and he missed. For a few moments it went on, the spade awkward and heavy, the dog in a panic yet never barking, only the low whimpering as it leapt and scraped itself out of danger. They struggled there, man and dog, lurching and stumbling, the edge of the spade cutting into the soft brown soil at each miss. Steam came from the dog's soaked coat, the man's breath ragged gauzes. At last the blow was struck and the brute howled, its back broken. The man struck twice more and then stood leaning on the spade, breathing hard while out of the dog's wounds seeped the day's first hue. Cuffee mounted and left them there, executioner and victim, the simplicity of death expanding in his mind like a stain.

All day his thoughts were of death and mortality, the cold comfort of earth and the end of air. It was a dead land he passed through. He saw few people and those mostly at a distance and always with their faces averted. Against his will he felt longings for Gerda's scented breasts, for the rank aura of life that was hers. He wanted a woman to warm his limbs and empty his mind. But in the grey houses that he passed no such creature lived, only upright bones with hanks of hair, heartless things no man could lie with. As night came the low sky was filled with the ragged banners of rooks, black flapping flags. Rather than stop he drove himself on, the white stick of his lamp tapping ahead. Without admitting it he would not commit himself to sleeping out, the craving in him for fire and companions was stronger than he could deny.

A farmhouse by the roadside drew him to its window. Within the scene was as a distillation of every interior he had ever seen or imagined. A man and his wife, three children, an old woman and a dog, sat at table and by hearth, in a yellow light in a room with the burnish of brass and the dull gleam of delft. They seemed not to move or speak but simply to be there, content with their good fortune, safe in their nearness.

Cuffee almost imagined them a figment, some tantalizing vision, but the man suddenly rose and came towards the window so that he feared himself discovered and stepped away into the dark.

Once he had dismounted though he could not bring himself to go upon the road again. He put his bicycle behind a hedge and carrying his bags crept among the outhouses until he found one open. Within was a great bunker of grain, dry smelling and clean. He slipped inside and spread his bag out on the grain. He lay silent listening for sounds of discovery. But none came and he relaxed. Only the darkness disconcerted him and so he switched on the lamp and began to read his father's notebook to keep him company till sleep came.

> 18th Oct.
> To one who has never been there the
> desert is a place of dust and discomfort,
> of hot inhospitable sand. But it is not.
> Above all it is clean, cleaner than anything
> that can be imagined. Nothing grows there
> and so nothing dies, and thus there are
> no symptoms of decay. There are only the
> endless billows of sand and the great abrasive of
> the sky. And of course the sun, devoid of any
> metaphor in its utter aridity. That is all there
> is. The desert challenges the very root of
> one's ideas about oneself. It asks a question,
> offers a challenge that makes it impossible to
> take refuge in the illusions which have sufficed
> hitherto. There can be no other place which
> shrinks a man to a speck and yet makes him feel
> such exaltation in his minuteness. No wonder the saints
> and the prophets sojourned here. Only here would
> their ideas seem less than ludicrous. Here asceticism is a
> condition of survival.

Reading of it in the feeble shine of his lamp made him long for it, its blinding light, its empty wastes. It was where, when he had found Uta, he must go and find himself.

The farm in the morning glistened with dew and a horse stood still as stone by a gate. The sun gilded everywhere and caused palest blue shadows to spill. It was earlier than Cuffee could ever remember. Gone were his dreads of dark and death, he felt absurdly hopeful of something, as a child feels waking on a holiday morning before memory serves, an exhilaration both diffuse and sweet, hopefulness that is never simply for fête or carnival but wells up from some unplumbed source of optimism. It flooded up in Cuffee now, this wet-eyed morning, and he sought to pay it homage, to express fitting gratitude. At the edge of the field, almost at the horse's front hooves, he saw a poppy. The horse moved off as he climbed the gate, its canter spangled with diamonds of dew, tossing its long head, making the whole green field spin around him. He plucked the poppy and smelled its pale, bitter breath. He held it up to the horse, now watching him, shaking its neck and blowing white breath from its nostrils. He ate the poppy, remembering Ruth in the wersh fleshes of the vivid bloom.

His thoughts as he travelled were now of golden things, of moments when the world was luminous with promise. The sun shone and the wind it blew from the south, hinting at warm far groves and spiced gardens, harbinger of summer in the greying land of winterset. Soon he would turn his face into it, ride down its long incline to the swallows and the sun.

He remembered as he lay in a hedge eating cheese and drinking a bottle of wine, remembered a moment such as this when nothing was lacking yet everything was still to come. Travelling in the Army in large trucks, passing through a village he saw a woman washing a window, her breasts moving in her blouse like some exquisite, unreachable apples. Later in the day they stopped at an orchard and several of them crept in to steal fruit. All were cautious except he. The laden, drooping trees intoxicated him and in a great rage of lust he ran among them, shaking their trunks in both hands, the apples showering down, drumming on him, bouncing and rolling in the grass and he remembered the woman at the window and the smooth skin of her, sweet to bite and her waist throbbed in his hands as he shook her like a slender appleful tree. His companions stood around, abashed at his excesses. Then fearful of discovery they fled and he ran from tree to tree, profligate in his joy, the apples falling around him like fat rain.

That afternoon he reached the frontier at Aachen, a striped bar that moved up and down on a counterweight. Then, a hundred yards on, another, and he was in Germany. He did not pause to consider what watershed he had traversed but pushed on to his journey's end.

THE CASTLE

Vilich Beuel lies some twelve kilometres from Bonn, in low land that rises in places to small eminences. The village itself grows round and upon one and a kilometre further the small Schloss of Heinrich Zimmerman raises itself out of the level to look across the land, in the early evening light a squat and powerful shape, set around with the long quills of poplars, ringed by a small moat, the bridge of which remains permanently down. The Schloss, which was really little more than a fortified manor house with an air of the grandiose, had passed through many hands in its two hundred years. The village had always known it, in its ringed insularity, withdrawn yet overbearing and despite the modernity of the times the villagers still maintained an attitude of resentful subservience to it and its occupants.

In a way Cuffee felt it the first moment he saw the place. He came swinging down through the village in the early evening and as he turned right it was there, growing massive in the dusk, flying an idle flag at its staff. His heart fluttered wildly and caused the bicycle to wobble. He pulled in to the verge and lit a cigarette, calming himself. It was the suddenness after all this time, the confrontation and the impending moment of meeting. Perhaps she would no longer be here, have gone any of a hundred unreachable places. Perhaps the castle would be empty and dark and he would beat on its doors in vain. And if she was there would she remember him, and if she remembered him would she care. Against these mounting doubts he had no course but to go on. The sooner he knew the sooner he could make his next choice, his next act of will.

The road which led to the Schloss was earth-surfaced and bore the marks of men and horses, and the deep ruts of cartwheels. It wound between lanes of poplars and the shape of the castle lay sometimes ahead and sometimes on either hand. Overhead in the stretched sky a flight of ducks headed arrow-like down under the walls and in the quiet air he heard their calls as they settled in the moat. He dismounted to cross the bridge.

He found that he could not recall her face and that the earth beneath him seemed strangely distant. At that moment the whole momentum of his journey, its fears and hopes, was exhausted and he with it. He could not summon up an image of himself as he approached the door, had not the energy to process this reality in his imagination so that he could be convinced of its purpose. In this moment of nakedness he was aware of the innumerable protective layers his mind was accustomed to, how much of the function of imagination was to prevent moments like this from occurring, standing in front of closed doors, wishing them to open for no other reason than that one wished to be taken in.

The sound of the bell died far within. There was a pause that began to yaw into silence and he was about to ring again when the sound of footsteps came towards the door. A man in a dark suit, dim light behind him, his face in shadow.

"I have come to see Fräulein Uta Wittner." There was a pause, Cuffee prepared to repeat the words. The man made a short nod. His English was slow and precise.

"What is your name?"

"Peter Cuffee."

"You will be pleased to wait," and stepped back, closing the heavy door over without completely shutting it.

When he came back he would say, what did it matter what the words were, any one of a number of things, but all meaning the same thing. He stood looking down into the moat. You spent all of your life avoiding this situation, this dependence on another, this being without, seeking entrance, and then suddenly as though there had never been a dread it was there, present. Maybe now he would learn what it was to be rejected, to be faced with that "no" which could not be wooed or coerced or defied. Perhaps this had been what his journey was for, to bring him face to face with that over which he had no control. Even as he was gathering together the ravelled ends of his will to meet this refusal the door opened behind him and he heard feet, running. The light was behind her, haloing her white dress. She called his name and came running towards him, "Peter," and her pale face floated beneath him and her mouth dark damson burst on his, her tongue hard as stone, in his hands her hands burned cold, she smelled of flowers and warm winds and her body pressed up, long and endlessly close as she sighed his name.

"Peter, aaahh my Peter, you have come, you have come."

"Yes."

"You have been a long time. Often I thought you never would."

"I am here." Her fingers searched his face, tracing the path of his scar. Her sigh was both of content and sorrow as she found it.

"Yes, you are here."

"I want you to come away with me, Uta."

"Where, to where do you want me to come?"

"South."

"South?"

"Yes, that is where we can be happy you and I. Where the sun is. Will you come?" She stepped back and for the first time he could focus on her face, all its features, blurred from innumerable recall, crystal at last in his eye. She was more beautiful than he had known, rarer, more perfect, the wide em of her upper lip, the far apart eyes, the nose almost severe in its straightness. He held her cupped in his palms.

"Uta, will you come?"

"It is not as simple as you asking and me saying yes." But it was, really, under everything that was exactly how easy it was. She had taken his hand and was leading him to the door. He wanted her to say "yes" before the others, whoever they were, came into the scene. On the threshold he stopped her.

"Uta, will you come away with me?" The light was on her face, her hair shone like red gold. She laughed, her laugh dizzied him with its brightness.

"Oh Peter, of course I will go with you to your South, wherever that may be," and so saying she drew him inside.

They were four for dinner. Herr Zimmerman at the head, Cuffee at the foot, Uta on the right hand and Yani on the left. Cuffee's impression of Zimmerman was of a rather short man of considerable breadth and with long arms. He wore a close, dark beard and his eyebrows, which were heavy, almost met

above his nose. His handshake, after this aura of physical
strength, was unexpectedly mild. Yani was as he remembered
her, still wan, withdrawn, in her greeting she kept her gaze
from his eyes and the small hand was damp and loose. Uta had
changed into a blue caftan edged with silvering and sat erect,
watching him ardently for short spells, then looking away.

A servant poured wine into long-stemmed goblets, a purple
colour that drowned the tint of the wine and set down
smouldered like cobalt flowers on the snowy cloth.

"How long have you been travelling?" Herr Zimmerman
asked.

"Five days."

"How did you come?"

"On a bicycle."

"Ach so. And sleep, where did you sleep?"

"I have a sleeping bag." The expression puzzled him and he
looked at Uta who translated it for him with a smile.

"Ah I see. You were self-contained then."

"Yes."

"You came through France or Belgium?"

"Belgium."

"On a bicycle that was very wise." Uta was turning her
head between them as she spoke, as though the question and
answer was in contest and making Cuffee feel that the whole
conversation as something he might well lose.

"What did you think of Belgium?"

"It seemed flat." Zimmerman smiled, as though prepared to
accept this as a witticism.

"Yes. That is the best description of Belgium. It is a flat
country with a flat people thinking flat thoughts. Do you believe that people are like the places they come from?"

"Possibly. I think some must find other places because they
cannot live where they are."

"No. I disagree," and he was emphatic. "A man's identity is
in the country of his birth. People do not change, if they try
to they destroy themselves. I would be surprised if you were
not an Englander, under everything. It shows in the way you
travel, self-reliant, insular."

"You may be right."

"Do you speak any German?"

"No."

"French?" and when Cuffee shook his head, "Italian?"

"No."

"How do you expect to be understood?" He held up a hand, small and shapely, "No, I will tell you. You expect that other people will speak English. Is that not so?"

"Probably."

"Is not that very English?" Cuffee made a gesture that admitted such might be the case.

"A fellow countryman of yours said there were three main reasons why people travel. Infirmity of body, imbecility of mind, or inevitable necessity. Which is your cause?" Cuffee could see Uta watching him, her goblet burning like some night flower as she raised it to her lips. Was that what she was then. His inevitable necessity. Needs must.

"It will have to be the third."

"And what inevitable necessity drives one so young?"

"I think I am one of the ones who must find somewhere else to live because they cannot live where they are," and as he said it he had an image of his father looking out over the garden at Knutsford, searching his long lost deserts.

"And where do you think you will find this place?"

"South. Somewhere the landscape is larger than the figures."

"You are a seeker of solitude then?"

"No, I have found solitude. I only wish to be where people will not interrupt it."

"That has the sound of metaphysics to me. That at least is un-English. But I have never understood what makes a man leave his homeland and go to foreign parts to find himself. Surely if he is to find himself anywhere it will be in the land of his birth?"

"Sometimes the land of your birth does not hold your true landscape."

"In that we Germans are more fortunate than most. We have a landscape to meet all of our needs."

"Where are your deserts?"

"We have had our deserts, young man, but we rebuilt

them," and his tone was almost harsh with authority. Cuffee nodded.

"Yes, but there are other things to be done with deserts. That is what is wrong with England. It has no deserts." Zimmerman stared at him a moment then he reached out for the fruit bowl.

"That is what other nations cannot understand about us, that we are proud to be Germans."

"I don't know. There are many Englishmen proud to be English."

"Ah yes, it is so everywhere. But here, here it is something more, something greater. People do not understand. They did not understand why Hitler could have so much support. They could not see that he touched the pulse of a great nation, that he made them proud to be German. If you understand that then you understand the Third Reich. If you don't you simply think Adolf Hitler was the anti-Christ."

"These are things I know nothing of."

"Well then, perhaps while you are with us I may hope to enlighten you. The only thing I have against young people today is that they will wear their ignorance as if it were something to be proud of. Now if you will excuse me. There are certain things I must attend to," and he rose and after kissing both Yani and Uta on the cheek he shook hands with Cuffee and left the room.

They sat at the table, constrained in Yani's presence. She seemed to sense this and slowly peeled herself an apple, the yellow ribbon of skin spinning out under the knife as she turned the fruit round and round. When it was finished she looked up at them and put the apple on her plate.

"Good night." And they sat looking not at each other but at the naked fruit. After a moment Uta said,

"What did you think of Herr Zimmerman?" Cuffee pretended a vagueness he did not feel.

"He seemed all right." The reply obviously did not satisfy her.

"All right? What does that mean?"

"Decent old stick," which made her angry.

"He is not an old stick, he is a very clever man."

"Yes he's all right," then as she looked away, "come on, I'm only joking."

"Why, what is there to joke about. You come to ask me to go away with you and you joke abut Herr Zimmerman. He is not a joke."

"No," Cuffee said and blew out smoke. "No. He isn't. It's up to him whether you go or not, isn't it?" Uta stretched across and took Yani's apple.

"He has been very good to me. He has been as a father to me. I will have to discuss it with him of course."

"And of course he will say no."

"It will depend on how well he likes you."

"That's good news. I can tell you now he won't like me."

"How can you be sure, he might like you very much." Cuffee knew why he wouldn't like him, and why the dislike would be reciprocal. He must not spend too much time fighting with Zimmerman. She must make up her mind soon and they must leave. They had a long way to go and winter was coming. Almost as an afterthought he said,

"We will be going by bicycle, I hope you can ride one."

"By bicycle?"

"Yes. It takes a long time but it's worth it when you get there." On the road he would make her his own. By the time they reached the sun he would have made her forget this place and these people, he would bind her to him as in blood.

From his window he could see the moon, risen to zenith, and the earth held in its pale cast. The houses of the village had drawn together for comfort and massed in black shadow, an occasional roof slope giving back a dull pewter shine. The air was cold and a rime of frost held everything in delicate vice. The poplars rose swift and straight, frozen fountains of brumal night.

How far the warm south seemed with its tawny beaches and orange sun. As remote as his father must feel them to be, dreamscapes. He felt the cold clench in his bones, a foreboding of winter and its dark domain. Yes, soon, soon he must go. He had a vision, as from a great golden height, of two naked figures dancing on the shore, with waves in pearly ruffles around their feet. Perhaps in that burning air there might be found the shapes he could need to paint, the blazing images of a sun-struck world that would find response in his heart, his invisible sun burning darkly within him. When both worlds, within and without, were as one, then he would be free. This was all that life was about, finding that place that revealed you to yourself, allowed the corollaries of each individual proposition to exist most fully. He searched his father's words for an instance of that sense of location that makes the problem of identity seem an irrelevance.

2nd Nov.
To see someone travelling across the
desert, a man upon a camel, at some
distance, it brings the heart into the
mouth with the sublimity of what it
expresses, carrying the imagination
beyond the reach of language, even
thought. All the ideas I ever had
of beauty, all that I could conceive
life to be, they all were dispelled as
I looked into those opaque terrible
distances and heard that wind, that
empty wind which had touched no green
thing in a day's blowing.
Once I had seen the desert I knew I
could never be the same again. It
told me things of myself that I had
assumed only God, if such there is, could
know. Had I been born there I would know
myself, as we are told God knows himself.
As it is I see it with a fracturing lucidity,
the aridity and limitlessness of my soul.
It both frightens and comforts me at one
and the same time.

This paradox of the father comforted the son as he lay in his strange bed. He too was both troubled and consoled by what lay before him. Looking back he could see that the source of his father's feeling was the proximity of reality, more than proximity, the immediate presence of that which is undeniably real. By this token perhaps he too was face to face with his reality. Whatever the outcome he would not end as his father had, trapped in his semi-detached villa, longing for what might have been. At some crucial moment he must have failed to choose, made the pretend choice with its pretend rationalizations. He, Cuffee, wouldn't make that mistake, no matter what the outcome.

He awoke in the morning in the wide bed and as soon as his eyes opened he knew where he was and why and a throb of excitement quickened him so that he could not bear to lie a moment but rose and washed, towelling himself briskly as he looked out over the morning scene. It was early and there was a faint ground mist which hung against the walls and obscured the water of the moat. Unseen the ducks squabbled and splashed. In a small tree in the grounds a bird flicked from branch to branch, curious little bead. Even at that distance he could see its red breast, the faintest twinge of colour. The village had not yet convinced itself that the night was over, except for certain chimneys, threading thin smoke upwards, grey orisons to the silver dawn.

After breakfast he tried to draw Uta aside that they might walk outside the castle but she made some excuse and departed with Yani leaving him in the room with Herr Zimmerman who was reading the morning papers and drinking coffee. He looked up after a moment.

"Ah, they have gone. Leaving us together." Cuffee nodded.

"Looks like it."

"Well we must put the opportunity to good use. Perhaps I can show you the rest of the house."

"Thank you."

"Or better still, perhaps I can show you my pets." When he received no response he went on, "Did Uta not tell you of my hobby?"

"I don't think so."

"I keep hawks and falcons, would you like to see them?"

"I would, yes."

They climbed an iron staircase to the aviary. The whole of the top floor had been taken for the birds and there was a pungent smell of meat and cages.

"Do you know anything of falconry?" Cuffee shook his head.

"It is a very ancient sport, although that is not the word for it. We have no words for the important things, have you noticed? In German death is *Tod*. Isn't that a stupid word for something so important."

"On your tod."

"What is that?"

"Just a foolishness. What kind of hawk is that?"

"Ah. That is a goshawk. He is mad that one."

The hawk sat in its long cage and stared at them with yellow wild eyes, an expression of permanent outrage in its unblinking gaze. The white featherings of its legs ended in rapacious talons, hooked over the perch, glossy blue black and perfectly pointed.

"He was taken by a method that is almost ended. He was netted in flight when almost full grown. He knew what the free air was like and it has never left him, his resentment of capture. He hates, that one."

"He feels trapped I suppose."

"Perhaps that is so. Even when he is flying he must know he cannot escape."

"Maybe some day he will just go on and on and you'll never see," and he wanted to say "her" but couldn't bring himself to it, "him again."

"That is a chance you take every time you release any bird of prey. Even these and they are not as that one."

"What are they?"

"They are peregrine falcons, they are the most beautiful of all God's creatures." It rather surprised Cuffee to hear God's name mentioned as it was a concept with which he rarely troubled himself. He remembered his father had written it in his book and the word had jarred his eye. He turned his attention to the peregrines who sat in their black, grey tinged feathers, lemony white on the chest, darkening to buff leggings, the talons red buff and finer than the goshawk's. Their

273

eyes, although inscrutably alien, were yet more witting of relationship, the beetling of the low brow not quite so severe. One of them, the larger, jumped down on to the floor of the cage and in a jerky strut walked to the end and turned, made a raucous yawk and bounded back beside its mate.

"That is the female. In birds of prey the female is always the larger. Do you find that a significant fact?" Cuffee shrugged, disguising his amusement at the man's obviousness.

"Perhaps if I were a bird of prey it might seem more important."

"There are some women who are like hawks," Zimmerman went on, intent upon his theme, "you do not have them in your mythology, your women are all beautiful and true and meek. Not so with us. With us the women can be as strong, stronger even. Do you know the story of Siegfried and Brunnhilde?"

"No, I'm afraid not." Zimmerman looked at him with what Cuffee took to be contempt.

"No, of course not." He walked on, past the other cages. "These are little hawks, what you call windhovers and merlin. Ladies' hawks and peasants'." He went up another flight of stairs and Cuffee followed him without glancing at the birds. "In medieval times all men had their hawks, a king had an eagle and a peasant had, what is your name for the one that hovers?"

"A kestrel."

"Yes, a kestrel. Every man had a hawk befitting his station." The morning stunned the eye with its bright crystalline glitter, frost and high cold sunlight everywhere.

"This is no longer the middle ages though," Cuffee said, noticing that the stairs had put Zimmerman somewhat out of breath. He looked at Cuffee and the challenge in his words.

"You think I am an eccentric. A middle-aged business man who lives in a castle and keeps hawks. You see me as absurd, is that not so?" Cuffee shook his head but Zimmerman went on, "You cannot help it. It is your age, you believe in nothing except doing what you want. Some of you invent philosophies to justify that, the rest just practise it, not knowing why or where it will take them. I have seen young people who believed in things, who had a purpose. They were like a race of young gods, they had a meaning in their lives. And that meaning was made possible because of religion. And the prophet of that religion was the man you know as Adolf Hitler. I know that he was mad, I know that he was responsible for terrible things, but he had the vision of a great prophet, and more, he had the power to make people see his vision." He stopped and looked out over the countryside. His face was flushed and his breathing remained uneven. "Is the world not a beautiful place? Look my young friend and tell me, is it not a beautiful place?"

Below them the landscape spread, perfect in its jewelled detail. A man led a brown horse towards the castle, pulling a cart laden with sawn logs. Their clean ends showed and the horse had a white blaze on its forehead. Plumes of steam came from its nostrils. The air around them glittered, empty of softness. Far away there were royal blue hills. Cuffee instinctively thought of them as being south. His hands ached from the coldness of the stone as he leaned. He rested on his forearms. He did not wish to oppose this man. He only wished to reach those hills and run down their far slopes. Perhaps for the first time in his life he was near, and wittingly so, to what he wanted of life. Uta was part of it. Uta or someone like her. Someone who could match what he knew to be in himself, that empty, monotonous simplicity that was so constantly being frustrated. He had seen it most clearly with the friend of Harry's who came, a small, dark, endlessly complex little man. In some way he had made Cuffee realize how uncomplicated he was, not uncomplicated like Harry because Harry was an innocent, with no energies, no appetites, no lusts. But in a cruel, selfish, direct way he was quite without problems. Only the landscape in which he lived would not admit of such simplicity but intruded endlessly its guilts and responsibilities. That was why he must leave it and take with him someone of his own kind, whom he could not hurt like he had hurt those others, those vulnerable others. Yes, the world was beautiful, but before it could be enjoyed it had to be ordered, as in his own way doubtless his host endeavoured to order it. He turned to Zimmerman, filled with the sudden feeling that he might tell him these things and be understood. Zimmerman still looked out and away from him.

"Herr Zimmerman, I would like to tell you why I have come here."

"I know why you have come," he said, without looking round.

"I have come to take Uta away with me."

"I know that."

"Do you approve or disapprove?"

"Uta is a rare person. She means much to me. As much as my own daughter." More, Cuffee thought, much more than your own daughter.

"You cannot keep her here for ever." Zimmerman turned, his face hypnotic with rage. Cuffee felt himself sink until it seemed as though he was looking up at Zimmerman, gazing up at a steep angle into the fierce face, the eyebrows in a bar above the bright angry eyes.

"Keep her? I do not keep her here. What do you know to talk of keeping? She is free, free to leave when she will, to go and never come back. She is not a prisoner here." And slowly the level returned, slowly until they were eye to eye again and Cuffee felt his heartbeat slacken.

"You have come for Uta. Very well. Be my guest here while you speak with her. Talk to her, find out about her, what she is like, how she thinks. Then ask her. If she will go with you take her and go. If she will not then leave, go upon your journey alone. Will you accept that?" He distrusted this openness, this fairness, but there was nothing he could do but agree and admit it generous. They shook hands on it and Zimmerman clapped his shoulder. Cuffee did not like it, this ease of manner, but in default of alternative he could do nothing but endure its familiarity.

When he went to his room he was surprised to find Yani sitting by the open window. From below in the moat the ducks could be heard, their liquid dashes filling the room with ripples. Yani said nothing but looked out of the window. Cuffee lay on the bed and smoked a cigarette. After a time Yani rose to leave. As she reached the door he said,

"What do you think?"

"About what?"

"Me. Being here."

"It is not my concern."

"You know why I am here."

"It is not my concern."

"Even if Uta decides to go with me?" Yani stared straight at the door.

"She will not."

"How do you know?"

"My father will not let you take her."

"He might not be able to stop her." Yani looked at him for the first time.

"It will be best if you understand that she will not go. It will save a lot of your time."

"Has anyone ever asked Uta to go away?"

"Some have."

"Have you?" She almost looked but checked.

"What do you mean?"

"If you and she could go away would you not go?"

"We do go away."

"But you always come back."

"This is our home. This is where we live." He sat up and caught her arm.

"Uta and I are alike. She has lived here too long. And so have you." Yani extracted her arm and to his surprise she smiled, wan but not unamused.

"Are you asking me to go with you?" Cuffee lay back on the bed.

"No, Yani. You will have to lose her some time. Best for you if it's clean. You wouldn't want to watch her being in love with me." He wanted not to have said it almost at once but as there was nothing he could do he watched the little face go bleak with hurt. She opened the door and stepped out. Then he heard her feet clattering quickly along the corridor. Poor little creature. She was going to lose whichever way it went.

He lay back and smoked, thinking of Zimmerman and his almost absurd, somehow forbidding, postures. He was a strong man, strong in his obsessions, strong with single-mindedness. He was a man of authority. He, Cuffee, had always found authority a goad, but perhaps this time it would be best to avoid any conflict. Nothing would be served by opposing his host. Uta must come with him for reasons that circumvented Zimmerman completely, giving no grounds for contest. She must come to love him. It did not seem such a simple thing to manage, now that he needed it. Before women had loved him and he had scarcely noticed. There had always been someone, wanting, longing. It came to him that for the first time he had outdistanced his lovers, the pursuers, shaken them off one by one. In order to need the love of someone else. He could see no sense to it, no pattern. He went to the window and threw his cigarette end to the ducks. They came rushing up, then turned away with a squabble of disappointment. When he turned Uta was in the room, by the door.

"I didn't hear you."

"Peter, I have good news for us. Herr Zimmerman is going away tomorrow."

"For how long?"

"I don't know but several days. We can be together all day." Cuffee wanted to ask why they could not be together anyway but she had come up and put her arms round his neck. "Aren't you pleased?"

"Yes, of course. When did he decide to go?"

"I don't know. He has only just told me."

"Good. Perhaps when he comes back we can tell him that you are coming with me." She kissed him.

"Do you remember when we met, at that party? Did you think I was beautiful then?"

"Yes."

"Did you hate me after I left you in the hotel, after Yani wounded you?"

"I wasn't very fond of you for a while." Her fingers soothed the scar in his eyebrow.

"I did not know what I was doing." That was something Cuffee was not sure about. He would have preferred her to know perfectly well. It did not seem to him improbable that such an act could be an expression of love, of a sort of love anyway. Certainly it was that more than any other single thing about her that had brought him back.

"It does not matter."

"Oh, but it does. I wish it had never happened, or that I had stayed to look after you. But we were so frightened. Yani thought she would be arrested so we . . ." but he cut her off. He did not want it explained away.

"It does not matter. The cut was no worse than I might have

got in a street fight. I did not mind that. It was afterwards that was bad."

"Why, what happened afterwards?"

"I was ill. I got very wet and very cold and they took me to hospital. That was much worse. Then I was helpless. That is the worst."

"Yes, I know. I have been helpless, and those I loved also. But I will tell you these things tomorrow, in order that you may know about me, and what I am like." Even as she said it it sounded odd, he could hear Zimmerman's voice advocating it, stepping aside to facilitate this process of comprehension. He distrusted it, the glibness. He was being denied choice by having all given to him. The only thing he could do was to place Uta's response beyond doubt by the time that Zimmerman returned.

He saw him leave in the morning. Footsteps on the cobbles brought him to the window and he was crossing the bridge, unaccompanied save for his pale shadow. Between the poplars he went, a small dark figure who did not look back at the castle. Cuffee watched him, wondering what his thoughts were, if this were all a ruse, an elaborate display of contempt. Well they would see. He waved derisively to him but was not seen. In the tree below the window the robin perched until Cuffee's wave disturbed it and it went looping away. Herr Zimmerman turned a corner out of sight and in an instant the landscape was quite devoid of movement, frozen before his sight. Disconcerted by its abrupt emptiness he retired once more to his bed, using as pretext the earliness of the hour.

THE IDYLL

They walked in the circular grounds, through grass stiff with frost, white blades that bent underfoot, leaving black tracks behind. The edges of the moat were lacy with ice, the tree, bereft of leaf, writhed in the iron ground. The sun shone red and round in a blanched, taut sky. All around the horizon an umber haze hung, sealing them within this dying world. The day ached with a cold, fierce pain, remembering in its stony bones the innumerable past onsets of winter, a memory more than human, but including humanity's short recall. As they walked in the redraw sunlight, circles within circles, her story was told.

"I was born in a small village outside Frankfurt. I was an only child. My father was a baker before the war but of course I never knew those times. When the war was over he could not work as a baker and we came to Frankfurt so that my father could get work in the rebuilding of the city. You cannot imagine what these cities were like that had had the bombing. There was nothing left only broken stones and walls with holes where the windows had been and the smell of ruin everywhere. He worked as a labourer my father and he was not strong enough for such work and when he came home at night he would be so tired that he would fall asleep in the chair still wearing his boots. I would sit and unpick the knots in the laces so that I might take them off. They were covered in mud and clay and sometimes the knots had got wet and were so tight that it would take me nearly an hour to undo them. There were times though when he was not so tired that he would make me up some dough and bake a few small loaves. That was what made me happiest in my childhood, to see my father's face as he brought the new breads out of the oven and the lovely smell of the crust and the white powdery flour on his hands and arms.

"But when I was only seven there was an accident at a wall my father was working on and he was trapped under the stone. When they got him out his legs were crushed and his back was hurt and he could not walk. They brought him home and put him on the couch by the stove and he lay there, helpless. So then my mother was the only one going to work and I could not go to school as I had to stay and look after my father. He worried that I was losing my education and so he tried to teach me things himself but he did not know very much except about baking and the only thing I can remember now that he taught me were the stories from a book about the heroes and the gods. I loved one story best, the story of Siegfried and Brunnhilde and when she had Siegfried killed by betraying his weakness where the leaf had fallen on his back I always wept.

"My father also told me about his childhood and about where he grew up, a little village in the Black Forest and told me of the strange things that happened there, of trolls and hobgoblins and werewolves and fox-demons. I think it was when his pain became very bad that he would tell me these things to help him suffer. Of course, I did not understand this when I was a little girl but only knew it was necessary for him to talk to me of such things even though it made me very frightened to hear of them, and sometimes at night I would wake up screaming from the bad dreams.

"The worst of all the stories was about the fox-demon. It was the story of a little girl who was out in the forest playing and she went too far into the trees and lost her way and it began to grow dark so she grew frightened for her parents had warned her of the fox-demon who lived in the forest and how when the light was fading he came out looking for all the lost creatures. But the more she hurried to find a way out the deeper she went into the forest. Then to her terror, as she came into a clearing among the trees, she saw the fox-demon sitting, cleaning his paws. He lifted up his long foxy face and when he saw her he smiled for he knew he could catch a little girl like that very easily. When the girl saw his red eyes and his long bristly snout she turned and fled as fast as she could, not considering where she ran but fleeing only from the fox-demon. Every time she looked back she could see him coming, his eyes shining and his breath panting.

"She ran and ran until she was exhausted and could run no

further and was almost ready to lie down and let the beast devour her when she saw a light through the trees and she ran towards it and to her joy she saw it was a cottage with a lamp in the window. With the last of her strength she reached the door and beat on it with her hands, terrified that it would not open in time for she could hear the fox-demon close behind her. But then the door opened and an old man looked out.

" 'What is wrong, my child?' he asked. 'Please save me, the fox-demon is close behind and he will eat me if you do not let me in.' 'Quickly, come inside,' the old man said, and she leapt into the warm lighted cottage and heard the door being closed and bolts secured. She fell upon the floor and began to weep for joy at having been saved. 'Now my dear, do not cry,' she heard the old man say and when she turned to thank him for saving her life she saw that his face, which had been round and kindly before, was growing long and pointed with hair sprouting on it and she recognized once more the face of the fox-demon."

It was a parable Cuffee knew without telling. It was betrayal such as only love or trust could suffer. It was like a warning. Love is the fatal flaw, like the leaf on Siegfried's back. Trust is the final desperation. The starkness contained its own comfort, like all nadirs. The true shape of things, the leafless tree. But looking, in the skeletal branches the robin remained, judas blossom, heart flower, growing once in the moment of betrayal. He had never loved, not anyone, not truly. Not only that he had made others unhappy, but that he had never let himself care enough for any save himself. He could see quite clearly then what he must do, it burned in his mind until he was dazzled. Then the robin flew up out of the tree and his epiphany with it. Bereft, he stood, his thoughts writhing in the iron earth. Uta went on, tugging his sleeve.

"My father's condition got worse as time went on and finally he had to be taken up to the bedroom and he had to stay in bed all the time. About then my mother began to bring home things she received from a soldier, cigarettes and food and soap and then one night she brought the soldier home and I was sent early to bed so that they might be alone downstairs. She never told him about my father upstairs because he was not a bad man, even though he bought a woman with these articles he was only doing what they all did and I am sure if he had known that the woman's husband was lying upstairs unable to walk he would not have come to the house. My father must have known for he and my mother used to quarrel and they would shout at each other but there was nothing he could do because she said she would leave us and I would be taken and put in a place and he would not even be able to come and visit me. I think he did not care about himself any more, only that I would be all right but there was nothing he could do about it.

"One night I had a very bad dream about the fox-demon, and I woke up screaming only it wasn't me but my mother who was screaming and when I ran in my father was lying half on the floor and half on the bed and all over the sheets was blood where he had cut his wrists with a piece of broken mirror. My mother tried to say afterwards that he did it because of the pain he was in, but I knew it was from lying upstairs at night listening to her and her soldier.

"After that when the soldier came they stayed in the room my father had had and I used to hear them and the noises they made. I could never imagine what it was they did to cause such noises and I would cover my head with the pillow to shut out the sound. In those days the thing I wanted most was to grow up so that I could be a nun. I had started to go to school again and it was a convent school and it was from there that I got the idea of becoming a nun. I loved the clothes they wore, the white so white and smooth and the many folds of black and how sweet their faces looked inside the cowls. It was more like a little house each of them lived in separately and I wanted to be in one, safe and clean and never unhappy any more. The only other thing I like to do was to skate. I was very good at it and it was the only thing which made me really happy. The nuns did not make me happy. It was just that I longed to be one, but to skate made me really happy, gliding along and everything so smooth and like flying and the thrill the ice gave in your ankles like an electric current. The only trouble was that I didn't have any skates of my own and I had to borrow those belonging to others. It was when I was wearing a pair of skating boots that belonged to someone else that I had my accident. I skated on a pond near the school and in the middle of the ice there was an iron post that stuck up from the bottom of the pond. I was skating very fast one day and trying to do a turn that was quite difficult when my ankle turned over because the boots were too large and I crashed into the post with my face. The force of it made me completely unconscious. The next thing I knew was that I was in hospital and my whole face was bandaged. My nose was broken, my forehead and both my eyes were so damaged that they thought I might not be able to see. And even if I could see, they told my mother, my face would always be scarred because of the way that the flesh had been torn. My mother said to me the best thing would be if I were to go into a convent. She did not know why that made me laugh so much. It was at this time that Herr Zimmerman found me."

Later, from his window, Cuffee watched the sun enter the brown rim of murk around the skyline, its bright red growing lurid till an ominous russet twilight lay over the land. The shadows under the wall turned into solids of gloom and the day died in throes of magenta and ruby, a great holocaust in the west. It matched his mood, sombre, yet gaudy from the melodrama of Uta's story. He pondered it, remembering her rapt, almost spellbound telling as if it fascinated her more than it could any other listener. Most of all the plight of her father touched him. He was, to Cuffee's mind, not unlike his own father and there was a way in which he himself could appreciate his need to choose in the face of the implacably malevolent universe. That is what he would have done, had he been unable to kill the woman, or the soldier, or both. He would have exercised his final choice. In a way that would be less terrible than Mr. Cuffee's slow atrophy. What had happened to him was perhaps the cruellest thing of all. To have his dream made so unmistakably manifest that no evasion is possible. His vision of reality had been honed to such an edge as would cut him to the bone for the rest of his life. Cheshire and Knutsford must seem most cruel ironies with their thick green glut and park-like pleasantry.

> Oct. 2nd.
> I rode out some miles until only
> desert lay around and then stopped.
> As soon as the engine died the
> silence came pouring in. With my
> binoculars I scanned the sand,
> letting my eyes caress the sculpted
> surfaces like fingers, trembling with
> excitement as they plunged into some
> blue pool of shade, taut with passion as
> they explored voluptuous dunes. Later
> in the brothel, I let my fingers walk over the
> desert of my purchase, remembering behind closed
> eyes the prone wastes of the land. It was the
> flesh of women that was as sand to me, and the
> desert was the flesh that gave me solace.

But he had returned, come back to his wife and children, to teaching, to a life sentence. Why? Because he could not choose, could not flex the muscle of his will sufficiently to make the break. Instead of the clean selfish act, the long festering years of frustration. Somewhere, far in the past, he had made the wrong choice, or failed to make a choice at all. It was all a warning, all pointing his way. He must not make the same mistakes, there must be profit from his father's failures. That much he owed him. He looked out into the night, now moving swiftly into darkness, arrested by the admission that he owed his father anything. He tried to think of some moment between them when anything approaching affection had existed. But all he could see was his father administering punishment. Left hand, right hand. It was scarcely a memory appropriate to this change of heart. He came from the window and washed before dinner.

His dreams that night were strange and tinged with fear. He dreamed of empty streets and sudden confrontations on corners where meaningless conversations tried, dimly, to discover some secret, some whereabouts of someone whose identity remained obscure throughout. It was a woman but it might have been anyone and although he searched for her he was also apprehensive of finding her. It seemed to him in the dream that perhaps he sought her for no other reason than to know who she was but this in no way helped him. The fear came from the landscape, bleak buildings and inexplicable ruins, doors which opened from bare streets into further bare streets, dogs which came running, barking, only to become blown newspapers flapping round his legs when he tried to stroke them. On one of the newspapers there was a photograph of a nun he recognized as the one who had looked after him when he had been ill in France. He woke once, shivering from having kicked off his eiderdown, still lost in the midst of his dream, and fear knotted in him and sent him scrambling for his cover, under which he hid, taking care that no part of him was left outside.

When they went next day to walk in the grounds the moat was iced on both edges, only a narrow channel in the middle remained free and the ducks paddled it in single file. The trunks of the trees were stockinged in frost and the grass crunched underfoot. Beneath, the earth lay rigid, old cadaver. In cyclopic scrutiny the sun, red-eyed, watched, and like some smallest reflection the robin, bloody-breasted, bobbed before them.

"The doctors told my mother that my face would be ruined and that I would be very fortunate if I could see properly. When my mother heard this she said it would be best for me to take the vows of a nun when I was old enough and become the bride of Christ. What she meant was that I would never be the bride of man with my face as it would be. I tried to be happy that I would be a nun as I had wanted but I was sad because I would be so ugly. When I cried the salt tears would sting in the wounds and make me cry even more.

"I had been in the hospital for several weeks when one day I heard a voice that I had not heard before. I knew all the voices of the doctors but sometimes they brought new ones to look at my face and I thought this would be another. But it was not, it was Herr Zimmerman. He had heard of my accident and come to see me. The doctors told him how badly my face was hurt and that there was not much chance of it healing without leaving bad scars. He spoke to me and asked me what I wanted to be and I said a nun. This made him laugh. I remember his laugh and his hands, one very loud and the other soft and gentle. He said he had seen pictures of me and I was too beautiful to be a nun. I said I wasn't beautiful and if he saw under the bandages he would not say I was. He said he could make me beautiful again if I really wanted it. I did not believe him but he said he could so I believed him. He went away and came back with a very important specialist and this man examined me and said he could save my sight. Then Herr Zimmerman brought another important doctor who had made many new faces for soldiers who had been wounded in the war. He said he could make an operation that would leave very little sign of the wounds.

"My mother had to sign papers to allow them to operate but what I did not know at the time was that she also signed papers that let Herr Zimmerman adopt me. They did not tell me at the time because they thought it would upset me while I had the operation but they did not know how glad it would have made me.

"So they began the operations and there were very many of them and each night I had to be strapped down on my bed and given something to make me sleep so that I wouldn't move or cry out lest it damaged the work they had done on my face. My eyes were closed for a very long time and after my mother stopped coming to see me I did not know what any of the people looked like, all I knew were their voices and the smell of their hands when they fed me. Sometimes I would try to feel through the bandages what my new face was like but my fingers could tell nothing, only where the features were, not what they were like. I would lie there at night, unable to move and everything as black as black and the air full of the smell of flowers that Herr Zimmerman sent and it was like being in your own coffin under the lid with the flowers piled on top and each night I was sure it would never end and that I was really dead and buried and the black pressing down on my eyes was earth and the sweet smell dying flowers. Then I would try to come awake into the daylight and see the sun and colours but I was strapped down and could not move and cold sweat would cover my body so that I started to shiver."

That was the terror of no choice made absolute Cuffee thought. It seemed now that even the memory of his father, offering him a choice of hands before he punished, was one that he might cherish. It did not now, hearing Uta's tale, seem so pointless to be offered, in the face of inevitable punishment, an iota of free will in order that he might not be totally helpless before a malevolent universe. "It is the hallmark of the solitary man that he can choose, and his prime virtue." And yet perhaps it would have been better if he had not been a solitary, if these experiences of childhood had not shaped him as he was now so that the process of achieving freedom was such a tortured one.

"At last the operations were over and they took off the bandages and the first person I saw when I opened my eyes was Herr Zimmerman. Even though I had never seen him before I knew it was him as soon as I saw his face. When I saw him I cried which pleased all the doctors very much because it showed them that the tear ducts had not been impaired. I thought that it was all over then but when I saw my face I realized it was not. My nose had to be re-set several times before they could get it right and even then they could not get it quite straight and that is why it has this ridge on it. But the real difficulty was with my eyebrows because if they had put new skin there I would have had no eyebrows and yet the way the wounds had been to join them up made very bad lines. So they had to open the cuts and sew them up again and put new skin in at the corners of my eyes and on the bridge of my nose and that was very delicate and the new skin did not join properly and had to be done again. So with everything I was in hospital for nearly a year.

"Even when they had finished with me and said I could leave I still did not look very nice. The new skin was a different colour from the old and the lines where they joined were red and I had no eyebrows yet and with lying in bed and all the good food I had become fat. No, I was not very beautiful then.

"When I left the hospital Herr Zimmerman had me taken to his hunting lodge in the Black Forest. I was to stay there until I was quite well. It was good for me because I did not want to meet anyone for I was very self-conscious about my appearance. I did not mind the Kemmels, who were the couple who looked after the lodge, but I did not want to meet any of Herr Zimmerman's friends or his daughter until my face was quite better. So all of the summer and through the autumn I was at the lodge and I had a pony to ride and every day I would go riding in the forest and if I ever got lost I did not have to worry like the poor girl in the fairy story because the pony knew the way home and I would just sit on his back and let him walk and dream that I was Brunhilde waiting for her Siegfried to return to her and imagine how I would be beautiful like the warrior queen and when I galloped my hair would stream out behind me for it was very long now, never having been cut since I had my accident.

"The Black Forest is a wonderful place. It is like an enormous cathedral, so large and cool and quiet and the light comes down through the columns of the trees in great shafts and I would ride along with my head back and my eyes closed and when we passed through a beam of sunlight it was as if a bright golden lantern was lit inside my head and then it would all go dark until the next time.

"I think being alone so much and dreaming of things made me a very strange girl. I did not talk to the Kemmels much and always liked to slip away and be by myself. They had no children of their own as their three sons had been killed in the war but they were not unhappy and they were very kind to me. At the end of the autumn Herr Zimmerman and the doctors came up to see me and they were all very satisfied that my face had healed so well. My eyebrows had grown in and they covered the marks of the scars and the skin on my nose had joined beautifully and with the tan I had from being outdoors you could hardly see any lines at all. So at the end of their examination Herr Zimmerman said I could leave the lodge and come to live with him and his daughter in the castle. Although I was sad to leave the forest and my pony and the Kemmels I was also excited to be going to where Herr Zimmerman lived for I knew by now that I would not be going back to my mother any more. This did not distress me at all, in fact I could not remember very clearly what she looked like. So, just before the snows started, at about this time of the year I left the Black Forest and came to live in the castle."

After they had come in Cuffee went to his room. A growing sense of unreality had him and as he stood at the window looking out he felt uncertain, dubious almost of his central purpose. In Uta's telling there was a kind of barrier between them. Rather than making her better known, closer, it seemed only to reinforce the identity she possessed here, with Zimmerman and Yani, in the castle. Their talk should not be of the past, from which he was excluded, but of what they would do when they left here, together.

A grey, livid cast had set everywhere and the air was thick and weighed with silence. The light was slowly being squeezed out of the day by the low, leaden pressure of the clouds. In its place there was a sort of twilight, a crepuscular murk that saddened him as it quenched all colour, embalmed the day in funereal gloom. He remembered being ill as a child, the bitter tongue-curling doses of medicine, and lying back, his mouth slowly losing its horrible taste, watching the sediment settle in the bottle, being borne down with it into realms of ineffable sadness, pure nameless misery. This moment, on the threshold of mirkshut, was an echo, a reflection of those childhood descents into the vale. Then he had saved himself by turning to the adventures of *Strang the Terrible* or *Morgan the Mighty*. His hero now was at one and the same time infinitely more remote and unbearably closer.

> Feb. 9th.
> Some thoughts on the desert.
> Vistas so sensuous, so exquisitely moulded
> they awaken longings such as one might have
> for the flesh of a woman.
> Scarves of sand blowing across its tawny
> breasts.
> The desert, lying in robes of silk,
> awaits her lovers to trace in her trackless

sands their own erotic intent.
Farthest gauzes, shimmerings of disbelief.
Against the fullest possible curvature a
scarped edge so keen that the thought of razored
flesh could not be avoided.
Any empty thing which is empty by its inmost
nature, not simply devoid of ornament, such a
thing will endlessly feed the mind. The emptiness
of the desert is of this kind.

His dreams, when they came, were all terror. Faces; Uta's
first, peeling and splitting, features breaking away until it was
no longer her but another, a dead other one and in the grave a
dog rotted, its flesh melting on its bones, the fur dripping from
the snout like putrid velveteen and the steady grimace of its
teeth shining in the buried dark. A scarecrow in a field, ragged
face split in idiot mirth. He could see himself curled in his
dream, dreaming and tried to wake himself but only rained
kicks on the face of a woman and then poured milk on to her
to revive her but it ran into the dark holes of her eyes and he
tried to shake her by the shoulders and she broke, crumbled as
he held her.

There had been a fall of snow, not deep but leaving the
landscape pied and strange, destroying perspective and achieving patterns of simplest contrast, abstractions of white on
black. They walked this time in a silent world, leaving their
trail behind them until they met it again and proceeded on
their circular way. The snow lay across the moat and the
ducks had departed. The robin throbbed across their path and
made Cuffee think of the brief blooms of flowers and the nub
of a man's arm, glowing in the hedgerows. In his mind they
coalesced, these gules, to make a blazon in which the red of life
stood against the empty white of death. For the colour of
death he perceived now was not black but the bleak blank of
white. Black was blindness, was the dark in which the mind
that did not know life lived.

"When I came here I was nearly fourteen and did not know
what would befall me in my new life. When I saw the castle as

we drove up I was very frightened, it looked so dark and ominous. I was taken up to my room and soon Herr Zimmerman came with Yani. She was much then as she is now, pale and quiet and her eyes always looking away. She was only a little older than I and Herr Zimmerman left us together to be friends. From the first he treated me exactly as he did Yani.

"In those days the castle was very mysterious to me and there were places in it that Yani had never been. Many of the corridors frightened me and especially was I afraid of the one with the heads of the animals in it. I would never go along that corridor alone and even with Yani I would always run. We played at games with the dresses that had belonged to Yani's mother. We would dress up in them and play at being princesses in the castle or pretend that we were prisoners and were waiting a knight to rescue us. We would tell each other what our knight looked like, how brave he was and noble and what deeds of courage he had done, each trying to outdo the other in details of how he would be dressed and what he would say. I suppose we were strange children but it would have been surprising if we had not been, growing up in a place such as this with Herr Zimmerman so often away on his business and the governesses who changed every few weeks for none of them could stand living alone here.

"I do not know if I was happy. I could hardly remember if I had ever been happy before and I accepted my life as being the only one I had ever known. My face was completely healed now and as I grew older it was obvious that I was going to be much more beautiful than Yani. I tried not to take pleasure in it but I could not help it and I would sit in front of the mirror combing my hair until Yani would start to cry and run out of the room. When I realized how unhappy it made her I was upset, but also, inside I was pleased, for it gave me a power over Yani that I could use when we quarrelled. I think it was a time when one is naturally cruel and I made poor Yani very unhappy in a great many ways. Afterwards I would be sorry but that would never stop me doing it again.

"Then one night just as we were going to bed I told Yani the story of the fox-demon and that night she had terrible dreams and woke up screaming. She screamed so loud that it wakened Herr Zimmerman and he was very angry when Yani told him what had happened. It was the only time he ever punished me. He sent Yani to his room to sleep and made me stand in the corner of our bedroom. There he said I could stand until I had learned my lesson. He wrapped himself in a blanket and sat in a chair. It was very cold and I only had my nightdress on and I soon was shivering and trembling and after a time I began to cry but Herr Zimmerman would not listen and made me stand there till I could stand no longer but crouched in the corner. I must have gone to sleep for I had a very vivid dream of skating on a pond only I had no clothes on and I had to skate very fast to keep warm only the faster I skated the colder blew the wind until I was so cold I wanted to be dead and when I saw the pole sticking up out of the ice I did not hesitate but skated towards it and crashed myself against it so that I might be dead and out of the wind and in the dream it was as if I did kill myself for I could see my body as if I were high above it, lying on the ice and blood from where I had driven myself on to the post.

"I do not remember getting back into bed so I suppose Herr Zimmerman must have put me there. But next morning I had a chill and it got worse in the next few days so that I had a fever and could not eat. Although I did not know it then I was very ill, all I can remember was that I had many terrible and strange dreams and I told them all to Yani and made her promise to write them all down. She didn't, however, and if I ever ask her what they were about she says she cannot remember as what I told her was very confused. Sometimes even now I still think I am going to remember what they were but before I can they always go away again. Perhaps it was meant that I should not know them.

"After a long time I got better and it was only then that the doctor told me that I had nearly died and that they had had to feed me with tubes while I was unconscious. I knew nothing of all this, only that whatever it had been it had taken away the last of my fat and it was as if I had grown up suddenly from a girl into a young woman and since then I have always remained slender."

He looked at the face, glowing in its fur cowl, miraculous reborn face. He touched it to make sure it was not a dream face, conjured out of his needs. Her lips clung against his knuckles, soft red petals. Her smile assailed him, like perfumed air he drank in her nearness. Looking past her he saw the world he inhabited. Its wastes caused his heart to contract in its arctic grasp. Pity for the loveless beasts of the black and white fields stirred in him, prompted by the perception that until this moment he had been one of them. They tread no sweet greens, nor munch the carmine poppy, on them falls not the rosy apple rain.

"I must needs love you, Uta. I have no choice." Words of surrender, accepted by her with a kiss of consolation.

"Does it make you so sad then?"

"No. It's only that I have never loved anyone before."

"Neither have I."

"It's not easy. I don't know what I expected but I feel as though a great weight had settled on my shoulders. I don't know why. I expected to feel free, but I don't."

"Don't feel trapped, Peter. I will do what you want, go where you want to go. I will not be a weight on you."

"Yes, but why should you want to go anywhere? You are happy here, what can I give you?"

"I hate it here, I have wanted to leave for longer than I can remember." He looked at her, astonished by the vehemence of both her words and their tone.

"But why, why have you not left long since?"

"Because you always need someone to help. No one is strong enough on their own." Echoes, echoing chords, the same words, different speaker.

"Why do you hate it here?" She looked away.

"I don't know, something, I don't know, I am unhappy."

"Yes, but why?"

"Let us go away, Peter, to the south or wherever, away from here. We will be happy."

"All right. When will we go?"

"When he comes back. I will tell him and we will leave."

"Are you sure you can tell him? I know it is cowardly but why not let your absence tell him?"

294

"No. Then I wouldn't be free, I would only have escaped."
"All right. You tell him and then we will go."

That night they lit a fire in his bedroom. The logs flared and cracked and around the walls great shadows leaped and ran. The warmth leaved them and softened their bones, letting them form the mould of lovers, melting in embrace while the ceiling swam with tawny light. Their mouths shaped themselves one to another and under his hands her clothing parted, till magical, her flesh grew. She lay over his knee, her back arched and her face hidden, only the sharp white vee of her underjaw showing. He kissed her throat, bit blue the stretched tendon of her shoulder, found high and firm the little half handfuls of her breasts. He took a nipple between finger and thumb and watching intently, his face close to her other breast, tortured it delicately until her whole body trembled on the threshold of pain. His eye was distorted by the enormities of nearness, flesh that stretched into untravellable distances, proximities so close as to defy sight. Under the raised welt of her ribs her belly scooped down into darkness. When the light lurched it lit her thighs orange and black. For Cuffee it evoked the images of his father's book, he let his fingers skim her skin, disturbing the tiniest particles of pleasure. She sighed and her body flexed and slackened, in her throat thickenings and the pulsing of an artery.

"Will you be my desert, Uta?" inaudible asking against her flesh. She held his head against her and her movements became more rapid, bringing her knees up and thrusting away from her. Far back in her throat she called out, not a name, a thick choking protest in German. As he tried to hold her she flailed away with her legs, her head turning back and forth wildly and he saw in the firelight how she held her upper lip with her teeth and blackly, blood trickled down over her chin. Then she screamed and nothing he could do restrained her as she twisted free, over the edge of the bed and on to the floor. Her hair slid slowly after her, through his fingers until she slumped, face down, and sobs shook her and filled the room with their quaver.

Cuffee waited until she was quiet before trying to talk to

her. He lifted her up on to the bed and put the eiderdown around her. The lip she had bitten had swollen already and her eyes were puffy from crying.

"Can you tell me what is wrong? Did you not want me to touch you?" She shook her head and pulled the eiderdown closer around her. "Were you afraid of me?" Again she shook her head. "What is wrong then?"

"I am cold," and to mark the words great convulsive shivers rippled through her.

"Come and sit by the fire." They sat side by side on the floor, Uta still wrapped in the eiderdown. "Is that better?"

"Yes."

"Are you afraid to make love, Uta?" She looked at him and her teeth sought out again the swollen lip but he laid his hand against her mouth. "Why can't you tell me, did I do something wrong?" She drew her head away and stood up.

"It is not you. It is me. Please forgive me. I do not know what made me behave like that." She was distant, controlled and cold. He rose to face her.

"Uta, what is wrong? You sound angry."

"No, I am not angry. Why should I be?"

"I don't know. I love you."

"Why do you say that now?" Why indeed. Meaningless phrase. He used it more as punctuation than anything, spacing out his thoughts.

"Because I do. I love you." She looked into his face, then at the fire.

"I must go. Yani will wonder where I am." It was wrong, he should stop it, stop it now, choke back his love and the weakness that went with it and make her his, take her. But he couldn't, the moment of choice was gone and he stood still as she gathered her clothes from the bed and went, still wrapped in the eiderdown.

His dreams were all of a fall, a fall down through the branches of a tree, many multiple fallings as in the free fall of apples, one single fall as his fall through the green heart of the tree, each branch breaking in turn, treacherously snapping to let him fall further, hands red from torn holds, red that showed on the apples as they fell in a shower of bloody rain, each apple a broken grasp and he plummeting down, uncaught, red-handed, guilty of falling, fall-man falling, knowing that to land was quite certainly to be dead yet almost wishing that to end the agony of his descent.

THE TRIAL

Zimmerman returned the next day. They were having breakfast when he arrived and after saying good morning he went
straight to his study. When Yani left them Cuffee asked Uta to
go to Herr Zimmerman and tell him of their decision.

"But he is only this morning returned."

"The sooner you tell him the better."

"It will do no harm to wait to this evening."

"Then I must tell him this morning, now."

"Why, why must it be now?"

"Because you do not want it to be now. That is why." She
sat a moment, unspeaking.

"All right. You do as you think best." He wanted to ask her
for reassurance, to tell him that she wanted Zimmerman told
but was afraid herself. But since she showed no signs of giving
it he bit back the impulse and went upstairs to see Zimmerman.

His study was entirely panelled in wood and had a large
desk at which he sat, reading through some typewritten sheets
and marking places with a pencil. There were many framed
photographs around the walls, many of them of Herr Zimmerman in uniform. On a table against the end wall there was
a pietà, a savagely carved piece in which the figure of the
crucified Jesus lay like a hideous old child across the lap of
Mary. There was a terrible vigour about the figures and the
crudity of the carving was echoed in the vehemence of the
colour, the naked torso chalk white and the loin cloth blue,
while the sunken, dead face was daubed and spiked vermilion.
High on the side was a deep red cut where the spear had
pierced him. His mother, her face a hack of grief, looked
down on the remains of her son.

"That was carved by a distant relative of mine," Zimmerman said. "It is very old, nearly six hundred years old. Always
someone in my family has worked in wood. That is what
Zimmerman means, a worker in wood, a carpenter. My father
was a carpenter. I too would have been one had I not shown

other talents. But come, sit down. You did not come to see me to hear about me and my family. What is it you have to say? About Uta I have no doubt."

"I have asked her to go away with me."

"And what has she said?"

"She said yes."

"I see. You are quite certain then."

"Yes."

"That is always a great advantage with a woman. They are impressed by certainty, whether wise or unwise."

"You think it unwise?"

"I think you simplify things in order to achieve certainty. But that is an effective way of overcoming obstacles. I myself used that method when I was young."

"But now you have more wisdom."

"It is not wisdom which prevents me. It is only that there is not the same kind of energy available to drive single-mindedness to a satisfactory conclusion."

"I think I have enough energy."

"I also think you have the energy. But I think you are only using Uta as a means to express that energy."

"I love her," and he could have bitten his tongue as it slipped out.

"Love is the greatest consumer of energy in the world. Of course you love her, it is inevitable that you do. What else could you do here in this situation? No, I do not doubt that you love Uta. It is your knowledge of her that I doubt."

"I have come to know her better in the last few days. When we are together then we will discover each other."

"But even from what Uta has told you you must realize she is very different from yourself."

"She is different yes, but not so very different."

"She has told you of her childhood?"

"Yes."

"And how she came to be here?"

"Yes."

"You would not say then her life has been normal."

"Normal does not mean very much to me."

"Perhaps not. Still the most important difference is one that Uta herself cannot express. The fact that she is German."

"I don't really think that is such an unsurmountable difficulty."

"But that is only because you cannot comprehend what it means to be German."

"Is it so different from being English, or French, or anything else?"

"If you are my kind of German, or Uta's kind, yes it is."

"What is so different? The fact that you lost the war?" Zimmerman smiled, not a lot, but a smile to show that he knew Cuffee was trying to prod him.

"The war, won or lost, is but an aspect of it, not even the most important aspect. It was an aspect which you may think marks the greatest difference between you and Uta, since it killed her parents and caused her to spend so much of her life in camps and institutions, but it is not because those experiences were not specifically German."

"In what way do you mean then?"

"To tell you that I would have to tell you about Germany and what it means, I would have to explain history to you, teach you philosophy. I would have to re-educate you."

"Wouldn't it just be possible to tell me, to say it is because of this and that. All this knowledge you would have me have before I understood sounds a bit dubious." Zimmerman smiled and nodded his head.

"Germany is the nation in which the archetypal emotions are most directly accessible. In Germany resides the potential of human greatness and human infamy in a more pristine form than in any other nation worthy of the name. All the others have achieved some means of disguising their humanity, in the fullness of the meaning of that word. Here in Germany, we are exposed to our potential in a way no other nation has ever been. But to make this intelligible I must describe to you how we see the very nature of being human, because whether you can allow for it or not you see the human condition as an Englishman and how a German sees it would make very little sense. As I said before I started, to tell you anything is to re-educate you. Do you want me to try?"

"Can I stop you?" Zimmerman laughed quickly and went on.

"If we look at history we see that among all the various patterns to be detected there is one grand pattern, one inexorable rhythm. War and peace, peace and war. For some people this is to say good and evil, evil and good, with the moral judgement that these words carry. They constantly preach the good of peace and the evil of war, they are horrified at evil and delighted at good, or they pretend to be. They are not prepared to look at history and draw the inescapable conclusion, that war and peace and good and evil are dependent one upon the other. They would rather believe that man was an animal who did not want war but couldn't help getting involved in it, who detested evil but failed to avoid it. They will not accept that they cannot be separated in history but continually reproduce themselves and since they cannot do that they cannot go further and realize that since history is only the consciousness of the humans who comprise it, projected into actions, then what is true of history is equally true of individual humans. In humans there exists not two opposing polarities, but a dualism in which good and evil are inevitably and rightly present, and I say rightly because there is a way in which that which exists is right and proper simply because it exists. Human thought has long concerned itself with unpicking the weave of our nature, dividing the sheep from the goats. It is one of the achievements of the German consciousness that it has finally made this dichotomy almost impossible. With the advent of Adolf Hitler a blow was aimed at the conventions of morality from which it can never recover without reverting to the most blatant hypocrisy. In most humans, even most great historical humans, it is apparently possible to separate their good actions from their evil ones. With Adolf this comforting division is impossible. His life destroys the meaningfulness of the terms good and evil. He lived with a total absorption in life, using his enormous, incredible energy to drive first himself, then his party, then his nation, and finally the world, onwards. By onwards I do not mean forwards as opposed to backwards, nor do I mean progress. I simply mean onwards. If Adolph Hitler had died at birth the world would not have observed a sixty years silence. History would have taken some other form. But it took the form it did because he lived and, in the end, dominated all the other energies of the world. To call him evil is to call the winter cold, it is a judgement of crudest comparison. When we consider his life we see, as if for the first time, what the potential of life really means. Life is energy, human energy is directed towards power, to have the power to modify the world according to one's desire. We all want to do this and we are insecure and unhappy inasmuch as this power is denied us. What other ideologies see in economic or spiritual terms we see most clearly in terms of power. This desire for power lies within us and our lives are spent trying to exercise it. When a genius comes along and unifies the individual needs of many many millions into a single national need he is called a fascist. All that one can say with certainty about fascism is that it is always an antidote to impotence, to frustration. Perhaps that means it can never, by its nature, be a stable political form but then to call fascism political in the first place is a misconception. Fascism is the most highly organized form of existential being, of direct involvement in the actual world. The fact that it springs from impotence guarantees that its most striking manifestation will be violence. In Hitler fascism discovered its supreme apologist. He knew that violence lurks within us, that frustrations erode us, hatreds twist us. He told us that these things were justified and showed us how to use them. The fact that he told us lies as justification is hardly the point. The emotions he appealed to weren't lies. He knew that fascism might not be an acceptable political creed but he knew that in one form or another it was everyone's personal politics. He distrusted the intellectual because he had so many ways of frittering away his latent violence. He distrusted the imaginative mind because it could indulge its violence vicariously. He distrusted the upper classes because they had institutionalized their emotions. Only the masses he was sure of. He did not love them or respect them but he knew them. When he said that power lay with the masses he was not mouthing democratic pieties, but speaking of the raw energy, the crude fuel of the historical vehicle. He knew that in those frustrated, inarticulate minds lay the source of all real power, political power, which every politician desires to canalize to serve his ends. Hitler was the political animal. Through political action and only through political action did he express himself. In every other field of human activity he was a nonentity and worse. But he succeeded as no one ever has before in forging a nation into a personal instrument of violence and with it, for the most personal of reasons, he bludgeoned the world into recognition of his identity."

After a moment Cuffee concluded that he had finished. "What has that to do with Uta and me?" Herr Zimmerman smiled, then laughed.

"You are not the philistine you pretend."

"True, but irrelevant."

"At the moment you feel Uta is your soul-mate, your anima. Take care she is not your doppelgänger."

"What is that?"

"It will do you no harm to learn one word of German the hard way. Look it up."

"I don't quite see why you told me all that about Germany and Hitler. It told me nothing about Uta that I can see."

"Perhaps it was not intended to tell you about Uta."

"Who then? You?"

"Or perhaps yourself. There is an aphorism from the Greek that I believe. 'Character is fate.' I think this is especially true of you." Cuffee rose to go. Zimmerman sat, his hands locked into one fist. He looked up.

"I do not wish to seem inhospitable but it will not be convenient if you stay on longer at the Castle. I have several business friends coming tomorrow and despite its size this place has not as many guest rooms as I could wish for. Your room will be needed."

"Fine. You've been very kind as it is. Goodbye, Herr Zimmerman," and he held out his hand. Zimmerman seemed disconcerted but shook hands. "I don't suppose I'll see you again. Don't forget you said you might let that goshawk go one day."

"No. I will remember." And Cuffee left him standing at his desk and went out.

The man was a dangerously astute plotter. He had tried to

seduce him with his rhetoric, prodding where he thought most receptive. He had been right too. Cuffee knew that much of what Zimmerman had said were his own thoughts and feelings. It was a slight shock to realize that he would probably have been a young Nazi had he been born there and then. But then it would have been because of his overpowering frustration. Now the blandishments of violent solution to those frustrations were grievously lessened. He was at last moving out into the air, into the light, into freedom.

In his room he rolled up his belongings in the sleeping bag. It was good to be leaving. He had almost stayed too long as it was. Now there must be no more delay. Uta must decide and his choice must be unaffected by her decision. He tied the bag securely and put his father's book into his pocket. There was a knock at the door. He opened it. It was Yani.

"My father says you are leaving."

"That's right."

"Uta is with him now. She will come in a moment."

"Tell her I will be in the shed where my bicycle is."

"You will not wait here?"

"No. You can have your room back." Yani looked surprised.

"How did you know it was ours?"

"Whose?"

"Uta's and mine."

"I didn't. When was this?"

"When Uta came here at first."

"Oh well, I didn't mean that. I just meant 'yours' not 'mine'." Yani walked past him to the window.

"This is my best room in all the house."

"This where you had your nightmares about the fox-demon?" Yani did not look round.

"That was poor Uta, not I. One of the serving women told her that story and it kept her awake for night after night. She said if she stayed awake the fox-demon would not be able to creep up on her." Cuffee stopped at the door.

"Yani, what happened to Uta's parents?"

"Did she not tell you?"

"Not exactly."

304

"They were killed in the war. She was too young to re-member them I think. Perhaps her mother a little." Cuffee came back and crossed to the window beside her.

"What happened to Uta's face? What caused her accident?" But Yani looked at him, suspicious.

"Why are you asking? Why do you not ask Uta?"

"Because I'm asking you."

"I do not want to tell you." Cuffee stood a moment, then shrugged.

"All right. No matter. Tell Uta where I'll be," and he left.

He was strapping the bag on behind the seat when Uta came down. She seemed angry.

"You would go without speaking to me?"

"Don't be stupid."

"What do you mean stupid?"

"Stupid. You know I wouldn't go without speaking to you. But I don't have much to say. Only are you coming with me?"

"When?"

"Now."

"Now?"

"Yes."

"But I can't come now."

"Why not?"

"Because Herr Zimmerman is here, he is just returned."

"What's that got to do with it. You couldn't go when he was away, you can't go when he's here. That means you can't go."

"Not this moment. I can't go now."

"And when can you go?"

"In a few days."

"Why a few days?"

"He has guests coming. He will expect Yani and me to help him entertain."

"Nonsense."

"It is not nonsense. Do you think I can just walk out. . . ."

"No. I don't." He took her shoulders. "No. I don't. I don't think you can."

"You said you loved me."

"I do."

"And I love you."

"But . . ."

"But what?"

"But you can't come with me."

"In a few days, when the guests have gone. If you love me can you not wait a few days?"

"I'll tell you what I'll do. I'll wait for you until Sunday. That's four days. If you haven't left here by then I'm going."

"Why are you like this, so hard?"

"Because I have to choose while I can. I've spent too much time here when we could have been cycling south. So now it's final. I'll wait for you until Sunday at nine o'clock in the morning. Then, I'm off."

"I will be there. I promise, Peter."

"All right. I'll find a bicycle for you. Don't bring too much stuff. Remember you'll have to pedal it to Spain and further."

"Oh I love you, Peter, I do."

"Good, I love you."

"I will give you the name of a place where you can stay. It is a students' place in Bonn and it will cost you nothing to stay there. Go to Bonn and find the road to the Venusberg. Just before you come to it there is this student house on your right. Ask for Franz Staffel. I will speak with him on the phone and tell him you are coming."

Cuffee got on his bicycle. Uta stood holding the handlebars.

"Uta, if you do not come I will still love you. But I won't wait." And then he went, feeling the pressure lift from him as he rolled out, over the moat and down between the trees.

The student house was a large grey air-raid shelter. The walls were rough concrete and windowless. The only door was small, wooden and set back almost a foot into the wall. The road ran on past it and turned left up to the Venusberg. It was a slightly derelict suburb, trees and houses in uneasy conjunction. The door opened to a push and admitted him to an interior dim and warm, the air smelling second-hand and the drone of the ventilation machinery steady on its monotone. The light was of a kind that had nothing to do with illumination, being rather an absence of darkness. It was an atmosphere which immediately ingested him, the step through the door was one which led not simply from the street to an interior but into a world so pervasively subterranean that he found his breathing suddenly quicken and his heart beat more rapidly.

It did not surprise him to find that Franz Staffel was a dwarf. Perhaps in the daylight he would have only been very short but sitting at a table in his cubicle room, his overly large head supported by a cupped palm, he was, to Cuffee's unsurprised eyes, a dwarf. His face as it turned to greet Cuffee's entrance, was extraordinarily beautiful. A high, smooth forehead, hollowed at the temples, straight firmly grained eyebrows and exquisite violet eyes that reminded Cuffee at once of Patsy, the first time he had thought on her for a long time. Staffel had a long aquiline nose, sensitive at the nostrils, and a wide mouth, thin along the upper lip but almost pouting in the lower. His smile when he rose to greet Cuffee was quite ravishing.

"You must be Peter. Uta has told me to expect you."

"Yes. You are Franz."

"Come in, let me make you some coffee." He poured some water from a kettle into a small pan and placed it on an electric coil. "It won't take many moments. Please, have a cigarette." He had long slender hands and the backs showed blue risen veins. "Uta said you would only be staying until Sunday, is that so?"

"Yes, I'll be leaving at nine o'clock."

"Yes, well I have found you a room on this corridor, at the end. It was a store room for mattresses but it has been cleared. You may stay there without charge until Sunday."

"Thank you. Are there many students here?"

"Oh yes. Some hundred and fifty."

"It's very quiet."

"That is so but mostly the students use it only to sleep and eat their meals in the mensa and study at the University. So it is only a dormitory." Cuffee looked around him at the books and pictures.

"But you don't use it only as a dormitory?" Staffel smiled his beautiful smile and dropped his eyelids.

"No, I am the student house guardian. I arrange the accommodation and see to the store and make sure everything is in order. I have a small grant from the Student Union for these services and also I have my room free. Thus I can study in comparative comfort."

"What are you studying?" Staffel smiled and his large pale hands spread like wings.

"Everything."

"Everything?"

"Yes. I am a storehouse of knowledge, I am the last of the encyclopaediasts." The gentian eyes looked into Cuffee's then lidded themselves again.

"What will you do with all this knowledge?"

"Nothing. It is all quite useless. But it keeps me entertained."

"How long have you been studying?"

"Nearly fifteen years."

"Always here, in Bonn?"

"Yes."

"Always here in this student house?"

"Yes. The other students call me Lord Bunker, 'bunker' is the German word for air-raid shelter or dug-out, they think I am mad."

"And are you?" The smile, ineffably sweet.

"No. Not at all. I am from time to time a little melancholy but I am not at all mad." The water boiled and Staffel made the coffee, his hands sensitive and precise in their motions so that Cuffee saw them as a silent dance as they flitted around the cups.

"You remind me of someone I left in charge of my cats when I came away from Manchester. A little girl she was, called Patsy. She had eyes like you. Same colour."

"I would like to have a cat, it would be very comforting, but it is against the rules."

"These cats used to come swirling round your legs in the

morning when you got up, their fur would be all cool, rubbing their heads against your ankles." Staffel gave him a cup of coffee. "Thank you." They sat and drank their coffee and Cuffee felt curiously at ease, as though the tensions and doubts of the days at the castle had never been. He wanted to know about this strange little man, rare emotion for him he felt liking for Franz Staffel, and the warmth of sympathy for another human gave him, for the moment, peace.

His room was smaller than the one Franz had. It had no furniture other than a bed. The light was set in the roof in thick opaque glass and the little square cell was painted white. Franz told Cuffee to come and see him whenever he wished, then he closed the door and left him alone. The sound of the air conditioning droned on steadily. Cuffee sat down on the bed and laid his bag at the end for a pillow. Then he stretched out and looked at the ceiling. When he fell asleep he was thinking about Staffel and his fifteen years under the earth as custodian of the labyrinth.

When he woke he did not know what time it was or how long he had been asleep. The light still shone, illuminating nothing. The air was still wearily forced into the room and still smelled of previous usage. His only sense as he lay awake was one of being trapped, in a cul-de-sac devoid of meaning. He rose and went out, taking several wrong turns and coming upon the exit by accident. To his surprise it was still light. Which meant it was still the same day, that only some hours earlier he had spoken with Uta, questioned Yani, been lectured by Herr Zimmerman. It was unreal and improbable, he seemed to have been a dweller in the bunker for longer than he could tell. To dispel such notions he rolled the bicycle down the slope and cycled slowly into the town.

By chance and a preference for the older streets to the busy ones he came into a small square, surrounded by tall houses where a man with a barrel organ played, sitting on a folding chair, winding the handle and coiling out the slow tumbling-over melody, endlessly joined, endlessly commencing out of its cessation. Under tall trees he sat, with soft brown leaves around his feet and the sky grey upon the houses. He felt himself to be alone, only the organ man's arm turning over and over, releasing the plaintive catena of song. He sat for a long time until he noticed the music had stopped and looked up to see the man wheeling his hand barrow away in the closing dusk and all around the square houses lighting their windows against the dark. Cuffee rose and made his way back to the bunker.

Staffel had known both Uta and Yani for some time while they had studied at Bonn University. Uta had been a brilliant student but erratic while Yani had never shown any particular aptitude academically. He had visited the castle on many occasions. Cuffee asked what he thought of Herr Zimmerman.

"Well, of course, he is one of the new Germans, he is a very ambitious man and he hopes one day to have political power. He is very clever and has more intellect than most. But he knows how to wait his time."

"Is he a Nazi?"

"It has been said of him. He was in the Nazi Party before and during the war but so were many men now in high places. He could not be called a Nazi now. He is too busy being above party strife, waiting for the need for a saviour to arise. In that respect he is a very cynical man. He believes that the government of this country will end in chaos and that there will be need for drastic remedies. But in other ways he is a good man. He has been very good to Uta."

"Yes. She has told me."

"There again, of course, there was an element of calculation but one cannot blame him completely for that."

"What do you mean?"

"When he adopted Uta, he had been appointed to the department that was responsible for the re-planning and re-building of a section of Frankfurt. There had been a very bad accident at an orphanage when a wall collapsed on a large number of children. Uta was one of them and she had severe facial injuries. Herr Zimmerman paid for her to have the very best surgeons and at the time much was made of it in the press that this bureaucrat had a heart as well. That much was probably political crowd-pleasing. But to go on and adopt the child and bring her up with his own daughter, that was something

310

more, wouldn't you agree?" Cuffee nodded, thinking of this further discrepancy between Uta's story of her life and its seeming actuality.

"Would you say that Uta was, I'm not sure of the word, but does she make things up, is she a fantast?" Franz looked dubious.

"I do not know about that. She is very imaginative, she was very sensitive some years back when she had a complete breakdown."

"What was that?"

"I know very little about it. Only that one night in winter she took off her clothes and went out and lay on the ground and when they found her and took her to hospital she refused to eat anything and had to be fed by means of intravenous injections."

"And what happened?"

"I do not know. She left the hospital and went to the Black Forest to convalesce. When she came back I was employed by Herr Zimmerman to coach her so that she should make up the studies she lost while she was away."

"Did she ever say anything about why she had done what she did?"

"She did not talk much of it, except to say how beautiful the Black Forest was. She would talk endlessly of that. The only other thing she said was that she wanted to feel something very strongly, that was why she had lain out on the ground, in order to experience the cold."

"Did she fully recover from it?"

"Oh yes, although she lost interest in her studies after she returned from the Black Forest and she and Yani did not return for the next term."

Cuffee pondered these things in his room, trying to shake the facts and the lies into some pattern, to see the shape of the truth in this melange. But something yet was missing, some root factor, some germinal secret.

In order that he might reflect upon it further he took his bicycle and cycled to the top of the Venusberg. It was a cold clear night and among the ruins on the crest of the hill the half moon made a frailest chiaroscuro, painting palest shapes on the darkness, conjuring with shadows. He thought of Uta and tried to untangle her from her lies and her dissemblings. He loved her, simply to look out across the night towards Vilich Beuel and to think of her in her bed was to make his heart wince. Love, whatever it was, paid no heed to Uta's deceptions, love possessed a certitude against the imperfections of its practitioners that gave to the condition its exalted melancholy.

The moon had begun to set and in the black sky the poniards of the stars had thrust myriad wounds. Their bright crystal blood dripped into his eyes. He had not wept since he was a boy. The night, ablaze with pain, trembled on the edge of grief.

There was no means of separating night from day in the bunker. Possessed of no windows, allowing no fluctuations of temperature, peopled by strangers, devoid of clocks, it was a limbo that quickly eroded any sense of time or place. When he awoke from sleep he had no way of knowing if he had been asleep for ten minutes or a whole night. Once, convinced it was morning he had risen, dressed and gone out to find the streets dark and deserted and a clock striking eleven. Stricken he had returned to an endless sleepless era in which he set his mind over and over to unloosen the knot which bound Uta and kept her from being his companion.

Finally he was forced to consult Staffel. As always he was awake, sitting up in bed reading, the clothes up under his chin. Seen thus he seemed to be no more than a head, a talking skull, some animate oracle.

"I love her, and there is something about her, something strange. I don't know what it is but I have to find out."

"Why?" Staffel asked, his face concerned and alert, the long slender fingers clasped on his chest. "Why do you have to find out?"

"Because she is lying."

"I dare say she is but what of it? Are you on such good terms with the truth that you must baulk at her lies?"

"But why does she lie?"

"Because she has to. Is that not possible?" Cuffee agreed that such might be the case. Staffel smiled at him and clapped his wrist.

"I am more concerned about your claim to be in love than I am about Uta's lies."

"Why?"

"Because I have not as yet managed to understand quite why human beings are compelled to love each other so vehemently. It seems to me a quite unnecessary excess," here again he smiled, "I agree that I am scarcely the person to pontificate on this subject having never wittingly been the object of the emotion and never been in the position where I might meaningfully say I loved someone."

"Well until now I don't think I've ever really loved anyone."

"In what way then does it differ from previous emotions? Is it stronger or more constant, or does it make you happier or less happy, what is it that makes it different?" Cuffee thought, trying to dissect the close bond of the heart, put words to feeling, make shapes in the wind.

"It pierces me more," was finally all he could say.

"Pierces? You mean causes pain?"

"No, pierces, penetrates. Enters into me. I just feel it more, not just feel the love, but feel everything, everything is raw, new, is sensitive."

"And for her, what for her do you feel?" Again he toiled in the inchoate dark to bring forth.

"Breathless."

"Ah, breathless," Franz said as though it explained much. "It seems to me that humans can only love each other, in the way you describe, for fallacious reasons. What you can tell me of your love confirms my other gleanings on the matter. You are pierced, and you feel breathless. These are good words, not overly rational. They are words which belong to another awareness also, that of isolation. Do you ever feel isolated?"

"You mean lonely?"

"No, not lonely. Loneliness is an emotion based on the failure to understand the true nature of isolation. We each of us exist in a total isolation just as surely as we exist in space or time. Isolation is a dimension also. The dimension of otherness.

313

We, as individual consciousnesses, could not exist without such a dimension. It is ours from almost the moment of birth, we are other than anything else."

"I know that, I know what that means, what you are saying."

"Yes, but knowing is not understanding, or understanding is not knowing. There comes a moment when isolation ceases to be an idea and becomes a fact, an inescapable fact. This moment can be brought into being by many things. One of these things which most commonly causes it is the desire to possess another human being and the inevitable discovery of their otherness. That is why when you said 'pierces' and 'breathless' I recognized the emotion as being one of intense revelation. You 'love' at the moment at which you discover the object of your love to be unpossessable. Love is in fact the most intense of the nostalgias."

"But nostalgia for what? If you say isolation is our condition, if we have always been isolated one from the other, how can we be nostalgic?" Here Franz smiled his seraphic smile and spread his hands.

"That is the question. That I deem to be where people talk of God and Paradise and the collective unconscious. I do not know."

Thinking of it later, when sitting in the square listening to the barrel organ revolving its song, his loneliness seemed, no matter how fallacious, undeniably real. It was not surprising that humans so afflicted should invent a myth of love and believe in it with all their heart. Maybe after the manner of paradox, such a lie, believed in forever, became the truth. Love may well be an illusion but only those able to pretend hard enough can make it real. Could he possibly pretend to such a pitch, which like the reputed love of God, passed all understanding.

Lying in the throbbing dark something that Staffel had said itched at his mind. "It has never been satisfactorily resolved whether the world is out there or in here" tapping his forehead with a finger like an ice pick. At that moment this seemed a genuine dilemma. Was the bunker perhaps not just the spatial extension of his mind and Franz not simply his own knowledge personified? So then Uta, was she out there or in here? What was she, his "doppelgänger" hadn't Zimmerman said, he must ask Franz what that meant. Uta was his doppelgänger then and Herr Zimmerman was what? Suddenly, bringing him upright with a swift crawling coldness, he knew Herr Zimmerman, knew his role in this whole melodrama. Herr Zimmerman was his father. He was the repository of authority, the that which must be opposed. He had been so busy with his dead father in the journal that he had failed to see the chair of reckoning had been reoccupied, by one in whom the power still flowed, who had as yet to be defeated. You run as far as you can but you still end up in the same place, seeing the same face, making the same choice.

Yet it simplified everything, even in its terrors there was the comfort of the known. The most difficult thing was to break the pattern, escape the imprisoning dictates of one's own nature. To be able to do so in this case would require that he give up his claim to Uta. Even to phrase it in his mind was to know that he could and would not. What had Zimmerman said, "character is fate"? So it would seem. With that realization came the attendant knowledge that there was no longer any need to wait. Sunday was not a day of decision. It would only be reached when he faced Zimmerman. He commenced to pack at once. He passed through the empty corridors without seeing anyone, nor did he attempt to visit Staffel. At the Studenthaus store he stopped and filled his pockets and bag with biscuits and chocolates and cigarettes, leaving a note in the register of goods purchased, "who won the war anyway." Outside the night waited, exhilaratingly cold.

The castle was dark as he came to it, winding between the trees, the frosted earth crackling beneath his wheels. He beat on the door, hammering the iron knocker until he could hear the interior fill up with the angry insistent sound. He felt almost gay, near hysteria. Ever since his recognition in the bunker he had been close to a kind of panic. Everything was poised now, his whole life focused on this moment. He was on the rare threshold of rebirth, conscious of the fact and conscious of his consciousness.

315

A man opened the door. Since it was not Zimmerman Cuffee
went past him and up the stairs, disregarding the man's protest.
As he reached the next floor Yani came towards him, in her
nightdress, her face anxious.

"What are you doing, why are you here?"

"Where is your father?"

"Why have you come?"

"Where is he?" Uta came out of a room, her hair loose on
her shoulders. She saw him and shook her head as though in
disbelief.

"Peter. Why have you come?"

"To see Herr Zimmerman."

"But we said Sunday."

"That was when I was to see you. This is to see Herr
Zimmerman."

"And what did you want to see me about?" He came down
the staircase, wearing a dark blue robe. He did not seem angry.
Cuffee went to the foot of the stairs.

"I have some things to ask you and some things to tell you."

"Did you have to come at this hour of the night?"

"Yes. I couldn't wait."

"Well, what are these things?"

"They concern you and me, but they are about Uta and
why she is as she is. I know something about Uta that there
can only be the one reason for. You are that reason. I want to
ask you about that. Shall we talk in private or here?" Zimmerman looked at him steadily but Cuffee knew he was afraid.
He knew it because he had to be afraid. Things were as they
were because they could not be other.

"Come with me," he said after a moment. Uta came up and
caught Cuffee's arm.

"Peter. You said Sunday."

"Never mind Sunday, it will all be settled tonight." He followed Zimmerman upstairs and along to his study. Inside he
closed the door and went to look again at the pietà.

" 'My God, my God, why hast thou forsaken me.' Isn't that
how he put it. Nobody seems to have been satisfied with their
parents."

"Why have you come here tonight?"

"Why did Uta take all her clothes off and lie out in a winter's night? Why does she lie about having smashed her face on a post rising out of the ice? Why is she terrified of the fox-demon who pretends to be kindly old men, why is she sexually in terror of the male's approach, why is she afraid to leave here and why does she want to flee? Take your time and answer in any order." Zimmerman stood behind his desk, the light masking his face.

"You think you know something."

"I know Uta is living in a world of unreality, she is frightened of something and that something would appear to be you."

"Uta is like my own daughter."

"No, not quite. Yani never had to stand in the cold until she cried to be made warm, Yani never had to feel you on top of her, inside her, Yani didn't have to try to forget with every fibre of her being until she snapped."

"You are suggesting that I violated Uta?" and his voice attempted outrage but broke in desperation.

"Violation, seduction, rape, it doesn't matter what you call it. All that matters is that I know and that I am taking her away."

"You will tell her this, these obscenities, you would try to poison her mind against me?" Cuffee came down and caught him by the front of the robe, pulling faces close.

"Her mind is already poisoned. It's only got a tight cork on it just now. Sooner or later it will come out, sometime she'll feel cold, or you will touch her, or she'll remember the fox-demon and it will all be with her again and then she will hate you, really hate you."

"And you propose to be the one that tells her?"

"No, not necessarily. She's put a lot of work into hiding the truth from herself. I don't know that it will serve much purpose to undo that work."

"Peter, if you love Uta you must leave her here. The last time when she met you she was very upset after it. If she goes away from here she may not be able to pretend any longer."

"Tough. Then we'll see if she can take it or if she breaks."

"You said you loved her. What sort of love is that?"

317

"I'm in love with life too. If Uta can't stay alive I can't go on loving her. I don't complain about the methods she uses just so long as they work. So I'm taking her away, I'm going to let her fly. That is, if she still knows how to. I just wanted to tell you."

He turned and went towards the door.

"Peter." When he looked back Zimmerman was seated.

"Yes?"

"I will not let you."

"How can you stop me?"

"In the only way left to me."

"By force?"

"Yes."

"What will you do Herr Zimmerman? Shoot me? Challenge me with sabres?" Zimmerman leaned forward, extended both arms.

"Which hand?" he said. For a moment Cuffee thought he might faint, a cold sweat broke on his arms and thighs. But he steeled himself, it had to be this way, there was no alternative. He came towards him.

"Which hand?" Zimmerman asked again.

"The right," Cuffee said and sat down opposite him.

Zimmerman cleared the desk and then rolled back his sleeve. He placed his elbow down, carefully, and extended his fingers to allow Cuffee to grasp them. They felt cold. Cuffee noticed his nails, grooved like the shells of hazelnuts, rounded and ribbed. His own hand was damp. He wiped it on his trouser leg and took a grip. Their hands were not greatly dissimilar in size, except his fingers were longer than Zimmerman's. He kept his grip loose, letting it settle into its hold and gently bringing his elbow down. Zimmerman indicated that his free hand was going behind his back and Cuffee followed his example. It left the engaged arm unprotected and vulnerable. In reaction he clasped and Zimmerman gripped too, both of them clasping fiercely yet without applying leverage. Then simultaneously they thrust one against the other and their breath came, hard and short and then a long sigh as they took in air again. Zimmerman's body was further over than Cuffee's and his head was turned away. Cuffee slowly judged the amount of pressure required to resist and maintained it, making no actual attempt to force Zimmerman's arm down. He waited for him to attack. There was a curious equipoise, one almost of peace, as they both refrained from the first move. Then Cuffee felt it, growing in the other's arm, hardening, forcing. Cuffee gave him an inch and held, his left arm pressing desperately against his spine to hold his body rigid. The pressure eased and Cuffee slackened and at once Zimmerman was at him again. This time Cuffee gave nothing but held until Zimmerman restrained. Their breathing was in marked contrast, Cuffee in short explosive gasps, the other slow, near sighs. Again he pushed and judging it to the instant Cuffee pushed back feeling for the first time the arm against him yield. At that moment he slackened and felt Zimmerman slacken too. At once Cuffee had him, driving all his body weight behind the arm, smoothly over and back so that Zimmerman's arm was almost on the table before he could summon up the first resistance. At such an extreme angle he could not sustain it and Cuffee put him back the last inch until his knuckles rapped on the desk top.

Slowly Zimmerman slacked his grip and withdrew his arm. He sat a moment looking down, his breathing heavy and slow. Finally he said,

"So. I did not think you would be strong in the arms," and he put his left arm up. Cuffee felt sorry for him. He could not prevent himself. He was beaten and he knew it. What did he expect, he should have known one day there would have to be someone who would want Uta enough to take her despite the obstacles. He put his left arm up with a grimace of regret. Their hands met and as the pressure began Cuffee resisted only partially. Zimmerman increased his weight and Cuffee let his arm bend, slowly topple until it was flat on the desk. Zimmerman looked at him, coldly.

"You think that I need encouragement, or is it that you wish to prolong what you believe to be your moment of triumph?"

"One each."

"Very well. One each. But you will not play games this time," and he rose and went to the cabinet behind the desk and took out two glasses.

"What difference will it make who beats who? Why don't

we just leave it as it is?" Zimmerman sat down again. He held the glasses out, one in each palm.

"Would you say that if you thought you could not win the third time? Come, be honest."

"Perhaps not."

"No. Well this will make sure at least that you are trying," and he knocked the glasses on the edge of the desk. They broke with short high chimes. Zimmerman placed them at the points where the hand would fall.

"You agree?" Cuffee hated him then and feared him also. The unswervable mind of the dogmatist. He longed to destroy it, to crush it once and for all into abject impotence. And yet so many battles in the past had been lost to it. He put up his right hand and looked at the spike of the broken glass, it was slightly cracked at the slenderest part. He could imagine it breaking as his hand struck down on it, imbedding a splinter in the flesh. He had a swift sense of how bony and exposed the back of his wrist and hand was, the tendons, the bones it would pierce. His glance strayed to the pietà at the end of the room and he remembered the figure on the hospital wall, stretched by the hands in his God-forsaken agony.

"Are you ready?"

"Yes. Yes, I'm ready."

Almost at once he knew he had lost. The arm against him gave no hint of hesitation. A great surge of force flowed through it against his desperate opposition. He bent as though his arm was waxen. The glass lunged up and at the very last second he closed his eyes as though in some way it might minimize the pain. But it came, first from his hand, then as his mind accepted the barbarity, in great waves of nausea. His clenched teeth were no defence against the scream that tore in his chest. He lost consciousness for a moment and when he opened his eyes it was to see, very close to his face, the glass still in his hand and blood, astonishing in its redness, dripping into it. Zimmerman still held him down, no longer driving him on to the spur, but holding, steadily. Cuffee tried to move but the slightest twist of the glass so sickened him that he stopped at once and rested his face on his forearm, eyes averted from his impaled hand.

"Do you know how a hawk is manned? There is, of course, the modern method. There always is a modern way. But the way hawks were manned when men knew what it was to identify themselves with a bird, that was something that took not only strength but will. The man carried the wild bird upon his arm, he gave it no food and no rest save that it would take on his arm. He carried it all day and all night and all the next day until his will had mastered its will, and it sat as though he were a tree and his arm a branch. All of those birds above I carried so, on this arm. And all of them bowed to my will in the end." He stood up. The movement almost made Cuffee faint again. He saw him walk towards the door and then his vision became blurry. He turned his head to see his hand. It lay on its back, the fingers open and spread like the dead legs of some crab thing. As though some enormous weight were on the end of it he slowly twisted his arm up, to free it of the glass, but it remained fixed, blood still dropping into its bowl. He knew all he need do was shake it and it would fall free but he couldn't bring himself, the idea of the glass slackening its hold in his hand was even more unbearable than his present plight. Entranced, he watched it, slowly filling up with his blood. His mind, dizzy with pain and horror, made wild calculations to determine when there would be a sufficient weight of blood to pull the glass free. As his arm slowly began to drop again he reached round his free hand in support. He did not hear Uta as she came in. It was her cry that made him turn. The glass was jerked loose at the movement. Uta stood in the door, her hands on her face. Cuffee started to get up and she turned and ran. He sat down again, holding his right wrist with his left hand.

Zimmerman came towards him.

"I think you had better go. Uta is very upset. I told you that this might happen. You made some arrangement to wait for her until Sunday. It might be better if you were to revert to that plan." His tone was calm, his words reasonable. Cuffee got up and went out, dripping blood on the floor.

The bunker awaited him. Once within he might never have left. Only the crescent-shaped wound on the back of his hand, the flesh puffed around it, going a bluey grey colour and the blood slowly welling up, thickening, then breaking free and coating his wrist and his fingers purple red. He went straight to Staffel's room, entered without knocking and held out his pain.

"My hand," he said and with that began to weep, choked, bitten back at first then fully, openly, in full spate, amazed even in the middle of it by the vehemence of such grief.

When he stopped he was in Staffel's bed and his hand was being bathed with rapt solicitude, held tenderly and touched with the utmost gentleness by swabs of cotton dipped in warm water. "This is a bad wound. You must have a doctor. How did it happen?" Cuffee did not answer him but only looked into the beautiful face, the violet eyes of love.

"Tomorrow you must see a doctor. It may be infected. It is very deep."

"You must phone her, Franz, and ask her to come." The gaze he received was fraught with concern.

"She will not come, Peter. I know her and she will not come, it will be necessary for you to forget her."

"She will come if you ask her to."

"It can only cause you more pain. She will not go away with you, you must know that."

"Tell her I want to see her. Just once. She will come. That is in her nature."

"I will ask her but I do not think she will listen to me. You must sleep and tomorrow you must see a doctor. There is one who attends the students, I will get him to see you." He carefully bandaged his hand and laid it on his chest. Then he put out the light and sat in the chair beside the bed.

"Franz, don't go away."

"No. I am here."

Once in the night his hand slipped from his chest on to the bed and the pain woke him. Franz was beside him, gently lifting the arm back, wiping his face. He reached up and touched his shoulder.

"You will ask her to come?"

"Yes. I'll ask her."

When he awoke in the morning the pain swallowed his mind

at once. His hand beat with a savage hot throb that made his voice quaver as he called Franz. The room was empty but pinned to the door was a note that said he had gone for the doctor. Cuffee did not look at his hand but lay back and let it pound.

Franz returned with the doctor after about an hour. The doctor was a brusque, elderly man who did not speak English. The bandage Franz had put on was stuck to the wound by a small rosette of dried blood. The doctor eased it off. Cuffee could scarcely bring himself to look at it. His hand was badly swollen. The cut was almost closed and set in red, risen flesh. He swabbed it with liquid from a bottle in his bag, talking as he did so to Franz. Then he put a yellow pad dressing on it and bound it firmly with white, fresh bandage, the sight of which soothed Cuffee somehow.

Then he took a small phial and a hypodermic and, still talking, loaded the syringe and gave Cuffee an injection in the upper arm. He looked at him a moment and said something in German, then left with Franz. After a few moments Franz came back and began at once to make some coffee.

"He asked me what had happened and I told him you had an accident and fell on a broken bottle. He did not believe me but agreed to attend you. I said you were a student studying at the University. He wanted to know why you did not speak any German but I said . . ."

"Did you speak to her?"

"No, not yet."

"Go and phone now. Tell her I want to see her. Tell her I must see her. Please Franz, now." He shook his large head in resignation and put the cups down again.

"All right, I will phone her." He went to the door.

"Franz."

"Yes?"

"What is a doppelgänger?"

"A doppelgänger. It is an apparition that a man sees before his death. It is a strange word to translate, it would mean something like 'double goer' in English."

"Phone her now."

"Yes. Now," and he went.

Cuffee waited all day and twice more he sent Franz to call her. Each time he said that he could not speak to her, only to Yani. On the fourth occasion Cuffee told him to say that if she did not come he would come to the castle. Franz came back and said it was still only Yani he had spoken to and that he did not think she would come.

But she did. Cuffee had moved himself, despite Franz's protests, to his own cell and lay there, propped against the wall, his hand lying on his chest like a heavy hot stone. The door opened and it was Franz. Behind him was Uta.

He stepped aside and she came in. She wore a white belted raincoat with epaulettes and large leather buttons. Her hair was caught high behind her head in a bronze knob.

"Thank you for coming," Cuffee said when the door was closed.

"I did not want you to come to the castle again."

"No. I didn't think you would."

"Herr Zimmerman has asked me to give you this." She held out an envelope. Cuffee took it.

"Thank you." She looked at him, her eyes close to contempt.

"What did you want to say to me?"

"Nothing."

"Nothing? You wanted me to come all this way to say nothing?"

"I wanted to see you again. Before I left."

"You realize that I cannot go with you."

"Of course."

"It was all foolishness."

"It was."

"I am glad you agree." She paused, searched for something to say, then put out her hand. "If there is nothing to say, then goodbye." Cuffee let her hand remain extended, then gestured with his bandaged one. "Oh yes, your hand. Well then, goodbye."

Cuffee came a little closer. He looked down at his hands.

"It only seems like a choice, left hand, right hand. It's the illusion of free will when in reality there isn't any. My father, God rest him soon, used to go in for little pieces of sophistry like that. Like father like son they say." He held out his hands to her.

"Which one?"

"What do you mean? For what am I to choose?"

"Because that's all the choice you have. Which hand, left or right?" She looked puzzled, her eyes went from his face to his hands.

"This is stupid."

"Which hand?" Her manner hardened, she shrugged.

"There is no choice. You only have one hand. That one," and she tapped the palm of his left hand with her finger.

He hit her very hard in the stomach, just below the buckle of the belt, his fist sinking into her unprepared body and driving all the wind from her so that her eyes opened wildly and as she sat down slowly her mouth desperately sought air. Cuffee caught her by the hair with his left hand, low down near the nape of the neck, and twisted her round so that she was looking into the wall. He lowered his mouth to her ear. All the while her body tried convulsively to draw air into it.

"See that wall? That is the wall of no choice. It's your turn to go to it," and saying that he drove her, open-eyed, against the stone, once, then again; then coldly, leaving no room for remorse, twice more. When he let loose her hair from among his fingers she slid down the wall, leaving a red smear on its whiteness from her destroyed face.

THE FLIGHT

Once he was clear of Bonn his panic eased. He had left his bicycle behind and taken one loaned by Franz. They would think he had gone by train, they wouldn't think he'd be cycling steadily along. His bandaged hand was hidden under a glove, he was a nondescript, going nowhere in particular from nowhere special. On either side of him were fields that rolled slowly past. He was on a river, a slow steady current carrying him away from all the past weeks. He had become temporarily confused. That thing which happened to rivers had happened to him. An oxbow. He had taken an oxbow but now it was all right, he was going ahead again, steadily, slowly, stamping down on the pedals, keeping his bandaged hand on his thigh. He did not need anything now except to keep moving. Distance and time. They would take him to where he was going. Franz would tell them he had left his bicycle. They'd think he'd taken a train. Franz would not betray him. Beautiful eyes. He would paint Franz when he reached the place he was bound for. Paint those beautiful eyes. And the little girl's eyes. They were the same. The same eyes in two different people. They would not betray him. His hand throbbed in time to his head, keeping his thoughts company.

At the first steep gradient he dismounted and walked slowly smoking a cigarette. He had plenty of money now. They would be sure he had taken a train or an aeroplane. At the top he remounted and released himself to the other slope. The descents were long dizzying falls, the wind streaming around him, the wheels whirling on the flying road, rolling round the bends letting the machine lead his body, then his bell trembling along the walls of the small hamlets at the foot of the hill. All he had to do was to travel ever south. When he reached there he would be well again, purged of his humours, clean again and self-contained. Only his hand was outside the blankets. Anything outside the blankets might be seized in the dark. It throbbed sometimes when he jarred it and to cool it he took off his glove and held it up into the wind. When he was far enough away he would have it attended to. Until then he would cool it in the wind.

All the first night he cycled driving his tiredness before him and stopping only when the dawn came. He sat a moment by the edge of the road and then went on again, tired but not yet prepared to rest. Only that night, cycling towards the cluster of lights in a small village, did weariness claim him. The lights started to go off and on again, in unison. There must be some fault at the power station. A short circuit. When the lights went off people must be doing something and left standing or sitting or walking or lying down until they came on again. They must be quite at a loss whether to go on with what they were doing or just to sit and wait for it to be mended.

The bicycle ran on to the verge and the hedgerow rattled against his shoulder. He swerved wildly and braked, and was wakened sharply by the swift stab of pain in his hand. It made him realize he had been falling asleep as he cycled. Shaken, he dismounted and walked slowly until he found a gate into the field. He woke late in the afternoon to find several children standing round, looking stolidly at him. Things repeat themselves. Violet eyes and wakening in strange hedgerows. His hand was beating steadily as he pushed out on to the road but it wasn't so hot. It was as if it was his heart, the life pulse of his body. He rested it inside his jerkin and rode with one hand.

Later he bought some cheese and a loaf and drank a bottle of milk. Once he had crossed the border he would stop and have his hand made well. Rest a few days, visit a prostitute. Then he would go on. He had a scratch on his face from where he had run against the hedge. But he felt well. He was his own man again. When he got there he would sort it all out, until then it could stay at the back of his mind. First he must escape them. Later there would be time to know what it all meant.

That day and night was a hard one. He stuck to it, pushing hard on the flat and walking doggedly up the hills, arms resting on the handlebars. Only down hill could he relax and imagine his goal rushing up to meet him. At the foot of each hill, however, the level waited and reduced him to a more sober pace.

He slept at down behind a low dyke and awoke well into the

day in a steady, cold rain. The land looked sodden and cheer-less, the green a wet dull hue and the heavy dark earth louring through. He squatted against the dyke and ate bread and cheese till it suddenly made him feel sick and he threw it away. The movement caused his hand to gout suddenly and after it died away he felt the glove excessively tight on it. He eased it off and felt with relief the coolness of the rain on the bandage. The bandage was dirty but showed no sign of slack-ening. He noticed as he cycled on that he had a soreness under his arm. That was from resting the hand too much. He mustn't favour it. Other parts of his body were protesting. This was a time when there must be no dissension in the ranks. He must use that hand as he used the rest. He gripped the handlebars firmly and tried to avoid anything on the road that might jar him.

As darkness came on again he ate a meal in a roadside café and studied a map on the wall to see where he was going. The road he was on would take him to Luxembourg. That would be the place to rest and get rid of the bicycle. He had plenty of money. He could take a train. But would they not be check-ing passports on the train? Perhaps. He must wait until he was in France before he boarded a train then there would be no borders for a long way and before they reached Spain he would get off and buy another bicycle and cross the border that way. He sat on in the café, drinking cognacs and postpon-ing the moment when he would have to go out again. He fell asleep and it was his hand hurting that wakened him. He rose and went out. The rain had stopped but there was a wind. It was almost eleven o'clock and there was no moon. He pushed off behind the feeble ray of his lamp. The big camions went by with a ripping crash, causing him to wobble into the hedge each time. He couldn't really put his right hand on the handle-bars for long now, it pained too much. He let it dangle and pedalled on.

The Luxembourg frontier came upon him by surprise. A descent and a bend to the right opened to reveal a long straight stretch of road. About quarter of a mile down it the black and white box of the frontier guard. He let the bicycle free wheel almost to a stop and then cycled slowly up to the barrier. For a time he thought they were checking on him when a second man joined the first one and looked at his passport photograph and then at his face. The wind soughed in the trees behind the road. Cuffee didn't care if they did catch him. He was very tired and his hand hurt. The wind didn't love him. They would only put him in jail. They would look after his hand. The man asked him where he was going. He said "south." The man asked him where. "Spain." There was a pause and the wind rose and fell, sad and cold, passing through leafless branches. The frontier official went inside and Cuffee saw him talking to another man. In a moment they would come out and tell him he was being detained. He was glad. This authority was too big, too impersonal to be worth fighting. He closed his eyes and confronted his hand. After a moment the man came out.

"You have money?" Cuffee looked at him. He was tapping the passport against his thumb.

"Yes."

"How much?" He took Herr Zimmerman's money out of his pocket. The man counted it quickly.

"If you have this amount of money why do you travel like a tramp?"

"I am an eccentric," Cuffee said and held out his hand. The man deliberated a moment longer then handed him back his money and his passport.

"You should clean yourself. You look as though you had no money."

Cuffee did not reply but rode on, very slowly, suddenly tired by his reprieve, uncertain as to whether he was glad or not. At the other frontier they stamped his passport without delay and let him through. The little boxes of warmth receded. The men in their secure uniforms watched him before going back to their coffee and night-long companionship. Cuffee, outcast, went slowly along the road and into the dark.

Just over the border the road rose in a long steady hill. A post told that the gradient continued for twelve kilometres. It was possible to cycle up but it needed both hands to control the bicycle and now any pressure on his right hand made him nauseous with the pain. He got off and walked. On either side of the road there were trees. His route lay directly through a forest. It stood, dark and solid, only the wind moving in it, causing a hundred sibilants to blend in long undulant sighs. Cuffee thought of the rise and fall of telegraph wires from the window of a train, travelling south. He stopped, dejected, the enormity of his journey suddenly overwhelming. He couldn't cycle on like this. He must leave his cautions behind. At Luxembourg he would get the train. He would go no further tonight. Tomorrow morning he would go on to Luxembourg and take the train. The forest stood, indifferent to his decision, denying him shelter. He could not simply lie down in its dank, dark depths with the wind moaning around him. But he couldn't walk to the top of this hill, it was too far. He tried to cycle but after a hundred yards his hand hurt so much he had to stop.

Ahead of him, at the side of the road and set into a small clearing, was a wooden hut. The forest grew close round it, undergrowth on two sides. He tried to see through the window but it was dark. He knocked but there was no reply. The door was secured by a padlock on a light hasp. He found a stone and awkwardly, with his left hand, steadying the padlock with his right, he broke it open. It made a considerable amount of noise but the forest absorbed it without trace. Nothing howled or flew, there was no sudden hush. The wind went on heedless of this intrusion. Only Cuffee's breathing was new, quick and harsh as though from exertion. Inside appeared to be a place for storing tools. There was a wide shelf running along one side and on it were shovels and hoes and the hafts of axes. He cleared them off and spread out his sleeping bag. Then he took the bicycle in and pulled the door closed. The hut smelled of damp wood. He got into the bag awkwardly, his hand hurting him every time pressure was put on it. It was cold but he pulled the bag over his head. As a child you kept all of you under the blankets. Under the blankets was safe. Tomorrow he would be safe. Safe and warm. He solicited sleep in the smothering folds of the bag. His hand was like another being lying alongside him. He tried to disassociate himself from its pain, to merely sympathize. He thought of good things, of things that held no pain. The bright clear water of a river where he had bathed. Cats swirling around his bare legs of a cool morning. Violet eyes, clouds seen like elephants, summer sun drying beer on a wooden table, a tree he had climbed into to carve his initials, the orchard with the rain of falling apples. His mind sought peace in this anthology of well-being, and partially comforted he fell asleep.

It was as though the dream was at him immediately. He lay beside a precipice with his arm hanging over the edge. His arm was enormously long and hung all the way down to the ground far below. It was so heavy that it threatened to pull him over the edge. He clung to some grass with the other hand. When he looked over he could see there was a red dog holding his hand in its teeth, and as he watched it began to eat it, biting into the flesh, tearing at it so that he threatened to be pulled over. In some way his hand had got out from under the blankets and fallen over the edge. The dog must have been waiting and seized it. If only he could find a stone to throw at the dog. He could feel the bones crunching in his hand and the tug as the flesh came away in strips. It was his right hand it was destroying. He must free himself. Summoning all his effort he jerked away from the beast but all he managed to do was to lift the animal clear of the ground where it hung for a long agonizing moment by the teeth until he felt himself begin to overbalance and despite everything he could do to prevent it, he fell.

He woke on the floor, still half in the bag, dizzy and sick with the force of landing. At first all he could hear was the sound of himself moaning from the pain of his hand, but after a moment he heard the other noise. At once he knew what is was and his body went rigid. It scratched against the wall, close to the door. Then it stopped and then it started again, this time on the door itself, scratching, searching for an entrance. He was crying now, trying to be quiet at first but as the scratching went on in great gasping sobs, through which he begged to be spared, promising to be good if only it would go away.

For a long time he crouched, abject in his weeping. Then slowly he realized that the scratching had stopped and his tears subsided also. He listened, holding his breath, but there was no sound at all. But he knew it was still there, waiting beyond the door, silent, red-eyed in the dark. It was waiting for him to come out, or to go back to sleep. Best thing he could do was to stay awake until morning, it would go away in the daylight. Outside a stick broke, snapped and snapped with it his control. His scream was rage and terror and hysteria all at once. Without thought he seized an axe handle from the floor and threw himself out into the night, ready to meet it, to feel the hot stink of its breath, the red burning eyes, to feel its teeth in his throat.

Nothing moved. No sound. Except himself uttering a garble of prayer and threat, of promise and plea, calling up his father both in heaven and upon earth to save him. Silent, dark. Not even the sound of the wind in the trees. Except for himself the night was empty.

He began to shiver, all his body, a trembling that he could not contain. Against the wall he leaned but it did not abate. Slowly he walked around, shivering and nursing his hand in which the pain quivered feverishly. There could be no thought of sleep now. When he was steady enough he got the bicycle out and mounted up. When his hand hurt he snatched it away then replaced it at once. Inside him was a great self-disgust that could find no expression. He despised himself for behaving as he had in the hut but he realized that his behaviour then was the outcome of his previous behaviour, and that of earlier, and earlier of even prior actions. He despised himself now in an unrelieved awareness of his unworthiness. Pushing up between the dark walls of the trees he came to the end of his excuses for being alive.

Luxembourg was yellow, haggard and deserted. Its emptiness went beyond an absence of people. It was dead, a mortuary through which Cuffee rode heedless of anything save his gnawing hand and its accompanying self-hatred. In the yellow light the stain on the bandage bloomed purple black. He rode through and on, no longer fleeing, not wishing to escape, all haste gone, welcoming the pain in his hand as his deserts. Sooner or later he would be able to go no further. Then he would stop.

His progress was almost leisurely save for the agony of his

hand. He moved at whatever pace he could manage. He saw things clearly but in swift surging glimpses, riding for long periods in a near coma of inwardness. He took such turnings as presented themselves, he stopped twice to eat and the second time was sick. Night came and went and he slept under a cart and woke with frost in his hair. His hand stopped paining him so much, only his arm felt very heavy, heavy enough to over-balance him. He kept it carefully propped on the handlebars. From time to time he would cry for no reason at all and the road and hedgerows would all melt and mingle through his tears. He didn't think of much but felt very weary. Soon all choice would be taken away and he would be safe. After the pain they would bring him down. He would be all right then.

He was in the square in front of the station. He looked at the entrance to the hall and it came back to him, from far away. So he was here again. He got off, propped the bicycle against the wall and went through the doors into the main hall. It was bare and empty. He stood looking at it, trying to re-member how many steps it had taken to walk right round it. The old man stood in the same place. He should have known, of course, that he would be there, waiting for him to return. Cuffee went to tell him that it was all right, he had arrived. He must have known all this time that Cuffee would be back and waited here.

He touched his shoulder and the old man at once began to walk, out across the hall to the other side.

"No, no," Cuffee said, "It's all right now. You don't have to walk any more," but he went stumbling on, Cuffee walking beside him. He wanted to tell him he had read the book and he understood about the hand, it didn't matter which one you choose, he wanted to explain it was all right but he kept walk-ing away from him. Cuffee caught his shoulder.

"It's all right. Listen. I want to tell you . . ." but with a lurch and a jerk he freed himself and went on. Cuffee was suddenly very angry, he didn't want to be but he was. It throbbed wildly in his head and he ran forward and stepped in front of the old man, who was forced to stop.

"I'm talking to you, don't you understand?" But he only

turned to go in another direction. Cuffee dragged him back by the neck. He was surprisingly light and once he had started pulling him he went on, dragging him back to where he had started from.

"Back we go," he said, "back we go." The old man stumbled and nearly fell. He was making cracked, protesting noises as Cuffee jerked him upright.

"Come on, up we get," and finally he had him over against the wall. "Listen now, let me tell you," but the old man screamed, the ruin of his face twisted with fear, he screamed and tried to push Cuffee away and Cuffee started to hit him, swinging punches to his face until the pain flowed up his arm and cramped his neck and burned, explosive wild blinding head pain that made him stagger and almost swoon then break in his throat, spilling out above the sound of his victim whom he had released and who crouched against the wall.

Stiff bars of pain ran through his arm. He tore at the bandage. It wouldn't come free. His hand had swollen so much that the bandage was bitten deep into the flesh. Only his fingers protruded, but not his fingers, dead fingers sticking up above the swollen gouting carcass of his hand. It was going to burst with the pain. All he could feel was his hand, it was enormous. Enormously big, enormously painful. He raised it with his other hand to bite at the bandage with his teeth. At each throb of pain he kicked the old man to ease it, to pass the suffering on to another. The smell of his hand revolted him, a rank gone green odour. He knew it, it was the old man's smell and the damp smell of things becoming vegetable. He ripped at the bandage with his teeth in a frenzy of revulsion until it finally ripped. The old man lay on his face now, moaning. Cuffee paid him no further heed now, concerned only with his hand, rocking it to and fro to ease the pain, slowly unfolding the bandage. Hush a bye baby in the tree top. He remembered the branch that broke. When the wind blows the cradle will rock. And how he fell. The two gendarmes came running towards him, clattering across the hall. He was unwinding the bandage when the first one stopped him. The other one ran on to the old man. The gendarme with Cuffee caught him by the arm, the right arm. Cuffee screamed, involuntarily, and swung his left forearm hard against his captor. The gendarme staggered and Cuffee ran, as much to escape the pain in his hand as anything. It was filling him up, he could feel its rise, threatening to drown him in its fierce bile. He ran out into the square and pushed his bicycle out and rode, swaying wildly across the cobbles.

They called on him to halt but he did not hear, nor had he heard would he have understood, nor had he understood would he have obeyed. Holding his burning hand up into the sky he drove the bicycle forward, seeking a wind to cool his pain. The bandage fluttered behind him, bloody pennant nailed to his martyred hand. The bullet as it entered under his armpit was only a violent extension of the other, primary pain. He fell, over the handlebars, rolling over twice, ending on his back some ten yards from the machine. It was just getting light he noticed and was not that rain? He could see his hand, enormous above him. It only seemed like a choice. Poor father, perhaps he didn't know.

The cycle lay, spinning its wheel slowly, without haste now. Beyond it, arched in death, the rider reached above himself for some last hold on life. When the wheel stopped its stillness was that of an inanimate thing, as though it had never known movement. Equally final was the torsion of Cuffee, though life had been but recently his.